He frowned and rumbled,
"Do not be afraid.
I will keep you safe."

Normally, a comment like that would have annoyed Pet and she would have told him she didn't need his protection. But Pet knew what immortals could do and . . . she was afraid.

"Pet?"

Her gaze had drifted down to his chest while she thought. Pet lifted her eyes now to meet his and blinked when she noted the silver growing in the black of his irises . . . like mercury in a thermometer expanded when the temperature rose. It was absolutely beautiful, she thought, and then realized his eyes were coming closer.

His head was slowly lowering . . . as if he intended to kiss her. She recognized that, and had plenty of time to rebuff him, but didn't. She was curious, so she lifted her head to him and let her eyes drift closed, and then his mouth was on hers.

By Lynsay Sands

LYNSAY SANDS

THE TROUBLE WITH VAMPIRES

AN ARGENEAU NOVEL

AVONBOOKS

An Imprint of HarperCollinsPublishers

Excerpt from *A Lady in Disguise* (previously published as *The Reluctant Reformer*) copyright © 2002 by Lynsay Sands.

THE TROUBLE WITH VAMPIRES. Copyright © 2019 by Lynsay Sands. All rights reserved. Printed in the United States of America. No part of this book may be used or reproduced in any manner whatsoever without written permission except in the case of brief quotations embodied in critical articles and reviews. For information, address HarperCollins Publishers, 195 Broadway, New York, NY 10007.

First Avon Books mass market printing: May 2019
First Avon Books hardcover printing: April 2019

Print Edition ISBN: 978-0-06-285517-6
Digital Edition ISBN: 978-0-06-285518-3

Cover design by Nadine Badalaty
Cover illustration/photographs by Tony Mauro
Cover photographs. front: © Howard Sandler/Dreamstime.com (house);
© Spiroview Inc./Dreamstime (driveway); stepback: © Howard Sandler/
Dreamstime (house)

Avon, Avon & logo, and Avon Books & logo are registered trademarks of HarperCollins Publishers in the United States of America and other countries.
HarperCollins is a registered trademark of HarperCollins Publishers in the United States of America and other countries.

FIRST EDITION

19 20 21 22 23   QGM   10 9 8 7 6 5 4 3 2 1

THE
TROUBLE WITH
VAMPIRES

Prologue

"**911.** *What's your emergency?*"

"*Hi . . . um . . . I'm not sure if I should be calling you or the police.*"

"*Is this an emergency?*"

"*It might be. I'm not sure . . .*"

"*Just tell me what's happening, son. Is someone there sick or injured?*" When the boy didn't respond at once, the operator asked, "*Are your parents arguing and it's scaring you? Are they getting violent?*"

"*No! No. It's our neighbor. Well, not really our neighbor, but his cousin who's visiting. He . . . er . . . he's sick . . . I think.*"

"*You think?*"

"*No. He is. He's sick. And I think he may be dangerous. I'm afraid he'll hurt Mr. Purdy.*"

"*Mr. Purdy?*"

"*My neighbor.*"

"*Right. And you think this cousin who is visiting*

him is sick and dangerous?" the operator asked, doubt obvious in her voice. *"If so, why hasn't this Mr. Purdy called instead of you?"*

"I'm worried maybe his cousin won't let him."

There was a long pause, and then the operator sighed and asked, "What kind of sick is dangerous, son?"

"He . . . er . . . I think he might be suffering from Renfield syndrome."

"From what?"

"Renfield syndrome," the young voice repeated reluctantly.

"What's that?"

"It's . . . er . . ." The boy paused, and when he continued, there was a grimace in his voice. *"It's a sort of vampire personality disorder. The—"*

"Vampire!" the 911 operator squawked. *"You think your neighbor's a vampire?"*

"No! No, I think his visiting cousin *thinks he's a vampire. That's what Renfield syndrome is and—"*

"Honey, there is no such thing as vampires," the 911 operator said over the boy's explanation.

"But he—"

"There're no buts here, kiddo. You need to cut the nonsense and get off the phone. You can get in a lot of trouble for crank calling 911. There are real people out there who need help and calls like this might prevent them getting through. Someone could be dying while you're wasting our time with this prank."

"This isn't a prank," the boy said earnestly. *"I really think he thinks he's a vampire. He has fangs and—"*

"And I really think you need to stop watching horror

movies and take yourself to bed. I'm writing down your number, boy, and if you call again, the police will be dispatched to your house and they could arrest you for this. Don't call again."

A sharp click sounded. It was followed by a dial tone.

One

"You shot me!"

"Yeahhh." Pet drew out the word on a wince. "Sorry about that, kiddo. It was an accident. I was shooting at the mutants and your big butt got in my way."

"Yeah? Well, this is an accident too," Parker snapped, turning his gun on her character.

"Oh, come on!" Pet squawked, quickly moving her character behind the cover of some trees to avoid the rapid-fire spray of bullets. "It was an *accident*," she protested. "Jeez. I thought we were on the same side."

"You shot me first," Parker pointed out, making his character rush after hers.

"Friendly fire. You'll never make it out of the next level without me, Parker. Just—" A shriek from downstairs caught her ear, and Pet lowered her game controller and glanced toward the bedroom door.

"Is Oksana watching TV or some—?" she began, but

stopped when the shriek ended and the housekeeper began shouting, "Home invasion! Home invasion!"

"Crap!" Dropping her game controller, Pet jumped up from the floor and rushed to the door. Once there, she hesitated though, and then cracked it open to listen. A frown claimed her lips when she heard the deep rumble of an unfamiliar male voice below and then silence.

Reaching for her cell phone, Pet glanced around for Parker and scowled when she saw that her nephew hadn't moved. The eight-year-old was busily shooting her video game character while she was distracted.

"Parker!" she whispered anxiously as she punched in 911 on her phone. "Stop that! We have a situation here. Didn't you hear Oksana yelling home invasion?"

"She always yells home invasion," Parker said with a shrug. "Oksana forgets to close the front door after checking the mail, grabbing the newspaper, or sweeping the front porch. Everyone from neighbors to delivery guys have come in afraid something was wrong 'cause the door is open. When they do, she shrieks home invasion every time. She even yelled home invasion when Mr. Purdy's cat came in yesterday. It's her thing."

"Oh," Pet breathed, relaxing a little. She didn't hit the call button on her phone, but she didn't delete the numbers she'd entered on the keypad either. Oksana still hadn't spoken again. Pet was debating whether she should call out and ask if everything was okay, or keep their presence in the house a secret and tiptoe to the end of the hall to get a look at who was in the entry, when she heard a soft whisper and then a deep male voice boomed, "Hello? Neighbor!"

"That's not a neighbor."

Pet jumped a good foot in the air when Parker spoke those solemn words right next to her. Clutching her chest, she briefly closed her eyes before letting out a slow breath and asking, "How do you know?"

"Because no one in the neighborhood has an accent like that. At least I don't think anyone does," he added with a frown.

Pet hadn't noticed an accent. It had only been two words for heaven's sake. How had he picked up an accent in two words? She gave her head a slight shake. The kid was just . . . different. Super smart and different. Letting her hand drop from her chest, she said, "Well, could it be a *new* neighbor then?"

"I guess," Parker agreed dubiously.

"But," Pet added, debating the matter aloud, "it's hard to imagine Oksana mistaking a neighbor for someone committing a home invasion."

Parker arched his eyebrows. "You heard the part about Mr. Purdy's cat, right?"

Pet merely scowled and shifted her feet as she listened anxiously for Oksana to say something. When there was nothing but silence, she glanced to her phone and then hesitated. She didn't want to call the police only to find out that it really was a new neighbor just checking on them. Sighing, she asked, "Do you have a phone in here?"

"Yeah. I got a cell phone for Christmas."

"A cell phone?" she squawked. "You're like *eight*. Who the hell buys an eight-year-old a cell phone?"

"Mom and Dad," he said with a grin.

"Right," she said with disgust, and then added, "Fine. Then grab your cell phone and stay here. I'm going to go downstairs and see what's happening. But if I say 'Spidey, come on down,' lock your door, hide, and call 911. Okay?"

"Spidey?" he asked, wincing slightly. "Seriously?"

Pet rolled her eyes at the complaint. "If they know your name is Parker Peters, they'll just think it's a nickname. Get it? Parker Peters? Peter Parker? Spiderman?"

"I got it before you explained it," he said with derision. "But it's just so juvenile and lame."

"Are you calling me lame? An hour ago I was your favorite aunt, and now I'm lame?" she asked with amazement, and then realizing this wasn't the moment for such a discussion, muttered, "Whatever. Look, sweetie, this is serious. Just call 911 if I call you Peter then, okay?" She waited for him to nod, and then turned and eased the door open, pausing only to hiss "stay here" before easing out of the room.

The hallway was surprisingly dim for seven o'clock in early June when the sun stayed up until nine or so, but it was light enough to see still. Pet had crept about halfway to the stairs at the opposite end of the hall when a voice called out, "Hello?"

The voice this time was female . . . but not Oksana's. Pet paused to snatch up a crystal vase from a side table, hid it behind her back, and moved to the railing that overlooked the front door entry.

Her eyes widened slightly when she saw the group of people crowding the large entry. Four men and a woman surrounded Oksana, and every one of them was dwarfing the housekeeper, who was a few inches taller than Pet's own five foot two. They were also all staring up at her, she noted, and then her gaze settled on the couple next to Oksana.

Pet felt her shoulders relax as she recognized the pair; Marguerite and Julius Notte. They'd been on the front porch talking to Pet's sister, Quinn, when she'd arrived that afternoon, and had stuck around long enough for introductions before heading back to the Caprellis', where they were staying for a couple of weeks. They were house-sitting while the older couple visited their daughter in Texas.

Pet's gaze slid to the other three men now, and her eyebrows rose slightly. All of them were big, but while two were just tall and muscular, the third was a complete behemoth, taking up twice as much space as anyone else in the entry. He was the biggest man Pet had ever seen, and that was saying something. She dealt with a lot of jocks in her work, but not one of them could have measured up to this guy. The shoulders on him! Good Lord! She'd heard black was supposed to be slimming, but the black T-shirt he wore just seemed to emphasize the width and muscle it was stretching to cover. His black jeans, on the other hand, were making his hips look tiny, or maybe they just *were* tiny in comparison to his shoulders. She followed the line of the jeans down to the black Doc Martens he wore and then ran her gaze back up again, taking in his shaved head and the fact that he wore rings on every one of his fingers. They could have been mistaken for brass knuckles except that they were silver. All told, the guy definitely didn't look too safe to be around.

"Hello, Petronella. How nice to see you again."

Pet forced her gaze back to Marguerite and almost sighed aloud with depression. Honestly, the woman was everything she wasn't but had always longed to be—tall, curvaceous, and beautiful with long, wavy auburn hair and perfect pale skin. Marguerite was wearing a pretty summer dress and sandals that just emphasized her femininity and made Pet feel like a slob in her T-shirt and shorts.

Realizing they were all waiting for her response, Pet forced a smile and murmured, "Hello again."

"We just came by to introduce you to our nephews and their friend. The boys stopped by on their way back from the East Coast and have decided to stay awhile. We didn't want you to be concerned if you saw them coming and going," she explained, and then smiled wryly and added, "But we got here to find the front door wide open. When we didn't see anyone around, we thought we'd better make sure everything was all right. I fear we startled your sister's poor housekeeper."

"Oh," Pet breathed, glancing back to Oksana. A frown curved her lips downward when she noted that the woman was just standing there, staring straight ahead at nothing. Although, she could be watching out the side window for her husband, Pet supposed. Oksana's husband was supposed to pick her up at seven. Pet shifted her attention back to Marguerite, stilling slightly as she noted her eyes. Marguerite and Julius had both been wearing sunglasses when she'd met them that afternoon. They weren't wearing them now, though, and she could see that Marguerite's eyes were blue while Julius's were black, but both had silver flecks in them. It was as if someone had blown glowing silver glitter into—

"You know these people?"

Pet turned in surprise to see Parker at her side. The boy was frowning down at the people in the entry with

THE TROUBLE WITH VAMPIRES   11

Oksana. Taking her nephew by the arm, she gave him a push, trying to send him back the way he'd come. "You were supposed to wait in your room."

Ignoring her urging, Parker held his ground and said, "They don't live on this street."

"Your mother introduced me to them when I got here. They're house-sitting for the Cabellies," she explained, still trying to urge him back toward his room.

"Caprellis," he corrected even as Marguerite did.

"Jinx," the woman said lightly, her smile widening. "It's a pleasure to meet you, Parker. Your mother and aunt were bragging about you this afternoon. Were your ears ringing?"

Parker shook his head, and then asked, "Who are you?"

"Marguerite Argeneau Notte," she announced, and then began introducing the others. "And this is my nephew, Zanipolo Notte—" She gestured to the man on her right who was tall and slender with lean muscle and long black hair pulled back into a ponytail. Pointing to the man just past Zanipolo, she continued, "A family friend, Justin Bricker."

Pet noted his short dark brown hair, handsome face, and laughing green eyes . . . again with silver flecks.

"And our nephew Santo Notte," Marguerite added, smiling at the bald behemoth.

Pet slid her gaze over the taller man's eyes. They were as black as Julius Notte's, but there was much more silver in his eyes, and the lighter color seemed to be growing, she noted grimly.

"And of course my husband, Julius." Marguerite turned and placed a hand on the arm of the man on her left. He was the only man not wearing black. The other three were decked out in black jeans, black T-shirts, and black Doc Martens. It was almost as if it were some sort of uniform. Julius, however, wore the same blue jeans and white T-shirt he'd had on when Pet had met him earlier.

Every one of the men were over six feet tall, but Justin Bricker and Zanipolo were closer to six feet, while Santo and Julius were at least six foot six or better. The two shorter men were also lacking a lot of the muscle Santo had. They were still muscular, but with a leanness to them rather than the solid bulk he had. Julius was somewhere in the middle.

"Where are the Caprellis?" Parker asked suddenly, sounding suspicious.

"Texas." The answer was a rumble of sound from the behemoth Marguerite had introduced as Santo. Pet had always gravitated toward deeper voices, and his seemed to vibrate right through her.

"They wished to visit their daughter," Marguerite added now, drawing Pet's reluctant gaze away from the big man. "I gather she moved there last year and they've been missing her and their grandbabies, so they put their house up on the House Swap exchange. We saw it and applied for a trade."

Parker immediately relaxed and began to grin. "I signed them up on the House Swap site," he announced gleefully, and was suddenly racing eagerly down the stairs.

Cursing under her breath, Pet immediately gave chase. She caught up with Parker as he reached the group in the entry, and started to reach for him, only to realize she still held the vase. Flushing guiltily, she set it quickly on the hall table and then caught Parker by the shoulders and dragged him back until his back bumped against her front.

Hardly seeming to notice the protective maneuver, her nephew exclaimed, "I didn't think it would work this quick, though. So you guys are from Texas?"

"Italy," Santo said, and Pet couldn't keep from looking at him again. He really was beautiful, with high, carved cheekbones, and full sensual lips.

She avoided looking at his eyes and glanced down at her nephew as he asked, "Italy?" She noted the suspicion returning to his face, and unconsciously tightened her hands on his shoulders, drawing him more firmly back against her.

"There was a couple in Texas who wanted to see Italy," Marguerite explained with a shrug. "And we wanted to come to New York, so we did a three-way swap. The Caprellis went to Texas, the couple from Texas went to our home in Italy, and we came here."

"Oh," Parker breathed, his eyes wide. "I didn't know you could do three-way swaps, but that's cool."

"Yes," she agreed. "But I understand and appreciate your concern for the Caprellis. They were waiting to give us the house keys when we arrived, and they seem like a very nice couple."

"Yeah, they are," he agreed.

"Are all your neighbors as nice?" Marguerite asked.

Parker nodded. "Yeah. But the Caprellis and Mr. Purdy are the best."

"Mr. Purdy?" Marguerite queried with interest. "Where does he live?"

"He's our neighbor on the other side," Parker explained, but his voice was quiet now, almost fretful, Pet noted with concern. She peered at him for a moment and then glanced to Marguerite, whose expression was oddly concentrated as she looked at Parker. So were the men's, Pet realized, and had to fight a sudden urge to drag her nephew upstairs and away from these people.

"Ach," Oksana said suddenly. "There is husband. Time to go."

Pet blinked at that announcement from the housekeeper and turned to see her gathering her purse from the hall table.

"We should probably go too now that we've introduced the boys," Marguerite announced as Santo opened the door for the housekeeper to leave. "As I said, we just wanted you to know who the boys were if you saw them coming and going."

Pet shifted her gaze from the old Ford truck that had pulled into the driveway, and to the others as they now followed Oksana out of the house.

"Make sure you lock up," Marguerite suggested as she led the men across the porch. "This is a nice neighborhood, but leaving the door wide open is a bit risky."

"Yes. Good night," Pet said as she watched them leave, but doubted if they'd even heard her. There hadn't been much power behind the words. She watched Oksana hop up into the truck, but as it pulled away, her eyes shifted to Marguerite and the men. Her wary gaze followed them until they disappeared around the hedges that lined the driveway between her sister's house and the Caprellis'.

"Come on," Parker said, heading back upstairs as she closed and locked the door. "I left the game running and we're both probably dead by now. We'll have to start from the last save."

"Are you sure you want to play with me? I mean, if I'm so lame . . ." Pet drawled dryly, still smarting from the earlier comment.

"Well, it's not like there's anyone else here to play with," he said, pausing on the steps to grin back at her.

"You hugged me when I got here and said I was your favorite aunt," she reminded him with exasperation. "Now I'm lame? Which is it?"

"Both," he said with a grin and then pointed out, "You're my *only* aunt. That makes you my favorite, lame or not."

Pet's gaze narrowed. "When did you become such a little smart-as—aleck?" she ended, catching herself before she finished the cuss.

But not quick enough. She could tell by Parker's knowing look before he shrugged and said, "I don't know."

Scowling at him, she started up the stairs.

"But Dad blames you for it," he added.

Pet stopped, her head snapping up with shock. "What?"

Parker nodded. "He thinks I spend too much time under your 'undue influence' and it has led to a bad attitude. His words," he added.

Pet ground her teeth with irritation. Her sister was married to an arrogant asshat. Pet had never liked him and had no idea why Quinn had married the man.

On the other hand, if she hadn't, there would be no Parker, and Pet did love the little smart-ass dearly, so . . . Giving him a push to get him moving up the stairs again, she growled, "I'm so gonna shoot you in the butt. On purpose this time."

"You can try," Parker taunted, rushing eagerly up the rest of the stairs.

Pet followed more slowly, her smile fading and gaze sliding back to the front door as her troubled thoughts returned to her sister's temporary new neighbors . . . and their glowing eyes.

Two

"So that's the boy who made the 911 call."

Santo glanced to Bricker when he made that comment as they filed into the Caprellis' country-style kitchen. Noting Bricker's frown, he asked, "Problem?"

"No." Bricker settled into one of the chairs at the table. "I read him when Marguerite asked about neighbors, and he's definitely worried about this Mr. Purdy."

"Sì." Santo leaned against the light-colored kitchen counter and crossed his arms over his chest. Smiling at his aunt, he added, "It was clever of you to ask that."

"Yes," Bricker acknowledged as Zani settled in the chair next to his. "It made Parker think of his worries for the old man. His call definitely wasn't a prank."

"We told you that when you got here," Marguerite reminded them as she put the teakettle on to boil.

"Yes, but you hadn't talked to him yet," Bricker pointed out. "And you hadn't talked to Purdy either, so you couldn't know for sure."

"I told you, the boy was in school when we got here," Marguerite said, sounding irritated at the implied criticism. She walked to the table and sat down across from Bricker and Zani before continuing. "We would have gone over after he came home but were waiting on you boys. We didn't want you to arrive to an empty house."

"And we did try Purdy's house," Julius added, stepping up behind Marguerite to rub her shoulders soothingly. "We were hoping to resolve the matter that way, but there was no answer when we knocked. Unfortunately, we could not break in to see this cousin for ourselves. This neighborhood is surprisingly busy during the day. In fact, the Caprellis were out working on their front garden at the time and would have seen us. It's part of the reason we came here to talk to them."

"And we learned quite enough from the Caprellis to justify further investigation," Marguerite added firmly.

"What was that?" Santo asked solemnly. He, Bricker, and Zani hadn't had the chance to ask any of this when they'd arrived. They'd been asked by Garrett Mortimer, the head of the immortal Enforcers, to stop in Albany on their way back to Toronto from a job in New Brunswick. Once here, Marguerite and Julius had played them the 911 call and then herded them next door to meet Parker. And the aunt, Santo thought, an image of the petite woman popping up in his mind and making him smile.

"The Caprellis are a nice retired couple who like to keep an eye on the neighborhood," Marguerite explained. "They told us that the Peters are both doctors, and Parker is their only child. He attends a special school for gifted children, is very helpful and respectful, and not prone to playing pranks. We also learned that the Caprellis too had noticed some odd goings-on when it came to Mr. Purdy."

"What kind of odd goings-on?" Zani asked, sitting forward in his seat.

"For one thing, they haven't seen the gentleman for nearly a week, when they would normally see him out in his garden every morning and afternoon," Marguerite said. "The Caprellis have also spotted other people entering the house at odd hours, mostly late at night, which is apparently unusual too. The couple were becoming concerned to the point that Mr. Caprelli was considering going over to check on the man today. Our arrival prevented that."

"Probably a good thing," Santo rumbled, thinking that if Mr. Purdy's visitor was actually a rogue immortal, he might be a danger to anyone who confronted him. Well, any mortal who confronted him anyway.

"We thought so too," Julius admitted quietly. "We decided that between the Caprellis' own concerns for Mr. Purdy and their opinion that Parker wouldn't make crank calls, it was enough to at least warrant looking into the situation. We called Mortimer, and he agreed."

"So you sent the Caprellis to Texas and moved in," Bricker suggested with amusement.

"Yes." Marguerite smiled with satisfaction. "The Council bought them plane tickets and rented them a suite in a nice hotel near their daughter."

Bricker nodded but then raised an eyebrow and

asked, "But why do we need a base? Why not merely raid the house and sort things out quickly?"

Santo noted the way Marguerite glanced at him, and away, and felt his gaze narrow with suspicion.

It was his uncle who answered that question. "Because Mortimer looked into Max Purdy. He felt sure the name sounded familiar. It didn't take much searching for him to realize where it had come up. Purdy is a second cousin to Dr. Dressler."

Santo stiffened, his body going hot and then cold as a sudden rushing sound filled his ears. While he grappled with the cacophony of emotions swamping him, his uncle went on.

"Mortimer wants to move very cautiously here. Dressler is a top priority target. He wants no mistakes that might allow the man to escape us again. He is rounding up as many men as he can spare to join us. In the meantime, he wants us to watch the house twenty-four hours a day and try to discern if the cousin is Dressler or not."

There was a moment of silence during which Santo was aware that everyone was looking his way. He knew they were awaiting a reaction. He could feel their tension and knew they were preparing themselves to stop him if he suddenly ran from the room. No doubt they expected him to try to charge straight to Purdy's home and crash through the door to hunt Dressler. Santo almost would have expected that reaction himself and was quite sure that was exactly what he would have done before his trip to Punta Cana and the counseling he'd agreed to after. But now, as the first shock and emotional rush began to wane, he found himself oddly calm.

Realizing they needed some response before they would relax, he gave an abrupt nod and muttered, "Makes sense."

He almost smiled when everyone exhaled in audible relief, but the urge died quickly as he realized what their reactions revealed. His family had obviously been worrying about him. He disliked troubling others.

"Well," Bricker said, and then cleared his throat before asking, "Wouldn't it have been easier to watch Purdy's place from the kid's house? We'd have an unimpeded view of the Purdy house from there."

"True," Marguerite agreed. "But it would have meant controlling the Peters, and then Pet plus the maid nonstop, and though both doctors are away at the moment, the mother will be back this weekend, and we have no idea when the father will return. It could be tomorrow. Meanwhile, this investigation could take weeks. We decided there were too many opportunities for mistakes that way."

Bricker glanced from Santo to Zani and then back to the couple to point out, "You could have sent them away for a long period like you did—"

"They are doctors, Bricker," Marguerite reminded him sharply. "Mr. Peters is an oncologist and Mrs. Peters is a surgeon. They have patients and schedules and—" She shook her head. "It is one thing to send a nice retired couple on a vacation they wanted to go on anyway and quite another to disrupt the lives of two doctors who have important positions keeping mortals healthy and even alive."

Santo grunted in agreement and then straightened away from the counter and slipped out of the kitchen. He followed the hall to the front of the house and then ducked through the last door on the left. It led into a small sitting area. Santo crossed to a side window and tugged the drapes aside to peer out. This house sat farther forward on the street than the boy's. He had an unhindered view of the front of the house belonging to Mr. Purdy. He stared briefly at the two-story clapboard building, noting that the drapes were all closed and the yard empty. He then turned away and abruptly paused when he saw that everyone had followed him.

A wry smile tugging at the corners of his mouth, he nodded and then moved past them to make his way back down the hall to the rear of the house. He took the last door again, but now it was on his right, directly opposite the kitchen. This was a dining room, and Santo moved to the last side window to peer out again. It looked out over a stretch of grass, and then the garage next door blocked anything else from view.

"There is a tree house at the back of this property," Marguerite said as she joined him at the window.

Santo glanced around at that soft announcement and then followed her pointing finger. A large oak tree stood at the back of the property and he could see a wooden structure perched in its branches.

"It is a little old," Marguerite continued. "But Julius checked it out and said it is still sturdy and allows a very clear view of the back of the Purdy house."

"A tree house?" Bricker asked with dismay, joining them at the window to look out with a scowl. "I'm guessing it's not air-conditioned?"

"No, and no electricity or furniture either," Julius said with exasperation as he entered the room with Zanipolo on his heels. "It is a kid's tree house, Justin, not a four-star hotel."

"I'll watch from the tree house," Santo said as Bricker opened his mouth on what would no doubt have been another complaint.

"Did you read Petronella, Santo?" Marguerite asked suddenly.

"The aunt?" he asked with surprise, his mouth turning down at the name. He hadn't heard it in at least a century. It wasn't used much anymore. He could understand why. He didn't care for the name.

"Yes, the aunt," Marguerite said dryly. "She's Parker's mother's twin sister. Did you read her?"

"No," he admitted, and was surprised himself that he hadn't. He should have. Normally he would have, but Santo had found himself distracted just looking at the woman. She was a cute little bundle. An inch or two above five feet, willow thin, and with long black hair. The name Petronella hadn't really suggested an Asian background. Neither did Parker Peters, for that matter.

Thinking of the boy made him recall how protective Pet had been of him. Santo had noted the way she'd clutched at his shoulders, keeping him close. He'd got the distinct impression she'd wanted to push him behind her, as if she felt she needed to put herself between him and the world. Or Parker and them, Santo thought, not liking that idea. He worried it was himself who'd intimidated her. He knew most people found him alarming because of his size, and didn't like the idea that she might fear him.

A sigh from Marguerite drew his attention, and he raised his eyebrows in question.

"You should try to read her the next time you meet," was all his aunt said.

"Was there something she knows that I should learn?"

Marguerite hesitated and then simply said, "I did not see anything of use to the case, but you might learn something I missed. I think you should try to read her."

Santo nodded and determined to remember to read Petronella the next time they met. If there even was a next time.

Parker was in the kitchen with his head in the refrigerator when Pet finally made her way there.

"What are you doing?" she asked as she checked the back door to be sure it was locked. At least it wasn't wide open, she thought with a shake of the head. She couldn't believe Oksana would leave the front door wide open, but from what Parker had said, it was a common occurrence. She'd have to keep an eye on that when the woman was here.

"I'm looking for something to eat." Parker pulled his head out to glance around. "What are you doing?"

"Just making sure everything's locked up," she muttered, checking the window over the sink.

"Again?" Parker asked with disbelief. "You did that after Oksana and the neighbors left."

Pet ignored the comment and instead asked, "Why are you looking for something to eat? You can't be hungry again. You scarfed down half a pizza at supper."

"That was hours ago," he said on a moan.

"It was only . . ." Pet cut herself off as she glanced at the clock over the window and realized it was nearly nine o'clock. She'd picked him up from the piano lessons he had after school at five o'clock and then had taken him out for dinner. She'd given him the choice of restaurant, and he of course had gone for pizza. They'd been done and on the way home by five thirty.

"We finished dinner three and a half hours ago," Parker pointed out. "I'm starved."

Recalled to the matter at hand, Pet suggested, "Then grab a banana or something and eat it while you get ready for bed."

"Bed?" he asked with dismay.

"In five minutes it will be nine o'clock, Parker," she said firmly. "Your mother said—"

"Yeah, yeah, I'm going," he grumbled, grabbing a banana from the bowl on the counter and pretty much stomping out of the room.

Pet smiled faintly at his attitude as she checked the window by the kitchen table, but paused as she glanced out and noticed movement in the Caprellis' backyard. It was Marguerite's nephew, the big one, walking toward the back fence.

Santo. She tested the name in her head. The man was huge, and gorgeous, with a voice so deep it actually gave her shivers, but Pet was distracted from her thoughts when Santo paused at the large oak tree at the very back of the yard and started to climb up the ladder to the old tree house. Her sister, Quinn, had once mentioned that the Caprellis had built it for their daughter decades ago, and Pet frowned slightly, wondering if it was safe for a big guy like him to climb up into, and why he'd want to. She watched him disappear into the wooden structure, and waited for him to come back out. Several minutes had passed when Parker yelled from upstairs.

Pet turned away from the window and moved out into the hall, flicking off the kitchen light on the way. Her nephew was on the landing upstairs, hanging over the railing, looking for her. She turned off the hall light as she reached the bottom of the stairs and then started up, asking, "What?"

"Can I get a glass of milk before I brush my teeth?" he requested, meeting her at the top of the stairs.

"Yeah. Drink it in the kitchen and put the glass in the dishwasher after, though," she said as she moved past him to start checking the upstairs windows. The kid nodded and was gone like a shot, rushing down the stairs and up the hall to the kitchen.

Pet considered telling him no running in the house, but then didn't bother. He was young, full of energy, and it couldn't hurt to use up some of that energy before he went to bed. She was checking the windows in his parents' bedroom when he found her several moments later.

"I came for my kiss good-night," he announced, hurrying to her side.

Pet eyed his blue pin-striped pajamas with amusement. He looked like a little adult, but his face was pink from scrubbing, and there was a smudge of toothpaste at the corner of his mouth. Bending to hug and kiss him, she asked, "Don't you want me to tuck you in?"

"I'm too old for that," Parker informed her firmly as he gave her a squeeze and peck on the cheek. Pulling away then, he rushed for the door, calling, "Good night."

"Night." Pet watched him go, thinking he was growing up so fast. But then time seemed to pass quickly. It seemed like the older she got, the faster time sped by. Shaking her head at that, Pet moved back to the window. It was locked. Every door and window in the house was. Now she peered out toward the tree house next door. It was still light out. The sun was hiding behind clouds as it made its way toward the horizon. Even so she had no trouble seeing the tree and the tree house in it. Unfortunately, she couldn't tell if Santo was still inside or not, or what he was doing if he *was* still up there.

Giving up on the mystery, Pet headed into the bathroom to brush her teeth and clean her face. After changing into her pajamas, she slipped downstairs to get a glass of water. Pet took it back to her room, collected her iPad from her bag, curled up in bed, turned out the light, and opened the iBook app to the novel she'd been reading.

Santo caught movement out of the corner of his eye and tore his gaze away from the Purdy house to see what was moving in the Caprellis' backyard. Recognizing Zani's lean shape heading toward the tree, Santo turned back toward the houses next door, his gaze skating first over the house where Parker and Pet were, noting that the lower lights were all out. The lights on the top floor were blinking out now too, one after the other. Petronella must be going to bed, he thought, his mind throwing up pictures of her walking through the house, flicking off switches as she went, and then making her way to the bedroom she was using and slowly peeling off her clothes to reveal the compact body beneath.

"Hey, *cugino*. I thought you might be needing some refreshments by now."

Santo turned at that greeting as Zani climbed through the small door and dropped to sit next to him on the tree house floor before offering him two bags of cold blood.

"Grazie," he grunted. The way his fangs dropped at the very sight of the blood told him he was in some need. Accepting the bags, he let one plop into his lap and popped the other to his fangs as he glanced back out the small tree house window. The Purdy house was dark and had been all night, but there was still one light on in the house where Pet and Parker were. The bedroom light, he guessed, even as it blinked out too.

"Anything happening?" Zani asked, peering out the window with curiosity.

Santo shook his head.

"Yeah. Bricker says he hasn't seen anything either. No lights, no movement, nothing."

Pulling the now empty first bag away from his mouth, Santo raised an eyebrow. "He's watching from the front?"

"Yeah. Marguerite and Julius are going to take over for him in the morning, and I'm going to spot you," Zani announced.

"You should sleep then," Santo said before slapping the second bag of blood to his fangs.

"Sì, I should," Zani agreed solemnly. "But I'm too wired to sleep right now."

Santo merely nodded, his focus on the two houses in his view.

Pet flipped the lid closed on her iPad and stared around at the dark shadows cast in the room by the night-light. She'd intended to read for perhaps fifteen minutes or so and then go to sleep. Instead, she'd finished the book. It had taken three glasses of water and as many hours to do it, but the book was done. It hadn't been a great read. That wasn't why she'd kept going. It was her own nerves that had kept her up. She'd sat there, skimming pages and glancing nervously around at every creak in the house. Which was just ridiculous. She'd never been this nervous in her sister's home before, or her own, for that matter. Pet wasn't a nervous person by nature. She knew she could take care of herself. But she kept seeing Santo's eyes in her mind and—

Pet cut off her thoughts and tossed the duvet and sheets impatiently aside to get out of bed. The three glasses of water were working together so that she had to pee now. Muttering under her breath, she made her way to the door by the dim glow of the night-light. When she opened the door, a line of night-lights greeted her. They seemed to come from the bottom of every plug socket, three little pinhole lights each, every six feet, lighting up the floor of the hall that stretched out to either side of her door.

It was actually pretty handy, Pet decided as she slid from her room and headed for the bathroom. The last time she'd stayed here, she'd had to turn on the hall lights to move around at night. Now the newly installed night-lights made it easy to find the bathroom. There was a brighter night-light in the bathroom, so she didn't bother to turn on the light in there either, but quickly relieved herself, washed her hands, and then ran her toothbrush briefly over her teeth again for good measure.

Once done, Pet slipped back out into the hall. She was still wound up and knew getting to sleep was going to be hard, but it was after midnight now, and she had classes the next day. She also had to get Parker to school first. It was going to be an early morning, Pet thought grimly as she made her way back up the hall.

Pet was passing Parker's room when she heard what sounded like a low growl. Pausing abruptly, she stood still, her ears straining. She frowned when it came again. It was definitely a growl, this time ending in a hiss. And it was coming from Parker's bedroom. The moment she realized that, Pet relaxed. The little bugger must be playing video games rather than sleeping, she thought, and stepped to the door.

It opened silently, and Pet swung the door several inches inward before pausing abruptly. The room wasn't completely dark. A night-light next to the bed added a little light, but moonlight was also splashing in through the windows, casting a dim glow across the bed to highlight her nephew's sleeping form.

She stared at him for a minute, and then another spitting hiss drew her gaze to the figure on the foot of his bed. It took Pet a moment to recognize that it was a cat, hunched up and glaring, growling and hissing toward the window. Even as she noted that, the moonlight creeping through the open curtains shifted slightly. Pet glanced toward the window and then froze as she spotted the dark figure outside. With the moonlight behind him, it was impossible for her to see anything more than that it was most probably male, and he was trying to open the window.

"How long do you think it will take Mortimer to gather men together to send out here?"

Santo pursed his lips as he considered the question. Every Enforcer who worked under Garrett Mortimer would be out on jobs right now, hunting down rogue immortals who broke their laws. He knew that, because everyone was always out on jobs since Venezuela. At least half of Mortimer's Enforcers had been sent to the South American country to track down Dr. Dressler, a scientist who had discovered the existence of immortals and started kidnapping them for experimentation. Mortimer still didn't have all of his Enforcers back. A few had remained on the small island off the coast of Venezuela to help. It left him shorthanded as he tried to deal with the rash of rogue activity that had erupted the minute half his Enforcers had been pulled away. The old saying that "while the cat's away, the mice will play" had turned out to be true when it came to rogues and Enforcers. It seemed that the absence of Enforcers had been seen as permission for anyone even considering going rogue to do so and cause trouble. They were still cleaning up the mess. Which meant it might take a while for Mortimer to get men together to send here.

Santo turned his gaze out the window again as he opened his mouth to answer, but paused as he caught movement next door. A dark figure was on the second-floor balcony that ran along the back of the Peters' house. The figure was standing at a window at the far end. He appeared to be trying to open it.

"That's not the aunt, is it?" Zanipolo said grimly, and Santo glanced to the side to see that his cousin had followed his gaze.

"No," he said with certainty.

"I'll get Bricker." Zani disappeared out the tiny door of the tree house.

It took Santo longer to follow than he would have liked. The tree house was small, and he wasn't. He had to crawl to the entrance Zani had just disappeared out of, and then twist slightly to get through the tiny opening. Once he did, though, Santo simply leapt from the tree branch to the ground. When he landed and straightened, a glance showed him that Zani was already at the back door to the Caprellis' house. As he started across the yard at a dead run, Santo saw Zani tug it open and heard him shout that someone was trying to break in next door.

Three

Pet stood frozen in the door, gaping at the figure outside Parker's window until her nephew suddenly shrieked and sat up in bed. When he grabbed the cat and drew it protectively against his chest, she shook off her shock and began to move. Thrusting the door wide, Pet raced to the bed and scooped up Parker, blankets, cat and all, and then turned to rush out of the room.

Her phone was plugged into a charger in the bathroom, which was also the only room with a lock. Pet took Parker there at a run, set him down abruptly, and snatched her phone off the sink counter.

"Call 911," she instructed firmly, holding out the phone as she backed toward the door. "I'm going to—"

"No!" Parker shrieked. Clutching the cat closer, he took a step away from the phone as if it were the devil and shook his head frantically. "You can't leave me! You're supposed to be looking after me."

Pet frowned at his panicked expression, and then glanced toward the hall. She wanted to go see that the intruder hadn't got the window open and actually intruded, but she couldn't leave Parker like this. Releasing her breath on a sigh, she pushed the bathroom door closed.

"Okay, honey. I'm not going anywhere," she assured him, locking the door. "See, I'm staying."

When he just stood staring at her as if still afraid she might disappear, she caught his arm and pulled him to her, then hugged him against her side and raised the phone in her other hand to dial 911.

"There was someone outside my window," Parker said shakily, obviously overwhelmed by everything.

"Yes, honey, I saw," Pet murmured, placing the phone to her ear before glancing down at him. She felt her heart squeeze in her chest as she took in his pale and frightened expression.

"What if they get in?" he asked worriedly, absently soothing the still distressed cat.

The animal definitely hadn't liked whoever was outside, Pet thought, and then wondered where the cat had come from. "Parker, whose cat—?"

The question died in her throat as the ringing stopped and a calm voice said, "911. What's your emergency?"

Pet quickly explained that there was someone outside trying to get into the house through a window. At least she hoped they were still outside.

Several questions followed, including the address. Pet was responding automatically when Parker said, "That's your address, Aunt Pet."

She blinked at him briefly, realizing her mistake.

Deciding she must be more rattled than she'd realized, Pet quickly gave her sister's address instead.

"I've dispatched the police. Have you heard the sound of glass breaking, or anything else that might indicate he's penetrated the house?"

Pet shook her head and then grimaced when she realized the operator couldn't see that and said, "No. Nothing."

"Where are you in the house?"

"The upstairs bathroom," she answered. "It's the only room with a lock."

"Your nephew is with you?"

"Yes."

"Are you safe there until the police arrive?"

Pet turned to peer at the door. It was a door. Wood, probably not solid wood, though, and the lock was your average bathroom lock—stick a narrow bit of wire or something similar in the hole on the outside and the lock would be undone.

Cursing, she glanced around at the small bathroom and then dropped to sit on the floor and braced her back against the toilet and her feet against the door. She had to slide her butt forward an inch or so to manage it, but hoped that would help keep the door closed if the lock was compromised.

"Ma'am? Are you safe in there?" he repeated.

"I—" Pet paused and turned to look over her shoulder at the window over the tub as shouting erupted outside. It was quickly followed by pounding from somewhere in the house. The noise was muffled by the door. Even so, it didn't seem close. It sounded like—

"I think someone's banging on the front door. Could the police be here already?" she asked hopefully.

"Just a minute . . . No. They're still four minutes out."

"Oh," Pet said weakly.

"Is it the police?" Parker asked anxiously, shuffling closer to her until he leaned against her shoulder.

"No, honey," she said forcing a smile. "But they're only four minutes away."

He didn't look any more reassured than she felt by that news, and Pet urged Parker to sit next to her on the floor. He dropped at once, still holding the cat almost desperately, and she slid her free arm around his small shoulders and tried not to think about how quickly one person could kill another. It took less than a second to pull a trigger if the would-be intruder was armed. Wishing she had a gun, Pet began to chew on the inside of her mouth as the pounding sounded again and then was followed by a crash.

"What was that?" the man on the phone asked with concern. She wasn't surprised he'd heard the noise, it had been a damned loud crash. Like wood splintering and slamming to the floor.

"I think we've been penetrated," she said grimly, using his word from earlier, and then closed her eyes briefly as she heard it come out of her mouth. Penetrated? It really just sounded wrong.

"The police are almost there," the 911 operator said soothingly. "Just stay calm."

Pet almost snorted at the advice. The man was miles away, safe in some cubicle somewhere with a headset on, or a phone to his ear. It was easy for him to say stay calm. She had a frightened eight-year-old on her hands, a cat who was suddenly trying to claw his way up on top of the kid's head, and a ridiculously thin bathroom door between them and some lunatic who peeped in windows and broke down doors. She'd like to see him switch places and "stay calm," Pet thought as she grabbed the cat by the scruff of the neck and dropped it back onto Parker's lap. Her nephew immediately wrapped the blankets around the animal, trapping its legs to prevent it clawing its way out again.

"Petronella? Parker? Are you okay?"

Pet stiffened at that call from downstairs. It was female, and familiar, but it wasn't until she heard a deep, rumbling male voice with an Italian accent say, "Upstairs. The bedrooms," that she realized the woman must be Marguerite, because she was quite sure that low growl of a voice that had followed was Santo.

"Oh, I do hope they are all right. You say you heard two screams?" Marguerite's voice was drawing nearer. Pet presumed that meant they were climbing the stairs.

"*Sì.*"

"That does not sound good at all. Petronella? Parker?"

"In here!" Parker shouted and launched himself to his feet to hurry to the door.

"Is it someone you know?" the 911 operator asked, obviously having heard the voices.

"The neighbors," Pet answered, scrambling to her feet as well. "I think—Parker, wait!" she barked as he unlocked and started to open the door. She leapt toward him but was too late and came to a shuddering halt behind him as he stepped into the hall and the lights suddenly came on.

Blinking against the blinding light, she lifted her gaze to the couple in front of Parker. Marguerite and Santo—she in a long white silk nightgown, and he still in the black jeans and T-shirt from earlier.

"Oh." Marguerite smiled with obvious relief. "We were so worried when you didn't answer the knock. The boys saw a man creeping around your house and heard two screams, and we were afraid your intruder had got in and harmed you before we could get to the house."

"We're fine," Pet said. Her mouth tightened, but she didn't comment on the fact that they were able to hear Parker scream when the windows in the house were all closed.

"I only screamed once," Parker said suddenly. "When I first saw him. I was surprised," he added as if to excuse screaming at all.

Pet placed her hands on his shoulders and instinctively drew him closer as she reminded him, "You also screamed 'no' when I was going to leave you in the bathroom to go see if he'd got in."

"Oh." He flushed slightly and nodded. "Yeah. Maybe I did."

Pet glanced back to Marguerite. "Thank you for your concern. I . . ." Her voice died in her throat as she noted the woman's eyes. They were more silver than blue now, as if the excitement of the moment had changed them somehow. Pet stared at the woman's alien eyes and for a minute they seemed to steal her breath as well as her ability to think.

"You are safe with us, dear," Marguerite said quietly, reaching out to touch her wrist gently. Pet felt those words to her very soul. She was safe now that

Marguerite and Santo were there. She knew it and felt herself relax.

"I think your caller is worried about you. Perhaps you should assure him you are all right," Marguerite said gently.

Pet peered down at the phone in her hand with surprise. She'd forgotten all about the 911 operator. Raising the phone to her ear, she heard his anxious cries, "Hello? Hello! Miss? Is everything all right?"

"Yes. Sorry," Pet said as soon as the phone was at her mouth. "Everything is fine. I—"

"Marguerite?"

Pet paused and glanced to the stairs at that concerned call from below.

"Up here, dear," Marguerite responded, turning her head toward the stairs.

"Your neighbors are there now?" the 911 operator asked.

"Uh-huh," Pet murmured as Marguerite's husband appeared on the landing. The concern she'd heard in his voice was equally apparent in Julius's expression as he came into view. It didn't ease until his gaze had slid over the four of them there in the hallway, she noted as he hurried toward them, and then her attention returned to the phone as the 911 operator spoke again.

"I'll warn the officers so they don't mistake your neighbors for the intruder," he assured her, and then added, "They're arriving now, so I'll let you go so you can talk to them."

"Thank you," Pet murmured, hardly hearing his words as she watched Julius Notte reach his wife and slide an arm around her waist.

"Everyone is all right, then?" he asked, pulling

Marguerite close and kissing her forehead. He was bare-chested, with only a pair of loose pajama bottoms hanging low on his hips. The couple had obviously been pulled from bed.

"The police are here."

Pet shifted her attention back to the stairs as Justin Bricker and Zanipolo appeared. Like Santo, they were still dressed.

"The police are asking to speak to the homeowner," Justin announced, glancing to Julius. "Should I—?" He stopped and glanced down with surprise when Parker suddenly launched himself forward, rushing for the stairs.

"Parker!" Pet hurried after him. The boy was still holding the cat and blanket, the latter of which was long and she was sure would trip him up. But he made it to the bottom of the stairs unscathed and didn't stop until he'd placed himself in front of the police officer just coming through the broken front door.

Pet slowed to a halt at the bottom of the stairs as she took in the damage Santo had done. Good Lord, he'd smashed it to pieces. It now littered the floor in short broken slats, leaving a gaping hole where the door had been.

"This is my house."

Pet glanced to Parker at that announcement and forced a pained smile to her face when the police officer blinked down at her nephew and then raised his gaze to her and arched an eyebrow in question. He was a nice-looking man. Tall and burly with dirty blond hair and clear blue eyes. His name tag read Cross.

"Thank you for coming, Officer Cross," she murmured, moving to stand beside Parker. "My name is

Petronella Stone and this is my nephew, Parker Peters. His parents own this house, but I'm watching him while they're both away."

Officer Cross nodded, and then his gaze dropped over her as he pulled out his notepad. When his movements stilled and his eyes widened suddenly, she glanced down at herself and nearly groaned aloud. She'd forgotten she was still in her nightwear. Pet had worn a cropped T-shirt and boxers to bed. The boxers were a pair an old boyfriend had left behind and never asked to have back. They were comfortable and large enough that they hung from her hips rather than at her waist. Her T-shirt stopped several inches above the boxers, leaving a lot of skin on display. It also clung to what little skin it did cover. It read simply:

> You.
> Me.
> Bed.
> Now.

The officer's stern expression cracked into a smile that made her assume he approved, and then a low growl had Pet glancing over her shoulder to see that Marguerite and all four men were coming down the stairs. She couldn't tell where the sound had come from, but did notice when Marguerite reached out to clasp Santo's arm as if to soothe him.

Santo felt Marguerite's touch on his arm but didn't take his gaze away from the petite woman in the entry and the tall policeman looking her over so lasciviously. At least the man had been before Santo had growled. Now the officer had his cop face back on and was eyeing Santo and the others narrowly as he opened his notepad and retrieved a pen.

Forcing himself to relax, Santo frowned slightly at his possessive reaction to the officer's obvious interest in Pet. It had caught him by surprise, coming on rather abruptly, and violently. He'd wanted to plow the man in the face and then pluck the eyes from his head for daring to look on her so.

But then, Santo acknowledged, he seemed to be having odd reactions to Pet as well. For instance, he'd been desperate to get to her when he'd spotted the man creeping around the house. And the scream he'd heard had scared the hell out of him. The second scream had just added to his concern. While his cousin, uncle, and Bricker had chased after the dark figure, he'd gone to the door and been about to crash through it when Marguerite had caught up to him and insisted he knock first. He'd reluctantly done so and then barely waited the length of a breath before knocking again. But that was all he'd managed before he'd sent a fist through the door, grabbed both edges of the hole he'd made, and literally torn the wood apart.

His relief on spotting Pet safe and well upstairs had left him weak and almost gasping. Or perhaps her outfit had been responsible for the breathless part. The woman was a sexy little bundle in the boxers and cropped T-shirt. The top clung lovingly to her skin and was so damned thin he could see the color and shape of her nipples through it. The saying hadn't helped any. *You. Me. Bed. Now.* Good Lord! He'd been hard pressed to think of anything else after that and had stood there like a drooling idiot while everyone else had spoken.

Santo was distracted from his thoughts when a second officer appeared behind Cross and tapped him on the shoulder. They exchanged a few words and since he couldn't hear them, Santo slid into Cross's mind to read what they were talking about. It seemed Zani and Bricker had spoken to the men briefly before coming inside, and while Cross had come to the door, the second officer had gone around to the back of the house, taken the outside stairs up to the balcony, and checked all the windows. Finding one had marks on it as if someone had tried to force it open, he'd then used his flashlight and walked around a bit outside, scouting the area. There was no sign of the would-be intruder.

"Right," Cross said suddenly and turned back to Pet to offer her a smile. "Petronella, you said? Can you spell that for me?"

Santo noted that the man still had his cop face on, but his gaze kept trying to skitter down over Pet's body as he waited, pen poised, for her to spell her name. It was Parker who answered.

"*P . . . E . . . T . . . R . . . O . . . N . . . E . . . L . . . L . . . A,*" Parker spelled out, and then added, "*S . . . T . . . O . . . N . . . E.*"

"Thanks, little guy," the officer said with a grin. "I figured Stone was spelled that way, but it's good to be sure, and Petronella is an unusual name." His gaze slid back to Pet as he added that, his grin widening.

"It is unusual but not unheard of," Parker assured him solemnly. "For instance, there were six female babies named Petronella in 1924. There were 1,161,210 babies born that year, making it only one in 193,535 babies given the name. But it's much more popular in Europe. There have been explorers, Olympic sailors, swimmers, a painter, a poet, a British journalist, and loads of other women with the name. There was even a Doctor Who character named Petronella Osgood."

"My nephew; the walking dictionary," Pet said. Her tone of voice was wry, and Santo noted that she took Parker's arm to draw him in front of her so she could rest her hands on his shoulders. It also helped cover her skimpy outfit. At least it did in the front. He was still getting an unobstructed view of her from behind and found his gaze lingering on her lovely legs.

"Nobody uses dictionaries anymore, Aunt Pet," Parker said, craning his neck to look up and back at his aunt. "They Google things . . . like I Googled your name one time because no one else seemed to have it."

"Of course you did," she said affectionately.

"So," the officer said now, trying to get the conversation back on track. "You called 911 about someone trying to break into the house?"

Santo noted the way the man's gaze slid past Pet to him as he stepped off the stairs to stand behind her. He was aware that the others followed him, and saw the officer's eyes track that as Pet said, "Yes. Parker and I were both in our beds. I got up to go to the bathroom, and heard the cat hissing and growling, opened his door, and there was a man outside Parker's window, trying to open it."

"Can you describe this man?" Cross asked at once.

"No," she said, sounding weary and apologetic. "He was just a dark shape with the moonlight behind him."

Santo saw his own disappointment reflected on the faces of both officers at this news, but Cross made a note in his book, and then asked, "What happened next?"

"I grabbed Parker out of bed, took him into the bathroom with me, locked the door, and called 911."

"She wanted to leave me in the bathroom and go see if the guy had got in, but I wouldn't let her," Parker announced, sounding upset that she would have left him alone.

"Good job, son," the officer said solemnly. "You were both safer waiting in the bathroom for us to arrive."

"Yeah, but we came out when Marguerite and Santo broke in and came looking for us," Parker pointed out.

Both officers immediately turned their gazes back to Santo and his relatives. Pet glanced around as well, her eyes widening when she saw that they had all spread out behind her and Parker in the entry.

"I fear Parker is right, officer, we did break down the door," Marguerite said smoothly. "We're staying next door, you see, and while Santo and Zani were out in the backyard talking, they spotted someone on the second-floor balcony over here and then heard screaming. Well, we all rushed over to try to help. Bricker, my husband, Julius, and my nephew Zani all went after the intruder while Santo and I came to check on Pet and Parker. When they did not answer the door, Santo broke it down." She glanced at the pieces of wood all over the floor and then assured them, "We will of course, call and get someone in first thing tomorrow to repair it. And Pet and Parker can come stay next door with us tonight."

"Oh, no, that's not—" Pet began with a frown, but Officer Cross interrupted her, saying, "That would be a good idea. You can't stay here without a door. Chances are it was just a Peeping Tom and your neighbors scared him off. But if he does come back . . ."

"He is right, dear," Marguerite said, her voice solemn. "You cannot stay here without a door. Besides, we have the room. And Zani and Bricker can stay here and guard the house until the repairman comes tomorrow," Marguerite assured her.

Pet opened her mouth, and Santo was quite sure she'd intended to refuse the offer, but then her gaze slid to Parker and she paused. The worry on his young face brought a frown to hers and she asked, "What would you like to do, Parker?"

The boy peered unhappily at the gaping hole that used to be a door and shook his head. "I don't think we should stay here, Aunt Pet."

"Right," she breathed.

"It is all decided then," Marguerite said cheerfully, moving past Santo to begin herding Pet and Parker toward the door. When she paused suddenly to frown at the cat and long blanket trailing behind Parker and then glanced to him, Santo uncrossed his arms and moved around Pet to scoop up the boy. He carried Parker out the door before Pet could protest, but knew she would follow. She was very protective of her nephew. Still, she must have hesitated, torn between following and staying to deal with the police officers, because he heard Cross say, "We just need to look at the boy's room and question the men. We don't need you for that."

He could tell Pet was already hurrying after him

as she called back to the officer, "Parker's bedroom is the last door at the end of the hall on the left. The room I'm using is the last on the right just past it."

Santo smiled with satisfaction and then quickly hid the expression behind a solemn look as she reached his side and tried to get a look at her nephew.

Her face full of worry, she said, "If Parker is heavy, I could—"

"He's not," he interrupted. "And you are barefoot. You need to watch where you are stepping. Carrying him would make that difficult."

"Oh, right." Pet sounded disappointed. Santo got the distinct impression she wanted to snatch Parker from his arms. He moved more quickly, to ensure she couldn't.

Four

"I think we need some hot cocoa and cookies before bed," Marguerite announced as she opened the door to the Caprelli house. She turned back to smile at Parker in Santo's arms and added, "What do you think, dear?"

"Yes, please," Parker said primly.

Pet managed a smile for the woman when what she really wanted to do was snatch up Parker and run back to her sister's house. She wasn't pleased at the thought of staying in the Caprelli house with these people. She'd rather stick Parker in her car and take him to a hotel for the night. Unfortunately, she hadn't been quick enough to say that before Santo had scooped up the boy and carried him off. She supposed everyone had assumed her saying "Right" in response to Parker not wanting to stay at the house had been agreement to staying at the Caprellis'. Now she didn't know how to get herself and Parker out of there without insulting their hosts or making them suspicious.

Sighing, she followed Santo into the house, aware that Marguerite was behind her.

The big man was very gentle with her nephew, Pet acknowledged as she watched him set the boy carefully down in a chair at the table. But when Santo stepped back and she saw the cat still in Parker's clutches, Pet frowned slightly.

"Parker, whose cat is that?" she asked abruptly, knowing it wasn't his. Her brother-in-law, Patrick, hated cats and claimed the only thing they were good for was oven mitts. He was also allergic to the felines. He wouldn't even have allowed the cat into the house and would freak if he ever learned it had been there. Even if it *had* saved his son from an intruder.

"This is Mrs. Wiggles," Parker said, stroking the animal's head. He no longer had it bundled in the blankets to keep it still. It was remaining in his lap, on top of the blankets by choice.

"Mrs. Wiggles?" Marguerite asked with interest.

Parker nodded, and explained, "Mr. Purdy's cat."

"The home invasion cat?" Pet asked, recalling his earlier story.

"Yes." He smiled, apparently pleased that she remembered.

"Okay," Pet said slowly. "But why was she in your room? And just how did she get there? She wasn't in your room when we were playing video games earlier in the evening. I would have noticed. And I didn't see her anywhere in the house. Did you let her in the window after you went to bed?" The very idea terrified her. If he'd been letting Mrs. Wiggles in as the man had come up to the window . . .

"No," Parker said quickly, apparently seeing her

mounting alarm. "She was in the basement all day until I went to bed." Looking guilty, he admitted, "I didn't really go down to get a glass of milk, I—"

"Went to get the cat," she finished, putting it together now.

Parker nodded. "I didn't want you to know she was there."

Pet tilted her head and eyed him with confusion. "Why?"

"Because you might have made me put her outside, or decided to take her back to Mr. Purdy yourself," he admitted quietly.

Pet considered him briefly and then sighed and said, "And you're right. I would have." When his eyes widened with alarm, she added solemnly, "She's not your cat, Parks. You can't just keep her. And Mr. Purdy is probably missing her," she added firmly.

"Yes, but—"

"And your father is allergic to cats. He won't be pleased to know you had one in the house."

"He knows," Parker countered quickly.

"What?" she asked with disbelief. Knowing Patrick Peters the way she did, Pet was sure that couldn't be true. Her brother-in-law would have thrown a fit.

"He *does* know," Parker insisted. "He saw her in my room yesterday night when he came home. He was upset, but when I told him what had happened, and that I'd called 911 and—"

"You called 911?" Pet interrupted with surprise.

"Yes, but they thought I was making a crank call and wouldn't do anything. When I told Dad that, he said Mrs. Wiggles could stay for the night, but he'd take her back to Mr. Purdy in the morning and check on him for me." Scowling, he added, "But he didn't. Instead, he flew off on business, and I'm kinda glad he didn't because I was worried for him. But he didn't check on Mr. Purdy, and the police wouldn't do anything about it and I don't know what to do, but I can't take Mrs. Wiggles back and let his cousin break her neck."

"Woah," Pet said, moving to his side to rub his back soothingly. "Slow down, Parker. Everything's fine. No one's going to break Mrs. Wiggles's neck."

"Mr. Purdy's cousin will if she goes back to the house. He said so!"

Astonished, Pet stared at her nephew and was about to reassure him that wouldn't happen, when Marguerite spoke up.

"Perhaps you had best explain what makes you think that, Parker," the woman suggested quietly. "Mr. Purdy is your neighbor on the other side, is he not?"

Parker nodded. "Yes. He's our neighbor . . . and a really nice old man. I helped him out with his garden last summer as part of a school project and we became friends. I usually stop there on my way home from school and we play chess and have tea and stuff, but . . ."

"But?" Santo prompted when he hesitated and Pet couldn't resist looking at the man. His voice had still been a deep growl, but it had also been softer than Pet had heard him use before. Almost gentle, she thought, and then glanced back to her nephew as he answered.

"But he has this cousin visiting and—" Parker paused and frowned briefly but then blurted, "He's a real weirdo, and I'm worried for Mr. Purdy."

Pet smiled faintly with relief. Weirdo wasn't so bad. Patting Parker's back, she said, "I understand that, sweetheart, but I'm sure your Mr. Purdy is fine. Everyone has a weirdo in the family. I'm sure this Mr. Purdy wouldn't let this cousin stay with him if he was dangerous."

"But I don't think he even wants him there," Parker said fretfully, and then explained, "Like I said, I normally stop by Mr. Purdy's on the way home and play chess with him. But then at the end of last week, I stopped and he answered the door but didn't invite me in like usual. Instead, he looked real uncomfortable, and he said he had company. His cousin had shown up unexpectedly and it would be better if we put off our daily visits until after he left." Parker paused briefly, a small frown tugging at the corners of his mouth. "I was okay with that. I mean, I understood. I usually skip our visits when I know Aunt Petty is coming too."

Pet smiled and nodded encouragingly when Parker glanced her way. "Go on."

"I did understand," he repeated for emphasis. "But Mr. Purdy was acting all weird."

"Weird how?" Santo asked in a rumble.

"Well, kind of twitchy," Parker explained. "Like he was afraid of his cousin or something. I mean . . . he was saying one thing, but his eyes were kind of rolling around and shifting from side to side, like they were trying to escape his head. It was really weird."

Pet noticed the exchange of glances between Santo and his aunt, and strained to hear what Marguerite said when she leaned closer to the man and murmured. All she caught was something about new turns not recalling or not yet able to control the expression, the eyes, or both while controlling thoughts. She was puzzling over that when Parker started speaking again, distracting her.

"Anyway, I was kind of freaked out and worried, so I kept an eye on Mr. Purdy's house and noticed some odd stuff happening."

"Like what?" Santo asked.

"Well, I saw his cousin come and go several times and he was a lot younger than I expected. I mean he wasn't a kid. He was old like you guys, but Mr. Purdy is ancient, he's like seventy or something, so for him to have a cousin so much younger seemed unlikely."

Pet grimaced at the "old like you guys" bit. Both Santo and his aunt looked to be in their mid to late twenties. Five to ten years younger than her own thirty-six years. Which she supposed meant her nephew saw her as ancient too. She said gently, "That's unusual but not impossible, Parker. My best friend in high school was a girl whose aunt was the same age as us. She even had some of the same classes as we did. And look at Marguerite and her nephews, they all look about the same age."

Parker just shrugged that away and continued, "And I haven't seen Mr. Purdy since the day he answered the door. His cousin comes and goes a lot, and he brings women with him that I never see leave, but Mr. Purdy hasn't come out again at all, not even to water his garden and he's usually always watering his garden in the summer." Shaking his head, he added with bewilderment, "His plants are dying and he's just *letting* them."

Pet was a bit concerned by that comment. Now that Parker mentioned it, that did seem rather odd. Her sister's neighbor had always had a beautiful garden. It was one of the things she'd noticed during her sporadic visits. The garden next door was lush, beautiful, and well-tended. She'd even seen the older gentleman Parker was talking about working in his garden several times as she arrived and left. Not this time, though. When she'd arrived earlier that day, she'd noticed that the usually gorgeous garden was beginning to droop and look a little abandoned.

"And the dogs and the cats in the neighborhood don't like Mr. Purdy's cousin," Parker continued earnestly. "They go crazy when they see him. Heck, they don't even have to see him. Mrs. Matherson's little schnauzer is usually the sweetest little guy, but he goes Cujo every time she walks him past the house. He just suddenly starts growling and barking and pulling on his chain as he lunges, trying to drag her away. He does it whether there's anyone outside or not, but he only started doing it since Mr. Purdy's cousin showed up."

"There are just some people that animals don't like," Pet said reassuringly, not wanting to add to his fears. But she was thinking that animals usually had good instincts when it came to people and if the pets in the neighborhood didn't like Mr. Purdy's cousin, he wasn't someone she would seek out.

"Yeah, but then yesterday after school, Oksana forgot to close the front door after getting the mail and Mrs. Wiggles rushed in. I told you about that," he reminded Pet. "About how Oksana started shrieking 'home invasion' until I caught Mrs. Wiggles and took her back outside. I was going to take her back to Mr. Purdy, but . . ." He looked away and seemed to shrink a bit, his shoulders hunching, and Pet reached out to squeeze his shoulder. He'd obviously been too afraid to knock on the door and was ashamed to admit it.

"You didn't want to bother Mr. Purdy while he had company," she suggested, giving him a way to save face.

Parker nodded and then straightened a little and cleared his throat. "So, rather than bother Mr. Purdy, I decided to put Mrs. Wiggles in the backyard so she could scratch at the screen to be let in. It's what she always does when she's finished with her wandering and ready to go back inside for the night," he explained. "She scratches the screen and Mr. Purdy opens it for her. But she didn't want to go anywhere near the door. I carried her over and set her down and she followed me back to the gate. I did that three times and then I finally scratched at the screen for her, set her down, and hurried back to the gate. I glanced back when I heard the door open and it was Mr. Purdy's cousin. He saw Mrs. Wiggles and . . ." Parker shook his head with bewilderment. "He kind of growled low in his throat, and then he opened his mouth and these fangs slid out and he actually hissed at her like he was a cat too."

Pet stiffened at this news, but Parker didn't notice and continued, "Mrs. Wiggles arched her back and hissed back, then rushed over and launched herself into my arms." Parker paused, his expression tightening with remembered fear. "That's when he noticed me and said, 'Bring that damned cat around here again, boy, and I'll break its neck!' and then he slammed the door."

Parker paused and let his breath out on a shudder of remembered fear. "He was real mean about it, Aunt

Pet. Real mean, and he had an accent. British, I think. But not," he added with confusion. "It's like he started out British and lived somewhere else that kind of changed the accent a bit if you know what I mean?"

"*Sì*," Santo said when Pet didn't respond. She couldn't; Parker's comment about the fangs had sent fear slithering down her back. She was suddenly desperate to get him away from the entire neighborhood. Forcing herself to remain calm, she blocked those thoughts and simply listened, but her eyes were sliding around the room, checking out exits and anything that could be used as a weapon.

"Anyway," Parker continued, "I was pretty upset. I mean, Mr. Purdy loves Mrs. Wiggles, but this cousin won't let her in, and that didn't seem right, so I brought her home. Dad wasn't here yet, and Mom was upstairs getting ready for work—she's been working nights in the ER the last week because one of the emergency surgeons was off sick," he explained, and when everyone nodded, continued, "Anyway, I knew Dad wouldn't be happy if he found Mrs. Wiggles in the house, but I couldn't believe Mr. Purdy would be happy with all this, so . . ."

"So?" she prompted, eyeing him with concern.

"I called 911," he admitted on a sigh. "I thought maybe if the police went there, they could . . ." He shook his head helplessly, and then his shoulders drooped in defeat. "But they thought it was a crank call." Parker scowled unhappily and then muttered, "I never should have mentioned Renfield syndrome. Maybe if I hadn't, they wouldn't have thought I was pulling a prank, and would have checked on Mr. Purdy."

"I don't understand," Pet said slowly. "Why would they think you were pulling a prank? What is Renfield syndrome?"

"Oh." He shrugged, looking suddenly uncomfortable. "It's just . . . it's a psychiatric disorder where the patient believes—" He paused abruptly and admitted, "Actually, it's never been officially recognized and published in the DSM or anything, so I'm not sure if it would be considered a true illness. But a psychologist named Richard Noll came up with the term and published it in 1992 as—"

"Parker," Pet interrupted patiently, knowing he'd explain absolutely everything he knew about the diagnosis if she let him. The damned kid was entirely too intelligent for his own good. When he stopped and peered at her in question, she said, "Just tell me what Renfield syndrome is, please."

Parker took a deep breath and then rushed out, "It's when an individual believes himself to be a vampire."

Pet stiffened but avoided looking at Marguerite and Santo and forced herself to remain calm as she asked, "You think Mr. Purdy's cousin *thinks* he's a vampire?"

"Yes."

Pet nodded, but her mind was racing. Her nephew was a fricking little genius, intelligent beyond his years. His parents had figured that out quickly and pulled him out of public school right after kindergarten to put him in a school for gifted children where they shaped the education to the child. There, Parker had already sped through the standard grade school curriculum, and at the age of eight was halfway through the high school curriculum as well. It was something

Pet didn't agree with. The kid was book smart, sure, but he had no friends and couldn't possibly grow up properly socialized this way.

Now she was wishing he wasn't so bright for other reasons. To her mind, his brilliant little brain was leading him to dance a little too close to the fire for comfort.

"And that's okay," Parker said now. "I mean, I don't care if he wants to run around wearing fake fangs and scaring the dogs and cats in the neighborhood, but I'm worried about Mr. Purdy. What if the cousin decides to bite him or something?"

"So, this visiting cousin has fake fangs?" Marguerite asked solemnly.

Parker nodded. "Yeah. The fangs are super real-looking, but they have to be fake," he assured them and then added an uncertain, "Right?"

"Yes, of course," Pet said quickly, but noted the glance Marguerite and Santo exchanged.

"Yeah," Parker agreed, seeming disappointed. But in the next moment he perked up and said, "I wish I knew where he got them. I'd be Dracula for Halloween, 'cause those fangs were super cool. They actually seemed to slide down out of his upper gums."

"Did they?" Pet asked weakly, and then decided it was time to get off this subject. "So, what happened after you called 911 and they didn't believe you?"

"Well, I took Mrs. Wiggles to my room. I mean I couldn't just leave her outside. She's a house cat. Mr. Purdy lets her out to sun herself in the garden during the day, but she always sleeps indoors," he pointed out, and Pet murmured an agreement when he seemed to be waiting for one. Once she had, he continued, "Everything was fine until Dad came home. He was late getting in, and I was already in bed. Mrs. Wiggles was sleeping with me, and Dad must have looked in on me, 'cause he freaked out and woke me up!"

Parker grimaced and then explained to Marguerite and Santo, "Dad's super allergic to cats, so wasn't too happy to find one in the house. But I told him what had happened and how worried I was about Mr. Purdy and what Mr. Purdy's cousin said he would do if he saw Mrs. Wiggles again, and Dad said she could stay for one night, but he was taking her back in the morning, and he'd check to be sure everything was okay with Mr. Purdy when he did."

"That would have been this morning?" Pet asked, just trying to be sure she was getting the time line right. When Parker nodded, she asked, "And was Mr. Purdy all right?"

The boy scowled, anger clouding his face. "Dad never went over. When I got up this morning, Mrs. Wiggles was still in my room and Mom was cussing and swearing on the phone to you about Dad taking off without even talking to her about it, and she couldn't believe he'd done that when he *knew* she had that big convention and she was the keynote speaker and everything."

Pet nodded solemnly. The phone call Parker was talking about was the reason she was looking after him. Her sister, Quinn, had been in a heck of a state when she'd called to ask if Pet could look after Parker for the week. She had a convention to go to and her husband, Patrick, was supposed to be the one looking after Parker while she was gone. But instead Quinn had received a text message on her way home from the hospital that morning, announcing that Parker was still sleeping and while Patrick had waited as long as he could for her to get home, he had to head out or he'd miss his flight. He was going out of town on business and would call when he could.

Fortunately, Quinn had only been minutes from home at that point, but she'd been livid. "A text message! Can you imagine? He left Parker all alone and didn't even have the balls to call me," she'd shrieked. "Probably because he knew I'd react like this. The convention has been on the calendar for almost a year. Patrick knew how important it is to me. He knew I counted on him to watch Parker, and then he just takes off 'on business' hours before I'm supposed to fly out? Leaving our son alone at home! What fricking business? He's an oncologist, not a stewardess."

"I think they're called flight attendants now," Pet had responded automatically. The silence that followed had clued her into the fact that it had not been the right thing to say and Pet had quickly offered to look after Parker while Quinn went to her conference. She'd then spent several minutes trying to calm her sister before she managed to hang up.

What had followed was a mad rush to pack up everything she might need while she stayed in her sister's home and looked after her nephew. Pet had then headed to work, knowing she would be coming here at the end of the day rather than her own place. Fortunately, UAlbany was on the summer schedule now and she only had a couple of lectures a day, so would be here when Parker got out of school. The private school he attended wouldn't stop for summer break for another couple of weeks.

"So," Parker continued, "I fed Mrs. Wiggles and tried to think what to do. I wanted to tell Mom about Mr. Purdy and his cousin and Mrs. Wiggles and about Dad not taking her home and checking on Mr. Purdy like he'd promised, but she was already so mad at him I thought maybe I'd better not. And then she was so grumpy, I decided it might be better just to put Mrs. Wiggles in the basement for the day and figure out what to do later."

Heaving a sigh, he shook his head and said, "Only I was so excited to see you when you came to pick me up after school . . . and then we went to dinner and came back and played video games and . . . I forgot all about her until bedtime," he admitted, shamefaced.

"Why didn't you tell me about her then?" Pet asked quietly. "I would have taken her back and checked on Mr. Purdy for you."

"I almost did," Parker admitted. "But then I was afraid the cousin might hurt you or something, and decided I'd better not."

Pet normally would have bristled at the suggestion that she couldn't protect herself, but this time, she didn't and simply nodded in understanding.

"The cocoa's ready," Marguerite said into the silence that had fallen over the room. Pet glanced around to see that the woman had moved away to prepare four cups of hot chocolate while she'd been distracted listening to Parker.

"Santo, why don't you carry the cocoa to the table while I plate the cookies?" Marguerite suggested and the comment made Pet blink with surprise. She hadn't heard anyone refer to plating food since her university days, when she'd worked waiting tables in a restaurant to make extra money. Marguerite obviously had a similar experience. That or she was a chef. The thought made Pet frown as she realized she didn't know a thing about these people. In the normal course of events she would have asked such questions. In this instance, she hadn't . . . and wouldn't.

Pet pushed that thought away as soon as she'd had it and forced a smile. "What can I do to help?"

"Nothing, dear. Just sit down. I'll be right there," Marguerite assured her. Pet could see that it was true. The woman had already retrieved a plate and was even now transferring cookies to it from a Tupperware container. Pet made herself remove the hand she'd had on Parker's shoulder almost since their arrival and settled in the chair next to him. She couldn't resist scooting her chair a little closer to his, though, and then Santo was suddenly leaning over her to place a cup of hot cocoa on the table in front of her.

Pet stilled, her body automatically going on high alert as it prepared for fight or flight. He didn't touch her, didn't even brush against her, but she was very aware of the heat from his body. His scent, a heady musk, briefly enveloped her and she found herself closing her eyes and inhaling deeply to suck the intoxicating aroma deep into her lungs.

"Here we are." Marguerite's voice was cheerful and drawing nearer.

Pet flushed guiltily and blinked her eyes open as Santo straightened and moved on to set down Parker's cocoa. She watched silently as the woman set a plate of chocolate chip cookies on the table. Marguerite then settled in the chair opposite Parker, leaving Santo to sit next to Pet.

"Hot cocoa and cookies are my comfort food," Marguerite said cheerfully as she took a cookie and then pushed the plate closer to Parker and Pet. "They always help me put things in perspective."

Pet managed a polite smile but didn't reach for a cookie. Parker immediately took one, though, and settled down to eating it and drinking his cocoa with an enthusiasm she envied.

"Aren't you going to have one, Petronella?" Marguerite asked gently.

Pet shook her head at once. "My stomach's still churning. Too much excitement I guess."

Marguerite murmured sympathetically, and Pet glanced away, her gaze landing on Santo. She stiffened when she noted the concentrated expression on his face as he peered at her. Shifting uncomfortably, she turned back to her nephew. "Hurry up and finish, Parker. You need to get to sleep. Tomorrow is a school day."

Nodding, the kid took another bite of his cookie and reached for his cocoa. Pet was watching him tensely when a dog barked somewhere in the house. Raising her head, she glanced to Marguerite, almost hopefully. "You have a dog?"

"Yes, dear. A Neapolitan mastiff," she said, seeming amused by something.

Pet almost shuddered with relief but tried to look regretful as she said, "Oh, well, we should probably go stay at a hotel then. I mean, I wouldn't want Mrs. Wiggles to be a problem."

"Nonsense, J loves cats," Marguerite said at once.

Pet frowned, seeing her chances of escape slipping away, and then rallied and said, "Yes, but I'm not sure how Mrs. Wiggles will react to him. She might swat him with her claws or something. I wouldn't want—"

"Let's see, shall we?"

Before Pet could protest further, Marguerite was on her feet and out of the room. A moment later, the soft clack of claws on hardwood announced her return as she led a huge leashed, black dog back into the kitchen. Pet's eyes widened as she stared at the beast. He was just short of three feet tall on all fours, but she suspected would be taller than her if he stood on his hind legs. She was equally sure he weighed a good fifty pounds more than she did, and all of that appeared to be muscle.

"J, this is Pet," Marguerite announced, stopping next to her.

Pet stared at the dog blankly and then blinked when the animal stepped forward and laid his head in her lap in greeting.

"It's all right. He won't bite," Marguerite said gently.

"He will drool, though," Santo said with amusement.

Pet smiled faintly and petted the beast's big head, surprised at how soft his fur was. She gave a startled laugh when the dog slid his tongue out to lap at her arm as she petted him.

"Good boy," Marguerite said, and then gave the slightest pressure on his chain. The big dog stepped back from Pet and turned to his mistress as she gestured to Parker and said, "J, this is Parker and his cat, Mrs. Wiggles."

The dog peered at the boy and cat and then tilted his

head and moved it slowly forward until it just rested on the edge of Parker's thigh next to the cat. Mrs. Wiggles sat very still, her eyes narrowed as Parker reached out to pet the dog's head, but then unbent enough to lean forward and lick the dog's snout once before relaxing back on Parker.

"I think she likes him," Parker said with a grin as he continued to pet the dog.

"I think so too," Marguerite agreed, returning his grin, and Pet sighed inwardly. Leave it to a cat to be contrary. She wanted it to raise a fuss and try to swat the big dog so she'd have an excuse to take Parker and the cat away. So, of course, the cat liked the damned dog.

"Eat your cookie, Parker. You need to get to bed," she said quietly after a moment, and her nephew acted as good as gold, nodding and giving J one last pat before turning his attention back to his cookie and cocoa.

When Marguerite returned to her chair and sat down, the big dog followed and dropped to lie at her feet. The moment he did, the woman bent to remove the leash.

"He seems well trained," Pet commented as Marguerite set the leash on the table. "How old is he?"

"Just over a year old." Marguerite bent to pet the big beast. "Julius got him for me about three months after we lost his predecessor to cancer."

"Oh, I'm sorry," Pet murmured, knowing how painful such a loss could be. They'd always had dogs as kids. She actually missed that.

"Thank you for the hot chocolate and cookie."

Parker's polite words drew Pet's attention to the fact that he'd finished his snack . . . which meant it was bedtime, and she hadn't managed to come up with an excuse to leave.

"I'll show you to your rooms," Marguerite said brightly, getting to her feet.

"Room," Pet said quickly as she got up as well. "I can sleep with Parker and Mrs. Wiggles. It'll be less work."

"As you like," Marguerite said easily as she headed for the door.

"Sleep well," Santo murmured.

Pet glanced back at that soft rumble from the big man and saw that the dog had moved to sit by him rather than follow his mistress. She mumbled, "Good night," as she followed her nephew and Marguerite out of the kitchen, but the truth was Pet didn't expect she'd sleep at all. Once the house was quiet and she was sure everyone was sleeping, she might even sneak Parker and Mrs. Wiggles out and leave a note with some excuse or other . . . if she could come up with one. She set her mind to that task as she trailed Parker upstairs but hadn't come up with anything when Marguerite stopped and opened a door halfway up the hall.

"This is the guest bathroom," she announced with a smile.

"Oh, good! I gotta go," Parker said with relief, and then hesitated before turning to Pet to offer her the cat and blanket.

Pet took the bundle of blanket and fur and watched solemnly as he closed the door.

"While he's in there, why don't I show you the room you will be using?" Marguerite suggested.

Pet hesitated, but then nodded and followed Marguerite to the next room down the hall.

"Here we go." Marguerite opened the door and led the way inside. "Julius and I are just across the hall, and Santo is in the next room up from this one, so you know where to go if there's a problem or you need extra blankets or pillows."

"Thank you," Pet said quietly as she set Mrs. Wiggles on the queen-sized bed. The cat clawed at the blankets briefly and then turned in a circle several times before settling down like a queen claiming her throne.

"Petronella," Marguerite said gently, drawing her gaze away from the cat. "We have no connection to the Brass Circle in China. In fact, we work with Enforcers who would hunt members of that group down should they ever try to move their activities into North America. You really are safe with us."

Pet's eyes widened incredulously. She'd been trying hard not to think about that boogeyman from her childhood called the Brass Circle ever since spotting the silver flecks in their eyes and recognizing that they were the result of nanos that made them immortal. Obviously, she'd failed. Enough of her thoughts had slid through for Marguerite to read them, and she was trying to reassure her. "I—"

"Hey! You left without me!"

Pet snapped her mouth closed and turned to the door as Parker rushed in. Managing a smile, she explained, "Marguerite was just showing me where we're going to sleep."

"Cool," he said, heading straight for the cat. Cooing soothing words, he gave the animal a gentle pet and then climbed into bed.

"Well, I should go and let you two sleep. Good night," Marguerite said solemnly.

"Good night, Marguerite," Parker chirped.

Pet murmured, "Good night," as well and watched the woman pull the door closed.

Five

Santo knew Marguerite was coming long before she appeared in the kitchen. He heard the whisper of her gown and the sound of her heartbeat before she'd made the bottom of the stairs. J raised his head and watched the door a moment later as he too heard her approach.

"How did you know?" Santo asked the moment his aunt stepped into the room.

Marguerite paused and peered at him with a smile just beginning to bloom on her lips as she asked, "You cannot read her then?"

Santo shook his head. "But you expected that."

"I did," she breathed, her smile finally breaking out. "The minute she pulled up in her car and walked up to join us on the front porch with her sister, I just knew she was yours."

"How?" he asked with curiosity. He hadn't recognized her at first. Oh, certainly, he'd found her attractive. But that attraction had been distracting enough that, despite Marguerite's suggestion that he read her, he hadn't thought to try until they were sitting here at the kitchen table. He'd only done it then because Pet had seemed so stiff and tense. She'd kept her expression composed, but he'd sensed that she was braced to leap up, snatch her nephew, and flee at the first provocation. It had made him curious enough to finally think he should read her. His shock when he'd found he couldn't . . . Santo still felt that shock again and closed his eyes briefly. His life mate. Dear God, he could hardly believe it. He had waited so long for her.

"It is hard to explain," Marguerite said finally, drawing his eyes open. "It is a kind of energy that comes off of you both. It is . . . not exactly the same, but . . ." She shook her head helplessly.

Santo nodded solemnly, letting her off the hook. He was about to ask why Pet was afraid, and—more important—if it was because of him, when they heard the front door open and close. J was on his feet at once and rushing from the room with a soft woof of greeting.

"Ciao amico," they heard from the hall and Santo sat back in his seat and relaxed as he recognized Julius's voice. His uncle entered the kitchen a moment later, petting the dog as he walked, but straightened as soon as he reached Marguerite. Kissing her firmly in greeting, he slid his arms around her waist and smiled down into her face as he asked, "How is my goddess?"

"Glad to see you," she said with a smile, placing her own arms around his neck. "Is everything okay at the house?"

"Mmm." Julius nodded and kissed her again before saying, "We handled the police and then took care of the gaping hole where the front door used to be, and now the boys are watching the Purdy house from there." Turning to Santo then, Julius arched an eyebrow. "Could you not have merely broken the door open without completely demolishing it? There was not enough wood left to even nail it across the hole. We had to break up a coffee table and a bed headboard and use them. Now we have to replace those as well."

"I will pay," Santo assured him.

"No, you will not," Julius said firmly. "The Council will pay. We are here on their behalf."

He didn't let Santo argue the point, but started to usher Marguerite to the door, saying, "Now I am taking my wife back to bed. You should retire too. You and I are replacing Zani and Bricker at the Peters' house tomorrow morning. Good night, nephew."

"Good night," Santo murmured as he watched them leave. For the first time, he didn't feel the pinch of envy that normally assailed him when he saw mated couples together. There was nothing to envy. He had met his life mate . . . Now, he just had to figure out how to woo and claim her.

Santo blinked as that thought ran through his mind. Good Christ! He had to woo and convince her to allow him to claim her. How the devil was he supposed to do that? Unfortunately, Santo didn't have a ready answer. It had been a hell of a long time since he'd wooed anyone. As in more than two millennia. He had some serious thinking to do.

Pet snapped awake and lifted her head, barely restraining a groan as her neck muscles protested. She was sitting at the top of the bed next to Parker and had nodded off, her head falling forward, so that her chin rested against her chest.

Grimacing, Pet rubbed the complaining muscles of her neck with both hands and peered around the room. She'd left the lamp on her side of the bed lit to help her stay awake. Sleeping had not been on the agenda. While Marguerite's assurance that they were not affiliated with the Brass Circle had at first reassured her . . . well, talk was cheap. She didn't know these people. Marguerite could be lying, so Pet had decided she'd remain on her guard until she could talk to the woman again and learn more.

Part of her brain was arguing that Marguerite had no need to lie. As an immortal, or what most people would mistakenly call a vampire, Marguerite could have just taken control of her and made her do whatever she wanted. That being the case, why would the woman waste her energy on lying? But the more cautious side of Pet, and much to her surprise there *was* a more cautious side, was arguing that it was better to be safe than sorry.

Pet leaned her head wearily back against the headboard and acknowledged that it was a relief to at least be able to think about this stuff now. Knowing immortals could read the minds of mortals, she'd been afraid to even think about the fact that she recognized from their eyes what these people were. She'd feared what they'd do if they realized she knew. In her experience, immortals could be wonderful or terribly dangerous. Pet wasn't sure yet which kind she was dealing with.

Sighing, she started to stretch her legs out from

their cramped position, only to pause at a hiss from Mrs. Wiggles. The cat was why she was sitting with her legs curled up almost under her. Parker had left the damned furball on one side of the bed and climbed under the blankets on the other side to go to sleep. It left Pet the top half of her side of the bed to sit on. Since she hadn't planned to sleep, she hadn't considered it a problem earlier, but there was no way she was going to be able to remain in this position all night. Her legs were already starting to cramp.

Muttering under her breath about cats who thought they owned the world, Pet shifted her feet off the bed, careful not to disturb her highness, Mrs. Wiggles, during the process. She carefully stood and paced away from the bed, smacking her mouth as she did. Thanks to sleeping upright, her mouth had apparently hung open and was now dry and nasty.

Biting her lip, she glanced to the door and then back to the bed, fretting over whether it was safe to leave Parker alone while she fetched a glass of water. She'd heard Marguerite and her husband retire earlier, and thought Santo had probably gone to bed too. Still . . .

Pet tapped her foot impatiently, debating the issue, but knew that aside from taking care of her dry mouth, water would help her stay awake. Mind made up, she moved to the door, listened briefly, and then eased it open.

The hallway light was off, but someone, probably Marguerite, had left the bathroom light on and the door open to allow that light to stream out into the hall. Pet slid out of the bedroom, pulled the door silently closed, and then tiptoed to the stairs at the end of the hall.

There was light coming from the kitchen when she turned into the downstairs hall, but it was dim, not the main light. Had Marguerite left a small light on there too in case she came down in search of water? Or was someone still up? Unsure, she approached the room just as quietly as she'd made her way thus far, and-rather than head straight in, she paused to peek around the door frame. Pet froze when she spotted Santo at the kitchen sink with his back to her. It was only now that she could hear the rush of the tap running. He was . . .

Pet blinked. The huge bear of a man was washing dishes while wearing a ridiculous frilly apron, she realized as he turned slightly to set one of the cups on the draining rack. She watched him set it down, and then glanced to his face, just glimpsing the blood bag at his mouth before he turned back to the sink.

Nothing could have stopped her startled gasp when she saw that, or her second gasp when Santo caught the sound and jerked around to gape at her with a half-full bag of blood stuck to his face. It was his expression and probably how ridiculous he looked in the frilly apron that pushed her past her first shock and horror and on to the realization that he was *drinking blood from a bag.* He wasn't one of the bad immortals that bit people and drank straight from the vein of their unfortunate victims. He wasn't one of the dangerous ones, her brain reassured her, but it hardly needed to. Honestly, the man looked anything but dangerous in that get-up, and the expression on his face was priceless. The man's eyes were wide with both guilt and horror above the bag at his mouth.

Just as she got past her dismay, Santo suddenly

reached up and snatched the bag away from his mouth. Big mistake, Pet decided, grimacing as the bag tore and blood went flying everywhere.

Cursing, Santo turned and threw the still bleeding bag in the sink, then just as quickly swung back to face her again, his expression now tormented, miserable, and almost hopeless.

Pet couldn't decide if he looked more like a serial killer or a serial killer's victim with the blood covering his face and shirt. It was on the counter and floor too, she noted, and shook her head at the mess he'd made.

"I . . ."

Pet raised her eyes back to his face, waiting politely for whatever he wanted to say. But he just gaped at her with such dismay she began to feel sorry for him. He was acting like he didn't know that she knew about his kind. Surely, he'd read her thoughts as Marguerite obviously had, and knew she knew about immortals? Maybe not, Pet decided when he continued to gape at her, his mouth moving slightly but no words coming out.

Deciding they would be standing there until dawn if she waited for him to speak, Pet finally entered the room and walked to the roll of paper towels that sat on a holder by the coffee machine. Ripping off several panels, she handed a couple to Santo to clean himself up, and then knelt in front of him to quickly mop up the worst of the blood on the floor and cupboard doors with the others.

When she finished and straightened, he was still staring at her with dismay. The paper towel she'd given him was crumpled in his hand and his face and chest were still awash with blood. The man seemed to be completely out of it.

Sighing, Pet tossed her used paper towels in the sink and snatched back the ones she'd given him, intending to clean him up. Unfortunately, he was ridiculously tall, and short of scaling his body like a mountain climber, she wasn't getting at his face.

"Bend down," she ordered.

Santo stared at her like she'd spoken Mandarin.

Pet scowled and then heaved out a resigned sigh and walked over to grab a chair from the kitchen table. She dragged it back in front of him and then climbed up on it. Fortunately, that put her face on a level with his and she was able to wipe the blood off his cheeks. But she was aware of the way his eyes burned into her as she worked.

"You . . ."

Pet paused and peered at him in question. When he didn't continue, she returned to wiping away the blood, moving from his right cheek down to his chin.

"I was just . . ."

She paused again to meet his gaze, but apparently, he couldn't come up with a feasible lie. That or he couldn't bring himself to admit what she'd caught him doing. Deciding to let him off the hook, she said, "You were just having a late-night snack."

When Santo stiffened, she added, "You're what some would call a vampire but is really an immortal. You need blood to survive and you get that blood from blood banks and yada yada yada," she ended on a mutter, returning to her efforts to clean him up.

"You know?" he breathed with amazement.

She met his gaze and said solemnly, "Yes. I know."

That helped chase the horror off his face, but now he just looked perplexed and she turned her attention to the blood dripping down his neck to give him some time to assimilate what she'd said. But when she began to chase the trails under the collar of his shirt, he caught her hand with his.

Pet froze. He wasn't hurting her, just holding her hand flat against his collarbone, but he'd moved so swiftly . . . She'd forgotten how quickly they could move, and felt now like she'd wandered heedlessly into a tiger's cage. Swallowing, she raised her head to meet his gaze.

They stared at each other for a moment, and then he finally asked, "Marguerite?"

"No, she didn't tell me," she said, easing her upper body back a bit, and then admitted, "I recognized what you all were the minute I saw your eyes." Her gaze shifted to his eyes now, and she stared briefly. They were beautiful, as deep and dark as space, with tiny flickering silver stars adding light.

"You already knew about immortals?" He asked the question slowly, as if trying to feel his way to the answers he was looking for.

Noting that his voice was deeper than usual and husky, Pet forced herself farther back from him and nodded. "I've known about immortals since I was three or four."

Surprise flashed again on his face and was quickly followed by a frown. "Yet you were afraid? Was it me? Did my size—?" He paused abruptly when she snorted at the suggestion.

"I get big guys in my classes all the time," Pet told him with amusement and then admitted, "Granted they aren't usually as big as you. Still, your size doesn't intimidate me."

Santo looked uncertain for a minute and then asked, "Then why?"

Pet shrugged. "I don't know you people, and not all immortals are nice, any more than all mortals are nice."

She could actually feel the tension in his body ease under where he had her palm pressed to his upper chest. But all he said was, "Now you are not afraid."

"You drink bagged blood. You're one of the good ones," she said simply, and then tugged on her hand. This time he released her. Pet immediately pulled away and climbed down off the chair. Picking it up to carry it back to the table, she said, "You'll have to wash off the rest. It's started to dry."

Pet heard the rush of water as he turned the tap on again, and realized only then that he'd turned it off when he'd heard her gasp. She slid the chair under the table and turned to see that he was dampening the paper towel she'd been using. Leaving him to it, she moved to the cupboard she'd seen Marguerite get the cups out of and opened it. As she'd expected, there were glasses there too, and she took one and then walked to the sink as Santo turned off the tap. She waited for him to move aside, and then turned on the cold water and ran herself a glass and gulped it eagerly down.

"Better?" Santo asked as she set the empty glass in the sink.

Pet turned to peer at him and couldn't hold back her amused grin when she saw the mess he'd made of his face. He hadn't got all the blood; there were still specks of it here and there. On top of that, though, he now had bits of paper towel all over his face, caught in the stubble on his cheeks and chin.

"Damn," Santo muttered, apparently taking her amusement to mean no, it wasn't better. Returning to the sink, he turned it on. This time he simply stuck his head under the tap and then scrubbed his face with his hands.

Chuckling softly, Pet picked up the dish towel and moved to his side. When he turned off the water and remained bent over, allowing the water to drip off his face, she pressed the towel into his hand and then stepped back as he straightened and dried his face and hands. Lowering the towel then, he turned and raised an eyebrow in question. "Better now?"

"Mostly, but you missed some on your neck," she said, and held her hand out for the towel.

He gave it up at once and Pet stepped forward and then frowned. It was the same problem as before. The man was ridiculously tall, and while she generally liked tall men, it could be pretty inconvenient for tasks such as this. She could reach his neck, but it would mean standing chest-to-chest with him to do it. Arching one eyebrow, she said, "Either you have to bend over, or I have to get the chair again."

Santo grinned at her annoyed words and then simply picked her up and set her on the counter next to the sink. He followed that up by stepping forward until his stomach brushed against her knees.

Pet stared up at him wide-eyed for a minute and then let her breath out on a small sigh and reached up to wipe at the spots of dry blood on his neck. It was a simple act, nothing sexual about it, and yet his closeness, the way his heat and scent enveloped her and the way his eyes were traveling over her as she worked made it feel very intimate. Trying to ease her own discomfort, she asked, "I'm guessing Mr. Purdy's cousin doesn't have Renfield syndrome?"

"No," Santo agreed solemnly, his Adam's apple moving in his throat.

Pet nodded, unsurprised by the answer. "He's immortal?"

"*Sì.*"

When he didn't offer more, she stopped wiping and leaned back to meet his eyes. "Someone you know?"

He hesitated and then admitted, "We suspect he is a known rogue."

"A known rogue?" Pet asked with a frown.

"A rogue we have encountered before," he explained.

"Okay," she said slowly. "But what is a rogue?"

"An immortal who has broken our laws."

"So he's a bad immortal," she said carefully.

"*Sì.*"

Pet bit her lip, her heart and mind both suddenly racing. She'd encountered bad immortals before . . . as a child . . . and they had torn her life and her sister's apart. Now another one had popped up right next door to her sister's home.

Santo caught her under the chin and lifted her face so he could see her expression. She tried to school her features into one of unconcern, but apparently not quickly enough, because he frowned and rumbled, "Do not be afraid. I will keep you safe."

Normally, a comment like that would have annoyed Pet and she would have told him she didn't need his protection. It was her standard response to men who wanted to play the protector, which was pretty much every man she met. For some reason, people equated her small stature with her being the equivalent of a child, someone to be humored, coddled, and sheltered from harm, but not to be taken seriously. It could be pretty damned irritating. But Pet knew what immortals could do, and how dangerous Purdy's cousin could be, and she was afraid. This was one time when she knew she couldn't defend herself properly. Even worse, she couldn't defend Parker against a bad immortal if he chose to harm him.

"Pet?"

Her gaze had drifted down to his chest while she thought. Pet lifted her eyes now to meet his, and blinked when she noted the silver growing in the black of his iris. Instead of stars in a dark sky, the silver was gathering and growing to block out the black, like mercury in a thermometer expanded when the temperature rose. It was absolutely beautiful, she thought, and then realized his eyes were coming closer.

His head was slowly lowering, Pet realized. As if he intended to kiss her. She recognized that, and had plenty of time to rebuff him, but didn't. She was curious, so she lifted her head to him and let her eyes drift closed and then his mouth was on hers.

Nothing could have prepared her for that kiss. Or, at least, not for her body's response to it. The moment their lips made contact, that earlier tingling she'd experienced when he'd pressed her hand to his chest exploded between them like fireworks on the Fourth of July. It started where his lips met hers but shot to every corner of her body, faster than electricity could travel.

While her mind was briefly stunned by overloaded synapses, her body responded like a sponge, soaking up the pleasure and expanding with it. Goose bumps rose on her skin, her nipples hardened and extended like rosebuds seeking the sun, and her arms moved of their own volition to embrace him as he stepped between her knees to get closer.

A shiver of pleasure slid through Pet when she felt his hands clasp her at the waist, and then his tongue urged her lips apart and she opened to him. As her own tongue greeted and dueled with his, her back arched, pressing her eager breasts against his huge chest, and her hands clutched at his back, pulling him closer to allow it.

Santo's hand began to slide up her sides then, pushing her cropped top upward until his thumbs rested against the bottoms of her breasts. When they stopped there, she let out the breath she hadn't realized she'd been holding on a groan that was caught by his mouth, and then gasped as he finally let his thumbs slide up to run lightly over her aching nipples. Her body jerked in his hold like a racehorse leaping forward at the sound of a starter pistol, and her legs wrapped around his, pulling in an effort to get him closer. He was already tight against the counter, though, and instead of moving him, her efforts dragged her butt forward on the counter surface until they were pressed tight together.

Santo broke their kiss and threw his head back on a groan as they ground together, then just as quickly lowered his head again. But rather than kiss her, he nuzzled her ear and then kissed and nibbled his way down her throat, urging her to lean back as he made his way down to one breast. His mouth found her nipple through the thin cloth of her top, and he tongued and then sucked at it through the material briefly.

Gasping and murmuring with pleasure, Pet shifted her hands to his head and caressed his skull, urging him on. She wasn't sure if he did it using his mouth or his hands, but suddenly the cloth of her shirt was gone and his tongue rasped against her sensitive skin without the barrier to temper it. Pet was nearly undone by the caress. Crying out, she dug her nails into his head, her hips shifting and grinding, and legs tightening so that she was riding the hardness pressing against her core. Just when Pet thought she was going to embarrass herself by orgasming through dry humping, Santo was suddenly gone.

Confusion at the abandonment drew her eyes open in time to see Santo's strained expression. In the next moment, he'd tugged her shirt back into place, lifted her off the counter to stand on the floor, and then moved to the sink and turned on the water.

Grasping the counter to help her stay upright on her trembling legs, Pet stared at him blankly, and then glanced toward the doorway in surprise when the man named Zanipolo entered. Understanding struck her then. Santo must have heard his cousin enter the house. That was why he'd stopped. The knowledge made her feel a little better, and then she frowned slightly. Santo was a stranger, and an immortal. She never should have let him kiss her, and she definitely shouldn't have responded as she had.

"Hi." Zanipolo's footsteps slowed as he noted her presence. "I didn't think anyone would be up still."

"I just came down for a glass of water," Pet murmured, noting the way his interested gaze was sliding between her and his cousin. Santo didn't even acknowledge his cousin's comment and still had his back to the room. Pet wondered about that until she noticed Zani's eyes drop to her chest and widen slightly.

Glancing down as well and saw that her nipples were still erect and poking at the soft material of her cropped top. She suddenly understood why Santo was keeping his back to the room. She'd felt him harden against her as they'd ground together and knew he was no doubt still sporting the proof of what they'd been doing in the form of an erection that would be making the front of his jeans bulge. Suspecting she was bright pink now, Pet mumbled, "Good night," and made her way out of the room as quickly as her shaking legs would allow.

She was a little steadier on her feet by the time she reached the stairs, and feeling almost normal by the time she made it to the bedroom she was sharing with Parker. She was also feeling lucky. If Zanipolo hadn't interrupted them . . .

Pet let out a shaky breath and paced to the window to look out. Her response to Santo's kiss and caresses had been . . . *unnatural*. That was the only word she could think of to describe it. All he'd done was kiss her and caress and suckle her breast, and she'd . . .

Pet shook her head. She was quite sure that if Zanipolo hadn't appeared when he had, she would probably be getting screwed on the kitchen counter right now. That just wasn't her. And her response to Santo had been too much too quickly, and too desperate. She still wanted him. Or did she? Pet knew immortals could control mortals. Had Santo been controlling her? Making her think she wanted him, making her feel this aching need?

She wasn't sure. Earlier in the kitchen when Marguerite and Parker had been there, she'd thought the man's scent was intoxicating. Surely he hadn't been controlling her then? But when she was trying to clean the blood away and he'd pressed her hand flat to his collarbone, her fingers and palm had tingled where they made contact with his skin. That tingle hadn't stopped in her hand. It had run through her body, setting off alarms like a pinball hitting bumpers. Had he been controlling her and making her feel those things then? she asked herself again. Pet didn't know, and because she didn't know, it seemed better to just avoid him.

As soon as morning came, she'd take Parker home and pack some of his clothes while he got ready for school. Then she'd take him back to her place when she picked him up from school. They'd stay there until her sister returned, and maybe even after that.

It wasn't just her unnatural attraction to Santo. Now that she knew that Mr. Purdy's cousin was one of the bad immortals, she wasn't risking Parker being here. She planned to get him as far away as possible from the lot of them . . . which was handy, because she was thinking that the farther she stayed away from Santo and his tingles, the better for her peace of mind.

"I just came to get a couple of bags of blood for Bricker and me," Zani announced, the words covering the sound of Pet's fading footsteps as she left the room.

Santo grunted and picked up the glass Pet had used. Grabbing the dishrag, he stuck the glass under the water and began to clean it. The activity gave him an excuse to keep his back to his cousin. While his body was starting to calm down now that Pet had left the vicinity, he was still sporting one huge and rather painful erection. It was going to take a while for that monster to go away.

"Do you want one?" Zani asked, opening the refrigerator door.

It took Santo a second to realize that Zani was asking if he wanted a bag of blood. Nodding, he growled, "Please."

Zani was immediately beside him, holding out a bag.

"Thanks," Santo muttered, turning off the water with one hand and taking the bag with the other. He remained facing the sink, though, and slapped the bag to his teeth at once, preventing further conversation. At least, on his side. It didn't, however, stop Zani from talking.

"Pet's a cute little thing, isn't she?" Zani commented as he retrieved a couple more bags from the refrigerator. "And she knows about us too. That's good. At least we won't have to constantly control or lie to her. Maybe we can even convince her to let us watch the Purdy house from her sister's place. It would make things easier," Zani pointed out, turning away from the refrigerator with four bags of blood cuddled in his arms. Not expecting a response, he nodded at Santo and then headed out of the room with a light "see you later."

Santo grunted what could have been taken as a response, but his mind was turning over what Zani had said. Pet knew about immortals. Zani thought that would make things easier in regard to their job here, but Santo suddenly realized it would also make things easier for him. Actually, it was one hell of a bonus. It meant he didn't have to explain everything like most immortals had to do with their life mates. He wouldn't have to try to find the most delicate way to explain that while most people would call them vampires, they weren't vampires. They weren't dead and soulless. They were simply mortals who had an extended life thanks to a scientific breakthrough back in Atlantis before its fall.

Extremely extended, he thought wryly, considering his own age, and then shook his head. He didn't think that meant all his worries were over. While she'd responded eagerly to his kiss and caresses, she'd also fled the room the minute Zani had appeared, rather than wait for him to leave. If she hadn't fled . . . His mind filled with images of his turning, picking her up, and kissing her the minute Zani left the room, and then carrying her to the table, laying her out on it, and—

Santo abruptly cut off his thoughts there. His body was responding to the images in his mind, his erection returning to full throttle and aching with the need to bury itself in her wet heat. Unfortunately, Pet hadn't stuck around for him to play out that scenario, which made him suspect she wasn't just going to fall into his arms like a ripe plum from a tree. She was mortal and was probably a little confused and maybe even overwhelmed by the desire that had exploded between them. He would have to be patient with her. He'd also probably have to woo her, and—

Straightening abruptly, he ripped the now empty bag from his fangs and muttered, "Shared dreams." Those were exactly what they sounded like—dreams shared between two life mates. They were apparently very helpful in winning a life mate over. They fanned the desire and encouraged intimacy before a couple was ready to claim it in reality. They were also supposed to be damned pleasurable. Which begged the question, what the hell was he doing standing here fretting when he could be in bed, enjoying the shared sex dreams life mates experienced?

Santo tossed the empty bag in the garbage and headed out of the kitchen. He'd go to bed, go to sleep, and just wait for her to join him in dreamland. Damn, shared dreams were supposed to be hot. He could hardly wait.

The sound of a door closing woke Santo. Knowing it wasn't likely to be Marguerite and Julius, who were late risers, he sprang from bed and hurried to the door, opening it just in time to see Parker disappearing into the bathroom. Thinking Pet must be awake too, Santo slid from his room and headed downstairs to put the coffee on. He was quite sure she would need one, because he was positive she hadn't slept at all last night. Otherwise they would have enjoyed some of those shared dreams he'd heard so much about.

Santo scowled at the lost opportunity, but suspected Pet had sat up through the night either worrying about the would-be intruder they'd scared off or fretting over the fact that she didn't have an alarm clock and might not wake up in time to get her nephew to school this morning. That, or she wasn't really his life mate after all.

Santo discarded that possibility at once. The way they'd gone up in flames last night after one kiss pretty much discounted that. Still, just the idea was enough to make him grumpy as he read the instructions on the coffee tin and tried to make coffee. It wasn't a task he'd ever attended to before. Santo hadn't drunk anything but blood in . . . well, he couldn't remember the last time he'd had an actual beverage that wasn't blood. Before Christ was born, certainly, he thought as he gave up on finding directions and just poured half the can of ground coffee into the machine, added water, and turned it on. That task done, he stood still, wondering what Pet would like for breakfast.

"Good morning!"

Santo turned at that cheerful greeting to find Parker looking wide awake and disgustingly chipper as he entered the kitchen.

"Morning," he growled and turned to retrieve a glass from the cupboard. Carrying it to the fridge, he asked, "Orange juice?"

"Yes, please," Parker said brightly.

Santo grunted, retrieved the carton of OJ and poured a full glass for the boy. After returning the carton to the fridge, he carried the drink to the table. Parker immediately scooted to the same chair he'd used the night before and sat down.

"What else?" Santo asked as he set down the glass, and then thinking about what Zani and Bricker usually had for breakfast, suggested, "Cereal? Toast?"

"Toast, please," the boy said promptly. "But I can make it myself if you like."

"No." Santo turned back to survey the kitchen briefly. He'd watched Bricker and his cousin make toast at least twenty times over the last month. It wasn't hard. If you knew where the bread was kept . . . and the toaster. Grimacing, he started opening cupboard doors until he found one and then the other. Santo set up the toaster on the counter, plugged it in, popped two pieces of bread in, and then grunted with satisfaction. Easy-peasy. He could do this, he thought, and then turned to Parker. "What do you want on it?"

"Peanut butter and jelly, please," Parker answered, and then added, "And butter of course. Or margarine I guess if you don't have butter."

"Right." Santo turned away to start his search. He found the peanut butter in the cupboard, the butter on the counter in a little white dish, and grape jelly in the fridge. He then grabbed a plate and knife. Once he had everything set up next to the toaster, he retrieved another glass and poured more juice, this one for Pet when she came down. He then moved back to the toaster to wait . . . and wait.

"How long does it take?" he asked finally.

"It'll pop up when it's ready," Parker assured him. "Are you sure you wouldn't rather I make it?"

"No," Santo repeated, and then turned back to the toaster as the bread suddenly seemed to try to leap out of it. Grunting, Santo snatched both of the golden brown slices and set them on the plate. He slathered one with butter and one with peanut butter, and then hesitated about the jelly. Finally, he just smeared some on both pieces of toast, stuck them together, cut the sandwich he'd made in half and carried the plate to the table.

"Thank you," Parker said politely, but Santo noted the way the kid eyed the toast uncertainly, before picking up one half and beginning to eat. It made him suspect he'd done something not quite right, but the boy didn't complain, so he decided he'd ask Marguerite later what he might have done wrong.

Heading back to the toaster, he set two more slices of bread in, but didn't press them down. He wouldn't do that until he heard Pet coming down the stairs. He'd get her a coffee then too, he thought as he glanced at the spitting coffeepot. That way it would be warm for her.

Nodding to himself, Santo turned to lean against the counter and crossed his arms as he watched Parker eat. The boy took his time, taking small bites and chewing each one about a thousand times before swallowing and taking another bite. At least, that's how it seemed to Santo as he watched.

He'd left the peanut butter and jam jars open, and their scents drifted to him as he waited, making his nose twitch. It was a scent he'd smelled each morning when Bricker and Zani had toast, and was usually a scent he could take or leave, or just didn't notice. This morning it actually smelled . . . good, he realized, turning his head to glance to the peanut butter container. He stared at it silently for a minute, then picked it up and dipped his finger in to catch a small amount on the tip. Drawing it out, he then popped his finger in his mouth and sucked it off.

Santo closed his eyes with surprised pleasure. It was creamy and thick and rich and . . . The taste was like nothing he remembered from when he used to eat. Although, he supposed they hadn't had peanut butter back then, at least not where he'd been born. Santo opened his eyes and dipped his finger in again.

"Don't let Aunt Pet see you sticking your fingers in the food. She'll give you heck," Parker warned.

Santo glanced guiltily toward the kitchen door at that news, but didn't stop eating the peanut butter. Instead, he grabbed a spoon out of the drawer to eat it with. When the peanut butter ran out, he turned to the jelly with curiosity and started on that. This was a totally different flavor, sweet and light on his tongue.

He was a much faster eater than Parker, Santo acknowledged when he finished and saw that the boy was only three quarters of the way through his sandwich. Parker was also humming and swinging his feet while he ate. Strange boy, he decided, and carried the now empty jars to the sink to rinse out.

Once that task was finished, Santo glanced around impatiently, wondering what was taking Pet so long. It wasn't like she had to dress and do her hair and makeup. They hadn't even thought to grab her toothbrush last night, let alone anything else. She should be down in the kitchen by now, he thought, and turned to Parker. "Your aunt is taking a while coming downstairs."

Parker stopped chewing to peer at him blankly and then said, "I don't think she's awake. She only fell asleep as I woke up."

"What?" Santo asked with surprise.

Parker nodded. "I woke up several times in the night and she was pacing every time. But then about an hour ago, she dropped onto the bed next to me. It woke me up. I tried to go back to sleep, but couldn't, so got up," he explained. "She was snoring when I left the room."

Santo stared at him with dismay for a minute, then

closed his eyes and bit down on his tongue to hold back the curse that wanted to slip from his lips. If he'd known that, he would have gone right back to bed on seeing the boy. They still could have had their shared sex dreams. And still might, he thought suddenly, blinking his eyes open.

"Bed," he announced, opening his eyes and straightening away from the counter. "No school today."

"What? No!" Parker cried, dismayed at the very thought. "I *have* to go to school."

Pausing on his way to the door, Santo turned to frown at the boy. "Why?"

He'd expected him to say he had a test that day or something else he couldn't miss. But the boy's answer was simply, "To learn. I like school."

"Of course you do," Santo muttered, thinking that was just his luck. Fifty million kids in America hated school and would use any excuse to avoid it, but Parker liked school and wanted to go. Perfect.

"Besides, there are only a couple weeks left before summer break starts."

Santo grunted at this news, but thought it was a shame it wasn't already on break. He really wanted to go back to bed, and was considering controlling the kid when the boy asked, "Do you think someone else can drive me to school this morning, though?"

He noted the worry on the boy's face, but before Santo could say anything, Parker added, "I don't think it's safe for Aunt Pet to drive me when she hasn't slept. According to the National Highway Traffic Safety Administration, there are at least six thousand fatal accidents each year due to drivers falling asleep at the wheel. And that doesn't count the seventy-two

thousand accidents caused just by drowsy drivers
who have trouble paying attention to things around
them, have slow reaction times, and make poor deci-
sions due to their drowsiness."

Santo stared at the kid with disbelief. "Did you just
make that stuff up?"

"No. I read it at the CDC website," Parker explained
before taking another bite of toast.

"The Centers for Disease Control and Prevention?"
Santo asked, recognizing the initials. When Parker nodded, he stared at him with bewilderment. "Why the hell
would they have statistics on driving while drowsy?"

When Parker just shrugged and continued to eat,
Santo shook his head and said, "Fine. I'll drive you
to school."

Parker stopped eating to peer at him suspiciously.
"Did you sleep last night?"

"Oh, yeah," Santo said dryly. "I had several hours
of uninterrupted sleep. No dreams at all . . . Not even
nightmares," he added with surprise as he realized it
was true. It wasn't the first time he'd managed a night
terror free. They had reduced in frequency since his
trip to Punta Cana, coming only a couple of times a
week now. But it had been four nights since his last
nightmare and he didn't usually go that long without
the memories of his years of being held captive and
tortured visiting him in his sleep, yet he hadn't had
one last night.

Santo was pondering that when Parker stood up to
carry his plate to the sink and began to rinse it. "I have
to go home to get dressed and get my schoolbooks,"
he announced.

"And brush your teeth and hair," Santo muttered

distractedly, his thoughts still mostly on this new sign that he was getting over a past that had haunted him for centuries.

"Okay." Parker finished with his dishes and hurried from the room. "I'll be back."

Santo hesitated, but then sighed and followed to walk the boy next door. Pet would never forgive him if anything happened to the little nipper. Hell, he wouldn't forgive himself either. He kind of liked the boy, he admitted.

Bricker saw them coming and opened the French doors in the living room for them to enter.

"What?" Santo asked with a scowl when he noted the way Bricker's eyebrows had risen. "I'm driving the kid to school."

"You might want to get dressed then, buddy," Bricker said with amusement. "You take him to school like that and his teachers are likely to think you're some kind of pervert. If you even made it to school with him and weren't pulled over by suspicious cops on the way."

Santo glanced down at himself and closed his eyes briefly when he saw that he was prancing around the neighborhood in his boxers. Cripes, he'd been in the kitchen waiting to greet Pet in them too. Wouldn't that have been a heck of a greeting?

"Damn skippy. Something has your boxers in a twist," Bricker said on a laugh as he watched the expressions traveling across Santo's face. "It's almost like you've met your life mate or something."

Santo eyed him sharply. "Marguerite told you."

Bricker shook his head. "Julius told us last night that Marguerite suspected Pet was your life mate. I'm guessing she was right?"

"Is she ever wrong?" Santo asked dryly.

Bricker eyed him with interest. "You don't sound happy."

"I'm happy," he growled, and turned on his heel to head back to the Caprelli house to get dressed. He ignored the be-robed man who had stepped out onto his porch across the street to get his newspaper and had stopped to gape at him. But when he spotted the middle-aged woman farther up the sidewalk, gawking as she walked her schnauzer, Santo sighed to himself and started to slow. If he didn't take care of the pair, he'd be the talk of the neighborhood.

"Go ahead, Santo. I've got them," Bricker said behind him on a laugh.

Growling "Thank you," Santo continued on to the house, entered, and started up the stairs, nearly mowing Marguerite down.

"Good morning, Santo," she said on a laugh as he caught himself at the last moment and stopped before her.

"Morning," he mumbled, stepping to the side, and then stopped again as it occurred to him that Marguerite and Julius usually slept late in the mornings. Turning his confused gaze to her, he asked, "Why are you up?"

"I was just going to make breakfast for Julius before the two of you head over to relieve Zani and Bricker. Should I make some for you too? Are you eating again yet?"

Santo simply stared at her. Dear God, he couldn't go back to bed and enjoy the shared dreams life mates experienced even after he got back from driving Parker to school. He had to take over watching the

Purdy house. The knowledge was enough that Santo could have wept. Instead, he growled a grumpy "no" to Marguerite's question and continued up the stairs.

He'd only taken a couple of steps when Marguerite suddenly asked, "What time do you think repairmen start work?"

Pausing again, he glanced back with confusion. "What?"

"I have to call and get someone to fix the door," she reminded him. "I was just wondering what time I should start making the calls."

"Oh." He shrugged. "Nine?"

"Right. Mortal hours. Well then, I guess I'll do that later." Beaming at him, she added, "I think I'll make bacon and eggs for breakfast."

Santo merely grunted and continued up the stairs. He wasn't hungry. He had to dress, drive Parker to school, and then relieve Bricker. There would be no shared dreams for him.

Six

Pet turned in bed and snuggled deeper into the blankets with a little sigh that turned into a yowl of pain as something stabbed her in the boob. Jerking up from the bed, she peered bleary-eyed at the ball of fur hissing at her with claws upraised. Right, it hadn't been a something that had stabbed her but several little claws, she realized with a groan, and then flopped onto her back away from the animal she'd nearly crushed.

Mrs. Wiggles. Damned cat, she thought with disgust, and then raised her head to examine her chest. A grimace claimed her lips when she saw the spot of blood growing on her cropped top above her left breast. The feline had got her good.

"Great," she muttered and sat up, then swung her legs off the bed. She'd spent most of the night pacing and fretting over Santo and whether he'd controlled her, and how dangerous Mr. Purdy's "cousin" might be. Then she'd switched to considering her plans to take Parker to her place after school today, and making a mental list of everything she should probably bring along with them. Aside from clothes and such, she knew the kid probably wouldn't go anywhere without his game setup. Which would mean taking the television from his room too since she considered them mind-sucking appliances and didn't have one.

And then there was Mrs. Wiggles. That could be a problem. She couldn't take her back to Mr. Purdy's house, nor would she just leave the poor thing to wander the neighborhood. Not that Parker would allow that. But her apartment was a pet free building . . . she'd have to sneak the cat into her apartment.

The cat, a litter box, kitty litter, and cat food, Pet corrected herself, and thought that could be tricky. The apartment manager of her building was a bored busybody who thought it was his right and duty to know everyone and everything that went on in the building. To that end, he had cameras everywhere and actually watched them like a reality show junky. They were going to have to be very clever to get the cat in unnoticed.

Pet had paced the room and fretted over that until sunrise, and then had stumbled over to sit on the bed as she continued pondering the issue. That was the last thing she remembered. Apparently, she'd fallen asleep during her pondering.

Sighing, she scrubbed her hands over her face and then glanced to the bedside clock. Pet stiffened briefly as she saw 11:14 on the digital display, and then cursed and swiveled around, already reaching out to prod her nephew awake before she realized Parker wasn't there.

Pet stared at the empty space on the other side of Mrs. Wiggles and then stood abruptly and ran for the door. The hall was silent and dim when she stepped into it. The bedroom door across from the one she came out of was wide open, revealing the empty room beyond. Marguerite and Julius were up then, she thought, and turned to head for the stairs, nearly tripping over Mrs. Wiggles as the cat came out the door she'd left open.

Cursing, she sidestepped the animal and then bent to scoop her up. The cat meowed in protest, but Pet ignored that and carried her with her as she hurried to the stairs and down them. She knew Mrs. Wiggles probably had to relieve herself and wasn't risking her doing it in the Caprelli house. She didn't set the cat down until she'd reached and opened the front door. She set her down on the porch floor then, and waited just long enough to watch her run into the garden before closing the door. She then started up the hall, reassuring herself that she'd find Parker in the kitchen, probably sitting at the table, chattering Marguerite's ear off as he drank juice and ate her cookies.

Those hopes died the moment she reached the room and saw that it was empty . . . as was every other room on the main floor, Pet discovered when she whirled and raced back up the hall, looking through each doorway she passed.

Pet almost went back upstairs to search every bedroom, but knew that if he'd been up there he would have been in the room with her and Mrs. Wiggles. He wasn't in the house. That thought raised such panic in her Pet could hardly breathe, and her next thought was the house. He had to have gone back home for some reason. That hope had her hurrying out of the Caprelli house and running down the driveway and around the hedge, desperate to find Parker and ease her building panic.

Santo was watching the Purdy house, his gaze sliding from the front of the house to the front yard, the road, and back to the house again when movement out of the corner of his eye caught his attention.

The lady with the schnauzer was back and he could see that she was straining to hold on to the leash as her little dog went "Cujo," as Parker had called it. It was a suitable description, Santo thought as he watched the dog snarl and bark and lunge madly about as if torn between racing up to the house to attack whatever was distressing him so, or dragging his mistress away to safety as quickly as he could. The woman on the other end of the leash was obviously distressed by his behavior. She wrapped the end of the leash around her wrist to guard against losing it and began to walk more quickly, but then suddenly glanced over her shoulder and then stopped dead, her eyes widening and jaw dropping.

Curious, Santo stood and walked to the front window to look out over the yard. His own eyes widened when he spotted Pet racing madly up the lawn toward him. Her hair was a wild black mass around her head, she was barefoot and still wearing the outlandish sleepwear she'd had on last night. Marguerite had mentioned giving her something to wear when she woke up, but if she had, Pet wasn't wearing it.

She also obviously wasn't wearing a bra. He'd noticed that last night, but was noting it now again as he watched her breasts move up and down with each running step. The shirt was moving too, riding up to reveal the bottoms of the small globes and then dropping to cover them again.

"Are you going to stand there gaping at her, or open the door to let her in?"

Santo glanced around at that dry question. Julius had joined him in the room and was looking out the window on the other side of the French doors. Santo's guess would be that his uncle had seen the lady with the schnauzer, noted her shock, and come to investigate as well. He knew he was right when Julius spoke again.

"I'll handle the dog lady while you tend to Pet." When Santo just stared at him, Julius then raised his eyebrows. "Well? Let her in, nephew. She has no idea where to go. The front door is just wood nailed over the frame still."

When Santo glanced back to see that Pet had mounted the porch and now stood staring with dismay at where the front door used to be, he quickly moved to the French doors and opened them for her.

"Oh, thank God!" Pet rushed forward. She actually tried to race past him, but Santo caught her by the shoulders to stop her and frowned when he noted her pale and distressed face. He hadn't noticed that as he'd watched her boobs bounce up the front lawn.

"What is it? What's happened?" Santo asked, and couldn't imagine what the answer might be. She'd been sleeping peacefully when he'd checked on her before heading over here, and Marguerite had been there to watch her, which made him ask, "Where is Marguerite?"

"I don't know," Pet gasped, clutching at his arms. "And Parker's gone! They both are!"

Santo felt himself relax at once. He had no idea where his aunt was, probably in the backyard with J, but he did know where Parker was. Trying to sound soothing, he growled, "Parker is fine. He's at school."

"What?" She seemed shocked at the possibility. "How?"

"I drove him," Santo said, and her eyes widened at the news as if she could hardly take it in.

"Oh," she breathed finally, and sagged slightly in his hold. "When I woke up and he wasn't there . . ."

"I am sorry," he said stiffly, thinking he should have left her a note. But he'd expected Marguerite to tell her where Parker was when she woke up. He'd never imagined Pet would have been left to panic at the boy's absence.

"No. Don't be. I just didn't know . . ." Giving her head a shake, Pet managed a weak smile and offered, "Thank you. It was kind of you to take him to school and I appreciate it."

"My pleasure," he muttered. Feeling uncomfortable with her gratitude, he turned it elsewhere by saying, "Marguerite called your work."

Pet's eyes widened incredulously. "Oh, God, I was so panicked about Parker I forgot all about missing work."

"Marguerite called," he repeated, thinking that should be sufficient to calm her again.

It was Julius who added, "She spoke to the head of your department and explained about the intruder, the destroyed door, and your being up all night. They were very understanding and said your . . . TA?" he queried, and when she nodded, he finished, "Your TA is taking your classes. You are to take as much time as you need. Just to let them know."

"Oh." Pet relaxed again.

"My wife also called the housekeeper, Oksana, and gave her the day off," Julius added. "There seemed little need for her today and we suspected the state of the door would just upset her."

That made Pet's lips quirk up with amusement, and she nodded. "No doubt."

Santo relaxed now that she was no longer distressed, and then, realizing he still held her by the shoulders, removed his hands and took a step back before her scent could tempt him to do something foolish like pull her into his arms and kiss her again right there in front of his uncle. Shifting uncomfortably, he tried to think of something to say, and then straightened slightly and asked, "Would you like coffee?"

Pet perked up at the word. "Is there some?"

"No," he admitted and when she started to droop again with disappointment, added quickly, "I will make it."

"Oh, dear God, no," Julius said abruptly. "You are *not* making coffee. Not after that mud you made this morning. *I* will make coffee."

Santo watched his uncle storm off to the kitchen, and then glanced to Pet to see her staring after him with twitching lips. When she turned to peer at Santo, the twitching turned into a smile that sucked all the air out of the room. At least that's how it felt. Santo suddenly couldn't breathe. She was so damned beautiful to him. Part of his brain could acknowledge that while she was pretty, she was no Helen of Troy. But that was only a corner of his mind. To the rest of his mind, she shone like spun gold, sparkled like diamonds, and was breathtakingly, heartbreakingly perfect.

"Oh."

When she glanced down suddenly, Santo followed her gaze and saw the cat had followed her in through the still open French doors and was winding around her feet, rubbing her sides against Pet's lower legs in a bid for attention. Santo turned to close the door as she bent to scoop up the cat.

"Did Parker feed Mrs. Wiggles before he left for school?" she asked as she straightened with the furball in her arms.

Santo shook his head. Parker had eaten his breakfast and then rushed over here to get ready for school. He probably hadn't even thought of the cat.

"Then I'd better go see if Quinn has some tuna or something to feed her," she said, turning away to head to the kitchen.

Santo automatically started to follow, but then paused as he recalled the task that he was here to do. Still, he stood, listening to the soft patter of her footsteps until they faded. Only then did he start breathing again. Giving his head a shake, Santo turned and moved back to the window. But while his gaze moved over the scene outside, his mind was full of Pet.

"Coffee will be ready in a minute," Julius announced, sliding the coffee carafe into the machine and turning it on as Pet entered the kitchen.

"Thank you." She offered a smile but passed him to begin opening cupboard doors in search of some kind of canned meat for Mrs. Wiggles.

"Ah, yes, cat food."

Pet glanced warily around when Julius murmured that, wondering if he'd read the concern from her mind or just guessed what the issue was. It was impossible to tell from his thoughtful expression. Shrugging the matter aside, she turned back to the cupboard and had just spotted a can of salmon when Julius spoke again.

"Would dog food do, do you think?" he asked, and then explained, "Marguerite spoils J horribly and will not feed him anything but the best canned food. I could go grab a can."

Pet considered the offer briefly but then shook her head as she retrieved the salmon from the cupboard. "That's kind, but I'm not sure what's good for dogs is good for cats. I mean we eat chocolate, but that kills dogs. Maybe there's something in dog food that's not good for cats," she pointed out, and then set Mrs. Wiggles down so that she could find the can opener and a bowl. "She can eat the salmon while I dress, and then I'll run out and pick up some cat food . . . and a litter box and litter and . . ." She shrugged helplessly, not sure what all she would need. The mental list she'd made last night had apparently fled her mind, chased out by the panic she'd experienced on finding Parker missing. She'd have to make a written list and maybe add to it when she got to the store and saw what was available. Pet had never had a cat. Dogs, yes. Cats, no. Patrick wasn't the only one allergic to the felines; her adoptive father, Randall, was too.

She should probably get two litter boxes, Pet supposed as she opened the can and then turned the salmon into the bowl. One for Mrs. Wiggles to use here until they left, and one for her apartment. It would be easier to sneak a clean, unused litter box and a container of litter into her building than a litter box full of used litter.

"Shopping."

Pet glanced to Julius with curiosity when he murmured that word. Her gaze narrowed warily when she noted the way he was looking at her. "What?"

"Nothing. I was just thinking," he said, and then smiled wryly and commented, "I am sure you noted the state of the front door?"

Pet snorted slightly at the question as she picked up the bowl of salmon and set it on the floor for Mrs. Wiggles. "It would be hard not to. Where did you guys get the wood you nailed over the frame?"

"We used the coffee table and a headboard from upstairs."

Pet straightened abruptly at that news, her eyes wide with alarm. "What?"

Julius nodded but shrugged his shoulders at the same time. "It was all we could think of at the time. Which is why, when you mentioned shopping for cat items, I thought . . . We need to replace the coffee table and headboard too."

"Oh, yeah, we do," Pet agreed, her tone dry as dust. She could just imagine Quinn's reaction if she came home to find them missing. She'd never hear the end of it.

"Of course, we will pay, and I had intended on

sending one of the boys out later today, but it occurs to me that they might not be able to find the exact same table and headboard."

Pet frowned slightly as she considered that possibility. Good Lord, the truth was, styles changed so quickly, it wasn't likely the stores would have the exact same coffee table, or possibly even the exact same headboard still in stock anywhere.

"Perhaps it would be a good idea if Santo went shopping with you for the cat items, and then the two of you could stop at a furniture shop to select a new coffee table and headboard that, if not exactly the same, might be acceptable to your sister."

Pet had stiffened at the suggestion of Santo going shopping with her, but by the time Julius finished speaking, she was seeing the sense behind his words. They needed to replace the items that had been broken up to block the door, and she would really rather have a say in what they were replaced with. She was the one who was likely to take the heat when Quinn got home and noticed the changed items if they couldn't find exact replacements.

"That might be a good idea," she agreed on a sigh, and glanced down to see that Mrs. Wiggles was gobbling up the salmon with enthusiastic speed. Fetching another bowl, she moved to the sink and began to run water into the dish as she added, "But I need to shower and dress first."

"Of course," Julius said solemnly. "I will have a word with Santo while you do."

Pet merely nodded and set the water dish next to the nearly empty salmon bowl and then led the way out of the room. She was aware that Julius followed her until they reached the stairs, but while she jogged lightly up the steps, he continued on into the living room. The soft rumble of the men's conversation started as she reached the bathroom, but Pet didn't stop to try to listen. The day was wasting away and she only had so much time before she had to go pick up Parker. A quick shower, a coffee to wake herself up, and they should be on their way if they were to get everything done in the allotted time.

That thought in mind, Pet was in and out of the shower rather quickly. She grabbed two towels from the cupboard under the sink, wrapped one around her long hair and used the other to quickly dry her body. Once that was done, though, she paused and looked around blankly as she realized she hadn't thought to stop off at her room to collect clean clothes to put on afterward. A really stupid oversight, Pet acknowledged, and not one she could explain, except that she hadn't had coffee yet and was still rather muddle-headed.

Blowing out an exasperated breath, she wrapped the damp towel around herself, snatched up her pajamas, and moved to the door. Much to her relief the hallway was empty when she eased the door open. She was able to slip out and pad to the guest room she always used while here at her sister's home. After a quick perusal of the clothes she'd brought with her, Pet settled on a pair of white capri pants, a red polo shirt, and a pretty pink bra and panty set. She dressed quickly, ran a brush through her damp hair, put it back into a ponytail, and then bypassed bothering with any makeup in favor of heading down to find the promised coffee. She seriously needed something to help wake her poor sleep-fogged brain.

Pet didn't encounter anyone on the way to the kitchen and couldn't hear the murmur of voices anymore from the living room either, so assumed the men had finished their talk and returned to their spots to watch the house next door. The coffeepot was just spitting out the last of its liquid when she entered the kitchen. Pet grabbed a cup, the sugar bowl, and the cream from the fridge, and set them down by the coffeepot. She then hesitated and glanced toward the door.

The polite thing would be to ask the men if she could get them a cup too, she supposed, and after debating the matter for a moment, clucked her tongue with irritation at her own reticence to deal with them. She found Julius in the den, peering out the window like a cat watching the world go by, but when she asked, he smiled and thanked her but said no. He'd had quite enough coffee that morning already.

Nodding, Pet backed out of the room and headed along the hall to the living room. Like Julius, Santo was positioned at the window, his gaze fixed on the house next door. But he turned to eye her the minute she stopped in the doorway.

"I was going to make myself a coffee and wondered if you'd like me to get you one too," she explained as her gaze slid over him. Dear Lord, he was something. Pet had a lot of varied interests on her bucket list. Mountain climbing wasn't on it, but this mountain of a man made her think it should be. She was quite sure she could spend hours exploring his peaks and crevasses.

Realizing where her thoughts had wandered, Pet stomped on them at once. She'd decided last night that those kind of thoughts were a no-go zone for her.

Whether or not Santo had controlled her and made her feel the passion she'd experienced, or they had been a natural result of her attraction to him, it didn't seem like a good idea to get involved with the man. Her prior experience with immortals convinced her that they were not safe to be around.

"Thank you."

The soft rumble of sound drew her gaze back to his face, and Pet's eyes widened slightly when she noted the surprise and pleasure on his face. It seemed obvious he hadn't expected such an offer. It made her wonder if maybe in her worry and fear, she hadn't been a bit rude when she first got here. Tilting her head, she asked, "That's a yes, right?"

He nodded, a smile claiming his lips, and Pet went completely still for a moment. The man was good-looking to begin with, but when he smiled like that he was absolutely gorgeous, she decided, barely restraining herself from fanning her face with one suddenly shaky hand.

Damn. He should come with a caution sign, Pet thought faintly as she turned away and hurried back to the kitchen. The sooner she got everything done and could head to her apartment, the better, she decided.

Pet was pouring the coffee before she realized she hadn't thought to ask Santo how he took his. That being the case, she ended up putting together a tray with two coffees, sugar, cream, and spoons on it to take everything out to the living room. She'd decided they'd have a quick coffee together before they left to go shopping. She had some questions to ask.

Santo was watching for her return and moved quickly to take the tray from her almost the minute she entered the living room. Pet murmured a polite "thank you" and then sat down in the chair next to the end table he'd set the tray on and quickly doctored her coffee. She watched Santo then prepare his own coffee, noting that he drank it regular like her.

Pet allowed herself a few moments to sip at her coffee, and then her gaze wandered to the boarded up hole that used to be the front door. She grimaced as she took in the table and headboard, or what was left of them.

"They'll be replaced," Santo assured her.

Pet glanced at him quickly to see that he had followed her gaze to the door. She nodded, and peered at him solemnly, wondering over the fact that the man rarely pieced more than three or four words together when he spoke. He was obviously one of those man-of-few-words kind of guys. Still, she needed info. "Do you know if Marguerite called about getting the door repaired? Or should I do it?"

"She did it."

Pet waited, and when he didn't elaborate, asked, "Is someone coming?"

"*Sì.*"

When he didn't volunteer anything else, she forced a smile and asked, "When?"

"In . . ." he paused to glance to his wristwatch ". . . about half an hour."

Pet glanced around for a clock and saw that it was nearly noon now. It didn't help her much. She had no idea how long it would take to replace the door. Hopefully it would be done before she had to go pick up Parker, though. Or shortly after she returned with him. She didn't want him staying here any longer than necessary today. In fact, she would have packed some clothes for him and not brought him back at all, but wasn't sure what he'd need or want to take with him and Parker could be particular.

Her gaze slid out the window to the Purdy house, and she peered at the windows, noting the tightly closed curtains that covered each one, before her attention went to the newspapers stacking up against the front door. There had to be half a dozen of them, delivered but never collected. Between that and the sad state of the garden and the fact that the yard was in need of mowing, the house almost looked abandoned.

Frowning, Pet cleared her throat and said, "I know Mr. Purdy's cousin is a bad immortal, a rogue, I think you called him last night?"

"Sì," Santo agreed. "A rogue."

Pet nodded. "A rogue then, but just how bad is this guy?"

Santo didn't hesitate. "The very worst."

"How?" she asked.

"In all ways."

Pet stared at him briefly and then heaved out an exasperated breath and asked, "Do you think you could elaborate on that a bit? Like tell me *how* he's the very worst?"

Santo didn't look as if he wanted to tell her anything else, but finally said, "He is dangerous."

"He's dangerous?" Pet echoed, her voice somewhat strangled with the frustration building in her. "That's it? That's all you have to say? He's dangerous?"

When Santo nodded, she set her coffee cup down with a sharp click and stood up. "We should get going. It's already noon and I need to pick up Parker at three o'clock."

Pet didn't wait for him to agree but walked to the French doors. She was just reaching for the handle of the door on the right when the door on the left started to open. Pausing, she took a surprised step back and then relaxed when she spotted Marguerite on the porch with her big dog at her side.

"There you are," Marguerite said with obvious relief when she spotted her. "When I went to check on you and found you gone, I did not know what to think. I started to worry that last night's intruder had returned and stolen you away."

"Oh." Pet's eyes widened, but she said quickly, "I'm sorry. I looked through the house when I woke up, but didn't see anyone anywhere and came over to find out where Parker went. I was in a bit of a panic myself."

"It must have been when I took J to the backyard," Marguerite said with a grimace. "I am sorry for the confusion. I meant to be there when you woke up to tell you where Parker had gone."

"Ah, well, best laid plans," Pet said with a wry smile, waving away the apology. "It's all good now, though."

"Yes." Marguerite glanced from her to Santo. "Were you heading somewhere?"

"Shopping," Santo growled.

Pet rolled her eyes at that and explained, "I mentioned to Julius about needing to get a few things for Mrs. Wiggles, and he decided it would be a good idea if Santo accompanied me. That way I can help pick out the coffee table and headboard to replace the ones they broke up last night."

"Oh, yes. A good idea." Marguerite smiled and moved inside and out of the way for them to leave. "I will go see if Julius needs a second pair of eyes watching the Purdy house while you are gone then. Have a nice time."

Pet managed a smile and murmured, "You too," as she led Santo out of the house and headed for her car. She was nearly to it when Santo took her elbow and urged her to continue down the driveway past it.

"What—?" she began.

"The SUV is bigger," Santo announced.

Pet glanced back over her shoulder at her pretty little red Toyota 86 and sighed as she realized that they wouldn't be able to fit a coffee table and headboard in it. The SUV would work better. Still, it would have been nice if he'd said more than *the SUV is bigger*. Shaking her head, she turned forward again and allowed him to lead her around the hedges to the black SUV parked in the Caprellis' driveway. Her gaze went from it to the huge RV next to it, and Pet commented, "When I first met Marguerite and Julius yesterday, they mentioned that they drove here in the RV."

"Sì," Santo said as he opened the door for her.

Pet climbed inside and turned just in time to see the door close. Sighing, she watched Santo walk around to the driver's side and slide in, but when he merely did up his seat belt and started the vehicle, she asked, "Why did they drive the RV? Why not drive an SUV like you guys did?"

They were the only two vehicles in the driveway, and the RV had been the only one there when she'd first arrived and met Marguerite and Julius, so it was a safe bet the men had arrived in the SUV, she thought as she waited for his answer. She just didn't understand what the RV was for. They were gas guzzlers. Not something you'd drive around in unless you needed a place to sleep, but they were all sleeping in the house.

"They were already in the RV," he said, and then added, "Do up your seat belt."

Pet reached for the belt and drew it impatiently across herself to snap it in its holder, but asked, "Why were they in the RV? Were they on vacation or something?"

"*Sì.*"

That was it. Just *sì*. Was he saying *sì* to the vacation or the something? she wondered grimly, and shook her head. It was like the man had no comprehension of how conversations were meant to go. That was a thought that recurred to her several times over the next two hours as they stopped first at the pet store and then at her sister's favorite furniture store. Pet was naturally chatty and cheerful, but it didn't matter what she asked Santo, his answers were either *sì* or *no*, with the occasional three- or four-word almost-sentence that revealed little more than *sì* or *no*. Frankly, talking to the man was hard work and exhausting. She soon grew tired of the effort and allowed a heavy silence to fall between them. She also rushed the trip along, eager to be done with it.

In the end, they weren't gone more than an hour. It felt like a hundred, and by the time he pulled into the driveway behind her Toyota, Pet was so angry she couldn't stand another minute with him. She'd decided that he definitely must have controlled her to make her want him last night, because there was absolutely nothing about him that was attractive to her now.

The minute the SUV came to a stop, Pet had her seat belt off and was sliding out of the vehicle. She had nearly two hours before she had to go pick up Parker, and she was thinking she should load everything she could into her car now, to save time later.

"Food?"

Pet was crossing the front yard to the porch when Santo said that. Pausing at the porch steps, she turned and arched her eyebrows in question. "I'm sorry. What does 'food' mean? Do you want some? Are you asking if I have any? What?"

Santo's eyes widened at her snarky tone, but he said, "I was asking if you are hungry."

"Well, then, why didn't you ask that?" she said with exasperation, and spun around to jog up the steps.

Santo stared after Pet for a moment, trying to figure out what had happened between the SUV and here to upset her. Everything had been going rather well as far as he could tell. They'd done all they'd needed to do, and managed it all rather quickly. A successful trip to his mind. Obviously, things hadn't gone as well as he'd thought, though. That, or he'd done something to annoy her. Or perhaps it was the front door that had been installed while they were gone, he thought as he watched her open the new door and enter the house. It was similar to the old door but not exactly the same. Perhaps that distressed her. Nodding at that thought, he followed her inside.

Pet was at the base of the stairs about to go up when he entered the house. Santo forestalled her by commenting, "You seem angry."

Pet snorted and started up the steps.

"Is it the door?" he asked solemnly.

"What?" Stopping abruptly, she whirled back with an expression of disbelief and then turned to look at the door and blinked. Her face softened at once, the angry tension leaving her as she moved back down the stairs and walked over to run her hand down the oak door. "Wow, they did a great job fixing it. I can't believe I didn't even notice. It looks good, don't you think?"

Santo grunted agreement, his thoughts on what might have upset her. It obviously wasn't the door. She appeared to approve of that, he thought.

"Tell me," Pet said suddenly, "when you grunt, is that a yes or a no?"

Santo glanced up with surprise at her question.

Before he could say anything Marguerite appeared in the hall behind Pet and came forward smiling. "You are back. How lovely. How was shopping?"

"It went well," he assured her and Pet swung on him, her expression shocked.

"It did?" she asked with disbelief.

"Sì," he said, surprised by her reaction.

"How did it go well?"

Santo's eyebrows rose slightly at the question, but he said, "We got everything."

When she narrowed her eyes at that, he added, "The table is nice."

"You liked it?" Pet asked, seeming surprised.

"Sì."

"And the headboard?" she asked now.

"Perfect. Almost exactly like the original."

"You liked that too?" she asked.

"Sì," Santo said, starting to frown now. She was getting more upset by the minute and he didn't understand why. She let him know why, of course.

"That's interesting," Pet said now. "Because when I asked you in the store for your opinion, all you did was grunt. In fact, all you've done since I got up today is give me grunts, *sì* or *no* answers, or very short responses to my direct questions. Honestly, getting information out of you is like pulling teeth. I can't figure out if you're just too stupid to be able to put more than three or four words together at a time, or if this is your way of letting me know that you consider last night a mistake and regret it. But, really, I don't care anymore. 'Cause I'm definitely over whatever craziness had me responding to your kisses. I'm done. The door's fixed. You've replaced what you broke. Feel free to go back to the Caprellis' and forget I even exist, because I fully intend on forgetting all about you."

On that note, she whirled on her heel and stomped upstairs, her ponytail swaying angrily back and forth.

Santo gaped after her, taken aback by her attack. At least it felt like an attack. But then most people found his size so intimidating that it was rare indeed that anyone even raised their voice to him, while she had not just yelled, she'd called him stupid. That made him scowl and wonder if she really was his life mate, after all. Were they not supposed to be your complement? The one you could not live without? Because he could certainly live without being called—

"Santo."

He glanced around, surprised to see Marguerite still standing there. He'd forgotten all about her, but her presence just made matters worse. She'd heard Pet call him stupid.

"A word, please," Marguerite requested gently.

"Go ahead," he growled.

But rather than start speaking, she glanced to the side. He followed her gaze to see Bricker sitting in the living room, watching them with interest. It seemed he too had witnessed Pet's tirade.

"The kitchen?" she suggested.

Nodding, he gestured for her to lead the way.

Seven

Pet strode into her room, snatched up her overnight case, and began replacing the few things she'd removed from it. There wasn't much. She hadn't really unpacked. Still, by the time she'd finished and zipped up the bag, the worst of her temper had run out and she felt stupid for losing it in the first place. She knew anger was a secondary emotion triggered by fear, whether it was fear of being helpless or trapped in a situation, fear for one's physical or emotional or mental well-being, or fear of rejection . . . which was the basis of her anger, of course. She'd only realized it, though, as she'd lashed out at Santo with the accusation that he was either stupid or trying to let her know that he was no longer interested in her. That had been the reason behind her mounting frustration during their outing. Fear of rejection.

Dear God, she'd decided last night that it was better to avoid Santo. But when circumstances had thrown them together for the shopping trip and he'd been so uncommunicative and short, she'd feared he was rejecting her and flipped.

"Ridiculous," Pet muttered, but knew the truth was she could tell herself that avoiding him was for the best, all she wanted, but that didn't mean she was suddenly going to just stop being attracted to him. And while she'd said she was done, Pet suspected if he kissed her again, she'd respond just as eagerly. She'd like to think otherwise, but just remembering those few moments in the kitchen had her body responding. Sitting next to him in the SUV had been worse, though. Being just inches away from him, surrounded by his scent, able to feel the heat emanating off his body . . . She'd wanted so badly to touch him, but he hadn't even seemed to want to *talk* to her.

"Pathetic," she said under her breath, and grabbed her bag. She'd start loading the car. She might not be able to pack for Parker, but there were other things she could load, starting with her bag.

"She *is* your life mate."

Santo came to a halt when Marguerite paused in the center of the kitchen and swung around to make that announcement. He scowled at the words and then shook his head. "But she—"

"Wants you to speak," Marguerite interrupted gently. "I know that is difficult for you. You have spent more than two thousand years avoiding people and not talking. It has only been the last couple of decades or so that you have allowed yourself to enjoy the company of others, and even now, you mostly listen rather than talk. But she is your life mate, Santo. And she is mortal. While she has some knowledge of our existence, Pet has no idea that she is a possible life mate to you, or what that means. You will have to explain it to her, and even then she will not automatically just fall in with it. She will need to be wooed, and she will need to get to know you. She cannot read your mind as I can and see how good and fine a man you are."

"You can read me," he said heavily. It wasn't a question so much as a resigned acknowledgment. Immortals as old as he could only be read when they allowed it, or for the first year or two after meeting a life mate. It was another sign that they had met one, they briefly lost control of their ability to shield their thoughts from others. If Marguerite, who was much younger than him, could read him, then Pet was definitely his life mate. The thought made him scowl and he complained, "She does not like me."

Marguerite smiled and shook her head. "She does not dislike you, Santo. She is just frustrated that you will not speak to her properly and is taking it as a lack of interest."

Santo's mouth tightened. Lack of interest indeed. He'd spent the last hour fighting the urge to take her in his arms, but all he said was, "I dislike talking."

"Well, you had best learn to like it, because you will not win Pet without it. The days of cavemen thumping women over the head and dragging them off to their caves are over."

"Pity," he growled irritably.

Marguerite rolled her eyes at that and said, "The modern woman is free to come and go as she pleases, so you had best start giving her a reason to want to stay."

Santo grimaced, but then stilled and lifted his head slightly as an idea struck him.

Obviously still reading his thoughts, Marguerite tsked with exasperation and said, "And that does not mean instigating life mate sex to try to tie her to your side."

"Why not?" Santo asked, almost embarrassed at how petulant he sounded. "It would bind her."

"So would rope," she snapped impatiently.

Santo nodded thoughtfully, almost wishing his conscience would allow him to actually do that. Not tying her up permanently, but just temporarily while he showed her what shared dreams could be like, which would hopefully lead to life mate sex, and—

"Santo," Marguerite said with a shock that assured him she was still in his head.

"It was just a thought," he muttered, avoiding her eyes.

Marguerite glared at him briefly, but then asked, "Do you want to be a true partner to her, or a vibrator with legs?"

"What?" Santo gaped at her. He thought he knew what she was talking about, but his brain was having difficulty putting the words together with the sweet, refined woman he'd always known as his aunt. Perhaps he was misunderstanding. English wasn't his first language, after all, so he asked, "What is a vibrator?"

"Exactly what you think it is," she said grimly, and then sighed and reasoned, "And if you use life mate sex to claim her and do not allow her to get to know you at the same time, that is all you will be to her."

Santo suspected that was supposed to sway him,

but really, what was wrong with being a vibrator with legs? She could use him, play with him, pleasure herself with him. He had no problem being used and played with, especially since her pleasure would be his pleasure, and he wouldn't have to talk to her—

"Santo," Marguerite gritted out, still in his head and obviously striving for patience. "Pet cannot love someone she does not know."

"She would get to know parts of me," he argued, still not convinced it would be a bad approach.

"She would get to know your penis," Marguerite said bluntly. "And a woman cannot love a penis, no matter how talented it is. She will use it and enjoy it, but not love it, and so she would have no reason not to leave it and go find another equally talented penis, one that might actually talk to her."

"That would be a very talented penis," Santo pointed out with amusement. When Marguerite didn't even crack a smile, he sighed and then shrugged and said arrogantly, "We are life mates. No other penis could pleasure her like me."

Marguerite arched her eyebrows. "No other penis could pleasure her like 'you'? Not 'like yours'? You realize you just called yourself a dickhead, which is how you are acting right now." When he flushed, she added, "And it is not necessarily true that no one could pleasure her like you. While it is rare for a mortal to be a possible life mate to two immortals, it does happen. As you well know," she added heavily.

Santo frowned. He did know. It had happened to his cousin Raffaele just weeks ago while they were in Punta Cana. A woman named Jessica had been a possible mate for Raffaele and another immortal. Santo briefly fretted over the possibility that such a thing could happen again, but then shook his head. "The chances of that happening—"

"Are not zero," Marguerite interrupted. "But even if that did not end up being the case for Pet, are you really fine with her walking away even temporarily to sleep with countless men to find out for herself that none can pleasure her like you?"

Santo stiffened at the very suggestion. No, he would not be fine with that. She was his.

"Me Tarzan, you Jane," Marguerite muttered.

"What?" he asked with confusion.

"Nothing," she said shortly, and then shook her head. "I am just a bit dismayed to realize that, despite your stalwart support of family members, and efforts to ease everyone else's situation, a Neanderthal has been hiding under that silence of yours all this time."

Santo clenched his hands at the insult. "I am not a Neanderthal."

"Then stop acting like one and acknowledge that to claim Pet you will need to win her trust and love," Marguerite suggested grimly.

Santo glowered at her, but after a moment, gave in and nodded. "Fine. How?"

Marguerite relaxed a bit and said quietly, "I told you. You need to speak to her so that she can see who you are."

"What do I say?" he asked, and when she gaped at him with disbelief, he said stiffly, "I am not trying to be difficult. I dislike talking about feelings and such feminine things."

"You do not have to talk about your feelings," Marguerite said soothingly, and then her lips twitched and she added, "In fact, since most of your 'feelings' for Pet right now seem to be centered in your lower regions, I would advise against it."

Before Santo could decide if she was insulting or making fun of him, Marguerite glanced at her wristwatch and murmured, "There are still a couple hours before she has to pick up Parker, and I do not think she has had anything to eat today unless the two of you stopped somewhere?"

Santo shook his head.

"Good," Marguerite said on a sigh. "Then I suggest you take her out for a late lunch and then talk to her. Just be yourself, but *speak* your thoughts out loud," she suggested as if it was easy as could be. Walking around him, she moved to the door and then paused to swing back and add, "Your less prurient thoughts, though, Santo. Save any sex talk for later. All right?"

She didn't wait for an answer but turned away, muttering, "I need to go talk to Julius. Maybe he will have some ideas on how to help you."

Santo stared at the empty doorway for several minutes after Marguerite left, feeling depression settle around his shoulders. He had lied when he'd said he disliked talking. It wasn't that he disliked it so much as he was out of practice and uncomfortable with it. It was part of the reason he'd refused counseling after the mess in Venezuela where he was kidnapped and tortured . . . He didn't know how to talk about it. And he didn't know how to talk to Pet.

Santo grimaced at how stupid that sounded, and then shook his head and left the kitchen to go looking for Pet. He didn't have far to go; he spotted her the minute he stepped into the hall. She was at the front door, her arms full of a bunch of equipment that she was trying to shift so that she could open the new door.

"What are you doing?" he asked with a frown, automatically moving forward now to take some of the items for her. His gaze moved over what he realized was a speaker and a gaming system as he took them.

"Thank you." Her voice was quiet and polite as she juggled the other speaker and game controllers still in her hands so that she could open the door before she answered his question. "I'm taking these outside."

Santo frowned, but followed when she stepped out on the porch. "Why?"

"To put in my car," Pet responded as she made her way down the steps and headed for the driveway.

"Why?" Santo repeated impatiently, trailing her to her red Toyota 86. It was a damned cute car, he noted not for the first time, and he thought she'd look good in it.

"So I don't have to later."

Santo glanced at her blankly, slow to put together that she was answering his question about why she was putting the items in the car. He paused next to her as she stopped at the trunk and popped it open, and then watched unhappily as she set the controllers and speaker inside. She then turned to take the game station and the other speaker from him and set them in as well.

When she closed the trunk and headed back the way they'd come, he followed again, asking, "Are they not Parker's?"

"Yes."

"Does he know?" he asked as they mounted the stairs to the porch.

"That I took them from his room?" she asked.

"Yes."

"Not yet."

Santo waited for her to explain and then scowled at her back when she didn't, annoyed as hell that she was being so reticent.

"Where are you going now?" he asked when they entered the house, and she started to jog lightly up the stairs.

"Upstairs," she announced as she reached the top of the steps.

Santo watched her disappear up the hall, and then muttered under his breath and strode into the living room.

"Problems?" Bricker asked with amusement.

"No," he snarled, wondering how he was supposed to ask her out to lunch when she was being so difficult. Or if he even wanted to. Seriously, he'd known claiming a life mate could be hard, but this was not the kind of difficult he'd expected. Shouldn't his life mate be someone who understood his silences and joined him in them?

A snort from Bricker reminded him that he wasn't alone and was easily read at the moment. He turned a baleful glare on the younger immortal, but it didn't seem to intimidate him.

"Buddy," Bricker said with a grin, "the last thing you need is more silence. Hell, I've spent half my time the last couple of weeks wanting to check to see if you're still breathing." When Santo glowered at him, he shrugged. "I'm just sayin' . . . I mean, at least Chewbacca squawks once in a while, you know?"

"What the hell is a Chewbacca?" Santo asked impatiently.

"Exactly." Bricker nodded solemnly, as if his question meant something. "You are way out of touch with society, my friend. And at least as bad as Lucian was at the boy-girl thing. You need help, and I'm just the guy to help you."

Santo arched his eyebrows and simply said, "The Bricker Lotto?"

Bricker grinned, apparently unembarrassed that Santo had heard about his explanations to his mate about their being life mates. "Yeah, all right, not my finest moment, maybe. But I got my girl, and that *despite* all the shade Anders and Decker were throwing my way, so . . . who's laughing now?"

Santo grunted at that, and then glanced around at the sound of the front door closing.

"It was Pet," Bricker told him.

Scowling, Santo strode out of the living room and hurried to open the front door. He peered out, then gaped when he saw that Pet was now carrying a television this time.

Cursing under his breath, he rushed after her, catching up just as she reached the back of the car.

"What are you doing now?" he asked with exasperation.

"Putting this in the car," she said, even as she did so.

"I can see that," he growled. "Why?"

"To take it somewhere else," she said simply, slammed the trunk and turned to head back to the house again.

"Why?" he repeated impatiently, beginning to feel like a parrot.

"So Parker can play his games."

"Well, he cannot play if they are not here," he pointed

out with exasperation, following her up the stairs to the porch and finding his attention briefly caught by the curve of her behind.

"He can," she assured him. "Someplace else."

That dragged his attention away from her butt, and he lifted his gaze to the back of her head with alarm. "Why would he not be here?"

"Because he'll be elsewhere," she said grimly and slipped back into the house.

Santo halted briefly, her words striking him like a blow as he realized she was taking Parker and his things and leaving. At least he thought she was. She was being so damned reticent he wasn't sure. Honestly, getting answers from her was suddenly like pulling teeth, he thought irritably, and then nearly gasped aloud as he realized those had been her exact words to him.

Son of a bitch, she was giving him some of his own back, Santo realized. And he didn't like it. No wonder she was annoyed with him. If she felt as frustrated by his lack of communication as he presently did with hers . . .

Muttering under his breath, Santo hurried after her. Bursting into the house, he glanced up the stairs, expecting to see her already halfway up them. She wasn't there, though. Instead, he heard her voice from the living room. He moved to stand in the doorway just as Bricker said, "Marguerite mentioned she didn't think you'd had breakfast or even lunch and might be hungry. Was she right?"

Santo saw the surprise that flickered onto Pet's face, and then she smiled wryly and nodded. "Yeah, I guess she is. I didn't even think of eating."

"Good. 'Cause I'm hungry too," Bricker said, and

then added, "I was thinking a nice juicy steak would be nice, maybe a baked potato . . ."

"That sounds good," Pet admitted solemnly.

Bricker nodded and then glanced past her to Santo and said, "Take her to that steakhouse we stopped at on our way here."

Pet swung around, her mouth forming an alarmed O as she spotted him and realized Bricker had set her up. She started to protest, "Oh, but—"

"They have aged steak there," Bricker said, talking right over her and taking her arm to steer her across the room to Santo's side. "And it was good too. Now, off you go."

Santo took her elbow when Bricker urged Pet toward him, and then turned to walk her out of the house. He suspected Bricker had taken control of her to prevent further protest. The fact that he followed them out onto the porch and watched them walk to the SUV just convinced him that was the case. Santo didn't know how he felt about that. Part of him didn't like Bricker controlling her, but another part suspected she wouldn't come with him otherwise and was grateful.

Sighing, he saw her seated in the passenger seat, and then started around the SUV.

"Hang on!"

Santo glanced around to see Julius passing Bricker and gesturing for the younger immortal to follow as he walked toward the SUV.

"Do you have the coffee table and headboard in the back?" his uncle asked as he approached.

"*Sì*," Santo murmured, realizing he'd forgotten to unload the items they'd picked up. "But they are in boxes and have to be assembled."

Julius nodded, not seeming surprised. "We will take them then. We can put them together while you are gone."

Santo walked around and opened the back. Julius immediately leaned in and pulled out the long thin box holding the coffee table top and its legs. After passing it off to Bricker, he leaned in to grab the longer box holding the headboard next. He didn't turn and head back to the house then, but paused to eye Santo solemnly.

"I had trouble talking to Marguerite when I first encountered her again," he announced abruptly.

Santo arched an eyebrow at this news and waited.

"But a mortal named G.G. gave me some good advice," he continued. "And that is that women like to talk."

Santo's other eyebrow rose at that. "Marguerite said I should talk more."

"She is a woman," he said with a shrug. "And you will have to talk *some*. Just try to pay attention to her questions. Your instinct will be to answer as economically as possible, from habit. Don't. Give her as much information as you can, and then try to find out what she likes and is interested in and ask her questions. Once she starts talking, you will be able to talk less."

Nodding then, Julius turned and carried the box with the headboard toward the house.

Santo closed the back and then hurried around to the driver's door. Pet was sitting silent and still in the front seat. Definitely controlled, he thought grimly and glanced toward the porch to see Bricker standing there, box in hand, still watching.

Wondering how long her subdued state would last

once they were out of Bricker's sight, Santo pulled on his seat belt and started the engine. As he backed out of the driveway, he turned over all the advice he'd been given. Bricker seemed to agree with Marguerite about the need to talk to Pet. And even Julius seemed to think he should, had even advised him on how to turn the tables and make it so he had to talk less later.

But it was his frustration with her bulleted responses that had made him realize how unpleasant his own lack of communication skills must make him seem to her, and he didn't want that. He wanted to talk to her. He just needed to figure out what to say, or what she wanted him to say.

"Here we are."

Pet glanced around with surprise at Santo's announcement, as startled by the fact that he'd bothered to make the announcement as by the fact that they were here. She'd been a little distracted during the drive. Actually, she'd been controlled at first. She knew that, had felt it, and had known it was Bricker controlling her. He hadn't tried to hide it. In fact, she'd heard his voice in her head saying this was for her own good as he'd sent her out of the house and into the vehicle.

His control had slipped once they'd driven out of sight of the house, and Pet had been absolutely furious. If Bricker had been there in the SUV with them, she probably would have punched him in the nose. But rather than turn her fury on Santo, she'd forced herself to calm down and look for the source of the anger. It was fear. She had been helpless, trapped in a body controlled by another. Yep. Fear.

Once Pet had acknowledged that, a lot of her anger had slipped away. Not because she wasn't afraid it could happen again. It could. But fear and anger wouldn't stop that. What would help stop it was getting away from these people, and she was doing that tonight. In the meantime, Pet was going to eat the most expensive damned steak on the menu, with a baked potato and beans. Oh, yeah, and maybe the combo platter for the appetizer, or fried pickles, or hell, both. She was planning on a big old doggie bag, and Santo was paying. He had to because Bricker hadn't thought to make her take her damned purse.

Pet undid her seat belt and started to reach for the door, but paused when she realized Santo hadn't moved. Turning her head, she peered at him in question.

He stared back silently for a minute and then cleared his throat and said, "I know Bricker controlled you to get you to come with me, and I am sorry about that. I should have stopped him once I realized it, but you did want to eat, just not with me, and I wanted to accompany you so I could make up for . . . earlier. I would like to have a nice meal with you and . . . talk."

The man damned near choked on the word *talk*, and Pet almost snickered but managed to hold it back. Partially because she was still annoyed.

"I will try to answer any questions you have," Santo added when she remained silent. "Whether they are about Purdy's cousin or myself or . . ." He shrugged, seeming to suggest he would talk about anything she wished.

Pet eyed him with curiosity. He'd sounded stiff, his

voice gravelly or even rusty by the end, as if he was not used to spitting out so many words at a time. She suspected he wasn't. But he was trying, she acknowledged, and wasn't sure how she felt about that. Part of her appreciated it, but another part was suddenly terribly frightened. She'd decided it was better to avoid him. His making an effort now might make him likeable. Add that to her attraction to him and avoiding him would probably become harder.

"Is that all right?" Santo asked solemnly. "Can you stomach eating a meal with me? Or should I take us back to the house?"

Pet almost went for the "take us back to the house" option, but that was her fear talking, and she knew it. Besides, she *was* hungry, and she still had questions she would like answers to. She opened her mouth to say she would eat a meal with him, but paused when her stomach answered for her with a grumbling that sounded loud in the suddenly silent vehicle.

It struck Pet as funny, and she felt herself relax. A smile even curved her lips as the long complaint ended and she said, "My stomach says yes, it would like to eat."

Santo relaxed and smiled back, and she was struck again by how beautiful the man was, and then he got out of the truck.

"What are you doing, woman?" Pet muttered under her breath as his door closed. Shaking her head, she opened her own door and followed him out.

Eight

"I guess I should have asked if this restaurant would do," Santo said solemnly as she met him at the front of the SUV. "I know Bricker suggested it, but you might have preferred something else."

"Actually, this is one of my favorite places," Pet assured him. It was a steakhouse chain that aged their meat and, much to her vegetarian sister's dismay, Pet was a big fan of steak.

"Good." Santo relaxed and offered her his arm.

Pet blinked at the old world action but then accepted the offered arm. This time she wasn't taken by surprise when a tingling started where her skin met his. Setting her teeth, she did her best to ignore it. But it was hard to ignore how large and firm the muscle of his forearm felt under her hand, and Pet squeezed gently as they walked to the door, testing the hardness. Santo didn't seem to notice, or if he did, he was too polite to mention it.

"Can I get you a table?"

Pet glanced around at that enthusiastic voice as Santo ushered her inside the restaurant. She watched with amusement as a middle-aged bottle blonde rushed toward them, her attention and wide eyes focused solely on Santo. The woman was practically shivering with excitement as she stopped in front of him.

"A table for two," Santo said in his deep rumble and the hostess breathed out a long "ohhhh" of wonderment. Pet could only presume it was at how sexy his voice was. She didn't think it could be with surprise at his asking for a table for two. There were two of them standing there, after all. The woman may not have noticed, though, Pet supposed. The hostess was positively eating Santo alive with her eyes.

Giving her head a shake, Pet released her hold on Santo's arm and followed when the woman grabbed two menus and started wending her way through the tables. She could feel Santo at her back and noted the other diners glancing their way. Pet was sure his size and the fact that he was gorgeous were the draw, and was relieved when the hostess stopped at a booth and announced brightly, "Here you go."

"Thank you." Pet slid quickly into the near side, leaving Santo to take the opposite booth seat.

The hostess gave them each a menu and told them that their server would be Dylan, before reluctantly leaving them alone.

It wasn't until after their waiter had taken their orders and then taken their menus away that Pet even dared to look at Santo again. She found him looking back, his gaze intense, and she quickly glanced away, wondering if he was trying to read her mind. She glanced over the other guests in the restaurant, noting that it was only half full at the moment. But then it was one thirty now, past the lunch hour rush.

"So," Santo murmured, drawing her reluctant attention back to him. "What do you want to know? What questions do you have regarding the . . . er . . . situation on your sister's street?" he explained, lowering his voice somewhat and glancing at the tables around them.

Pet looked around again as well, this time noting that there wasn't really anyone near enough to hear them. She then turned back just in time to see him straighten his shoulders as if preparing himself to face battle.

"I shall endeavor to do a better job of answering them than I did earlier," he assured her when she hesitated.

Pet felt her mouth twitch with amusement. Really, the man looked like he had just agreed to a root canal without Novocain rather than simply answering some questions. It made her wonder about his earlier annoying lack of communication. Perhaps it hadn't been deliberately irritating, or a rejection.

Sighing, Pet sat back and considered what she should ask. Her first concern was Parker. Not just his physical safety, which she intended to take care of by taking him to her apartment and keeping him there, but also his emotional well-being, which appeared to be tied up with concern for his friend and neighbor Mr. Purdy. "You said that Purdy's cousin is dangerous." When he nodded, Pet asked, "Do you think Mr. Purdy is safe?"

"I do not know," Santo admitted, but when irritation flickered across her face, he added, "As you know, we have been watching the house, but we have seen no signs of life. We may already be too late."

He didn't look any more pleased to make that admission than she was to hear it, she noticed. "Then why haven't you just raided the place or something?"

Santo hesitated, several expressions running across his face, and then he sighed and said, "Our orders are to watch and wait for backup."

"Because this cousin is dangerous?" Pet guessed, and before he could answer, asked, "Why? How is he dangerous? What has he done?"

Santo seemed to consider her questions for a long time before finally saying, "If he is who we think he is—"

"Who do you think he is?" Pet interrupted at once.

"Dressler," Santo answered simply, and then seeing her exasperation with his short answers, he expounded. "Dr. Dressler was a mortal scientist performing . . ." He hesitated, and then asked, "How much do you wish to know about Dressler? His recent history, or—?"

"All of it," Pet interrupted promptly.

"Right." Santo grimaced and then took a deep breath and said, "As far as we know, he started out performing genetic experiments on other mortals more than thirty years ago. But—"

"What kind of genetic experiments?" she interrupted again. This time he didn't hesitate to answer.

"Splicing human DNA with the DNA from various animals to create hybrids."

"Hybrids?" Pet sat back, a frown pulling at her lips. "You mean like snake men or cat people or something?"

"I did not see either of those," Santo said seriously.

"But there were winged mortals, mortals with change-able chameleon-like skin, creatures who looked like normal mortals but had both lungs and gills and could breathe under water as well as on land, and the boy in the cage next to mine had the body of a horse without its head, while where the neck would start was the up-per body of a mortal from the waist up."

"What?" Pet barely breathed the word, horror seem-ing to close her throat. "You mean like the mythical centaur?"

Santo nodded, his expression grim. "*Sì*. Like a centaur."

"Damn," Pet breathed, hardly believing it, and then she wondered, "What was this Dressler guy thinking? What kind of life will the poor boy have?"

"He will not," Santo said solemnly, and when Pet looked confused, he explained, "The boy died. His lungs were unable to take in enough oxygen to sustain what was essentially almost an entire horse body and half a human body."

Pet sighed sadly at that news, and then stilled as what he'd said earlier ran through her mind again. Horror growing in her, she asked, "You said he was in the cage next to yours?"

Santo stiffened, his expression closing. It seemed obvious he hadn't meant to mention that part, and while she was dying of curiosity to have him ex-plain that, she took pity on him, let it go, and instead prompted him to continue his explanations by asking, "So Dressler was experimenting with gene-splicing on mortals?"

"*Sì*," Santo breathed, some of the tension leaving him. He started to open his mouth as if to continue, but then paused and sat back as their waiter, Dylan, arrived with their drinks.

"Thank you," Pet murmured as the young man set a glass of Sprite in front of her and another in front of Santo. She leaned forward the moment the man slipped away, and sipped some of the cold sweet drink up the straw sticking out of it, noting that Santo aped her action, not picking up his glass, but leaning down to sip from his straw as well. She was just thinking that couldn't be comfortable for such a big guy, when he straightened abruptly and blinked at her. Unsure why he was reacting like that, she asked, "Is something wrong?"

"It is bubbly," he said with surprise.

Pet smiled faintly. "Have you never had pop before?"

"No," Santo admitted, peering down at his drink as if unsure what to make of it.

"Then why did you order it?" she asked with amusement. "Why not get something you like?"

"Because I did not know what I would like," he admitted. "I have never had any of the beverages listed on the menu but the coffee and did not want that, so just ordered what you did and hoped for the best."

"Wait. What?" Pet stared at him with amazement. "You've never had any of the drinks they serve here?"

"Immortals often tire of food and other things after a century or two," he explained quietly. "So while I consume meat and raw eggs on occasion to help sustain muscle without the need to consume too much blood, I do not usually bother with beverages."

"Hmm," Pet murmured, her gaze sliding over the muscles in question. He'd said after a century or two, but Santo had the kind of body she imagined medieval warriors or Vikings would have needed to wield their great swords. She was guessing he was older than a century or two. Forcing her attention away from his body and back to his face before she began to drool, Pet asked, "So did you like the flavor, or would you like something else to drink?"

Santo hesitated, and then leaned down tentatively to try the drink again. This time he actually sucked a good portion of it into his mouth, straightened, swished it around a bit as if testing a fine wine, and then swallowed.

"Well?" she asked with a grin.

"It will do," he decided.

Pet shook her head and took another drink before prompting him with, "So, you said this Dressler guy was experimenting on DNA-splicing with mortals?"

"*Sì.*" He straightened a bit in his seat, his expression turning grim again. "He did that for decades, apparently."

"Was it legal?" she asked, quite sure it couldn't be.

"I do not know," Santo admitted with a shrug, and then added, "Although, I would not think so, and the fact that he had moved his operations to a private island down in Venezuela would suggest not. It certainly was not legal for him to kidnap locals on the mainland, drug them, and harvest their eggs and sperm, and force the women to carry the resulting fetuses."

"He did that?" she asked with dismay.

Santo nodded. "He even harvested his own wife's eggs."

"And she let him?" Pet asked with amazement.

Santo shook his head. "Apparently, she was unaware until her son was born with wings."

"Oh . . . my . . . God," Pet breathed. "What a bastard."

"*Sì,*" Santo agreed, and then took another drink before continuing, "Unfortunately, a few years ago he encountered an immortal and found out about our existence. His interests turned and he dedicated himself to learning all he could about us."

Pet sat back in her seat, a small ball forming in the pit of her stomach as she saw where this was leading.

Santo was no longer looking at her. Instead, he kept his gaze on his drink and she suspected it was to hide some pretty heavy duty emotions. Clearing his throat, he said, "Of course, we are normally harder to kidnap and control than a mortal, but Dressler developed a drug that would knock us out. He then hired a small army of mercenaries and paid them handsomely to hunt down and kidnap immortals for him to experiment on."

"And he got away with this?" Pet asked with surprise.

"No one realized what was happening at first. We are . . ." He hesitated, and then sighed and said, "Most immortals live a largely solitary existence until they meet their life mate. They avoid other immortals to avoid having to guard their every thought."

Life mate. Pet considered the word solemnly. She remembered that word from her childhood and thought it was basically another word for wife or partner. Letting it go for now, she thought about what Santo had said about immortals living solitary lives. Pet shook her head and pointed out, "You don't. You're here with your cousin and aunt and uncle and that friend, Bricker."

"*Sì,*" he agreed. "But I have only started to spend more time around my family for the last decade or so.

Before that . . ." Santo shrugged. "I lived a very solitary life and probably would not have been missed for quite a long time. Perhaps even years."

Pet considered him briefly, wondering if that was the reason for his usually short answers. He'd got out of the habit of actually communicating with people while living alone and was still struggling to relearn how to actually talk to people. He was doing much better at it now than he had earlier, but his speech was still very slow, careful, and stiff, as if he was picking each word with care. She suspected this was an effort for him, and felt herself soften toward him in appreciation that he would make that effort.

Forcing herself back to the discussion at hand, Pet asked, "What kind of experiments was he performing on immortals? Not DNA-splicing," she guessed.

"No. Not DNA-splicing," he agreed grimly, and then paused briefly before saying, "His tests on immortals were to discover how much damage we can take and survive, how long it takes to heal, etc."

"So cutting, burning, shooting, maybe?" she guessed. "And then tracking how long the injuries took to close up and heal?"

"*Sì.*"

Santo was avoiding looking at her and she could tell he didn't want to talk about this. She also suspected he would talk about it if she insisted, though. But as curious as Pet was, she hadn't missed how pale he'd gone, or the way his hands were clenching on the tabletop. Whatever he'd gone through while in the cage next to the centaur boy, it hadn't been pleasant, and she didn't want him to have to go through it again there in a restaurant.

Deciding to move the subject along, she guessed, "But he also learned how to become immortal?"

"*Sì*." Santo relaxed a bit. "Ultimately, that was his objective. His experiments were simply to find out what he could expect to survive and such once he became immortal."

"And Mr. Purdy's cousin is this Dressler?" she asked, finding the idea alarming. The man sounded like he'd been a living nightmare as a mortal. As an immortal . . . She shuddered at the thought.

"We think so," Santo said carefully.

Pet's eyebrows rose. "Think? Don't you know? I mean, surely if he captured you, you've seen him?"

"I saw him as a mortal, an old man," Santo explained. "I have no idea what he would look like as a young man at his peak health. However," he added when she opened her mouth to speak again, "the man in Parker's memory is definitely an immortal. He is also tall and thin like Dressler, and Mr. Purdy is a second cousin to Dr. Dressler, so the chances are very good."

"Great," Pet said unhappily, and then sat back when she saw that their waiter had returned, this time with food. Her eyes widened and her mouth began to water as a plate of fried pickles and a combo platter with a variety of appetizers were set in the middle of the table. With her stomach urging her on, she barely managed to wait for their waiter to say a cheerful, "Enjoy," and walk away before reaching for a fried pickle.

"Professor Stone?"

Pet stilled, and lowered the pickle she'd been about to bite into as she turned her head to blink at the pretty young brunette standing at the end of the table. Forcing a pleasant smile, she asked, "Yes?"

"Sorry to bother you. I work here," she explained, holding up her small order pad as if to prove the legitimacy of her claim, and then added, "But I'm also a student at UAlbany."

"I see," Pet murmured. The girl had turned to Santo as she'd added that, her ponytail swinging and a huge smile stretching her lips as her eyes slid over his wide shoulders and muscled arms. Pet waited for the girl whose name tag read Brittany to continue, but when the girl just stared at Santo, Pet left her to her ogling and took the opportunity to bite into her fried pickle. If she hadn't been in public, she would have moaned when the flavor burst in her mouth. Pet loved fried pickles anyway, but hungry as she was they seemed extra delicious today so she wasn't pleased at the interruption when Brittany suddenly asked, "You teach Women in History, don't you?"

Pet stopped chewing and glanced up at that question, but relaxed and continued chewing when she saw the girl wasn't even pretending to look at her. She was still staring at Santo with hungry eyes. Pet shifted her gaze to the big immortal to see how he was taking the attention, and smiled with amusement when she saw that he hadn't noticed. His focus was totally on the chicken wing he'd chosen from the combo platter and was now demolishing.

Swallowing the bite of pickle, Pet cleared her throat and said, "Yes, I do."

"Huh?" The girl swiveled her head to peer at her blankly. "What?"

"I do teach Women in History," Pet said gently.

"Oh, good." Brittany nodded, and then turned back to Santo as he dropped the bones he'd gnawed clean and reached for another chicken wing.

Oh, good? Pet thought with exasperation. The girl obviously wasn't the least bit interested in anything she taught. She'd just used her as an excuse to get closer to Santo. Or maybe she was being uncharitable and the girl had really wanted to ask something but got distracted by Santo's impressive physique. *Been there, done that,* she thought, and decided to help the girl out by prodding her along with questions. "Were you interested in taking my class in the fall?"

"What?" Brittany glanced around, looking rather annoyed to have her ogling interrupted.

Pet narrowed her eyes but then offered a cool smile and said, "I presume that's why you came and interrupted my meal? So you could ask questions about the class Women in History?" She didn't add, *and not just to gawk at my hunky dining partner,* like she wanted, but simply said, "However, I do have office hours and I'm going to have to insist you use them and leave us to our meal."

Cheeks flushing with either embarrassment or anger, Brittany opened her mouth, closed it, and then turned on her heel and walked away. Pet was guessing she wouldn't see her in her Women in History class.

Grimacing, she turned back to Santo just as he started to open his mouth to ask something. To forestall him, she quickly asked, "So, do those nano things make you extra attractive to women or something?"

Santo closed his mouth, considered the question, and then nodded. "I believe so."

Pet's eyes widened. She'd actually been joking, kind of. The guy was a big beefcake and would attract female attention anyway. He had certainly caught her attention right away. But he seemed to be suggesting . . .

"Really?" she asked finally.

"No one has ever studied it that I know of," he said in a slow rumble. "But most of the advantages the nanos give us, such as speed, strength, better hearing, and so on . . ." He shrugged. "They all make us better hunters, to gain the extra blood we need. Making us more attractive to the opposite sex would aid in that too, so it seems likely the nanos make us secrete some kind of pheromone that would do that."

Pet sat back and tried to look at him objectively without her hormones giving their seventy-five cents worth. Santo was really a super gorgeous man. He was big, muscular, with beautiful eyes and sexy full lips. He would make any woman take a second look. But if he also secreted sexy pheromones . . . well, it was no wonder women acted like idiots around him. Including herself. The thought actually made Pet feel better about her own responses to the man.

"You are a history professor at UAlbany?" Santo asked suddenly.

He sounded surprised, and she asked, "You didn't know that?"

Santo shook his head. "I knew you worked at the university. Marguerite mentioned this morning that she was going to have to call there and explain your absence. But I did not know you were a professor. You do not look like a history professor."

That made her grin. "What does a history professor look like?"

"Old and dusty, with glasses and corduroy sport coats with patches on their elbows," he said without hesitation.

"And male?" she suggested with amusement.

Santo shrugged and picked up another chicken wing.

"So what would you have guessed I did at the university?" Pet asked with interest as she picked up another fried pickle.

Santo considered her briefly. "Something in the arts. Maybe music or dance."

Her eyebrows rose slightly. "Why?"

"I do not know," he admitted with a wry smile. "I just think of music when I look at you. Beautiful symphonies and—" Santo paused abruptly, embarrassment crossing his features, before he repeated, "I do not know."

"Actually, music was my major and history my minor my first year," she admitted. "But I switched them my second year."

"Why?" he asked at once.

Pet smiled wryly. "My parents. The idea of my majoring in something as fluffy as music nearly killed them."

"Music is not fluffy," he growled.

Santo sounded so outraged, she found herself curious, but merely said, "You have to understand, everyone in my family is a medical doctor. Both my parents are physicians with family practices, and my sister was studying medicine as well. I was expected to join the family business too. The fact that I didn't was enough to make me the black sheep of the family. But majoring in music nearly killed them."

"So you switched to history to please them," Santo said solemnly.

"With a minor in music," she reminded him. "I still play music. I even used to be in a band."

"Keyboards?" he guessed.

Pet grinned and shook her head. "Electric guitar. It was a hard rock band."

His eyebrows rose at that. "I play drums in a rock band."

"Really?" she asked with interest, and could actually picture him behind a drum set.

"*Sì.* We are called the NCs, for Notte Cuginos."

"Notte cousins?" she asked, recognizing the word *cugino*, and when he nodded, Pet asked, "And are you all cousins in the band?"

"*Sì.* But we have not played for a while."

"Why?" she asked at once.

"Gia, our singer, Christian, our violinist, and Raffaele, our keyboardist, have all found their life mates, and all are from here in North America. Christian's wife, Caro, has business concerns in Toronto she is still tying up, so they spend a lot of time there, Gia's husband is from California, and Raffaele's wife, Jess, is from Montana, so . . ."

"So the band has disbanded," Pet suggested when he didn't finish.

"For now," he allowed, and then added, "But it is fine. Julius has decided to open offices here, and Zanipolo and I will split our time between projects in Italy and here once Mortimer does not need our aid anymore."

Pet's eyebrows drew together with confusion. She

had no idea who Mortimer was. "I'm sorry, I don't understand. What offices are you talking about? I thought you guys were Enforcers who hunted bad immortals?"

"Bricker is the only one among us who is actually a full-time Enforcer. The rest of us are presently working as Enforcers to help them out. Mortimer calls it being deputized. Once things settle down and Mortimer has all of his people back . . ." He gave another shrug. "We will return to our usual full-time jobs."

"I see." Pet thought about that briefly and then asked, "So is the RV some kind of cover or mobile command center or something?" RVs didn't exactly jive with immortal Enforcers in her mind.

"No, it is an RV," Santo said with amusement. "Marguerite and Julius have not actually been working as Enforcers. They were on vacation, an RV tour with J. But when Mortimer got the tape of Parker's 911 call and realized it originated from Albany, which Marguerite and Julius were driving through, he called and asked them to stop and look into it. Once they'd spoken to the Caprellis and decided it should be investigated, they called him and he called us and had us stop here. We were in Newburyport, Massachusetts, at the time."

Pet blinked at that. "What were you doing in Newburyport?"

"Driving back to Toronto from New Brunswick using the American route," he said, and before she had to ask, explained, "We were investigating the purchase of a couple dozen coffins in New Brunswick to be sure it was not a rogue starting his own little army of immortals."

"Immortals don't sleep in coffins," Pet said with certainty.

"No," Santo agreed with a smile. "But some rogue immortals use the vampire myth to control their turns. They make them sleep in coffins with a bit of dirt in the bottom, telling them they have to sleep there or they will die or some such rot. It ensures they do not run off. They always have to return to the coffin and their sire."

"Smart," Pet commented, and then asked, "So, was it a rogue who bought the coffins?"

A look of disgust crossed Santo's face. "No. Someone calling himself an artist."

"Artist?" she echoed with disbelief. "Why would an artist need two dozen coffins?"

"To make an art installation," he said dryly. "He had arranged the coffins in rows in a gallery there, dressed up stuffed animals of all sizes and description, and then ripped off limbs or the head, or slashed open the gut so that the stuffing stuck out, and then he arranged one in each coffin and called it art."

A small laugh slipped from Pet and she shook her head. "You're kidding, right?"

"I wish I were," he muttered. "The gallery owner considered it high art."

"Are you sure you didn't misunderstand and he was telling you he was high when he agreed to give this so-called 'art' a showing?" she asked with amusement.

"I would not be surprised," Santo said with a grin. "I think both the artist and the gallery owner were high when we interviewed them. They actually sat there driveling on about how it was the artist's representation of the death of innocence. That was even the name of the art show, The Death of Innocence."

Pet laughed at that, and then as her laughter faded, she tipped her head and eyed him for a moment, before asking, "So, your temporary base is in Toronto?"

"*Sì.*"

"But you'll eventually go home to Italy?"

Santo hesitated, and then said, "As I mentioned, Julius is opening offices in North America, probably in both Toronto and New York, so I will most likely spend more of my time here in North America."

"Oh," Pet murmured and wondered why that made her happy. She'd already decided he wasn't someone to tangle with. Clearing her throat, she asked, "What are the offices Julius is opening for, exactly?"

"Notte Construction."

"You work for a construction company?" Pet asked, not sure why she was surprised. The man was huge. She could see him wrestling a jackhammer and such. But she'd never imagined that's what he did and still found the idea unlikely.

"I am a civil engineer," he announced as if guessing she'd been imagining him in a wife-beater and jeans, swinging a sledgehammer.

"Oh." Pet blinked and smiled. That seemed more his style. He was smart and commanding and she could imagine him strutting around a construction site in a hard hat with a clipboard in hand, ordering people around.

"Here we go!"

Pet and Santo both stopped and looked up at that. Their waiter had returned with the main course.

Sitting back from the table to stay out of the way as the young man set down the plates, Pet glanced toward the appetizers that remained. There wasn't much left. They'd both been eating as they spoke. Santo had eaten every last one of the chicken wings and between the two of them they'd eaten all the fried pickles and most of the potato skins. There were just a couple of jalapeño and cheese balls, and one potato skin left. In fact, Pet was actually kind of full now and eyed the steak Dylan set before her with a little regret. She would end up taking most of it home in a doggie bag, she knew. But it was best fresh off the grill, and now she regretted eating so many appetizers.

"Enjoy!" Dylan said cheerfully before moving away.

"Thank you." Pet picked up her knife and fork and set to it, determined to make a good showing.

They had eaten in silence for several minutes when Santo suddenly said, "You intend to move Parker out of the house after school today."

Pet glanced up from her plate and eyed him silently. His voice had been grim.

"That is your plan, is it not?" he asked quietly when she continued to stare at him. "That is why you were putting his gaming system and television in your car?"

"Yes," Pet said finally, and then set down her knife and fork and reached for her drink. She picked it up but then simply held it as she explained, "Parker was left in my care. It's my responsibility to keep him safe and between midnight creepers and the fanged visitor next door, the house isn't looking very safe at the moment."

"No," he agreed quietly, but much to her surprise he looked extremely disappointed by the news.

Pet wondered about that as she watched him reach for his own drink. Was he disappointed? If he hadn't controlled her last night when he'd kissed her—well, really, even if he had controlled her, no one had been controlling him, and there had been no mistaking the hard bulge in his jeans last night as anything but definite interest. So maybe he *was* disappointed at the thought of her leaving.

Of course, the more cautious side of her mind argued, men would screw a hole in the wall if it got them off, and she was the only female around. At least, the only one who knew about them and was easily available since she had been in the same house. That thought made Pet grimace as she watched Santo drink.

Bypassing the straw, he swallowed a large gulp of the clear bubbly liquid and then set it carefully back on the table before asking, "Where will you take him?"

"My place," she admitted, and took a drink of her own beverage. A wry smile claimed her lips as she set it back on the table, though, and she added, "Which ought to be interesting."

When he raised one eyebrow in question, Pet explained, "I live in an apartment building, which means more security and people around, which is all good, but . . ."

"But?" Santo prompted when she paused.

"But my building doesn't allow pets," she admitted. "Parker isn't likely to agree to leaving Mrs. Wiggles behind, though."

"So you plan to sneak the cat in?" he guessed.

Pet nodded. "Yeah, but getting Mrs. Wiggles and all that gear I just bought into my apartment without the apartment manager noticing and raising a fuss should be interesting."

Santo was silent as he placed his last piece of steak in his mouth. It was only after he'd chewed and swallowed that he offered, "Perhaps I can help."

"Schlepping all the stuff up?" she asked with amusement. "Or distracting the apartment manager with your magnificent yet intimidating physique while Parker and I sneak Mrs. Wiggles and all her gear in?"

Santo smiled suddenly, and she thought, pheromones or not, the guy was gorgeous enough to stop traffic. Then he asked, "You think I have a magnificent physique?"

Pet flushed, but snorted at the question. "Like you didn't know that."

"I did not know," he assured her.

She didn't buy that for a minute. Her expression becoming serious, she said, "I know you can read my mind, Santo, and so already know exactly how freaking hot and sexy I find you. Don't deny it," Pet said when he started to shake his head. "I knew about immortals being able to read and control minds before I encountered you guys. But even if I hadn't," she added firmly, forestalling him when he opened his mouth as if to protest, "Marguerite gave the game away when she reassured me that none of you were connected to the Brass Circle when I hadn't mentioned them to her."

Santo looked confused. "Who are the Brass Circle?"

Pet eyed him uncertainly. He really looked bewildered by the name.

"Is it a band?" he asked finally when she remained silent.

Her eyes widened at the question. Good Lord, he really had no idea who the Brass Circle was. Not that she hadn't believed Marguerite when she'd said they weren't connected to the organization, but since the Brass Circle had been uppermost in her mind since she'd noted the silver flecks in their eyes . . . Of course, she'd tried to block those thoughts the minute they'd cropped up in her head, Pet reminded herself. Still, Marguerite had picked up on them anyway.

"Pet," he said quietly, sliding his hand across the table to gently touch hers.

The tingle that charged through her at the innocent touch had her stiffening and staring down at their hands.

"I cannot read or control you."

She glanced up sharply. "What?"

"I cannot read or control you," Santo repeated solemnly.

Pet stared at him blankly for a minute and then asked, "Why? Marguerite can."

He withdrew his hand and straightened in his seat, but rather than answer her question, asked, "Just how much do you know about immortals? And how do you know about us?"

Pet peered down and picked up her fork to begin pushing her potatoes around on the plate. "I know that immortals started in Atlantis and have existed since before its fall. That their beginnings came from science and not some curse."

"Nanos," Santo said with a solemn nod. "Bioengineered nanos that were developed in an effort to create something that could heal people without the need for surgery and such."

Pet hadn't known that, but merely nodded and added, "I also know that while you're similar to vampires in that you need extra blood, are stronger, can see better, and hear better than mere mortals, you aren't dead and soulless like mythical vampires are supposed to be."

"Anything else?" Santo queried when she fell silent.

"You can read mortals' thoughts and control them," she said quietly.

"Yes, usually we can. However, I cannot with you," he assured her.

Pet was silent for a moment and then cleared her throat and asked, "So, last night, when we—when you kissed me . . ." She met his gaze. "You didn't control me in any way?"

Santo looked so surprised and even horrified by the question, she knew the answer before he said, "No, of course not. Even if I could have controlled you, I would not have done that at such a time. It would be rape."

"But Marguerite can read me," she repeated with confusion. "And I'm pretty sure she's controlled me a couple times too, and I know Bricker did to get me in the SUV."

"Yes." He nodded. "But I cannot."

"Why?"

Santo was silent for so long, she was sure he wouldn't answer, but then he sighed, shrugged, and said, "Sometimes that is just the way it is."

Pet's eyes narrowed. He was avoiding her gaze now and she suspected there was more to it than that, but he didn't leave her the opportunity to press him on the issue. Glancing around, he spotted their waiter and waved him over.

"We should get moving or we will be late picking up Parker," he said as he pulled out his wallet.

Santo was right, of course, Pet saw when she glanced at her watch and noted the time. They'd been sitting there for much longer than she'd realized. They really did have to go. But that didn't stop the questions now swirling in her head. Could he really not read her? Or was he lying? And if he was lying, why?

Nine

"This isn't going to work."

Pet rolled her eyes at Parker's prediction as he dragged the last of his books out of his school knapsack. It was at least the sixth time he'd said it, and it was the sixth time she responded with, "Yes, it is."

"The cat will be fine." Santo added the reassurance as he gathered the bags Parker had filled with things he "just couldn't live without" during his stay at her place.

Parker released an exasperated sigh and turned his bag upside down, shaking it to remove anything still remaining inside. When nothing fell out, Pet picked up Mrs. Wiggles from where she'd been napping on the bed while they'd packed Parker's clothes in his small suitcase. "Here. Open up and we'll put her in."

"She'll suffocate in there," Parker protested even as he opened the bag wide for her to set the cat inside.

"She won't," Pet assured him as she released her

hold on the cat and retrieved her hands. When Parker started to zip up the bag, she said, "You don't have to close the bag until we get to my building, and then you can leave it open just a bit so she can get air, but not enough that she can stick her head out. Okay?"

"Okay." He relaxed a bit and reached into the bag to pet the animal.

"Why don't you go downstairs?" she suggested. "I'll put your schoolbooks in a bag and bring them down."

Nodding, the boy headed for the door, his head bent to peer into his knapsack at Mrs. Wiggles rather than where he was going.

"He's going to fall down the stairs and break his neck," Pet muttered with a shake of the head.

"I'll keep an eye on him," Santo said and left the room on the boy's heels, several bags hanging from his shoulders and hands.

Pet smiled crookedly as she watched him go, and then glanced around, noting that the room seemed a lot larger without him in it. It also seemed to be cooler and have more air. Neither of which could be true, so she supposed that meant it was just her when the man was around. She got hot and bothered.

"Almost ready?"

Pet glanced toward the door and smiled as she watched Marguerite sail in, another lovely lightweight summer dress swinging around her long legs. "I just have to pack up Parker's school stuff and we'll be good to go."

"I'll help," Marguerite volunteered, moving to join her at the bed.

"You don't have to," Pet protested.

"I want to." Marguerite picked up a pencil case and notebook and put them into the large cloth bag Pet had liberated from her sister's pantry for the task. "I also wanted to thank you again for agreeing to let us use your sister's house to keep an eye on Mr. Purdy's place. It will make things much easier. The window in the den affords a view of both the front and back of the house, which means only one of the men will have to watch at a time, allowing them to take shorter, six hour shifts each, rather than the two watching twelve on and twelve off they started with."

Pet smiled faintly but shrugged as they worked. "It was hardly an altruistic decision. It isn't safe around here until Purdy's visiting cousin is taken care of and you guys are seeing to that. Besides, this way I don't have to worry about the creep who tried to get in the other night returning and getting in to steal stuff or wreck the place while we're gone. You guys can handle him."

"True," Marguerite said, sounding amused.

They both fell silent for a moment and concentrated on gathering everything Parker had removed from his bag. The sheer amount of stuff made her shake her head. She had no idea how he'd fit it all in his knapsack. There were at least six thick textbooks, several notebooks, two pencil cases, a sketch pad, an iPad, his laptop, various power cords, a ruler, and even some paint, paintbrushes, and charcoal.

"Ask me what you have wanted to ask me since returning from your late lunch with Santo," Marguerite said suddenly.

Pet stilled and raised her head, and then tilted it as

she considered the other woman. "You read my mind again."

It wasn't a question, but Marguerite nodded. "I apologize. It is a habit that is hard to break. However, that subject is what you want to ask me about anyway. Whether Santo was telling you the truth when he said he could not read or control you."

"Was he telling the truth?" she asked at once.

"Yes, he was. He cannot read or control you," Marguerite said solemnly, and then grinned and added, "I fear all that passion you experienced with him came naturally, not through any control."

Pet flushed with embarrassment but ignored the last part of what she'd said and pointed out, "But *you* can read and control me. Why can't he?" Pet didn't wait for an answer but quickly asked, "Can the other men read me? I know Bricker controlled me, so he must be able to read me too. But what about Julius and Zanipolo?"

"Yes. Everyone in this house can read and control you except for Santo. Well, and Parker, of course," Marguerite added with a little smile, and then, her expression turning solemn, she said, "But I fear I cannot tell you why."

"Because you don't know? Or—"

"Because it is not my place," Marguerite said, cutting her off. "Santo will have to explain that to you. When you are ready."

Pet was frowning over that rather enigmatic comment when Marguerite straightened with a pleased little sigh. "That is everything, I think. We should go below now. Parker and Santo are waiting." Turning, she headed out of the room, leaving her to follow.

Pet stared after her for a moment before picking up the cloth bag full of Parker's school items and following.

"Hurry, hurry, hurry."

Pet rolled her eyes at Parker's harassment as she unlocked her apartment door and said with exasperation, "I'm hurrying, Parker. Just—there," she said with relief as the lock clicked and she was able to push the door open.

Parker raced ahead at once and disappeared around the corner to the left.

"Take her to your room," Pet called firmly after her nephew as she led Santo into the entry. Both of them were weighed down by bags, but Santo had the majority of them, and Parker had only carried his knapsack with Mrs. Wiggles in it. Which was why he'd been desperate to get inside as quickly as possible. The cat hadn't moved since he'd zipped up the bag, and he was sure she was dying or scared or both. Pet thought Mrs. Wiggles was just a lazy old thing. She hadn't moved much when he'd been carting her around the first night either, except when she'd tried to climb his head and that had been purely out of fear.

"Your home is very nice."

Pet glanced around at that comment from Santo as they stepped out of the ten-foot-long entry and reached the main part of the apartment. From here they could see the high, light-colored walls and open concept layout. The kitchen was directly ahead of them with the dining area beyond it. Both were open to a sitting area on the right that was separated only by an island with a sink and indoor grill that ran the length of the kitchen area. Her office was beside them, running the length of the entry, but they could see part of the large, open living room beyond it from where they stood. To their left, a hall headed away, leading to the bedrooms.

Pet tried to look at it all as he must see it and mostly what jumped out at her were the large windows in every direction. The outer walls were pretty much made of them, which was what she'd loved about the place when she'd first seen it, and what she still appreciated.

"Thank you," Pet murmured, moving into the kitchen to set down the groceries she'd carried up. They'd stopped at the store after picking up Parker. She'd put the perishables in one of her sister's cooler bags once they'd got back to the house, so she didn't bother to put them away just yet. They would be fine for a few more minutes, so she started back toward Santo, intending to take a couple of the bags from him.

The man had her overnight bag, Parker's suitcase, the bag that held the boy's school items from the knapsack, and several more bags of Parker's. He also carried the bags from the pet store. Santo didn't let her take them, though. Raising them out of her reach, he said, "Lead the way and I'll carry them to where they need to go."

When she opened her mouth to protest, he added, "It means I get the tour."

Chuckling, Pet gave up and led him up the hall. Stopping at the first door on their right, she knocked lightly and then opened it to reveal a bedroom in pale blue. "This is Parker's room when he's here."

She stood back for Santo to enter, and then followed and closed the door to prevent Mrs. Wiggles from escaping. While he set down Parker's bags and the ones from the pet store, Pet moved to the bed where Parker was hovering over Mrs. Wiggles and petting her as he apologized for putting her in that "nasty old knapsack."

"She's fine, Parks," Pet said with amusement. "Look at her. She's purring."

"She is now that she's out, but how would you like to be zipped up in a nasty old bag?"

Pet rolled her eyes and walked over to set up the litter box. She followed that up by going through the bags and separating the food and food dishes from the toys and catnip. Santo helped her with that, and then picked up the bag she'd placed the food dishes and canned food in and followed her from the room.

"This is the guest bathroom," she announced, pausing by an open door to a compact but full bathroom in pale earth tones. As Santo glanced in with curiosity, she said, "There's also a half bath on the left of the entry."

When he nodded, Pet turned and continued down the hall to the next door on the right. "Another guest bedroom."

This one was done in earth tones like the guest bathroom.

"Nice." Santo nodded with approval.

"Thanks." Pet grinned and continued to the end of the hall where a door opened onto the left just before the hall turned away to the right. She opened the door and said, "Laundry room slash pantry."

Santo stepped into the long narrow room that stretched almost the length of the two bedrooms on the opposite side. The washer and dryer sat at the end to the right of the door, taking up the entire width of the narrow room, and long shelves on either side led away from the door to the left, running the length of the room.

"I have never seen an apartment with so much room," Santo said with wonder as he peered down the shelves holding everything from food to seasonal items.

"I wanted space," Pet said solemnly. "I get claustrophobic in small spaces. I'd be in a house except . . ."

"Except?" he prompted with curiosity.

"I don't like mowing the lawn," she admitted with a grimace. "Or shoveling sidewalks or weeding gardens . . . Besides, it's safer in an apartment building. At least it feels safer with the security entrance and people nearby."

Santo's eyes narrowed as she said that last bit, and Pet suspected he was wondering why security was such an issue with her. Since it wasn't something she intended to discuss, she quickly stepped back out of the room and led the way around the corner to the two doors at the end of this short hall. She opened the door on the right first.

"I guess this would be the master bath, though it's not actually attached to the bedroom," Pet pointed out as she stepped aside for him to enter the large room with a big shower, a spa bathtub, and a long counter with double sinks. Turning away once he'd looked around, she opened the door to her bedroom and then just shrugged and stepped back again, leaving him to enter alone.

The moment Santo stepped into her room, she felt ridiculously exposed. Calling herself a coward, Pet forced herself to join him inside as he walked up to her bed and set down her bag. But when she started wondering if the queen-sized bed would be big enough to accommodate his length, she gave her head a shake and gestured to a door on the left. "That's a walk-in closet. It's not huge or anything, but it's better than just the standard two-door closet."

Santo walked over to open the door and peer in and Pet hoped it wasn't a mess. She'd been in such a rush to pack and get out of here the other day after her sister's call, it probably was, but there was nothing she could do about that now. He shut the door and then moved to the closed curtains and drew one aside enough to look out at the view.

"The balcony runs the length of your apartment?" Santo asked, letting the drape fall back into place.

"Yes," Pet murmured, fighting the urge to turn and hurry up the hall away from him when he started walking back toward her.

"Aunt Pet-tee!"

Smiling wryly at Parker's call, Pet released the breath she hadn't realized she'd been holding and turned away from Santo to step out of the room.

"What?" she called back, leaving Santo to follow.

"Mrs. Wiggles is hungry," Parker announced as soon as she came around the corner.

"Then it's good we got her food, huh?" Pet said lightly and then glanced back to see Santo coming up behind her with the bag of cat food and dishes in hand. Turning back to her nephew, she promised, "I'll open a can and bring it to you and then figure out dinner. Good?"

"Good," he agreed.

Nodding, Pet took the bag from Santo and led the way to the kitchen. She set the bag on the island and quickly began removing items from it as Santo walked around the outside of the island until he stood opposite her. He then crossed his arms and leaned against the counter to watch.

Pet was very aware of his eyes on her as she worked and her gaze kept skittering to him and away. She was actually a little surprised that he was still there in her apartment. She'd driven her 86 back here, and he'd followed in the SUV with Parker for a passenger. The boy had insisted on riding with Santo, claiming the dark SUV looked safer than her little sporty Toyota. But Pet knew the truth was he disliked how she drove. To his mind, Pet had a lead foot and took the corners too fast.

Trying not to be offended, Pet had merely shrugged. Santo had planned on coming anyway to handle the apartment manager should he somehow figure out they had a cat with them and raise a fuss. But that hadn't happened. At least, he hadn't suddenly popped out in the hall in front of them as they'd carted everything in, which he always did. So, perhaps Santo's presence had actually helped, after all. Perhaps his size had been intimidating enough that the man had stayed safe in his own apartment instead of trying to harass her for a change. She knew it was all intimidation tactics. The apartment manager insisted he liked to run a "tight ship" and "keep his thumb" on things, but she'd noticed that while there were some men in the purchased apartments, he only rented to women, so suspected he just liked trying to keep *them* under his thumb. Pet was quite sure he'd be disappointed to know that she didn't find him intimidating so much as just pathetic.

Shaking her head, she retrieved the can opener from the drawer next to her and quickly began to open a can of something that smelled absolutely atrocious. Wrinkling her nose, she glanced to Santo again and found herself asking, "Do you want to stay for dinner?"

Pet had no idea where that question came from. If Marguerite hadn't assured her that Santo couldn't read or control her, she'd have suspected he'd made her say it.

"Not if that is what we are eating."

Pet glanced up swiftly to see the expression of distaste on his face and grinned with amusement. "No. I was planning to make chicken Caesar salad. This is for the cat."

"And she likes that?" he asked with disbelief.

Pet chuckled and shrugged. "Pets have different taste than ours. Heck, our dog used to eat poopsicles. This is better than that. Maybe," she added with a grimace as the rest of the food plopped into the dish looking like a cross between diarrhea and vomit. God, she wouldn't eat this stuff if they paid her. Glancing back to Santo, she raised an eyebrow. "You aren't asking me what a poopsicle is."

Santo stared down at the cat food with a sort of horrified fascination, but then seemed to remember himself and straightened. Meeting her gaze, he said, "My mother has always kept dogs. Some of them had the unfortunate predilection to enjoy eating other's frozen waste. I presume that is what you are calling a poopsicle?"

"Yes," she admitted with a chuckle as she turned on the tap to rinse the second cat dish. Santo had really been trying to make an effort to talk since their shopping trip, and she appreciated it. And when he smiled at her as he was doing now, she just wanted to crawl across the island, up his chest, nibble on his ear, and ask him to have mad, passionate sex with her.

"Yes."

Pet glanced up sharply at his words, her eyes widening. Had she spoken her thoughts aloud again? It was a bad habit with her. Something she'd already done with him once at least. So had she? And was he saying yes to having mad, passionate sex with her? And why did that thought please her when she'd decided she should avoid getting entangled with the immortal? Clearing her throat, she asked uncertainly, "Yes?"

"*Sì.* Yes, I will stay to dinner," he explained.

"Oh, well, shoot."

"You did not want me to say yes?" Santo asked carefully, one eyebrow rising.

"What?" Pet asked with surprise, and then realized she'd muttered her disappointment aloud, which she hadn't intended to do. "Oh, no. I mean yes, of course I wanted you to say yes. I was just thinking about asking you something when you suddenly said yes, and my first thought was that it was in response to my question, so I was disappointed when I realized it wasn't, which is silly, because I hadn't actually asked it out loud or anything."

Realizing she was babbling in her embarrassment, Pet cut herself off and then decided to move away from the subject of her thoughts and said, "But of course I wanted you to say yes to dinner, or I wouldn't have asked." Grimacing, she admitted, "Though, I'm not much of a cook, so it's just going to be a chicken Caesar salad and some frozen garlic bread. Well, hopefully the garlic bread's not still frozen when I serve it. But no promises," Pet added on a nervous chuckle as she decided the cat dish had been rinsed enough and straightened it to collect the water now. She kept her gaze focused on the dish then, very aware that Santo was staring at her, and hoping he'd let the original topic drop. Of course, he didn't.

"What did you wish to ask me?"

"Oh!" She raised a panicked gaze to him but quickly dropped it again and tried to think of something, anything she could say rather than the truth. When her gaze landed on the overflowing dish of water, she promptly pulled it out from under the stream of water and held it out to him. "Help me take the cat stuff in to Parker?"

Santo stared at her for a long minute before taking the water dish. He then leaned across the island to place his hand onto the dish holding the cat food as well. He didn't pick it up right away. Instead, he stared at her silently, his face just inches from hers and said, "I suspect that is not really what you wished to ask me."

"Oh?" she squeaked, eyes wide.

"*Sì*. And I think you should know," Santo continued in a gentle rumble and then leaned forward just enough that his words were a soft growl against her lips as he told her, "The answer will always be yes." And then he was gone. Pet could sense that before she opened eyes she hadn't realized she'd closed.

Swallowing, she peered at the empty space on the other side of the counter where he had stood, and then down at where the dish of stinky cat food had been, and then she wrapped her arms around her waist and bent over with a gasping squeal of, *"Oh, my God."*

Shaking her head, Pet straightened, but her mind was still squealing. The man was just so damned gorgeous. And he hadn't controlled her the night before. And he hadn't been rejecting her today. And she had no business being interested in an immortal. They were nothing but trouble. But he was so damned sexy! And he made her pulse race and her body scream with interest. And he'd said the answer would always be yes, and she so wanted to ask *that* question.

What was she going to do? How was she supposed to not melt into a puddle at his feet or throw herself at him? And he'd been in her bedroom! And why had she decided she wasn't supposed to ask that question anyway? She was finding it hard to recall now with her lips still tingling from the feel of his mouth brushing hers as he spoke. And—

"What?" Parker's shocked question sounded from down the hall, interrupting her mind's mad bouncing around inside her head. It was followed by a horrified, "Nooooooo!"

Frowning, Pet started toward the hall just as Parker came hurtling out at her.

"When you said you'd see to dinner, I didn't think you meant actually *cooking* it. Please tell me you aren't cooking! Please," he cried pitifully, collapsing against her with his face pressed to her stomach and his arms wrapping around her upper legs. "Please, Aunt Pet, I'll be good I promise. Don't punish us so."

Pet scowled down at the little twerp as Santo came out of the hall too. His expression was shocked and alarmed until she growled, "Ha, ha, very funny, Parks."

"I'm not being funny," he protested earnestly, pulling back to peer up at her. "You can't cook, Aunt Pet. You'll kill us all."

"Oh, for God's sake," Pet muttered, beginning to flush now with embarrassment. "I'm just making chicken Caesar salad, Parker. It will be fine."

"How old is the salad dressing?" Parker asked at once.

"What? I don't know," she admitted, clucking her tongue with irritation when he pulled away and moved to her refrigerator to search for the dressing. Sighing, Pet turned to Santo and reminded him, "I did mention I'm not much of a cook."

Head stuck in the fridge, Parker snorted with derision. "The last time she cooked for me I was sick for two days. Food poisoning."

"It wasn't food poisoning," she snapped. "You just had a tummy bug."

"Food poisoning," Parker insisted firmly. "And the time before that, she made chocolate chip and *bacon* cookies."

"No, I didn't," she said quickly, knowing her cheeks were probably red as apples now. "There was no bacon in them."

"No, there wasn't," Parker agreed. "But you made them with bacon grease. They were disgusting."

"It was the only fat I had," Pet said defensively, but could feel herself heating up even more. If her face wasn't cherry red now, she'd be surprised.

When Parker turned his head and arched one of his little supercilious eyebrows at her, she grimaced and glanced to Santo as she explained, "My sister, Quinn, is always on some diet or other. All she ever has in the house is green stuff. I wanted to make Parker cookies, but of course there was no butter. Not even margarine or shortening. The only fat in the house was the bacon I'd brought with me for Sunday breakfast, so . . ." She left the sentence unfinished and shrugged helplessly.

"So you fried the bacon and used the leftover grease to make cookies?" Santo guessed.

"It seemed like a good idea at the time," Pet said defensively and then wrinkled her nose and added, "Mind you that was on a Saturday night after two or three glasses of wine."

"It wasn't a good idea," Parker assured her.

"No, it wasn't," she agreed and then glanced to Santo and admitted, "They really were disgusting. But in my defense, that's around the time they started that campaign claiming everything is better with bacon so I thought it was worth a try."

"*Everything* doesn't include chocolate chip cookies," Parker said dryly, backing out of the refrigerator with the Caesar salad dressing in hand.

"Yeah, well, they put bacon on donuts now," Pet pointed out, and then bit her lip and tried to think when she'd bought the dressing he was now scanning in search of an expiry date. Surely it hadn't been that long ago? she thought, but sighed with resignation when he turned to her with his *aha* look. "What's the expiry date?"

"June."

"There," she began with relief. "This is June. It's fi—"

"Of last year," he interrupted dryly.

"Right." Pet sighed the word and then moved to the phone. "So . . . pizza? Again?"

"Yes, please." Parker threw the salad dressing in the garbage under the sink and hopped out of the kitchen, headed for his room and Mrs. Wiggles.

Pet scowled at his disappearing back, and then glanced to Santo as a low chuckle rumbled from his throat. He'd been grinning since Parker had started blabbing about the chocolate chip and bacon cookies. A mistake her nephew was never going to let her forget, she was sure. Still, her humiliation was almost worth it to hear that deep rich sound, Pet decided as something inside her vibrated in response. Giving herself a shake as her call was answered, she raised her eyebrows. "So? What do you like on your pizza?"

"Whatever you normally get," he said easily.

Pet nodded and began to speak to the waiting worker on the phone, doubling her usual order and then tripling it as her gaze slid over the huge man. It wasn't until she hung up that Pet remembered him saying that he didn't normally eat except for raw eggs and meat. Frowning, she started putting away her groceries, considering what she had as she did. She'd bought steaks and could cook them to feed him, she supposed.

"You look troubled," Santo commented, moving up beside her to help put the groceries away. "What are you thinking?"

"I just remembered that you don't eat except for meat and raw eggs," Pet admitted as she stretched up on her tiptoes to place a can of soup on an upper shelf. "I could grill up a steak if you'd rather, or—" The offer died in her throat when his hand closed around her fingers, and then he took the can from her and set it on the shelf for her before urging her around to face him.

Pet stared at the middle of his chest until he cupped her face and lifted it so that she had to meet his gaze.

"It is very sweet of you to offer to cook for me," Santo murmured, brushing his thumb lightly over her lower lip.

The small caress sent tingles rushing through her

again, and Pet's lips parted slightly on a small sigh. The moment they did, he slid his thumb farther forward to run between both lips, once and then twice.

"But I would rather not suffer food poisoning."

The words were so unexpected that it took Pet's mind a moment to register them, and then her eyes shot to his and she caught the wicked teasing grin on his face. She didn't even think, she simply bit down on the tip of his thumb. It had been meant to punish him for teasing her, but instead the action made him burst out laughing. He also withdrew his thumb, but then he pulled her close, pressing her face to his chest as he chuckled.

Pet scowled at his amusement and drew in a breath to lambast him for his bad behavior, but then paused as his scent assailed her senses. Damn, he smelled good. She didn't think it was a cologne or body wash. It just smelled too . . . organic. That was the only word she could think to describe it. There was nothing chemical to it, no floral undertones. He smelled clean and masculine, cool and spicy at the same time, like a walk in the woods or standing on a mountaintop with the sun beating down and a cool breeze brushing your skin at the same time. Pet inhaled deeply, unconsciously sliding her hands around his waist and pressing closer.

Pet was so distracted by her attempt to fill herself with his smell that she didn't notice when Santo's laughter faded and he went still. She gasped with surprise, though, when he suddenly caught her by the waist and lifted her off the floor. He turned at the same time so that he could set her down on the island counter next to the sink.

Cheeks pinkening, Pet started to open her eyes but

stopped with them half open when his mouth covered hers. She then let them drift closed again. Her lips parted slightly at the gentle caress. She slid her arms around his neck and then moaned, her back arching as his tongue swept through the opening to explore what she offered.

Pet hadn't forgotten the shattering passion she'd experienced during their first kiss in the Caprellis' kitchen, and still she was shocked when it exploded between them again so quickly. Overwhelmed by the force of it, she tightened her arms around his neck and basically held on for dear life as his mouth devoured hers, his lips and tongue feasting on the passion they were stirring to life.

When his hand suddenly closed over one breast, kneading her through her bra and shirt, Pet groaned and arched into the caress, her bottom rising slightly off the counter. Santo immediately slid his other hand under her behind and urged her farther forward on the countertop until their lower bodies rubbed forcefully together.

Moaning at the pleasure now bouncing through her, Pet wrapped her legs around his hips, pulling him tighter still, and then began to tug at his T-shirt, try-ing to pull it out of his jeans and drag it upward so that she could reach beneath and touch his beautiful chest. But Santo caught her hands and stopped her.

When she broke their kiss to protest, Santo growled, "Parker."

"Oh," Pet breathed, understanding managing to push through her passion-soaked brain. Parker. Of course. Just kisses, no clothing removal or touching. Parker could come out. She'd barely reasoned that out when Santo's mouth found hers again. This time, though, his kiss was a gentle grazing of his lips over hers, as if he were trying to cool them both down. But when Pet's breath slid out on a sigh in response, his mouth opened slightly as if to catch it and then moved over hers again, applying more pressure before his tongue slid out to lightly trace where her own lips barely met. Pet opened at once, inviting a return to the passionate kiss he'd first given her, and Santo gave into the request with a groan. His tongue filled her, sweeping away any common sense Pet had managed to grab ahold of.

Groaning, she pressed up and forward, the edge of the counter pressing into her upper thighs as her bottom lifted slightly so that she could get closer to him. Santo groaned again when her breasts rubbed against his chest, the sound vibrating through her mouth and then her body so that her response became almost frantic with the need it sent resonating through her. She hardly noticed when Santo shifted her hands behind her back and caught them in one of his large ones. She did notice when his now free hand then covered her breast again and squeezed before he found the nipple through the material covering it and began to rub his thumb back and forth over it.

Pet broke their kiss and threw her head back on a gasp at the fiery charges that sent through her, and Santo immediately began to lick and kiss and suck at a spot under her ear before following a path down the base of her throat, urging her to lean farther back as he went. He paused briefly when he reached the open collar of her polo shirt and then stopped toying with her nipple and reached down to drag the hem of her shirt up. Once he had the red material up above her breasts, though, he pulled back from her throat to look at what he'd revealed.

Santo's eyes burned over the pale pink cups of her bra, the silver in his eyes growing, and Pet swallowed, feeling suddenly self-conscious. She was about to remind him that Parker could come out, when he suddenly tugged one frail cup down and lowered his head to latch onto the revealed nipple.

"Oh, God!" Pet gasped, digging her nails into the hand holding both of hers as he sucked and laved the sensitive tip by turn. She could feel his hard erection pressing against her core, the heat of it burning through the cloth of his jeans and her capris, and she couldn't resist tightening her legs and shifting her hips to rub herself against him. The excitement that action stirred up had them both gasping and stiffening against each other, and then Santo let her nipple slip from his mouth and raised his head to claim her lips again, his tongue thrusting almost violently now, demanding a response Pet was happy to give.

When Santo suddenly released her hands to fumble blindly with the snap of her capris, Pet quickly undid it for him. She even lowered the zipper a little before he brushed her hand aside so that he could slide his fingers inside the lacy pink material of her panties and touch her. Pet gasped into his mouth at the first grazing and then cried out when one finger slid between her moist folds to explore what they hid.

"Aunt Pet! How long until the pizza comes? And can I bring Mrs. Wiggles out now?"

Ten

All Pet could think was that it was a darned good thing that immortals were fast, because while they'd heard Parker before he'd reached the kitchen, they'd only had a couple of seconds to break apart and straighten their clothes. Santo did all the straightening. In the blink of an eye, he'd removed his hand from her panties, closed the snap of her capris, though not the zipper, and tugged her top down to cover her exposed breast. He'd even moved to the side of her to turn the tap on, leaving her legs to help hide the raging erection presently trying to disprove the well-known fact that true jean material did not, in fact, stretch.

It was giving it a good try, though, Pet noted, staring down and to the side with fascination at the huge bulge in the front of his jeans. Dear God, he must be as huge there as everywhere else, she thought faintly. And he was going to have zipper prints embedded on his—

"Well?"

Blinking, Pet turned to see that her nephew had reached the kitchen. She stared at him with a mind that was completely blank of anything but Santo's zipper print cock. "What?"

Parker heaved out a most put-upon sigh. "I asked how long until the pizza comes," he said with exasperation. "And can I bring Mrs. Wiggles out now?"

Pet stared at him, trying to gather the remains of her scattered good sense, and then scowled. "First of all, we don't yell in an apartment. We come out and ask in polite tones so we don't disturb our neighbors," she began and immediately heard some apparently much wiser voice in her head say, *Oh, that's good, Petronella. Make sure you don't get any warning next time so that Parker gets an eyeful of you and Santo playing kiss and grope in the kitchen and is scarred for life.*

Ignoring that wiser voice, Pet continued, "Second, the pizza should be here in—" She glanced at the clock on the stove, did a quick calculation, and said, "Fifteen minutes."

"Ahhhh," Parker groaned. "I'm hungry now."

"And," she continued firmly, "no, you can't bring Mrs. Wiggles out until after the pizza delivery. I don't want her slipping out the door when it comes."

"Fine," Parker huffed, turning back up the hall. "Call me when the pizza is here then."

"Fine," Pet huffed right back, watching until he was out of sight, and she heard his bedroom door close.

She was starting to turn back to Santo when he was suddenly in front of her, tugging her shirt back up. Eyes widening, she glanced down, but he merely pulled the cup of her bra back up to cover her breast and then tugged the hem back down again. He didn't release it, though, she noticed. Glancing up uncertainly, she noted the struggle taking place on his face.

"I want to look at you," Santo admitted.

Pet blinked at the confession, and then she straightened slightly and cleared her throat and simply whispered, "Okay."

Some of the tension eased from him then, and Santo slowly lifted the hem he still held, revealing her stomach and then her breasts encased in pink lace.

"Beautiful," he breathed, reaching out with his other hand to run his fingers lightly over the tops of the lace cups.

Pet shivered and bit her lip as goose bumps rose in the trail of his fingers, and then he suddenly grasped the top with both hands and began to tug it up. But Pet caught his hands to stop him.

"Parker," was all she said, but it was enough.

Santo stopped, but he also frowned and then glanced around until his eyes settled on the door to her home office. "Can we go into your study?"

Pet hesitated, somewhat torn. She was still wet and aching, and she wanted him to kiss and touch her again, but—slamming the *but* door closed, she slid off the counter, took his hand, and led him into her office, her erect nipples pointing the way.

Santo released her hand the moment they entered the office and moved to turn on the light. He then closed the office door and turned to lean against it rather than approach her.

Pet peered at him uncertainly. "I thought you wanted to . . ." She shrugged.

"I am afraid if I touch you, I will start something we

do not have time to finish," he admitted, a small wry smile twisting his lips.

"Oh." She shifted her feet uncertainly and then asked, "Do you want to go back out to the kitchen then?"

"No. I want to look at you," Santo assured her, and then his deep voice dropping another octave, he said, "Take off your top for me."

Pet bit her lip and shifted again. It was one thing for him to tug her clothes off in the midst of passion, or even for her to help him take her clothes off in the midst of passion. But it was an entirely different thing for her to give him a peep show.

Although, a bra doesn't show any more than a bathing suit does, really, that voice that had seemed so wise just moments ago pointed out. *So what's the harm?*

"Right," Pet muttered aloud, and then rolled her eyes when she realized she had. Wasn't talking to yourself the first sign of insanity?

Shaking her head, Pet decided to handle it like removing a bandage and rather than a slow strip tease, simply grasped the bottom of her shirt, tugged it up and then over her head and off.

"Ta-da." It was meant to be a joke, that ta-da, but Pet's voice caught on the words and neither of them were laughing. Santo certainly wasn't. His eyes were filling with silver, as if liquid mercury was pouring in to cover the black. That was disconcerting enough, but not nearly as disconcerting as when he suddenly moved toward her using that immortal speed of his. One minute he was lounging lazily against the door, and the next he was just inches in front of her, and she was forced to tip her head back to meet his gaze. Pet loved his height, but seriously, sometimes it could be a pain, like now when she was sure she was going to get a crick in her neck if she had to keep looking up at him like this, she thought, and then glanced down when he took the shirt from her limp hand.

She watched him lean past her to set it on the desk, and then turned back to face him as he suddenly dropped to his knees in front of her. This was actually nicer, Pet decided, relaxing a little. At least she wouldn't get the crick in her neck she was worried about, she thought, and watched him look her over, his eyes traveling over every inch of exposed flesh. She could almost feel his gaze like a physical touch as it slid over her skin, and her body was responding as if he had. Her nipples hardened further, extending more, her stomach muscles rippled, and small shivers started rippling down her back. Pet bore that until she just couldn't take it anymore, and then she reached for him.

Santo caught her hands at once, preventing her from touching him. He clasped her hands lightly, but firmly, licked his lips, and then growled, "Take off your bra."

Pet might have balked if he hadn't sounded so tortured, but he sounded as affected as her. So, when he released her hands, she slid them behind her back and unsnapped the bra. She hesitated then briefly, catching the ends of the bra to hold it in place, but finally made herself release them and let the flimsy cloth slide down her arms to drop on the floor between them. Pet then stood silently before him. Waiting.

Santo closed his eyes briefly as if the sight of her burned his corneas. When he opened them again, they were blazing brilliant silver with not a drop of black left. His voice was a rough growl when he said, "I want to taste you."

Pet reached for him with relief, but again he caught her hands to stop her. Holding them out to the sides, he then leaned forward and caught one nipple between his lips. She watched it disappear into his mouth and then closed her eyes and moaned as he began to lave and suckle it. When he gave an answering moan in response, the soft hum against her sensitive nipple made her knees buckle, and she would have fallen if Santo hadn't released her hands to quickly catch her behind the thighs. Pet clasped his head then and let her own head fall forward, her long black hair a curtain stretching down to shelter them both as he held her up and continued to devour one breast before releasing it to turn to the other. He was just about to close his lips over the tip of that excited nipple when the phone rang on the desk behind her.

Both of them stilled, and then Pet sighed and whispered, "That will be the pizza."

"Of course." Santo's voice was rough with emotion, and then he cleared his throat and stood up, snatching up her bra and handing it to her as he did. Leaving her to put it on, he moved around the desk to answer the phone.

Quickly replacing her bra, Pet listened as he greeted the caller. Finishing with the task, she grabbed her shirt and turned to peer at him in the silence that followed, and saw when he looked down at the phone with confusion. Knowing he was trying to figure out how to let the delivery person in, Pet said, "Press the number sign below the button with nine on it."

She waited to see that he pushed the right button, and then shifted her attention to her shirt. It was inside out, and as she started to turn it right side out, Santo set the phone back in the receiver and glanced at her. A smile tinged with regret tugged at his lips, and then he said, "I will get the door while you finish dressing."

"My purse is on the island," she said. "Just grab some money out of my wallet."

"I shall pay," he said firmly, before opening the office door and slipping out of the room.

Pet watched the door close and then turned her attention back to her shirt with a sigh. She supposed she should feel bad that she had canoodled with someone she didn't know very well and who was an immortal to boot, but mostly she just felt disappointed that they'd had to stop. The man was like a drug . . . and she wanted more of it. She wanted all of him. She wanted him moving inside of her, his arms enfolding her, and his breath mingling with hers as they kissed and the world melted away around them.

Instead, she was going to get pizza and possibly a Disney movie on her computer, unless they set up Parker's television and connected her computer to it so they could watch it on the bigger screen. She had an iTunes account. Buying a movie shouldn't take more than a minute.

Damn, Pet realized suddenly. The television and Parker's gaming gear were all still down in the trunk of her car. Hmm. How had she forgotten all about that? The same way she'd forgotten that there were still groceries sitting on the counters in the kitchen, waiting to be put away, Pet thought wryly as she stepped out of the office and saw the evidence of everything she hadn't done yet. Man, throw one hunky beefcake into her life, and she became one useless creature, Pet thought with self-disgust.

Well, time to change that, she told herself firmly and walked over to her purse to dig through it for her car keys.

"Wow! Really? Thanks, man. That's an awesome tip."

Santo grunted at the delivery boy's gratitude, and holding the three pizza boxes in one hand, started to close the door with the other, only to pause and glance down with surprise when Pet suddenly ducked under his arm and hurried out into the hall.

"I forgot the television and gaming gear in the car," she called out as she rushed off toward the elevator.

"Wait, I will—damn," Santo muttered when the elevator door opened and she disappeared inside.

"Women, right?" the delivery boy said, shaking his head. "You can't live with 'em, and you can't tie 'em up to keep them where you want them."

"So Marguerite says," Santo growled, and then closed the door and quickly carried the pizzas to the island. "Parker!"

"Is the pizza here?" the boy squealed with excitement as he rushed out of his room and ran into the kitchen.

"*Sì*. Get plates and napkins ready and decide what you want to drink. Your aunt has gone down to retrieve your television and gaming system and I am going to help. Do not start without us, and do not let the cat out until we return," he added firmly and then swung around and hurried out of the apartment.

The delivery kid was waiting by the elevators when Santo stepped out into the hall. When the teenager smiled and waved, he nodded but turned to the stairs rather than wait for the elevator. Santo didn't bother holding back on speed. He didn't see cameras in the stairwell, so raced down the thirteen flights to the underground parking level at an immortal pace.

He and Parker had helped gather the groceries from her car earlier, he knew Pet's parking spot was actually on the other side of the elevator banks, so rather than take the door into the parking garage on this side, he took the door that led to the elevators. A frown claimed his lips when he spotted the hunched figure waiting at the end of this short corridor, peering around the corner of the hall. They were both in a short hall that turned left into a longer hall which ran in front of the elevators to a second short hall that turned back behind the elevators to another set of stairs on the other side, and another door leading out into the parking garage there. The figure was an old man who presently held the pose of a mischievous boy about to play a prank.

Curious, Santo slipped into the man's mind as he approached, his interest giving way to anger as he read the thoughts in the mind of the old pervert. It was the apartment manager, and he had been watching the camera displays in his apartment, so had seen Pet rush into the elevator. Suspecting she was going down to her car, he'd hurried out of his main floor apartment and down here in the hopes of *scaring the bejesus out of that snooty little China girl who thought she was so much better than him. He'd show her. Maybe he'd scare her so bad this time, she'd burst into tears and he'd have to comfort her. And maybe he'd get to cop a feel of those pretty little titties of hers as he did.*

Pausing behind the old degenerate, Santo poked him in the back and glowered down on the man when he shrieked and whirled around to gape up at him wide-eyed.

"Go home, turn off your cameras, and do not even think of spying on or bothering your female tenants again or I will find out and pay you a visit."

Santo hadn't really meant to control him but wasn't displeased when the man's face went blank and he walked to the door to the stairwell Santo had just come out of. Santo watched him until he heard the ding announcing the elevator's arrival. He then turned and walked over to stand in front of them so he would be the first thing Pet saw when the door opened.

"Oh, hi," she said with surprise as she stepped out. "How did you—oh, yeah, immortal speed, right?"

Pet didn't wait for an answer, just smiled and shook her head as she led the way around the corner to the door to parking.

"I thought maybe we could watch a Disney movie with Parker while we eat our pizza," Pet explained as she opened the door marked Parking and led him into a large dim concrete garage full of vehicles all lined up in their allotted spots. "But then I realized I left his television and gaming gear down here in the car, so thought I'd just nip down to get them. Hopefully, it won't take too long to set up. I wouldn't want the pizza to get cold, but I remember pizza night when I was a kid and it was always pizza and a movie, so . . ." She shrugged the rest away as she reached her car and moved around to the trunk.

"You didn't have to come help me," Pet continued as she unlocked the trunk. "That's really sweet of you, though. You're kind of a sweet guy under all those grunts and stuff, huh? At least I know that about you."

Santo frowned slightly at those wry words. It made him realize that despite the fact that he was finally talking, she still didn't really know much about him other than that he was a civil engineer who split his time between Canada and Italy and that he played drums. That, of course, was because all they'd talked about so far was Dressler and Mr. Purdy. He'd have to rectify that, though, Santo decided, and as quickly as he could, since Marguerite insisted he let Pet get to know him before he started any immortal life mate sex. He didn't think he was going to be able to go long without making her his, physically. The woman had a hell of a lot of passion in that petite little body of hers, and his body was roaring to explore it.

If not for Parker and the pizza delivery, they'd probably have already explored it and be passed out on the island right now. And while he'd told himself he wouldn't touch her in the office, that hadn't gone quite to plan either. He'd given up the not-touching-her thing pretty quick to latch onto her nipple once it was on display, and was sure if they'd had a couple more minutes he would have given it up completely and would have had her naked on the floor under him . . . and probably would have suffocated her when they both passed out as true life mates usually did when first coupling.

That was something to keep in mind for when they did finally mate, Santo thought grimly. She'd have to be on top.

"I should have brought a bag down to put the controls and speakers in."

Santo forced his attention to Pet as she scowled down at the items in her trunk. He considered them briefly, then urged her out of the way and picked up the television. He flipped it so that the face of it was down, then pressed the edge to his chest and said, "Put the game box and speakers on top. Then you can handle the controllers and doors."

"Oh. Aren't you clever," Pet praised with a grin. She lifted the game box out to set it and its cord on the back of the TV as he'd suggested. The speakers followed, and then she gathered the controllers and closed the trunk.

"Does Parker know where we went?" she asked as she led the way back to the door.

"*Sì*. He is getting plates and napkins and drinks. At least his drink," he added, turning sideways to slip through the entrance with his burden when she opened the parking garage door and held it for him.

"You must have tipped the delivery guy big time," Pet commented as she scurried around him in the hall to get ahead of him and push the elevator button. "I heard him thanking you so profusely as I came up behind you."

Santo grunted noncommittally. He always tipped big. He appreciated good service and had no problem paying for it, plus the kid had been quick, friendly, and polite. He wouldn't have bothered otherwise, Santo thought as the door opened and he turned sideways to move onto the elevator.

Pet glanced both ways up the hall, he noticed, before following and pushing the button for her floor.

"What were you looking for?" Santo asked, suspecting he already knew.

"Oh, the apartment manager usually likes to jump out and try to scare me whenever I'm coming or going. But I didn't see him when we arrived earlier either. It makes me wonder if everything is okay with him."

"Does he?" Santo asked, and when she glanced up at him, added, "Scare you?"

Pet snorted at the suggestion. "That old geezer? I could take him with both hands tied behind my back. Although," she added with a wry smile, "he did manage to startle me the first couple of times after I moved in." She shrugged. "I'm used to it now, though." Pet frowned before adding, "I do worry about the other ladies here, though. There are a couple of old biddies I suspect are terrified of him and I've been thinking maybe I should write a letter to the owners of the building and let them know what he gets up to. I swear he spies on everyone coming and going, which isn't so bad. I mean, no one's likely to get in without his knowing, but I think he needs to lay off the tenants. If he did that, he'd be the perfect manager."

Pet started to chatter about some of the other tenants in the building then. Santo suspected she was just babbling a bit because she was a little uncomfortable with him after what had happened between them. He listened to her with half an ear, but a good portion of his mind was now considering her words, and he was wondering if he should have given the manager the order to go home, turn off his cameras, and not bother his tenants again. It did poke a big hole in the security set up in this place.

He'd stop at the man's door and have a word with him on his way out tonight, Santo decided. Have him turn his cameras back on and watch them as he apparently did normally.

"Here we go."

Santo shifted his attention to the doors as they began to slide open, but let Pet get off first before turning sideways and following.

Eleven

"Well?"

Pet smiled faintly at Parker's impatient demand the minute the credits began to roll, but admitted, "It was good. I really enjoyed it."

"I *told* you it was good," Parker crooned, hopping out of the overstuffed chair he'd been sitting in and dancing excitedly around the room. "*Guardians of the Galaxy* rocks! I've watched it like thirty times and it's still good every time."

"What?" she squawked, grabbing the couch pillow beside her and tossing it at her excited nephew. She missed him by a mile, but he did stop and grin at her. Shaking her head, she asked, "Why did you want me to buy it if you've already seen it? And thirty times?"

"Because it's an awesome movie," her nephew said in a tone that suggested that should be obvious. "The second one is pretty awesome too. Not as good as the first, of course, but still good. Can we watch that now? Please?"

Pet glanced at the wall clock above the gas fireplace and shook her head. "Sorry, buddy, it's a school night. Bed for you."

"Ahhh," he whined. "Tomorrow then?"

"Maybe tomorrow," Pet allowed with a small smile. She really had enjoyed the movie.

"Awesome!" Parker squealed and then hurried back to the chair where he'd been sitting and snatched up Mrs. Wiggles from the huge cushioned footstool she'd been resting on in front of it. The poor cat had been sleeping. She woke at once and was obviously disgruntled at being jarred awake, but Parker petted her soothingly and headed out of the room, cooing, "Come on, Mrs. Wiggles. We have to get ready for bed. Tomorrow is a school day."

Pet watched him go, an affectionate smile curving her lips.

"You really love him."

Pet glanced to Santo at that rumbled comment. He was slouched on the opposite end of the couch with his ankles crossed, feet resting on the coffee table, and his hands clasped on his chest. He'd been so still and unmoving through most of the movie that she'd been sure he was asleep. But every time she'd looked at him, his eyes had been open, and she was quite sure she'd heard him chuckle a time or two.

"Of course I love him," she said finally. "He's my little man. And probably the closest I'll get to having a child of my own."

Santo glanced at her sharply, his eyebrows rising. "Why?"

Pet shrugged and sat up to begin gathering the glasses and plates on the coffee table from their pizza meal as she informed him, "I'll turn thirty-seven next month, without a serious partner or even any real prospects in sight. And I'm not the type to do the whole test tube baby thing and raise a kid on my own. Although, I did consider it earlier this year," she admitted, standing with the items she'd gathered and heading for the kitchen.

Santo and Parker had set up the television and her laptop on top of the fireplace mantel in the living room and connected everything while she'd transferred the plates and napkins Parker had gathered to the coffee table and fetched drinks. She'd then brought out the pizzas as well before using her laptop to purchase *Guardians of the Galaxy* on iTunes at Parker's insistence. It had been past seven when they'd sat down to pizza and a movie. *Guardians of the Galaxy* was two hours long. Of course, they'd finished eating well before the movie ended. But it had all been good. A nice family type night she thought they'd all enjoyed.

"You considered having a child on your own?" Santo asked, following her with the remainder of their detritus from dinner.

"Well, sure," Pet said as she placed pizza crusts and napkins in the garbage and put the plates and glasses in the dishwasher. Straightening, she added, "I mean, I'm a realist. It's getting late in the day to count on the right man coming along. And then you have to figure the time schedule."

"Time schedule?" Santo queried uncertainly.

"Well, the guy's not going to propose right away, so maybe you date a year, and then you're engaged for at least another year. Plus, few men would want to have a baby directly after marrying. Couples need to adjust to each other before they bring a baby into the equation, so figure at least another year before you start trying to get pregnant . . . And then there's the nine months for gestation. Even if I met Mr. Right tomorrow, and everything went perfectly I'd probably be at least forty-one, maybe even forty-two before I squeezed the poor kid out."

She shrugged. "But that's doubtful. Once you hit forty, fertility decreases, so I'm not likely to get pregnant on the first try. And then there are the increased risks for both the baby and the mother at this age. The risk of hypertension, gestational diabetes, and preeclampsia increase. So do the possibilities of miscarriages and chromosomal abnormalities." She sighed at the thought of it, and then said, "But even if I did get lucky and I had a healthy baby on the first try . . ." Pet grimaced and asked, "Having a baby at forty-one or -two? That means I'd be a tired fifty when they're an energetic eight, and I'd be sixty when they graduated from high school. And if they wait to forty themselves to have a kid, it's fifty-fifty as to whether I'd even be around to see my grandchildren. But if I was, I wouldn't necessarily be in the best physical shape to help out with things like babysitting and stuff."

Crossing her arms, Pet admitted, "So, I considered going IVF and having one right away."

"But you decided against it," Santo said quietly.

Pet hesitated, and then said, "I guess I'm old-fashioned. I believe a child should have two parents. I also believe a parent should have a partner or at least someone to back them up raising a child, and while I have my sister and my parents, they're all doctors, always busy. They don't have the time to be my backup. So . . ." She shrugged. "Barring a miracle, or an accident, I'm probably not going to have kids."

Pet fell silent then and waited for his response but began to feel uncomfortable when she noted the expression on Santo's face. The man looked like he'd just been hit by a Mack Truck. Raising her eyebrows, she asked, "What?"

Santo shook his head. "I can see where Parker gets it."

"What?" she asked on a half laugh, bewildered by the comment.

"His tendency to think so much and spit out facts and data," he said in a rumble.

Before Pet could respond, Parker rushed in to the kitchen. He was in his pajamas, face scrubbed clean, and teeth brushed, ready for his good-night cuddle. Pet smiled at the boy and bent to kiss his cheek and hug him. As she straightened, she reminded him, "Don't forget to set your alarm on your cell phone."

"I won't," he promised, and then surprised her by moving around her to give Santo a hug good-night too.

If she was surprised, it was no less than Santo. His eyes widened incredulously, but he did hug the boy back, and even ruffled his hair affectionately, before watching with a somewhat bemused smile as Parker ran out of the room again.

"Kids, huh?" she said with a smile, and then turned to the coffee machine and began to make a pot.

"Yes," Santo murmured, and then announced, "I would like to have another child. Actually I would like to have many more."

Pet stiffened and then turned to peer at him. "You have a child? You're *married*?"

"No, I am not married," Santo assured her firmly, and then added, "But I had children with a female immortal who was not my life mate. Five of them. Twin boys, twin girls, and then a lone boy." His jawline clenched briefly, and she saw pain flicker in his eyes, and then he added, "They are dead now, along with their mother."

Pet let her breath out slowly and then swallowed before turning back to the coffee machine and murmuring, "I'm sorry. What happened to them?"

Santo was silent for so long that she was sure he wouldn't respond. Pet didn't press him or comment, she simply continued going about the business of making coffee and then moved away to get cups, sugar, and cream. She had just finished gathering the items and returned to watch the coffee begin to drip when Santo released a long sigh and then said, "House fire."

Pet glanced quickly to him, but saw the closed expression on his face and merely murmured, "I'm sorry," again and turned back to the coffeepot. But after a moment, she couldn't stand the silence anymore and moved past him to enter the hall, muttering, "I need to use the bathroom."

Pet bypassed the hall bathroom and went around the corner to her own. Flicking on the light and fan with one hand, she closed the door with the other and then stopped when she saw herself in the mirror. She knew from the pictures she'd seen of her biological

mother that she looked like her, which she was grateful for. Pet had always thought her mother pretty, and
liked to think she was too. Now she examined herself
critically.

Her hair was long, straight, and jet-black. Her nose
was small, her cheekbones wide, and her mouth small
but plump, almost pouty-looking. Her eyes were a
boring dark brown, but big and round, with a parallel
crease. All in all, she was pleased with the face she'd
been given. It was her body she'd never been pleased
with. Short, whip thin, and with little to brag about in
the chest department. As a teenager, Pet had longed
to be tall and curvy like Marguerite, and had prayed
for a growth spurt to give her long sexy legs and some
curves. That growth spurt had never come. At thirty-
six, she was still short at five foot two and still lacking
the curves she would have liked.

While Pet had learned to live with what she'd been
given, now she was looking at herself unhappily and
wondering what the mother of Santo's children had
looked like. In her mind, she was picturing someone
Amazon tall with long legs and big breasts, and feeling completely inadequate in comparison.

"Idiot," Pet muttered to herself impatiently and
turned away from the mirror.

As she took care of the business bathrooms were
meant for, she told herself it didn't matter what the
woman had looked like, she was dead now. Besides,
Santo seemed to find Pet attractive enough. Not that it
mattered since she didn't intend to get involved with
him anyway.

But what about an affair? that part of her brain
that had earlier seemed so wise suggested now and

pointed out. *You don't have to get involved to have good monkey sex. Heck, he's not even going to be around long enough* to get *involved. Another day or two and that backup they're waiting for should show up so they can deal with the Purdy situation. They might even arrive tomorrow. He could be gone by tomorrow afternoon or night.*

Pet frowned at that thought . . . Santo gone from her life as quickly as he'd appeared. For some reason, that didn't please her as it would have the night Marguerite had shown up with the men and she'd noted their eyes and realized they were immortal. Which was just last night, she realized quite suddenly, and was shocked at the knowledge. Had he really only been in her life for twenty-four hours?

She shook her head at that and then considered the affair business. In truth, it wouldn't even be an affair really. Well, not if the immortals cleared things up and left Albany the next day, which was possible. So, if she walked out there and jumped his bones right now, it could be a one-night deal. A one-night stand, Pet realized, and while she didn't normally go in for that kind of thing, Santo was a pretty tempting treat.

Tempting is right, her wise voice assured her. *It wouldn't just be a one-night stand, it would be a best-night-of-your-life stand.* Pet nodded, pretty sure that was true. The kind of chemistry she experienced with Santo was rare, and the passion she'd experienced with him was too. What she enjoyed with him was the kind of thing she wasn't likely to encounter again in her lifetime, Pet admitted to herself as she flushed the toilet and stepped up to the sink to wash her hands. A short affair with him would give her something to reminisce over in her dotage. What was wrong with that?

"Nothing," Pet told her reflection as she turned off the water and dried her hands. "You're a big girl. You can handle hot meaningless sex with the big guy without getting emotionally involved. Just concentrate on sex and avoid talking so you don't get to know him any better and it should all be good."

They needed to talk, Santo acknowledged grimly as the coffee machine spat out the last of its brew. He'd known that was true as he'd watched Pet walk away up the hall, her expression shuttered. For a minute, when she'd bypassed the nearer bathroom and disappeared around the corner toward her room, he'd feared she'd recognized his lie when he'd told her how his children had died. He'd feared that after being so open and honest about her desire to have a child but her belief she wouldn't now, his lie had upset her so much she might close herself in her bedroom and not return. The thought had made his chest constrict with panic, and then he'd heard the bathroom fan turn on, followed by the sound of a door closing, and his common sense had returned. She wouldn't just leave him to see himself out. She was going to the bathroom.

But it had made Santo think. She was his life mate, his chance for peace and happiness and a life less lonely. With her, he could have incredible passion, a family, his other half. Knowing that, he could never just walk away from her. But Pet could. She was mortal and didn't know any of that. She had no idea how wonderful life could be for them. To her, he was just a guy she had admitted she found attractive and whom she'd experienced a taste of passion with. And it might not even be more passion than she'd experienced with mortal men. They hadn't yet enjoyed the full-blown passion they could have together. Pet hadn't touched him other than to put her arms around his neck that first time in the Caprellis' kitchen, and he hadn't let her touch him here earlier tonight. Knowing Parker was nearby and that the pizza delivery would show up soon, Santo had deliberately kept her from touching him to keep them both from losing control. That being the case, he had no doubt Pet could just walk away from him at this point.

He needed to change that. He needed to let her get to know him. And he needed to tell her the truth about how his children had died. Fire had been a part of it, but it had been so much worse than just a house fire. So bad, in fact, Santo had never been able to bring himself to talk about it, to anyone. Not even his mother knew the full extent of what had happened that day, and she knew more than most. But he could hear Marguerite's voice in his head telling him he needed to talk to Pet and let her get to know him, and he knew he should probably tell her about it since it was a large part of what made him who he was.

Grimacing, Santo moved to stand by the coffee machine as it finally finished. Yes, they definitely needed to talk, he decided as he began to spoon sugar into each cup. She had to know him. He wanted her to, he thought as he poured them both coffee and added cream. He'd reveal himself to her and, hopefully, earn a part of her heart.

And then he'd sew it up with life mate passion and ask her to be his life mate.

Satisfied with that plan, Santo stirred both cups of coffee and then picked them up and carried them out to the living room. Once there, he paused, though. While Parker had sat in the chair and they'd shared the couch earlier, he didn't think that was a good idea now. If he wanted to get any talking done, it was probably better if he sat in the chair, and she sat on the couch. There was less chance of an accidental touch or brushing of arms or legs, which might lead to a kiss, and then . . .

"Definitely better," Santo muttered, setting her cup down on the coffee table in front of the couch and then carrying his own to the end table beside the chair. He'd just set it down when he heard the faint sound of the bathroom door opening and the rustle of her returning up the hall. Pleased that he'd arranged everything so that they could have that talk they needed, Santo settled in the chair and tried to relax.

Pet's feet slowed as she stepped out of the hall and glanced around to see that the kitchen was empty. She was just starting to worry that all her fretting had been for naught, and Santo had left while she was in the bathroom, when he called out to her from the living room.

"I made both of us coffees and brought them out here so we could talk," he announced, drawing her head around to see him seated in the chair Parker had occupied earlier.

Pet's eyebrows rose and then lowered slightly. He sounded very serious, which made her nervous as she wondered what he wanted to talk about. In fact, his intention to talk didn't really fit with the decision she'd just made about having a short, completely sexual affair. She was thinking more along the lines of *not* talking and filling their time with crazy hot sex, so that at the end she could walk away as she would from a great, wild ride at an amusement park. One she might get to go on again someday, but might not.

"Come before it gets cold," Santo said when she simply stood staring at him.

Sighing, Pet moved reluctantly out into the living room to join him, but paused by the couch and frowned as she peered at him in the chair. It was going to be hard to instigate any hanky-panky with him so far away.

"Wouldn't you rather sit over here with me?" she asked.

Santo shook his head and picked up his coffee. "I am good here."

"Oh," she muttered, and settled unhappily on the couch. This wasn't working out the way she'd hoped, Pet thought grimly as she picked up her coffee and took a sip.

"I was born in 965 B.C."

The coffee Pet had just taken into her mouth came back out like water from a pinched garden hose as she gasped in shock, and then choked and sputtered over that announcement.

Santo was immediately out of his seat and at her side, his face wreathed with concern as he pounded her back. "Are you all right?"

"Y-yes," she gasped, holding her hand up to make him leave off thumping her. Good Lord, the man didn't know his own strength, she decided, relief rushing through her when he stopped pounding. In the next moment, he was gone, and Pet glanced around with confusion, only to see him already halfway back from rushing to the kitchen at immortal speed to grab some paper towels. He moved so quickly that she'd hardly realized that when Santo was already kneeling in front of her, mopping up the coffee she'd spat out onto the cream-colored carpet.

"I'll do that," Pet muttered with embarrassment, bending forward to try to take the paper towel from him.

"It is done," he said, and was upright and heading back to the chair before she could even get close to touching the paper towels or his hand.

Pet glanced at the carpet then, surprised to see that he was right and it was done. The carpet was Scotchgarded to protect it from staining. It now looked good as new.

Sighing, Pet started to reach for her coffee, then decided to leave it where it was and sat back in her seat to stare at Santo. After a moment, she arched one eyebrow and asked, "Did you say you were born in 965?"

Santo nodded warily and then added, "B.C."

"B.C.," Pet echoed, and closed her eyes as she tried to absorb that. He was born in the tenth century B.C. Before Christ. Dear Lord, he was older than Christ would be today, she thought with dismay, and then forced herself to stop thinking and breathe for a minute.

"Are you okay?" Santo asked suddenly.

"I'm fine," Pet said quickly, but even she could hear how high and strained her voice was. Clearing her throat, she said in a more normal voice, "Just give me a minute."

Santo grunted.

Pet ignored him and tried to think. She was a history professor. Even so, her training didn't generally stretch back that far. All she knew about that period was that it followed the collapse of the late Bronze Age in what they now referred to as the Near East, and that he was born in the century when the Early Iron Age started there, or at least really took hold.

Which didn't really matter, Pet supposed, because he wasn't from western Asia but Italy. Except that there had been no Italy then. Well, the land had been there, of course, but the country Italy hadn't existed. Dear God, he was older than Italy too. The man was just—

"Pet?"

Opening her eyes, she peered at him solemnly and said, "You're really old."

"*Sì*," Santo agreed solemnly.

"I mean, I was thinking you were old like fourteenth or fifteenth century old. But you're really, *really* old."

Santo merely grunted this time.

"It's no wonder you have a tendency to grunt all the time. You're like caveman old." His eyes were widening at that when Pet frowned and said, "Okay, not caveman old, they died out something like forty thousand years ago and you're a decade or two short of three thousand years old, but—oh, my God, you're a decade or two short of three thousand years old," she gasped with horror.

"Perhaps I should not have started with my age," Santo said dryly.

Pet blinked and asked, "Started what?"

"Talking," he said in a rumble, and then added, "Telling you about myself so that you can get to know me better."

"Oh," she breathed weakly, thinking, wasn't that just her luck? All she wanted from him was sex, and he wanted them to get to know each other better. Which was the last thing she wanted. Right now she liked him. But talking might bring about more liking, and possibly love, which was the last thing Pet wanted to feel for an immortal who was going to walk out of her life soon. She'd really been kind of counting on the hot monkey sex, though.

"Pet?"

Pushing her thoughts aside, she peered at him in question, but when Santo opened his mouth to speak, she stood abruptly and muttered, "I need wine."

Twelve

Pet strode into the kitchen with purpose. The apartment had come with a little wine fridge in the island. She went there now and opened it to consider her options. She wasn't much of a drinker unless with her sister. Then the two of them tended to get into the booze. Other than that, though, she really didn't drink the stuff. Which was a shame since wine was the go-to gift her coworkers and friends usually bought for any celebration. Birthday? Wine. Christmas Secret Santa? Wine. Get tenure? Lots of wine. Her wine fridge was stuffed with bottles that she'd received and never drank. Pet considered them now, wondering which, if any, would be good, and then simply grabbed the middle one on the top row.

It wasn't until she set it on the counter that she noticed that it was a rosé and had a screw top rather than a cork. She almost put it back then, sure that was probably a bad sign, but then thought what the hell, she wasn't drinking it for flavor anyway and the label was pretty. Pet fetched a wineglass out of the cupboard, then grabbed a second one in case Santo wanted to join her.

Pet opened the cap and started to pour, her eyes widening appreciatively when she saw that it was a sparkling wine. Santo joined her at the counter as she finished filling the first glass and started on the second. Pet glanced at him and then back to what she was doing, filling the second glass until it too was full.

"No. *Grazie*," Santo murmured when she picked up both glasses and offered him one.

Shrugging, Pet set one back on the counter and lifted the other to her mouth. The wine was actually quite nice. It was light and fruity but not overly sweet. Refreshing. It made her think of picnics and pool parties.

Curious, she turned the bottle so she could read the label as she took another drink. LOLA was in big letters with Pelee Island in smaller type beneath it and she now recalled where she'd got it. Jill Brandon was a professor in the social welfare department and a good friend. She and her husband had a cottage up in Ontario somewhere that they spent their summers and Jill had brought this back for her last fall, claiming she loved it and Pet had to try it. It had sat in her wine fridge ever since. But Jill was right, she liked it.

"Good?" Santo asked as she took another drink.

"Very nice," Pet murmured. "Sure you wouldn't like some?"

When he shook his head, she took her glass and headed back to the living room. She returned to her seat on the end of the couch, but when Santo headed for the chair again, she frowned and asked, "Are you sure you wouldn't like to sit on the couch with me?"

"It is probably better if I sit here in the chair," he said in that sexy rumble of his.

Pet took another drink, eyeing him over the top of it as she tried to think of a way to get him to her bedroom. Claim she needed a light bulb changed that she couldn't reach, lead him in there and "trip" into him, accidentally tumbling them both to the bed? No, she was too small and he was too big. Even if she tackled him like a linebacker, she probably couldn't knock him onto the bed.

"My mother is Calandra Notte," Santo said solemnly.

"That's a pretty name," Pet murmured. Perhaps she could claim she had to go check on Parker, then grab Mrs. Wiggles and put her in her room and say the cat ran in there and she needed help cornering the feline and—and what? If the cat was on the bed, he'd just grab her and put her back in Parker's room, and if Pet put her under the bed, he'd do the same. Neither would actually get him *on* the bed where she could strategically trip onto him and hopefully end up in a nice passionate—

"My father was Gasparo Carbones Notte," Santo continued. "My mother was two hundred and thirty years old when she met my father. He was fifty-one."

Maybe she could—Pet's thoughts died abruptly and she gaped at Santo. "Hold on, your mother was almost one hundred and eighty years older than your father?"

"*Sì.*" He nodded. "Why are you so surprised by this?"

"Well, you know, I mean, older guys get with

younger women all the time. And some women are getting together with younger guys now, but it's still not that common, and I mean, *come on*, she was almost a hundred and eighty years older than him. That's a super gap."

"But she looked about twenty-five," he pointed out gently. "And still does."

"Oh. Right," Pet muttered. "Just like you look like you're somewhere between twenty-five or thirty, but are really almost three millennia."

"Exactly," he said easily.

"Yeah." Pet nodded and then shook her head. Good God, the diseases he must have encountered over those millennia. The plague, smallpox, leprosy, tuberculosis, syphilis . . . Could immortals get herpes? Maybe she should rethink this. She had condoms still in her bedside drawer, leftover from her last boyfriend, but she wasn't sure they would fit Santo. If he was as big down there as he was everywhere else . . . Well, that could be a problem. She didn't know if they made Super XXX-sized condoms. Maybe they did come that big but were special order. This could be a serious problem and one she needed to sort out right away.

"I was born four years after they met and became life—"

"Do you have condoms?" Pet interrupted.

Santo blinked several times and then asked weakly, "What?"

"Condoms," she said clearly. "To prevent pregnancy and the spread of disease."

"I . . ." He looked at a loss for a minute. She suspected that was a bad sign. And then he cleared his throat, rubbed one hand over his skull, and said, "I have no need of condoms."

Pet narrowed her eyes. "So you've just gone bareback all these millennia?"

"What?" he asked with bewilderment.

"Bareback," she repeated, getting a little agitated at the thought that she had been messing about with him and he might be riddled with disease. "It means sans condom. Have you gone the last nearly three thousand years screwing women without protect—dear God!" she interrupted herself with horror as another thought struck. "How many women have you had sex with?"

"What?" Santo asked with disbelief.

"I mean, you're nearly three thousand years old, Santo," she pointed out as if he didn't know that. "Even if you only had sex with one woman a year, that's nearly three thousand women. If it's been two a year, that's nearly six thousand. I don't even want to think what the numbers are if it was one a month. That would be more people than live in all of the city of Long Beach, and almost a third of the population of Albany. And all bareback. Dear God! You could be a walking herpes simplex, riddled with syphilis, and—and gonorrhea. And I kissed you! I can't believe this!" she muttered, and then snatching her still nearly full wineglass, she stood up and downed it on the way to the kitchen.

"Pet," Santo said with a frown, following her. "I am not sure how you—why you are—I have not slept with more women than the population of Long Beach," he said finally with frustration, and then added, "I have not even slept with six thousand women, and probably not three thousand women either."

"*Probably* not?" Pet gasped, turning on him as she reached the sink.

Santo scowled and shrugged helplessly. "I do not know the number. I never counted, and even if as a foolish and prideful young man I had kept count, that was a long time ago and I could not possibly remember now."

"How long?" she asked at once.

"I have not had sex since 775 B.C.," he said solemnly.

Pet's jaw dropped at this news, and then Santo added, "Except to make my children. But that only took two tries in the summer of 1108 to make Cataldo and Romaso, once in 1212 for Dardi, and three in the spring of 1316 for Claricia and Fenicia."

"Twice in 1108 and once in . . ." She couldn't remember the second year, so just fell silent and stared at him with amazement.

"*Sì.*" Santo puffed up a bit. "I am very virile."

"And probably disease ridden," Pet snapped. "I'm quite sure they didn't have condoms back when you were sexually active, but I'm equally sure they still had STDs."

"I am not disease ridden," he said a little sharply, and then added more calmly, "I cannot be. The nanos would not allow it."

"They wouldn't?" she asked with surprise.

"No, they would not," Santo said firmly. "The nanos are programmed to keep us at our peak condition. That does not just mean to make us young and strong and repair any injury we might suffer. It means destroying and ridding the body of any foreign invader whether it is a virus, bacteria, a cancer cell . . ." He paused and then frowned suddenly and said, "Did you not know this?"

"No," Pet admitted on a sigh, and thought that was good news. But then she recalled the whole virile thing and frowned again. Her gaze dropping to the front of his jeans, she muttered, "A large-size condom probably wouldn't fit you, huh?"

Much to her amazement, the front of his jeans started to bulge outward as she looked at it, and then Santo cursed and turned sideways to lean against the counter.

"Why are you even asking me something like that?" he growled, and she glanced up to see that he was rubbing his head again as if checking for dandruff . . . or as if he were stressed.

"Because you're *virile*," Pet said dryly. "And while I would very much like to have sex with you, I don't want to get pregnant, so a condom is needed, and I only have large size ones. I suspect you'd take a triple X or something . . . if they even make condoms large enough to accommodate you," she added with a frown.

"Dear God." Santo leaned forward and began to bang his forehead on the island top.

Pet reached for his arm to stop him, but the minute she made contact, he jerked up and away until there were a good three feet between them. He then just scowled at her. Sighing, she picked up the glass she'd poured for him and took a drink. Just one, before commenting, "I'm not sure why you're upset, I'm just trying to be responsible here. I told you I didn't want to have a baby alone."

After a prolonged silence, Santo sighed and said,

"You would not be alone. But a condom is not necessary. As a rule, immortals cannot impregnate mortals."

"As a rule?" she queried, one eyebrow arching.

"It has happened twice in my lifetime that I know
of," he said solemnly.

Twice in almost three thousand years with numer-
ous immortals sleeping with probably countless mortals, she thought. Those were actually pretty good
odds. Better odds than the pill, which was supposed
to be 99 percent effective. Still . . . "So would large
fit? Or does one of us have to go to the drugstore?"

"Please stop talking about condoms," Santo begged,
running one hand over his head again.

"Why? We are both grown-ups, Santo. And we need
to think of these—"

"Because I want to be a talking penis and not just a
vibrator with legs," he growled. "But discussing condoms and when I last had sex makes me want to strip
your clothes away and ravish you."

Pet stared at him blankly. She had no idea what he
was talking about with the talking penis and vibrator
with legs business, but the stripping her clothes away
and ravishing her business sounded promising. Only,
it sounded like he wasn't likely to do that until they'd
"talked" and "got to know each other better."

That was a problem, Pet decided, and glanced down,
then paused when she saw the coffee staining her top.
Apparently it hadn't all gone on the floor. She scowled
at the discolored splotches, thinking that probably
wasn't helping her cause. Her outfit wasn't exactly sexy
to begin with, but having it covered with coffee stains
probably just made her look pitiful rather than someone
he'd want to jump . . . which gave her an idea.

Pet had no idea if the coffee would stain the top but was quite sure Santo wouldn't know either, so murmured, "Oh, damn," and set her glass down on the counter as she raised her other hand to touch her top where the worst of the stains were. "I'd better go change and put this in the sink to soak before the coffee sets and my shirt is ruined."

Pet didn't wait for him to respond, just moved around him and headed for her room.

Santo released his breath on a long sigh as Pet disappeared up the hall, then shook his head and walked back out to the living room. This talking business was more difficult than even he had imagined, and since he disliked talking to begin with, he'd feared doing so would be pretty damned hard, but—good Lord, her reaction to his age had been dismaying! And that business about how many lovers he'd had . . .

The truth was, Santo had been born and raised in Greece, where the people had been anything but prudes about sex. He'd had many lovers during the almost two centuries that he'd been sexually active before growing bored with it. But he'd never kept count and couldn't even guess at the number.

Sighing, he relaxed back in the overstuffed chair and gazed up at the high ceiling as he considered what he should talk about next with Pet. Obviously, just blurting out everything from his birth to now was not the way to go about it. He needed to be more circumspect, and to that end, he started going through his history, deciding which things he should probably leave out.

Santo doubted she would appreciate learning of the many centuries he'd spent as a warrior, first in Greece and later in Europe. While he would surely tell her about them someday, now might not be the time since, if he were to judge by how the conversation about sex had gone, Pet might ask if he'd killed anyone and then how many. He didn't want to upset her with the knowledge of just how many men he'd killed in battle over the last three thousand years. Not that he'd kept an accounting of that either, but . . .

Pushing the thought from his mind, Santo decided he would simply tell her about his day-to-day life outside of battle. As a history professor, she'd no doubt be fascinated by what he could tell her about life in ancient Greece.

But, Santo decided, he would have to stay away from the lustier aspects, like the celebration of Dionysius where the people had paraded through the streets carrying giant phalluses. Probably he should avoid talking too much about the symposia he'd attended too, at least the ones that had turned into all-out orgies when high-class prostitutes had been hired for entertainment. Keeping the conversation away from sex altogether seemed a good idea—

Santo's thoughts died as a whisper of sound caught his ear. Lifting his head, he turned to see Pet approaching the living room, and sat up. But as he noticed what she was wearing, he stiffened, his mouth dropping open with shock.

When Pet had said she was going to go change and soak her shirt, he'd expected her to change into another top or . . . something. Not the sexy, dark purple slip of a nightgown she was wearing. Pet had also put on a matching robe, but since it was just as short as the gown and she'd left it undone and open, the only things it covered were her arms. Everything else . . .

His gaze slid hungrily over the dark lace bodice that didn't really cover much of the breasts they were encompassed so lovingly, and then trailed down over the purple silk that did cover the skin beneath until it stopped high up her thighs. The gown and robe were so short that he was sure if she turned around and bent over, he'd get a lovely view of her panties. If she was wearing any.

Dear God, she wasn't wearing panties, Santo realized with dismay when Pet swung toward the couch and the gown swung with her, flaring out and lifting enough to give him a peek at the bottom of her bare behind before it dropped again.

"I hope you don't mind," Pet murmured. "But it seemed silly to dirty another shirt so late in the day and it's not like you haven't seen me in my pajamas before."

Santo blinked and shifted his gaze back up to her face as Pet settled on the couch. Her cheeks were flushed, as if she was a little embarrassed or uncomfortable and she was wringing her hands a bit nervously. He supposed his trying to devour her alive with his eyes had done that, and quickly looked away, managing little more than a grunt in response to her words. But she was right, of course. He *had* spent a good deal of time with her last night and earlier today while she was in her pajamas. But while the boxers and cropped T-shirt she'd worn then had been sexy in a cute way, this was . . .

His gaze drifted down to the lace hiding so little of her breasts and he swallowed thickly.

"Now . . . you wanted to talk?"

"Talk," Santo growled, grasping desperately onto that reminder. Yes. Talking. What was it he'd wanted to talk about? He searched his mind a little frantically, trying to recall what he'd been thinking about as he'd waited for her, and spat out the first word to enter his mind. "Sex."

Her eyebrows rose delicately and she stilled. "You wanted to talk about sex?"

"No," he assured her quickly. That was a topic he was supposed to stay away from, Santo recalled, but then realized he was also nodding his head even as he said no. Forcing himself to stop nodding, he squawked the next word that jumped out at him from his earlier thoughts. "Orgies."

Pet's eyes widened. "Orgies?"

"Phallus," Santo added, and then slapped his hand over his mouth, trying to stop the words that kept leaping out of his treacherous lips. He followed that up by closing his eyes on a groan of dismay and letting his head drop back to rest on the chair back. Good Lord, when had he lost his mind? And how was he supposed to talk to her about himself and his past with her sitting there looking so damned—

"Are you all right?"

It wasn't the words so much as how close they sounded that caught his attention. Opening his eyes, Santo lifted his head and then froze again when he saw that she had crossed the room to stand between his splayed knees. She was now bending forward as if to touch him.

Pet froze when Santo raised his head and looked at her. She'd been about to touch his arm and perhaps feign a loss of balance and then tumble decorously into his lap as part of her seduction routine. The nightgown had been the first part of her plotting. Actually, it had been all the plotting she'd managed when she'd gone to her room to change. Put on a sexy nightgown and hope he was so overcome with lust he forgot all about talking and they could get on to the good stuff.

Pet had always been impetuous by nature, but even she had got a little nervous once she'd changed into the nightie. She'd pushed those nerves aside, though, and headed out, stopping only to look in and be sure Parker was sleeping soundly, and not letting herself think much about what she was doing for fear she'd lose her nerve. Santo's reaction had been gratifying. At least at first. She wasn't sure what to make of the words he'd started barking at her, though. Sex? Orgies? Phallus?

Still, when he'd looked so pained, covered his mouth, and dropped his head back, she'd seen an opportunity to get closer to him under the guise of concern. The idea about tumbling into his lap had only struck her as she'd crossed the room to reach him. But the sight of his silvered eyes made her pause and catch her breath. They were so beautiful . . . and so hungry.

Pet was still staring at those eyes with fascination, when Santo suddenly lunged forward. Snatching her up, he pulled her off her feet and dragged her with him as he fell back in the chair again. Pet found herself on his lap in a cocoon made up of his chest and arms, but her smile of relief died on a gasp as his mouth covered hers.

There was no feathering of lips first, no soft seeking kiss. It was like she'd unleashed a beast intent on devouring her as his mouth claimed hers and his tongue swept in to conquer. Pet stilled briefly under the onslaught, but only very briefly, and then her own passion rose to meet his and she gave as good as she got. Battling him with her lips and tongue, she managed to free her hands from between them. One immediately slid to clutch at his shoulder, while the other went around his neck and then up so that she could scrape her nails over his bare head.

Santo murmured into her mouth at that, and then broke their kiss and growled, "We should talk," as he shifted her to sit upright in his lap and began to push her robe off her shoulders.

"We will," Pet panted, lowering her arms so that he could remove the silk cloth.

Santo grunted at that, and then caught her at the waist and shifted her to straddle him so that he could close his mouth around one nipple through the lacy covering of her nightie. Pet gasped and then bit her lip and groaned with pleasure as he tongued the sensitive tip through the thin material.

She was so distracted by what he was doing that Pet was barely aware of his urging her arms down to her sides until he stopped what he was doing and raised his mouth briefly from her breast. She glanced down then to see that he'd slid the straps of her nightie off of her shoulders and was urging them down her arms. She immediately shifted her arms so the straps slid down and off. It left her nightie to gather around her waist, leaving her bare from there up. Santo immediately took advantage of this and lowered his head to reclaim the nipple he'd been teasing through the lace.

Pet gasped and shuddered as he began to draw on the sensitive nub, her arms closing around his head. But when his teeth grazed the aching bud, she caught his ears and tried to urge him back to kissing her in a bid to stop the almost painful pleasure. Much to her relief, Santo released the excited nipple at once, but only to shift to the side and claim the other one.

Moaning, "Oh, God," Pet shifted her hands to his shoulders and dug her nails in, her lower body grinding against the hardness she could feel beneath her.

Santo groaned in response, the sound vibrating against her breast and then he suckled harder, almost painfully as his hands slid under her bottom and squeezed and kneaded eagerly.

Pet murmured something nonsensical even to herself and let her head tip back as her body responded to the caresses, and then gasped when his hands shifted lower and together so that his fingers were brushing against where the cheeks met and farther forward where she was most sensitive.

"Santo, please," she gasped, her bottom squirming into his touch.

He responded at once by letting one hand slide under to drift over the more sensitive area. Straddling his legs as Pet was, that part of her was completely open to him, and she shuddered and groaned as his fingers grazed her damp core.

"Yes," Pet gasped when the groan ended, her hips shifting into the caress, only to groan again as his fingers left her. But he was just moving his hand around to the front to caress her more easily, she realized when his hand slid between her legs again.

She raised herself to a kneeling position when he urged her upward. It lifted her breast out of his reach, but Pet didn't care when his hand began to caress her, his talented fingers gliding over her slick flesh in quick firm motions, and then slower teasing ones. He was very skilled, and Pet had the mad thought that she wished she could thank those three thousand women for their aid in making him so skilled.

She gasped in surprise when he nipped at her stomach and then pressed his mouth over the spot and sucked gently, and then his hand withdrew, and he caught her by the upper thighs and raised her in front of him, his tongue and lips trailing down her stomach. Pet's eyes widened and she grabbed for his head and then didn't even have that to hold on to as she found herself suddenly standing with her feet on either side of his hips as he buried his mouth between her thighs and lashed her with his tongue.

Pet cried out softly, her shaky legs collapsing, but he merely pushed the backs of her knees forward to press against the back of the chair as he continued to devour her. But when she curled forward, over his head, he suddenly shifted forward.

Eyes opening, Pet gasped as she found herself falling backward, but his hands shifted, holding her bottom and her back as he laid her down on the footstool in front of the chair. It was as wide as the chair, perhaps three feet by two feet, and he set her down so that her head rested just at the edge. She opened her eyes as she felt the cool cloth against her back, and then he raised up to kiss her.

He was kneeling at the end of the footstool now, her knees spread on either side of his hips, his body bent over hers and one hand keeping his weight off of her as his other slid between her legs to fondle her where his mouth had so recently been pleasuring her.

Pet moaned and slid her arms around his neck to kiss him urgently back. Her feet pushed at the floor, lifting her hips into his caress, and then he broke the kiss and his mouth moved to a spot below her ear, before sliding down her throat. He licked and nipped his way down to one breast and then over to the other, his fingers never stopping, but slowing and gentling just when she was sure she was about to tumble headfirst into the release that was waiting for her, only to start moving more quickly and firmly again once she'd calmed. He just kept pushing her to the edge and then pulling her back until she thought she might hurt him if he'd didn't stop, and then his mouth was traveling down her stomach.

The muscles in Pet's belly began to ripple under the assault, and she drew her knees up. Planting her feet on either side of his shoulders, she dug in, pushing her body up the footstool until her head was hanging off the end and her center was at a more convenient spot for his mouth to reach.

Apparently, recognizing what she wanted, Santo chuckled against the skin of her stomach, but he wouldn't be rushed. He simply shifted to continue nipping and licking her stomach, the hand between her legs driving her absolutely mad as his mouth made its desultory journey down to caress the crease where her leg met her body.

Pet was gasping and crying out, her body trembling and shuddering as his wonderful mouth followed that sensitive crease downward. But then he finally removed his fingers from between her legs, used both hands to spread her legs as wide as they would go, and then ducked his head between her thighs.

The first brush of his tongue across her sensitive skin had her covering her own mouth with her hand to keep from crying out in both pleasure and protest, and then he settled in and feasted on her. That was the only description for what Santo did, he nibbled and then suckled on the folds that sheltered her core, and then pressed them open and laved every inch of the flesh he exposed, before settling on the growing bud of her excitement and suckling at that.

Pet's heart was hammering like a drum, her head twisting frantically, she was clutching desperately at the sides of the footstool and murmuring nonsensical nothings as her body threatened to come apart, and then he slid one large finger into her as he sucked hard on her clit and the world exploded around her. Pet was vaguely aware of screaming and reached up quickly to cover her mouth, but instead she ended up biting it as wave after wave of pleasure crashed over her, until it finally dragged her into unconsciousness.

Pet woke up in Santo's arms. Blinking her eyes open, she peered up at him with confusion and then glanced around as she realized they were moving. He was carrying her down the short hall to her bedroom.

"What happened?" she murmured, giving her head a shake to try to wake herself up properly. "Did I faint?"

"*Sì.*" His voice was a soft rumble as he carried her through her open bedroom door.

"I'm sorry. I must have had more to drink than I realized," she muttered with embarrassment, and flushed with more embarrassment when she glanced down to see that her sexy nightie was now nothing more than a wad of cloth around her waist about the size of a belt. She'd barely taken note of that when he released her legs and then set her on her feet beside the bed. Her nightie belt immediately dropped to pool around her feet.

Pet stared down at it blankly, and then lifted her gaze to the man who had just given her the greatest pleasure of her life.

Santo reached for his shirt, hesitated, and then asked, "Do you want me to leave?"

"Oh, God no." The words were out of her mouth before she could stop them, but Pet didn't regret the admission much. They were true. She didn't want him to leave. Now that she was waking up and remembering what had happened before she'd passed out, that was the last thing she wanted.

Santo smiled and then tugged his shirttails out of his jeans and pulled the shirt up his chest to remove it.

Pet gasped as he did. The man was absolutely gorgeous. Exquisite. His muscles, his skin, the hair on his chest . . . all of it was perfect. He was a marble Adonis come to life and she fell on him like a slavering dog, her hands moving over his lovely skin even before he had the shirt off over his head.

She felt his hands come to rest on her hips once he'd finished with his shirt, but ignored them in favor of trailing her fingers over his six-pack stomach and then letting them glide up to explore his pecs. The man had a body to rival Dwayne Johnson's when he played Hercules, all muscle and power, and dear God, he was beautiful.

"Thank you," Pet whispered suddenly and pressed a kiss to the very center of his chest.

"What for?" The question was a husky growl that made her shiver and squeeze her thighs together.

"For the pleasure you gave me," she answered. Moving her head to the right, Pet gave the areola around that nipple a quick lick and added, "Now it's your turn," before closing her lips over his nipple.

Santo grunted in surprise and then let his breath out on a moan as she gave the small hard nib the attention he'd paid to hers earlier. She felt his hands glide into her hair and clasp her skull, but was distracted by the pleasure sliding through her own body as she drew on his nipple. It was almost like their roles were somehow reversed and he was doing the licking, nipping, and suckling to her body again. Or like she was experiencing his pleasure, Pet thought, which was impossible. She couldn't read minds.

When one of her questing hands drifted over to pluck at and toy with his other nipple while she continued to attend the first, her pleasure increased and Santo groaned, his hands dropping to her back and urging her tighter against him. The hardness that pressed against her stomach drew her attention then, and she released his nipple and glanced down as she reached for the snap of his jeans.

Santo immediately reached down to help, unzipping his pants himself. Her eyes widened incredulously when his erection immediately shoved its way out of the tight jeans. Oh, yeah, he was perfect . . . and the size large condoms she had definitely weren't going to fit.

No problem, Pet told herself. He'd given her pleasure, now she'd give him pleasure, and tomorrow she'd buy the largest condoms she could find and invite him over for dinner again. If he was still in town. That thought made her frown, but then she pushed it away to concentrate on what she was doing as her hand closed around him.

Her touch made Santo hiss through his teeth with shock, but Pet was too distracted by the jolt of pleasure that shot through her to notice. Fascinated by her body's reaction to touching him, she dropped to her knees and immediately took him into her mouth. Santo's hands knotted in her hair, and he groaned loudly as her lips closed over him. Pet groaned in response as her own body was assailed by pleasure and for one moment she froze, but then she went with it. She began to explore, moving her mouth slowly, then quickly, wrapping her hand around the base in front of her mouth and tightening, then loosening her grip experimentally as her hand followed her mouth's movement, and finally lashing him with her tongue too as she found the rhythm that caused the most pleasure in her.

Santo was alternating between groaning and muttering words to her in Italian that might have been endearments, praise, or a recipe for all she knew, but they sounded beautiful to her ears as she gave them both pleasure. Unlike Santo, she did not have the stamina to prolong this interlude. She wanted the release again, so when Santo pulled on her hair, trying to make her stop just as she was reaching that pinnacle of excitement before the tumble into ecstasy, Pet resisted him. In the end, he let her take them both over the edge. She heard him shout something in Italian that she was quite sure was a curse, but caught up in her own, stunning orgasm as she was, Pet barely had the presence of mind to remove her mouth to keep from biting him as she started to convulse before losing consciousness.

Thirteen

"Here you are, sir. Miss."

Pet managed a smile for the man holding out her chair, took her seat, and murmured, "Thank you." But the moment he moved away, she cast her eyes around the room he'd led them to with something approaching alarm. Santo had brought her to one of the finest restaurants in Albany, one where you usually had to book well ahead. She had no idea how he'd managed to get them in, especially in this private room, but knew it must be costing him a mint. It was a room that included a good-sized cooking area separated from the dining side of the room by an island. It also included a private chef who cooked where you could see the action. It was meant for smaller parties to have private celebrations. Smaller being ten to eighteen people, not two.

Shaking her head, Pet turned helplessly to Santo, feeling like she was heading for a cliff at top speed and not going to be able to save herself from going over. But then she'd been feeling like that since waking the second time last night. She'd woken up cradled in Santo's arms in bed rather than on her bedroom floor, which had been a nice surprise. But that surprise had soon been followed by concern as she acknowledged that she'd fainted again. That issue was soon pushed aside, however, by the memory of how her kissing and touching *him* had given *her* so much pleasure.

Pet had just decided it must be some immortal thing and raised her head to ask him about that, but the moment she lifted her face to his, Santo had kissed her. That's all he'd done, however. He'd given her a hungry, hard kiss that got her all worked up and then slid from the bed and began to dress.

"Where are you going?" she'd asked with dismay.

"I have to get back to take my shift watching the Purdy house," Santo had said apologetically.

Pet had been terribly disappointed but had climbed from bed to see him out, her mind fretting over whether she'd see him again. It wasn't until they were at the door that he'd said he'd be back today if that was all right with her. When she'd nodded in mute agreement, he'd cracked his first smile since waking and said not to worry about dinner. He'd take care of it.

It was only once she'd crawled back into bed and found her mind going back over the night that she'd realized she was obsessing like a teenager with a crush. Pet had reassured herself it was just the new sex. That always made it spicier and left you jonesing for more, she'd reassured herself. After the next night, she'd calm down.

Pet had spent the whole day at work today excited and looking forward to seeing Santo and getting to experience more of the pleasure she'd found in his arms. She'd even stopped at a drugstore after giving her last lecture of the day, and picked up the largest sized condoms she could find. Tonight, she planned on finally having him in her, and she'd thought of nothing else but that as she'd driven to Parker's school to pick him up. They'd go home, Santo would come over, they'd have dinner and watch another movie with Parker, then her nephew would go to bed, and she and Santo would play.

It was when she and Parker had got home that her plan had started to unravel. They'd arrived to find Santo, Julius, and Marguerite waiting. The presence of the other couple had been alarming enough, but Santo in an expensive and beautifully tailored dark blue suit with a pale blue shirt and bloodred tie had nearly had her hyperventilating as she worried over what was happening.

What was happening was that she was going on a date. It was Marguerite who had announced that tidbit, saying Santo had mentioned he wished he could take her on one, and so she and Julius had volunteered to keep Parker company while he did. A table was booked, he was all dressed, and Marguerite was going to help her prepare so they would make their reservation in time.

The woman had kept up a constant chatter as she'd fixed Pet's hair and makeup and then picked out her dress. Marguerite had chosen Pet's favorite. One she'd bought late last year but never had an occasion to wear. Or perhaps the nerve, she acknowledged. It was an off-the-shoulder sheath cocktail dress in bloodred satin. It was beautiful, and made her feel beautiful, and perfectly matched Santo's tie.

"What is wrong?" Santo asked quietly, taking in her expression.

Pet lowered her gaze as she began absently fiddling with the silverware next to her plate. "Nothing. This is lovely."

"But?" he prompted.

She hesitated, but then met his gaze and said, "But this is expensive, and you didn't have to do it. I would have been perfectly happy with fast food and a movie with Parker."

Santo nodded solemnly. "But then I would have missed seeing you in that gown."

When Pet's eyes widened in surprise at the compliment, he asked, "Do you not realize you are the most beautiful woman here tonight?"

Pet blinked and then grinned and pointed out, "I'm the only woman in here tonight."

Santo glanced around the room and scowled as he realized his compliment was ruined. Sighing, he said, "*Sì*. But you truly are beautiful, Pet. To me, you are the most beautiful woman in the world. The *only* woman in the world."

"Oh," Pet breathed, and then frowned down at her plate, trying to regain the equilibrium his words had stolen. She needed to keep a level head. He was immortal, she was mortal. He wouldn't be here long, she reminded herself, and then glanced up to their waiter as he approached the table. He set a menu before each of them and then poured water into their glasses and asked what they'd like to drink. Santo said he was fine with water. Pet asked for white wine and then turned her attention to her menu.

"What is pâté?" Santo asked after a moment.

Pet glanced up and smiled at his bewildered expression. "It's . . . Order it, I think you'll like it," she said in the end, deciding a description probably wouldn't sound as appetizing as it actually tasted.

"Do you like it?" he asked.

"One of my favorites," she assured him. "In fact, now that you've mentioned it, I'm torn. I was thinking of ordering the onion soup."

"We will both have onion soup and order the pâté as well then," he decided. "What is good for the main course, do you think?"

They looked over the menu together and decided on the handmade ravioli and beef scaloppine with roasted potatoes and seasonal vegetables. The waiter approached with her wine the moment they set down their menus. He whisked away their menus as he took their orders. He didn't write them down, simply smiled and walked to the island separating the open cooking area from the main part of the room and presumably gave the order orally. At least that was her guess. She couldn't hear what he said. The far end of the table was close to the island, with enough room for someone to move past the chairs at the end even if they were inhabited. But she and Santo were at the opposite end of the long table that was large enough to seat up to eighteen people. She couldn't hear the men talk and doubted the chef or the waiter, who had now moved behind the island to set to work, would be able to hear a word they said if they kept their voices down.

"It's her, I'm telling you, Randall. I saw her come in here and—there! See, I told you it was her. Petronella?"

Pet had recognized that soft voice and stiffened at the first words she'd caught of the conversation as the door to the private room opened, but sighed with resignation as her name was called. Grimacing at Santo, she muttered, "Hang on to your hat. The 'rents are here," and then standing, she turned to offer a reluctant smile to the couple by the door.

"Darling, I thought it was you!" Her tall, mostly still blond, and curvy mother rushed forward and enveloped her in her arms briefly before pulling back to frown. "What on earth is going on? I called Quinn and she said she was out of town at a conference and you were watching Parker because Patrick took off. But I've called the house several times last night and today and got no answer. We were starting to worry so much we were going to stop there on our way home after dinner."

"You should have tried my cell phone, Mother," Pet said calmly, thinking that Marguerite and the men obviously weren't answering the phone at her sister's house. But then that was probably a good thing. If Quinn called and a strange man answered, it would not be good. Her parents on the other hand, probably would have been ecstatic to think a man was there with Pet. They would have started planning wedding invitations. Rolling her eyes at that thought, she explained, "I took Parker back to my place. We're staying there."

"Why on earth would you roust the boy from his home when all his toys and things are there? And where *is* he?" she added, her eyes moving around the room as if expecting him to pop out from under the table.

"At my apartment," Pet said, and then added quickly, "with not one, but *two* responsible adults watching him."

Mary Stone's eyes narrowed at once. "Why aren't you watching him? You are the one supposed to be watching him."

Pet felt her teeth grind. No matter what she did, her mother always made her feel like she was in the wrong. Raising her chin, she said, "Actually, Patrick is the one who's supposed to be watching him, but he took off quite suddenly the morning Quinn was supposed to fly out for her conference and when she asked me, I stepped in to take care of Parker in his stead," she said firmly.

"Then why aren't you?" Mary shot back at once.

"Because I'm on a date, Mother," Pet said with exasperation. "Good Lord! You're always pestering me about finding myself a man and settling down. But here I am on a date, in the very expensive and very fancy private room of your favorite restaurant, and you're interrupting it and giving me hell because I left Parker with babysitters for a couple hours."

"Oh." Mary blinked, her brain doing a regroup, and then she planted a smile on her face and turned to Santo. "I'm so sorry to have interrupted your—*oh, my God!*"

"Mary?" Pet's father said with concern, finally moving away from the door to join them. Randall Stone had always taken a step back and allowed his wife to handle their daughters in situations like this. He stiffened, though, and grabbed her mother's arm to pull her back several steps when he got a good look at Santo.

"Crap," Pet muttered, closing her eyes. She should have realized how they would react the minute they saw Santo's eyes. And she should have maneuvered her mother away and back to the door where her father had been waiting before Mary could see that Santo was an immortal. This wasn't going to be good.

She turned to see Santo's raised eyebrows as he eyed her parents. He seemed stunned that they too knew about immortals.

"Petronella, come here at once."

Pet turned with surprise at the fear in her mother's voice, something she'd never heard before. Demand, command, disappointment, anger . . . those, she'd heard. But fear? Not her mother, the lioness. However, Mary Stone looked afraid and was holding her hand out almost desperately to her, while keeping her frightened gaze trained on Santo.

Sighing, Pet moved to join her parents by the door and said soothingly, "It's all right. He's one of the good immortals. Like Meng Tian."

"Meng Tian got your mother killed," Mary cried, clutching at her arm and trying to drag her to the door.

Pet's mouth tightened at the accusation, and she dug her heels in. Refusing to move, she said stubbornly, "It wasn't his fault."

"She'd be alive today if she hadn't got tangled up with him," Mary argued grimly.

"I know, but—"

"There are no buts. This date is over, and I never want you to see that . . . man, again," her mother said firmly, pulling harder on her arm.

Pet could have pointed out that she was a grown woman and could see who she wanted, and normally she would have, but the chef and their waiter were gawking at them, her mother was panicking, her father didn't look like he was doing much better, and she gathered her mother's strident tones were gaining attention from the rest of the restaurant because one of the other waiters had stuck their head through the door to look around to see what the fuss was about. In the end, Pet simply turned to Santo impatiently. "Will you take care of this, please? I know you can."

He nodded solemnly and then turned his gaze first to the waiter at the door, who suddenly smiled and backed out. Santo then turned his concentrated gaze on her parents. Both immediately lost all expression and turned to walk calmly out of the room. Finally, he shifted his attention to the chef and their own waiter, who relaxed and went back to work.

When Santo then turned to her, Pet sighed and muttered, "Thank you," as she returned to her seat. After taking a fortifying sip of wine, she asked, "What did you put in my parents' minds?"

"That they ran into you here, were happy to see you, and left you to your date," he said quietly.

Pet nodded just as solemnly and took another sip of wine, and then stilled when he said, "Will you now tell me how you know about immortals?"

"You didn't read their minds while you were controlling them?" she asked, one eyebrow arched, because she was sure he would have, might even have had to while in their minds.

Santo nodded once in acknowledgment but added, "It made little sense."

"What did you see?" she asked at once.

"Horror, fear . . . a child's charred body."

Pet blew out her breath and dropped back in her seat as his words brought her own unpleasant memories to the foreground.

After a moment, Santo asked, "Can you tell me now?"

"Does it matter?" she asked wearily. He was leaving soon anyway. Why did he have to open this can of worms? The very can of worms she'd wanted to avoid since realizing that immortals were staying next door.

"Marguerite seems to think it does," he said softly.

Pet frowned. Of course, the immortal woman had read it from her thoughts. It was how Marguerite knew about the Brass Circle. Pet had forgotten how hard it was to keep secrets from immortals. It had been a long time since she'd lived with one.

"Everything about you matters to me."

That made her stiffen and avoid his gaze as confusion swirled within her.

"She will tell me if I ask," he added quietly. "I would rather you tell me."

Pet almost told him to ask Marguerite, but just as quickly changed her mind. Though, she couldn't say why. Sitting up again, she kept her gaze on the fork she'd taken to rolling in its spot as she cleared her throat and said, "My biological mother was married to an immortal and became one herself."

Santo leaned back as shock rolled through him. He'd tried to think of possible explanations for her knowledge, but this was the last one he'd expected. A father who was immortal and a mother who was not? It wasn't impossible. While it was rare for an immortal to impregnate a mortal woman, it happened on occasion, and if the mother was mortal, the child, or in this case, twins, would be mortal as well. "Your father is—?"

"My stepfather," she corrected quietly. "Our birth father died shortly after Quinn and I were born. Two years later, my mother met and married our stepfather. *He* was my dad."

"And *he* was an immortal?" Santo asked, wanting to be sure he wasn't misunderstanding.

Pet nodded. "He had brown eyes with bright silver flecks in them. His name was Meng Tian."

Santo didn't recognize the name any more now than he had when Pet had told Mary Stone that he was a good immortal like this Meng Tian. But that didn't mean anything. While he knew the names of the families that had survived the fall of Atlantis, there had been so many new branches to those families over the millennia that it was impossible to know them all.

"I do not know him," Santo said finally, and noted the disappointment that flickered over her face in response. For some reason she'd hoped he'd known the immortal. Perhaps to save her having to explain, he thought.

"Well, Meng Tian was a good immortal," Pet said finally. "He and my mother were very happy. They loved each other very much, but they made sure we felt loved too. My childhood in China was full of good memories with lots of laughter and happiness. I always felt loved."

The fact that she'd repeated that her birth mother and stepfather had always made her feel loved, coupled with her reactions to her adoptive parents just moments ago, told him a great deal. Pet had said she was the black sheep of the family because she'd chosen history instead of the medical field like Quinn had, but he suspected it had started long before that. She obviously hadn't felt loved by her adoptive parents for some reason, and that angered him a great deal. No child should be allowed to feel unloved, but especially not his Pet, who was perfect in every way . . . Except perhaps cooking, if Parker was to be believed, he thought with a faint smile.

"I've thought Dad was a police officer since I was a child," Pet continued. "But I think now he must have been an Enforcer in China."

Santo's gaze sharpened on her. His voice was a low growl when he asked, "Why?"

"Because Mom always said 'he was like a police officer,' but he never wore a uniform that I saw. I didn't really know there were what basically amounts to immortal police until Marguerite said you were all working with Enforcers." She shrugged. "Now I think that's probably what he was. An Enforcer."

Santo nodded at her reasoning and suspected she was right. Immortals usually avoided mortals when they could. It was too hard to watch them age and die. Being a police officer in a mortal unit, working with them day in and day out, coming to like and care for them, and then watching them die before their time would be hard. It could also be dangerous for an immortal. In a job such as that, if a mortal friend and coworker were shot or seriously injured . . . In the heat of the moment, the immortal could be tempted to try to save the mortal by turning them. Which would be a death sentence to the immortal if he or she had already used their one turn.

"Anyway," Pet breathed out. "When Quinn and I were six . . ." She paused and seemed lost in her memories for a moment, and then frowned and continued, "Meng Tian usually worked at night after we went to bed. He was always home in the mornings and during the day while mother homeschooled us. We had to be quiet to keep from disturbing him."

"You were homeschooled?" he asked with interest, but then realized they had probably had to be since they knew about immortals. Attending a school, making friends . . . Both would have been risky. Pet and Quinn could have been tempted to tell about their immortal mother and father.

"Yes," Pet said now. "Mother made it fun despite the need to be quiet."

"Your mother didn't sleep during the day?" Santo asked.

Pet shook her head. "We all slept late, but she got up as soon as we stirred, fed us, looked after us, and taught us. Usually she took us out into the courtyard during the day so that we could play and learn without disturbing Dad, but she was always covered up despite the fact that she stayed under the sheltered half of the courtyard." Her eyebrows drew together. "For some reason, I don't think that cover over the courtyard was normal, so it was probably something Dad had erected to give added protection from the sun."

Santo nodded solemnly. Most immortals avoided sunlight to avoid the damage it did to all humans. The problem was that while a mortal's body basically just aged under the damage the sun's rays did, an immortal's body continually repaired the damage, using extra blood to do so. If her mother was out and about during the day to tend to Pet and her sister, a cover over a portion of the courtyard would have helped to keep her from sustaining the damage that would have led to a need for more blood. Adding it would have been the smart thing to do.

"I wish I could remember where we lived," Pet said suddenly. "At least the area if nothing else." She looked thoughtful and said, "I know China is supposed to have a population problem, but I don't have memories of a lot of people being around, so suspect we lived somewhere that was isolated or at least less populated. I remember our home being big with just us in it, not small and crowded. I don't remember it ever snowing where we lived, the willows were always green, so I suspect it was in the south of China. There was lots of water . . ." She shook her head, frustration crossing her face.

"What about your adoptive parents?" Santo asked. "Surely they know and can tell you?"

Her mouth tightened briefly, "I'm sure they could, but they won't. They both refuse to talk about my mom, dad, and our sister, Erika. They think it's better that I just forget all about it. Safer, they say."

Santo felt a flicker of surprise at the mention of a sister named Erika. It was the first time she'd spoken of such a person, but he wasn't surprised that her adoptive parents might be overprotective. While reading Mary Stone, he'd found a desperate need in the woman to keep Pet and her twin safe. He hadn't been able to tell if that was tied to the burned body or not.

It had felt like a litany that had lived in the woman's head for decades.

They were both silent for a moment, and then Pet said, "Anyway, one night when Quinn and I were six and Erika was ten, Mom roused Quinn and me from our beds in the middle of the night. I was half asleep at first and confused." She frowned. "I remember stumbling out into the hall and Erika and Dad being there. Meng Tian," she added to clarify which father, before continuing, "That was unusual. So was the fact that Dad was grim and quiet. He was always laughing and happy around us, so I knew something was wrong.

"Mom, her name was Feiyan, Meng Feiyan," she added, and then continued, "She didn't even let us dress. She'd hustled us out of our room in our night-gowns. They kept telling us to hurry, we had to leave. Dad scooped up Quinn and me the minute we left our room, and started running down the hall with us, while Mom snatched up Erika and followed . . . There was some sort of sound like breaking glass or a crash. I can't remember which, but Dad immediately turned, set us down, and pushed us toward Mom, yelling to run, he'd slow them down. Mom set down Erika and told her to run, then snatched us up. I guess at ten Erika would have been able to run faster than us," she murmured and then shook her head. "But Erika ran back the way we'd come. Mom followed, shouting at her to get to the kitchen."

Pet paused, looking thoughtful. "I remember there was a door out of the kitchen to a small garden with woods behind it. I think Mom meant for us to run out and hide in the woods or something, but Erika was in a panic and didn't listen. She ran back to her room and crawled under her bed. Mom ran after her, but when she stopped in the room, we could hear the pounding of feet in the hall. Dad hadn't been able to hold them all back. Mom hurried to the closet and set us down. As we crouched together in the very back of it, she told us we must stay quiet, not make a sound, no matter what. And then she closed the doors."

Pet stopped and Santo watched as she reached for her wine, then left it and picked up her water instead. She took a long gulp. Setting the glass back on the table, she cleared her throat and said, "The doors banged shut, but then bounced back open a little. Not a lot, just enough that we could see when Mom ran to the window across from the closet and slung a leg over the sill before pausing to wait. I was so confused. I was afraid she was leaving us, but she wasn't actually leaving. In fact, she only started moving again when men rushed into the room, and she was yelling, 'Run, get away, hide!' as if we were outside as she did. But by then it was too late, and they were on her."

Sighing, Pet murmured, "It wasn't until I was a little older that I understood she'd been hoping to trick the men into thinking the three of us had made it out the window in front of her and to the woods on that side of the house. I imagine she thought they'd drag her out of the room and down the hall or something. But they didn't. They dragged her to the bed, brought Father in, and made him watch as they took turns raping her."

The words were said as if Pet were discussing the weather, but he suspected it was the only way she could say it. There was no mistaking the empty look in her eyes. She'd separated herself from what she was discussing to get past the trauma. Santo's hands balled into fists and he withdrew them from the table and set them in his lap. He couldn't imagine the horror of watching your life mate abused so and being unable to do a thing. How much worse must that be for a child to see? But he didn't say a word. He simply waited, knowing she wasn't done.

After a moment, Pet let out a shaky breath and then cleared her throat and said, "Dad was badly wounded. His chest was sliced open from his shoulder to the opposite hip, and there were other wounds as well. If he'd been mortal, he'd have been dead already, but it hardly seemed to slow him down. He went wild trying to stop them from hurting mother. He almost succeeded too, but there were too many of them, and they were able to hold him back. They kept saying things like they'd *heard he was looking for them so came to see him*, and *this is what you got for daring to hunt the Brass Circle.*"

Santo noted movement out of the corner of his eye and glanced up to see the waiter approaching with their food. His gaze flickered over the food, but he slipped into the man's mind and sent him back as Pet continued.

"When they were done with Mom, they cut off her head," she said her voice turning shaky, and then she closed her eyes in pain before adding, "Quinn and I were in the closet, covering each other's mouths. We'd been so quiet like Mom wanted that whole time, but we both screamed then. Dad screamed louder, though, and they didn't hear us. His scream . . . I've never heard so much raw pain. I think even they were affected by it, because when it ended there was this heartbeat of complete silence . . . and then a small sob." She opened her eyes and looked at him sadly. "Erika didn't have anyone covering her mouth."

Santo cursed and lowered his gaze, knowing what was coming before she said, "Dad didn't even look up when they dragged Erika out from under the bed. It was like he was already dead. That might have been a small mercy, though. I think if he had looked up even once, they would have raped or at least tortured Erika too. But he didn't and the men just fed on her, one at her neck, one at each arm and leg. They drained her dry while she screamed in agony and terror and then snapped her neck. The minute that was done, they cut off Dad's head."

Pet cleared her throat and then her voice going flat again, she said, "After that, someone said, 'What about the twins?' The head guy started barking orders. I didn't catch a lot of it. Too horrified I guess. I know he sent some men to search the woods, and others to search the rest of the house. He must have sent someone to get gasoline or some other accelerant too, but . . ." She shrugged. "When he fell silent, he was the only one left in the room. He stood there for a long time and then looked around like he was searching for something. I don't think we made a noise or anything. Maybe he just started thinking about Erika under the bed, and maybe he'd noticed that Mom hadn't moved too fast to get away and realized that she'd sacrificed herself to try to save us all, but then he suddenly turned to the closet."

Pet swallowed and then admitted quietly, "I peed myself when he started toward our hiding spot. I know Quinn did too. I remember seeing two streams of liquid running toward the doors, and then he opened them and—I was praying so hard," she admitted. "I know he read me. I felt him in my head, a strange ruffling. He had brass-colored flecks in his eyes instead of the silver Mom and Dad had. He bent down with a mean smile and reached out to grab me, but then his gaze shifted to Quinn and as his fingers closed in my hair, his eyes widened and he kind of froze, just staring at Quinn. His expression became more concentrated, and then he looked shocked. Neither of us moved. He just stared at her for the longest time, and we stared back, shaking, and then the man who had gone for the accelerant came back into the room and the leader quickly released my hair, straightened, and closed the doors."

Pet shook her head with amazement even now at the memory. "I couldn't believe it. I felt sure he was just toying with us and would whip the doors open again and drag us out. But then I heard the other man ask something and him say he'd just been searching the room. The other man said, 'Nothing? The men haven't found the twins.' He said, 'No, nothing.' And then when the other man started to pour something that smelled like gasoline on my mother and father, the leader said, 'Take them out in the courtyard. I want a bonfire by moonlight.' They dragged their bodies to the window and tossed them out like trash and then grabbed Mom and Dad's heads and climbed out the window with them."

Pet lowered her head, staring at that spinning fork as she said, "We smelled the fire not long afterward.

Heard the men laughing and talking for a while and then silence. But Quinn and I were too afraid they'd come back to move. We just crouched there, still covering each other's mouths until well after the sun rose, and then we fell asleep huddled together in that small closet."

Fourteen

"Pet?"

She glanced up with surprise when Santo softly said her name. She'd been lost in the past, clinging to her sister and trembling in the dark closet, watching the monstrous shapes dance across the walls of the bedroom beyond the doors, cast there by the flames in the courtyard.

Sighing, Pet straightened in her seat. "Sorry."

"Do not apologize." He frowned and asked, "Do you want to stop now?"

Pet considered it, but then shook her head. Might as well finish, she thought, and cleared her throat. "Anyway, like I said, we fell asleep from sheer exhaustion after the sun finally came up. But Quinn's screaming woke me some time later. I'd barely opened my eyes when someone was picking me up. I started screaming and kicking and . . ."

Pet shrugged. "I guess I must have fainted. Every-thing gets kind of blurry after that. Like I'm missing bits and pieces." She narrowed her eyes briefly, but then continued, "The next thing I remember is waking up somewhere else. I think it was a hotel room. Mary and Randall, friends of my parents, were there." Her mouth twisted slightly. "They kept talking in sooth-ing voices, trying to reassure us everything would be okay, and asking where Mom and Dad were. But Quinn and I wouldn't talk, we just clung to each other and stared at them. I guess we were probably in shock.

"I'm not sure how long we stayed in that hotel room. It could have been a day or weeks. I don't know, I kept kind of zoning out. I remember other people came and went, people with silver flecks in their eyes like Dad's . . . and yours." She met his gaze briefly and then looked away. "I'd met some of the people who came before, knew they were family on Dad's side."

She was silent for a minute and then said, "I re-member we were never allowed near the window or out of the room, and then I remember a car ride, and then being on a plane, but not a normal plane with lots of people. It had tables and chairs, and a couch and it was just us and Mary and Randall. And then we landed. There was another car, and then we were in a house and they were telling us we were in America now. That we were now Americans, that they were now our parents, and our family name was now Stone."

Her mouth hardened at the memory. Everything had been taken from her, even her name. Pushing her re-sentment down, she drank more water and then sipped her wine before glancing up at him and raising her eyebrows. Her voice was back to normal when she asked, "Questions? Comments?"

Santo opened his mouth, but afraid he would say something sympathetic that would bring the tears on, Pet warned, "Don't do the whole pity thing. I don't need it. I, at least, remember Mom and Dad. Quinn doesn't remember a thing."

"Quinn does not remember that night?" he asked with surprise.

Pet shook her head. "Or anything else. Not even Erika and our parents. At least she says she doesn't. But she also won't let me talk about it to her, so maybe she just says that to shut me up . . . or maybe she doesn't *want* to remember." She shrugged wearily.

Santo looked thoughtful for a moment before asking, "These men were Brass Circle?"

Pet nodded and frowned as she tried to remember everything she'd heard about them. "I remember hearing Mom and Dad—Meng Feiyan and Meng Tian," she added a little wryly so he would know which parents she was talking about. "I remember hearing them talk a couple of times before that night. I remember Mom was worried, and Dad tried to soothe her, but I could tell he was worried too. But he said they had to hunt them and . . . something about . . . they were kidnapping mortals and making them blood slaves?" She looked at him uncertainly, a question in her eyes.

Santo's eyes widened and he cursed under his breath and then growled, "That is a term I have not heard in ages."

"What is a blood slave?" Pet asked at once.

For a moment, she didn't think he'd answer, and then he growled, "Human cattle."

Pet frowned at the brief explanation. "You mean kept on a farm, or . . . ?" She shook her head, unable to think of anything else it might mean.

"Large numbers of them kept in cages, fed slop, only brought out to be fed on, and leashed when they are." His words were cold and hard, but painted the picture pretty well. Sighing, he ran a hand over his bald head as if to soothe his temper, and then asked, "Who found you in the closet? Immortals?"

Pet shook her head. "Mary and Randall. Randall was the one who picked me up."

"They were there, in China?" Santo asked with surprise.

Pet nodded. "I guess while Dad was trying to soothe Mom, he was worried enough about retribution that he wanted to send us all away until the situation was resolved. Mary said later that someone he'd worked with had been found dead not long before the attack on us. They feared it was a retribution killing and were concerned he would be next. Mary told me that she and Mom had been roommates at boarding school, and they both got into Princeton and were roommates there too. She said they loved each other like sisters." Frowning, she added, "I remember Mary and Randall visiting us once or twice in China before that night, but Mother—Mary," she clarified, "she said she came twice a year before she married Randall and then once a year after that and that Mom visited her in America twice with our birth father and then with Meng Tian too."

Pet shook her head. "Anyway, Mother—Mary," she clarified, "Mary said while Mom—Feiyan—agreed to send Erika, Quinn, and me away for a while, she refused to leave herself unless Dad, Meng Tian, agreed to come with us. Mom arranged for Mary and Randall to come collect us, but unbeknownst to her, Dad had sent a message to Mary, explaining everything and begging her to help him convince Mom to leave with us when she got to China. He figured if anyone could, it would be her. At least that's what Mary said he told her."

She shrugged. "I guess their plane landed that morning, just hours after everything happened. They came straight to our home. They found the door broken open and started to look around. They found a child's charred remains in the courtyard first, but other than that, just a lot of ash."

"We are highly flammable and burn hot," he said grimly. "Ash would be all that was left of Feiyan and Meng Tian."

Pet filed that information away. "They didn't know that, so still hoped Mom and Dad and two of us kids were alive somewhere. They searched the rest of the house, found Erika's bedroom with all the blood, and then found us asleep in the closet. Randall picked up Quinn and passed her to Mary, then picked me up. That's when I woke, but I didn't know it was him at the time. His body was blocking the light, and he was just this big dark shape picking me up. I thought the bad men had returned."

Pet released the fork and sat back in her seat, relaxing a little now that the worst of it was over. "I guess Mary contacted Dad's family for help getting us out of the country. They arranged for the plane, and gave her passports for us with our names, now Petronella and Quinn Stone."

"What were your names before that?" Santo asked.

Pet was a bit surprised that he couldn't figure that out. She'd mentioned Meng Tian several times, but she answered the question. "Meng Petronella and Meng Quinn. We had taken Meng Tian's name when he married our mother. I guess over here it would be Petronella and Quinn Meng, but there the surname goes first."

"Your first names were Petronella and Quinn even in China?" he asked with disbelief.

Pet felt amusement try to lay claim to her lips as she took in his expression. "My mom fell in love with America while she was in school here. She loved everything American and hoped to move here permanently someday. So, when we were born, she gave us American names with meanings that were traits she hoped we would have."

"What do your names mean?" Santo asked with interest.

"Petronella means rock, and Quinn means wise and intelligent or something."

"Strong and smart," he murmured.

She smiled softly and nodded. "Our older sister's name was Erika, which means powerful ruler . . . or honorable ruler, maybe. I'm not sure anymore," Pet admitted, unhappy with herself for forgetting that. It felt like she'd let Erika down somehow. Sighing, she reluctantly admitted, "Erika wasn't our sister by birth. She was our cousin. Her mother was my mother's younger sister. She had no husband and died giving birth to her. Our parents, Mom and our birth father, were newly married but took her in and named her and raised her. She was four years older than us and a big sister in every way."

Santo nodded but asked, "You said Meng Tian's family arranged new passports?"

Pet quickly followed the switch in topic, and suspecting what he wanted to know, said, "And social security numbers and new birth records so that we were suddenly Americans. They also read our minds to learn what had happened to Mom and Dad." Her mouth tightened before she added, "They foolishly told Mary and Randall what they saw in our memories and Mary freaked. I remember that. I also remember her trying to convince them to blank out our minds to get rid of our memories," she added grimly. "They refused. Thank God."

He didn't comment, but Pet could see that he was thinking and wondered what about.

Santo was thinking that he wasn't surprised the immortals had refused. If they'd simply removed the memories of that night, those would have eventually returned, jostled back into Pet and Quinn's minds by other memories of their life with Feiyan, Meng Tian, and Erika. It might not have happened for decades, but eventually things like that came back. A trip to China, their own child hiding in the closet during a game of tag, a child wetting themselves, even a bonfire or a picture could have opened the door and brought it all rushing in . . . No one could know what would bring it back, or when. They could have experienced any one of those things several times and then the third or tenth time the memories could suddenly spring forth. And then the trauma would have been compounded by its unexpectedness. In his experience, children's minds were more adaptable than adults'. They could better handle trauma. Trying to hide something like that and then it's popping out ten, twenty, or even fifty years later could have caused huge psychological issues.

The only way Meng Tian's family could have ensured those memories never returned was to do a 3-on-1 on each child to completely wipe their minds. A dangerous thing to do with a lot of risks, including leaving them both beautiful little drooling idiots.

"Every time I remember Mary demanding they wipe out our memories, I just want to slap her," Pet growled, reaching for her fork again. "They were my parents and she wanted to take them away."

"Not your parents," Santo said with certainty. "The pain and trauma."

When she glanced at him with surprise, he reminded her, "I read her mind."

"And?" Pet asked, stiffening.

"She fears she failed Feiyan with you."

"Because I'm not a doctor like them and Quinn?" she suggested grimly.

Santo shook his head. "Because you clung to the past."

"What?" Pet asked with surprise.

"You call Feiyan Mom," he pointed out.

"Feiyan *was* my mom," she said resentfully.

"But you call Mary Mother."

Santo knew he didn't have to point out that Mom was a more affectionate title than Mother. He could tell by her expression that she saw that. But he did point out, "Mary has been a mother to you for thirty years, Pet, yet you show more affection in title for a woman who has been dead that long and was able to mother you for only six."

"It's hard to love someone who wants to take even the memory of your own mother from you. Memories were all I had left."

Santo could almost feel her pain in her words, but suspected it was just the tip of the iceberg. Pet and Quinn had suffered a terrible trauma, but Mary and Randall could never have taken them to a mortal psychologist to help them deal with it. Doing so would either have revealed the existence of immortals, and that they weren't legal Americans, or convinced the psychologist that they were delusional or suffering some other mental illness. It had left Mary and Randall to try to deal with their trauma on their own. Something they weren't really equipped to do. They had inevitably made mistakes with them that they hadn't even realized they were making at the time. Like this business about the wiping of the memories. Mary probably didn't even realize that Pet had heard that, or how she'd taken it. So had never corrected Pet's misconceptions.

It seemed he wasn't the only one needing counseling in this relationship, Santo realized, and almost felt better for it. He had just started talking to Marguerite's son-in-law, Greg, who used to be a mortal psychologist and now counseled both mortals and those immortals willing to seek such help. Perhaps he could convince Pet to seek him out too.

In the meantime, though, he might be able to help clear up some things for her, Santo thought, and growled. "What if Quinn was gang-raped and murdered?"

Pet blanched at the thought.

"Mary and Feiyan were like sisters," he pointed out. "That is how she felt."

Santo let her think about that for a minute, and then asked, "And if Parker witnessed his mother being raped and murdered? What would you want most in the world for him?"

"I'd want—" Her eyes widened and then closed on a sigh as she finished, "to take the memories away and save him from carrying that horrible trauma in his head."

Santo grunted and waited. After a moment, she opened her eyes, uncertainty on her expression.

"So . . . Mary wasn't trying to take my mother away and replace her in my memory?"

Even though Pet had concluded that she'd want to do the same thing for Parker as her adoptive mother had tried to do for her, Santo wasn't surprised she would have doubts. She had believed a certain story-line for so long that it would be hard to adjust her vision of events. Santo knew he could help her with that, though, and nodded before saying, "I read her mind. She was desperate to protect and care for you both. She still is," he added, thinking of the woman's reaction once she'd realized he was immortal. Mary Stone obviously held all immortals to blame for the death of Feiyan. Which was a shame, since this was one of the few times when a life mate wouldn't have had to leave her family behind. Mary and Randall knew about immortals, so Pet's not aging would not have had to be hidden once he turned her. Which made him wonder—

"Did Mary and Randall know about immortals before your mother's death?"

"I don't know," she admitted slowly. "I presumed so, but maybe not."

"But they definitely flew back to America with that knowledge intact," Santo muttered thoughtfully.

Pet eyed him with curiosity. "Is that unusual?"

"Sì." Santo nodded. It was very unusual, and normally wouldn't have happened . . . unless there was a concern that Pet and Quinn were still in danger from the rogue immortals who had killed the rest of their family. The Stones might have needed that knowledge to keep the girls safe.

He supposed, at the time, that threat would have been a definite possibility if someone in this Brass Circle had discovered the twins yet lived and where they were. While the very fact that these rogues had a name like Brass Circle suggested they were organized where most rogues weren't, there were other concerns here too that made that a possibility. The leader's letting the girls live, but not doing so openly, for instance. That was an indication that he either wasn't the actual leader, just the leader of that attack with orders to kill the whole family, or that he hadn't been confident enough in his control over the other men in the organization that they would have obeyed his decision to let them live. Had he worried others in the group might insist on killing Pet and Quinn?

Santo considered that briefly, and then pushed the thoughts away. It had all taken place thirty years ago. The chances were no one from the Brass Circle would come after Pet and her sister now. Still, it might not be a bad idea to get what information he could on the group. He'd have to ask around, Santo decided. Just to be safe.

"Sir?"

Santo pulled himself from his thoughts and glanced up at their waiter with surprise. He'd actually forgotten where they were and that they weren't alone.

"The restaurant closes at ten o'clock and it's nearly that now. I fear if you wish to eat the food the chef has prepared for you, you'll have to get started," the man said apologetically.

Santo caught the grimace that flickered across Pet's face, and knew she probably didn't feel like eating after the heavy conversation they'd just had. Come to that, he didn't either. But he knew he'd be hungry later, so said, "Wrap it up to go."

"Yes, sir."

"And throw in several of those desserts we saw on the way in," he added as the man started away.

"Of course, sir."

"I'm sorry."

Pet's soft voice made Santo glance around with surprise. "What for?"

"For ruining our dinner date with all of this. I know this must have cost a lot of money, and—"

"Pet," he interrupted in a gentle rumble. "Never worry about the money I spend on you. I have accumulated a good deal of it in my lifetime."

"Really?" She seemed surprised.

Santo wasn't sure if he should be insulted or not by that surprise, but simply said, "As you have pointed out, I am nearly three thousand years old, and I have worked nearly all that time."

"Yeah, well, I work too, but most of my money goes into that apartment I own. There isn't a lot left over to sock away and build a fortune."

"You own the apartment?" he asked with surprise.

"Yes. Most of the apartments are rentals, but the ones on my floor were sold to help finance the building. I saw it, I loved it, I bought it." Pet sipped the last of her drink. "Renting seems kind of . . . Well, you are basically throwing your money out the window. You pay your rent and that money is gone, never to be seen again. But when you buy a house or apartment, even if you are paying on a mortgage monthly . . ." she shrugged again ". . . you'll get that money back if you sell the house later. Unless, of course, the bottom falls out of the housing market again or something."

Santo nodded but then asked, "How long is the average mortgage?"

"Twenty to thirty years, though, I think you can get shorter ones."

"And that is the largest portion of everybody's monthly expenses, *sì*?"

"*Sì*, I mean yes. Most budgeting guidelines suggest housing should be thirty-five percent of your monthly expense," Pet admitted. "Although, for me it's more like fifty percent. But they also allocate five to fifteen percent for debts, and since my mortgage is my only debt . . ." She let the sentence trail off.

"So, once I acquired a house, my expenses dropped greatly," Santo pointed out, but thought to himself that Parker definitely got his habit of spewing out facts and figures from his aunt Pet.

She nodded with understanding and then murmured, "Let's see, you're two thousand nine hundred and eighty-four years old. Divide that by thirty years per mortgage . . ." She paused, her eyes widening incredulously. "That's like the equivalent of a hundred houses—99.467 to be exact."

Santo nodded solemnly and then said, "I have one home . . . and you must consider interest on the money from all those houses I have not bought over the years."

"Good Lord, you're rich as Croesus," Pet exclaimed, looking more dismayed than pleased by the news.

"Croesus may have been wealthy, but he was very ostentatious with it," he assured her and her eyes immediately narrowed.

"You did not know Croesus! He was . . . ah hell, he was around in five hundred and something B.C. You could have known him," she realized, and then asked with curiosity. "Who else did you know?"

Santo actually laughed with disbelief at the question. "I have been alive a long time, woman. I have known many people."

"Yes, but—" Pet paused to scowl and said, "You did not just call me woman."

A smile tugged at his lips as he took in her outrage and teased, "You would prefer, *mio amante*?"

"What's that?" she asked suspiciously.

Santo opened his mouth, but then paused and simply stared at her for a minute. She was so lovely. Her eyebrows were arched over her large dark eyes, her mouth was pursed into a deep red pout, and her long hair fell around her naked shoulders in black waves that stopped just above the figure-fitting red dress she wore.

"It means," he began, but his gaze dropped to the

deep V cut into the dress between her breasts, and his voice lowered with it into a hungry growl as he finished, "my lover."

Silence followed his announcement and lasted so long he finally forced his gaze up to her face. He saw at once that she was as affected by the simple word as him. The sexual desire he was suddenly feeling was reflected in her eyes and her lips had parted slightly as if inviting his kiss.

"Here you are," the waiter said cheerfully as he returned. "We put it all in bags to make it easier to—oh, th-thank you."

The man blinked in surprise as he found the bags gone from his hands and a wad of money in their place. Santo had stood, retrieved his wallet, pulled out the money, snatched the bags, and placed the money in the waiter's hands at immortal speed, leaving the man somewhat dazed.

Realizing what he'd done, Santo forced himself to slow down as he moved around the table to urge Pet from her seat. He managed to maintain that calm, measured pace as he escorted her from the restaurant and out into the night. He even managed to walk her across the now nearly empty parking lot to where he'd parked in the back corner. It was at the SUV that he lost it. Santo had opened the passenger door for her and then stepped back, but not far enough. When Pet's body brushed against him as she went to slide past him, he drew in a hiss of air, closed his eyes, and suddenly raised his arm to wrap it around her just below her breasts.

If she'd protested or even laughed when he then pulled her back against him, Santo might have been able to stop there, but she didn't. Not his beautiful, passionate Pet. Instead, she melted into him with a sigh, her head turning to the side against his chest, and her hands sliding back to clasp his behind and pull him tighter against her so that his growing hardness was cuddled against the top of her behind.

Groaning, Santo lowered his head and kissed the top of her head, his own hands moving up to cover her breasts through the soft silk of her gown. Pet moaned in reaction and then gasped and arched her back, thrusting her bottom against his erection, when he squeezed and kneaded the small mounds he'd claimed.

Santo groaned and thrust back, then turned Pet and pressed her back up against the SUV as he bent to kiss her. She responded hungrily, opening for him at once when he slid his tongue out, and sucking at it eagerly before allowing her own tongue to duel with his. He was holding her by the shoulders, his body slightly bent, but he wanted to feel her body against his, so shifted his hands to her waist and lifted her, then held her there against the SUV with his lower body so that his hands could find her breasts again.

Pet gasped into his mouth as he tugged the top of her off-the-shoulder dress down to free her breasts to the cool night air, then she sucked violently at his tongue, her hands clutching at his shoulders as his hands covered the flesh he'd revealed. Santo felt her excitement and pleasure double his own as he caressed and kneaded her bared breasts, then pinched her nipples.

He had broken their kiss and started to bend his head to taste one of those hardening nipples when he heard a door close and the sound of voices. Stiffening, he lifted his head to see that a group of people had come out of the restaurant and was separating into couples as they moved to three of the remaining cars.

Reminded of where they were, Santo quickly lifted Pet's gown back into place, then leaned his forehead against hers.

"Home," she demanded in a whisper, running her hand down his back. "I need you."

"Home," Santo growled, moving at once. Clasping her waist, he stepped back and set her down, then ushered her into the passenger seat. He stopped to pick up the bags of food he'd dropped, and quickly placed them in the back seat, then headed around to get behind the wheel. His only thought was to get her back to her apartment, rip that beautiful gown from her body, and plunge himself inside her.

Fifteen

"Do not forget you take over watching the Purdy house at midnight."

"*Sì, sì,*" Santo said impatiently in response to Julius's reminder as he tried to urge the man and his wife, Marguerite, out of the apartment. He was very aware of what time he had to start. He also knew that it was a quarter to eleven, which meant he only had an hour before his phone alarm would go off, telling him it was time to leave. He'd have more time had Marguerite and Julius left as expected when he and Pet returned. Instead, the couple had suddenly got chatty, asking about the restaurant and their meals, etc. Santo had answered with lies rather than force Pet to relive her memories yet again. They'd then discussed this and that and basically nothing for half an hour before finally making noises about leaving. Santo had immediately stood to see them out, leaving Pet alone in the living room.

"We had to stay," Marguerite said suddenly, inter-rupting his annoyed thoughts as she stepped into the hall. "You were a little wound up when you got back, your thoughts screaming your plans to rip that beauti-ful gown off Pet. It's too gorgeous for that. She never would have forgiven you."

Santo blinked at the words and then just stared at Marguerite as she smiled and leaned up to kiss his cheek.

"Life mate passion is all a bit overwhelming at first. Remember how strong you are and be careful with her," she warned in a gentle whisper before pulling back and allowing Julius to take her arm to walk her away.

Startled by the warning, Santo simply stared after the pair as they made their way down the hall. It wasn't until they disappeared into the elevator that he finally closed the door and made his way back to the living room.

He spotted Pet the minute he turned the corner out of the entry. She'd left the chair she'd been sitting in and now stood with her back to the room, framed in the large floor-to-ceiling window as she peered out at the dark night and city lights beyond. Her red gown was a bright beacon against that background, and his gaze slid hungrily over her as he approached.

Feeling himself immediately harden and his hands clench with the urge to rip the gown off so he could run his hands over the pale flesh it hid, he forced himself to stop and take a couple of deep breaths. Good Lord, he was like a bull ready to charge the matador's red cape, he realized, and shook his head.

He wanted to go slow here. Hard for life mates, but not impossible. He hoped.

Pet heard the soft rustle of his suit as Santo approached her, but continued to look out the window at the city below. Her eyes closed, though, when his big hands settled on her shoulders, and his thumbs began to rub back and forth over her naked skin.

They stood like that for a minute, neither of them speaking, and then Santo brushed the hair away from her neck and bent his head to kiss the sensitive skin there.

Breathing out a sigh, Pet tilted her head to the side, giving him better access as his mouth moved along her throat. The small caress sent shivers through her body and had her nipples tightening with anticipation. She was sufficiently distracted that it wasn't until her gown began to slide down her body that she realized he'd undone the zipper. Santo shifted his hands to her waist then and lifted her out of the dress as it pooled around her feet. He then stepped in front of the overstuffed chair she'd been sitting in earlier before setting her down.

When his hands left her, Pet sensed that he'd stepped back to look at what he'd revealed. She could feel his eyes trailing over her body. The gown hadn't allowed for a bra, and it had been too warm for stockings. She was standing there in nothing but red panties and the red high heels she'd worn with the dress, but waited patiently, allowing her anticipation to build.

"Turn for me." The words were a low rumble that vibrated through her body.

Pet turned slowly to face him, her anticipation growing when she saw that his eyes had gone silver. She stood still and proud as those eyes burned hungrily over her body, but her own eyes were moving over him too, taking in his large shoulders in the tailored suit, and his flat stomach, before dropping to the growing bulge pressing against the front of the dark dress pants.

"Sei bellissima," Santo murmured finally, and then reached out to brush his knuckles over one already erect nipple.

Pet thought that meant she was pretty or beautiful, but didn't bother to ask as he let his hand drop away and stepped closer to lower his head and kiss her. This was a sweet, teasing kiss, his lips feathering over hers and then nipping lightly.

She reached for him, wanting to slip her arms around his neck, pull him close, and deepen the kiss, but he caught her hands to stop her. Holding them captive, he continued to tease, lick, and nip at her lips until she moaned in frustration. Only then did Santo slide his tongue out to thrust it between her parted lips. It slid in for a brief sortie that had her responding eagerly, but then it withdrew again.

Pet opened her eyes in time to watch him sit down in the chair. Using his hold on her hands, he tugged her forward to stand between his legs, and then he suddenly leaned forward to press a kiss to her lower belly. Pet's stomach muscles jumped in response and she bit her lip as Santo's tongue slid out to run along the strip of skin above the line of her panties. But then he leaned back a little, grasped each side of the delicate cloth, and drew the red lace panties down her legs.

Pet stepped out of them when he urged her to, her now shaky legs wobbling a little on the heels, and then she watched him toss the scrap of cloth on her dress. Her head whipped back around, though, when one of his hands began to skim up the inside of her leg. Lifting his head to watch her face, he let his fingers drift up along her thigh until he could press the heel of his palm against her. Pet closed her eyes on a moan as he applied pressure, her hips instinctively pushing forward into the caress. And then she gasped and grabbed for his shoulders as he slid one finger up through her folds to find the moist heat already waiting for him.

"I want you," Santo growled as his finger moved against her flesh, running lightly over and then around the center of her excitement.

"Yes," Pet groaned, and reached down to cover his hand, urging him to move it so she could straddle him on the chair. But he wouldn't allow that and simply continued to caress her, his eyes hooded with desire as he watched her face.

"Santo," she protested on a gasp when his other hand glided to her breast and began to pluck and toy with her nipple, adding to the pleasure swelling within her. "Please."

"Not yet," he growled, and then claimed her other nipple with his mouth.

Panting, Pet shook her head but then cried out and threw her head back, her body stilling when he slid one large finger inside of her, slowly stretching and filling her.

"Santo . . . please," she cried to the ceiling, and then his hand left her breast, tangled in the hair at the back of her head and urged her face down as he let her nipple slip from his lips so that he could kiss her. There was no teasing this time. His tongue thrust into her in rhythm with his finger as it withdrew and plunged back in.

Pet kissed him back almost desperately, her fingers clutching at the shoulders of his suit, her legs trembling, hips thrusting as she rode his hand toward the release she knew waited. But just when Pet was sure she was about to find that release, his hand was suddenly gone from between her legs and his mouth left hers to press soothing kisses to her cheeks and then her neck.

Pet started to open her eyes on a groan of disappointment but ended up gasping instead when he suddenly sat back and caught her at the waist to tug her forward. She ended up straddling his lap on the chair, her legs bent and caught between his legs and the chair on either side. She could feel his erection beneath her, hard, hot, and exposed, and realized he'd unzipped his slacks and drawn himself out at some point.

She tried to rise up then to take him into her, but Santo caught her hips and held her still.

"If you do that now, it will be over," he growled in warning.

Pet hesitated, considering the benefits of prolonging this torturous foreplay versus the instant gratification of having him inside her, and then growled back, "I don't care."

Santo's eyes widened, the silver in his irises swirling, and then his grasp on her hips tightened and he lifted her slightly until she could feel his erection pressing at her opening. But he wasn't completely done tormenting her. With his hands on her hips, he kept her from plunging down on him as she wanted and eased her slowly down, filling her inch by inch.

"Oh, God," Pet groaned as her body fought to accommodate him. "Oh, Santo. Oh, please. Oh . . . oh," she breathed, opening eyes she hadn't realized she'd closed and meeting his gaze once they were completely joined. Panting heavily, she took in his burning eyes and clenched jaw, and suddenly smiled and said, "You feel *so* good."

Santo relinquished one hold on her hip then. Sliding it around her neck, he pulled her head to his for another kiss. Even so, this time Pet was the aggressor, thrusting her own tongue into his mouth as she began to move, raising herself halfway off of him, and then sliding back down. They both groaned as their bodies met again, the sound vibrating through their mouths and bodies and then she broke the kiss and sat up to watch his face as she began to ride him.

It was a short but very satisfying ride. Pet barely rose and lowered herself half a dozen times before the pleasure of release overwhelmed them, and she tumbled into the dark void that seemed to always follow when she was with him.

Pet turned off the hall light in passing and flicked on her bedroom light as she entered, only to pause in the doorway. The bed looked big and empty under the glare of the overhead light. She frowned at it briefly and then turned away, hitting the switch again as she did. Darkness instantly settled around her, but Pet knew her home well and made her way back through the silent apartment to the living room without a problem.

While her bedroom drapes had been closed and the hall had no windows, the blinds at this end of the apartment were always open. With moonlight gliding through the windows, she had no problem seeing, and her feet carried her straight to the chair she'd woken up in half an hour ago.

Santo had been asleep when Pet first woke, slumped against him in the chair. She'd taken a moment to peer down at his handsome face in rest. But hunger and the memory of their dinners in the refrigerator soon had her shifting gingerly to climb off of his lap. Of course, her movement had roused Santo at once, and he'd reached for her, but she'd avoided his hands and gained her feet. Naked and laughing at his grumpy mutters, Pet had fled the living room.

After hitting the bathroom, she'd moved on to her bedroom to find a robe. She'd pulled it on and tied it as she'd retraced her steps to the kitchen. Much to her surprise, Pet had found Santo there, unpacking their meal from the restaurant. His jacket was now missing, his shirtsleeves rolled up, but otherwise his clothes were back in order.

They'd worked together to heat up the food, and then sat at the island to eat. It had been pleasant but a little rushed. Santo had to return to the house for his shift watching Purdy's place and all too soon it had been time for him to go. She'd seen him out, then cleaned up the mess from their meal and headed for bed, only to come out here instead.

Pet pulled her legs up and curled sideways in the chair where Santo had shown her such pleasure. Closing her eyes, she pretended it was his chest she was resting against rather than just the back of the overstuffed chair. She had wanted him to stay, but had known he had to go, and now she missed him.

The acknowledgment made her swallow a sudden lump in her throat. This was exactly what Pet had wanted to avoid, and she didn't know how it had happened, but she was falling for the overgrown immortal.

Pet frowned and looked back out the window, wondering where it had gone wrong. She'd been upset about the date to begin with, knowing there was too much chance for him to tell her about himself and deepen her liking for him. That was why when he'd asked her how she'd known about immortals, she'd revealed her history to him. Pet had thought if she kept talking and kept him from telling her about himself, she could avoid getting attached. But somehow it had backfired.

Santo had listened attentively, asking just the right questions at just the right times. She'd watched the play of emotions cross his face—rage, pain, sympathy, and understanding—but never once had she seen pity there. And then there was the wisdom he'd offered about her mother, Mary. He'd helped her see things from a different perspective. One that she hoped would allow her to let go of her age-old anger and resentment and have a better relationship with the woman who had been her mother for nearly thirty-one years. And then too, she'd noticed when the waiter had approached the table with their meals only to suddenly stop and turn away. Pet had known that Santo had slipped into his mind and sent him off, and she'd appreciated it. Especially since she'd seen the flicker of hunger cross his face when he'd first spotted the food approaching.

And then they'd left the restaurant. Santo's touch and kisses in the parking lot had soothed her bruised soul and quickly turned her thoughts from her past. Pet hadn't thought once about her childhood as they'd driven back, instead her mind had been full of what would happen when they got here.

Of course, it hadn't gone quite as expected. Marguerite and Julius had stayed to visit for a bit. Pet had simply listened as Marguerite had chattered on for half an hour. She'd watched the men's faces, Santo's patient, Julius's full of love, and Pet had felt a yearning to be a part of that. A part of their family.

She was falling for the whole damned bunch of them, but her heart had opened to Santo tonight, and Pet wasn't sure she could close it up again. Sighing, she stood and moved into the kitchen to get a glass out of the cupboard. While the moonlight was bright enough that she could see darker shapes in the darkness, that didn't stretch to the cupboard, but Pet managed to find the right door and then felt around for a glass. Turning with it, she then ran some water into it.

Pet had to go to work again the next day and sitting up all night fretting about something she couldn't change was only going to make her a grumpy girl in the morning. So, water and bed was the plan.

Hopefully, if she lay there long enough she'd sleep, Pet thought grimly as she tipped the glass to her mouth. She stood at the island while she drank, trying not to remember Santo's kisses and caresses here the first time he'd come to her apartment. She then placed the glass into the dishwasher and turned to leave, only to pause as she heard the muffled jingle of keys through her door.

It was probably her neighbor across the hall, Pet thought, and took another step, but then paused again at the sound of her lock turning. Shocked, she stared at the dark entry, unable to make out even where the door was until it started to open.

Bright light splashed in from the hall as the door opened halfway to allow a figure to enter. With that light behind them, all Pet could see was a dark silhouette that was definitely male and also definitely not the apartment manager, Mr. Laurier. This was a tall slender man while Laurier was a potbellied old guy. But who else would have a key to her home?

That worry scattered when the door closed, blocking out the light and leaving the entry a black hole that hid her intruder.

Pet squinted, wishing she could see better, and then suddenly realized that while she couldn't see who had entered anymore now that they were cloaked in the darkness of the entry, she was standing in the moonlit kitchen and they could probably see her. Mouth setting, she started backing up, her gaze sliding along the counter on her right as she tried to judge where her knife block was by using memory and the dark shapes she could make out.

She heard the intruder coming at her bare seconds before he reached her. Pet barely had the time to draw her elbows in close to her body and raise her left hand in front of her so that the boney part of her wrist was pushed out with the fingers back. Even as she automatically did that, she slid her left foot back, shifting her weight and angling herself slightly so that whatever was coming wasn't head-on. Pet had just made herself relax when he was on her.

Some part of her mind recognized that she was witnessing immortal speed as the shape came out of the darkness in a blur, but Pet concentrated on simply moving. Her extended hand swept to the left to block his arm as his fist came at her head. At the same time, her right hand shot out and up at his neck. With fingers extended, she jabbed him in the throat and then shifted and brought her left leg forward for a front kick, bringing up her foot and then stamping it down on his knee.

Knowing she was up against an immortal, Pet had put all her force behind both strikes and wasn't surprised to hear her attacker make a hissing gurgling sound as her fingers hit his throat, and the cracking sound as she hit his knee. Thinking she'd crushed his windpipe and possibly broken his knee and had bought herself at least a few seconds, she dropped back in the original position and made her body relax again as she glanced to the side in search of the knife block.

That was a mistake. She might have done serious damage, but he was immortal and strong and as he stumbled, he swung out wildly with his left arm. Her moment of inattentiveness cost her. He caught her in the midriff, slamming her up against the refrigerator hard. Pet's head flew back, cracking into the metal door, and lights danced briefly in front of her eyes. But her body responded by rote, her hands and feet moving as she'd been taught as she fought for her life, blocking when necessary but striking back at the same time, jabbing at points along his centerline and sweeping his legs or kicking at his knee when the opportunity arose.

Pet had trained at martial arts for years, but even so she knew she was fighting a losing battle. Immortals were too strong, could take too much damage, and healed too quickly for her to win without a weapon. Preferably a bazooka or a machete to take off his damned head, she thought grimly just before he caught her with a blow that spun her around and sent her slamming into the counter. Her hands skidded across the countertop, one of them slamming into solid wood, and her head bounced off the upper cupboard, dazing her briefly.

Giving her head a shake in an effort to clear it, Pet started to push off the wood, intending to turn and prepare to continue defending herself and then realized what she was touching and went still. Pet felt a hand in her hair, pulling, and moved her own hand quickly up the block of wood to the larger knives, managing to grab one just before she was spun around to face her attacker.

She saw the moonlight reflecting off his eyes. Her head was yanked to the side, exposing her throat, and Pet could have sworn she could see his fangs in the darkness as he lunged for her neck. But those fangs never pierced her flesh. Grasping the knife firmly, Pet brought it around and up, jabbing it into the side of his throat with all her might. She didn't hesitate then. Even as her attacker stiffened in shock and pain, she tugged the handle toward herself.

Pet's knives weren't as sharp as they should be, and

slicing through half his neck was harder than she'd expected. It wasn't like cutting butter or a sandwich. It was like trying to push the edge of a knife through a raw roast without any sawing action. Ignoring the blood she could feel spraying warm across her face and chest, Pet ground her teeth and put all of her strength into the effort . . . and damned near slammed the blade into her own face when it finally cut through the last of his flesh and suddenly sprang forward.

She instinctively jerked her head back to avoid the blade, pushing against her attacker as she did, and managed to avoid stabbing herself. Pet also sent her intruder stumbling back. She saw his arms raise, his hands going to his throat, but he didn't go down. She couldn't believe it, but he merely sagged there against the island, holding his throat and making wet, gurgling sounds.

Pet had the terrible feeling that he might be healing even as she stood there looking at him. She didn't know if that was what was happening, or if it was even possible, but her vision was blurring, and she was woozy and nauseous. Afraid she was going to pass out and be at his mercy, Pet didn't stay to find out.

Clutching the knife to her chest, she slid sideways along the counter and then turned and stumbled out of the kitchen and down the hall. Even in the dark, Pet knew she was weaving. She nearly tripped over her own feet several times and kept bumping into the walls, but made it to Parker's room.

Eyes closed against the pain in her head, she fumbled for the doorknob, listening desperately for any sound that the attacker was following, but was afraid she'd never hear it over the agony thundering in her brain. And then the door opened, and she nearly trampled Parker as she staggered into the room lit only by a night-light.

"Aunt Pet?"

Ignoring him, Pet grabbed the edge of the door to help her stay upright and then shifted and leaned her weight on it, slamming it closed.

"Get. Desk chair," she gasped weakly from her position slumped against the door.

"What's happening?" Parker's voice was high and full of fear, but Pet didn't have the strength to answer. She was struggling to stay conscious.

"Jam it . . . under . . . the doorknob," she gasped when he returned dragging a chair with him, and then Pet slid to the side a bit to make room and sank down along the door to the floor, the knife still clutched to her chest.

"Aunt Pet? What happened? Aunt Pet? Are you all right? Aunt Pet!"

She felt Parker shake her shoulder, his voice panicked as he repeated her name, and opened eyes she hadn't realized she'd closed. Pet immediately moaned as light stabbed straight through her eyes and into her brain. Parker had turned on the light. She squinted against the brightness to look at her nephew and try to understand what was happening.

"What do I do?" he cried, tears running down his cheeks.

It took a moment for her to remember how she'd got there and why she hurt, and then Pet managed, "Call home. Santo's there," just before she lost consciousness.

Sixteen

"Mortimer's sending out blood, drugs, and chains with the backup when they come, so it's all here and ready for when you convince Pet to turn."

Santo grunted at that announcement from Bricker as the Enforcer entered the den at the Peters' house, putting his phone away.

"Did he say if he has managed to get enough men together yet, and when they will show up?" Julius asked, considering the cards in his hand.

"He's waiting on two more men. They should be back at the Enforcer house by tomorrow and will fly straight here. Mortimer has a plane and the rest of the men standing by," Bricker said, and then rubbed his stomach and glanced around. "Is anyone hungry?"

"I could eat something," Zanipolo said, leaning on the small card table where Marguerite and Julius were playing. Gaze sliding enviously from the husband to the wife and back, he muttered, "I wish I could play cards. It looks like fun."

"It is," Marguerite said with a smile. "But only because Julius and I cannot read each other so cannot read what cards the other has. Unfortunately, we can both read your mind, Zanipolo, which would make it much less fun for you," she pointed out.

"Yeah," the younger immortal said on a sigh.

"What kind of hungry are you, Zani?" Bricker asked joining them at the table. "Pop and chips hungry? Sandwich hungry? Burgers on the grill hungry?" He paused briefly before pointing out, "They have a gas barbecue out back and it *is* barbecue season."

"A burger sounds good," Zani agreed.

"How about you, Santo? A cheeseburger?"

"No," Santo growled with irritation as he wondered why they were all here. He'd had to leave Pet to take over his watch, but if he'd known they were all going to hang out in the den anyway, he could have left them to it and stayed with Pet to make love to her again. Any one of them could have kept watch in his place. They were here anyway. Why was he?

"You are here because it is your turn to stand watch," Julius said, answering the question in his thoughts.

"And we are here because we want to spend time with you," Marguerite said gently. "We are not likely to see much of you the next year or so if she agrees to be your life mate."

"She will agree," Santo said. He was growing increasingly confident that she would. There had been a couple of times tonight when she'd looked at him with a softness about her face and a yearning in her eyes that made him think she was starting to care for him, perhaps even love him.

"She is," Marguerite murmured, drawing his gaze around. "I read it in her mind tonight after you came back from the restaurant. She has opened her heart to you and yearns to be part of this family."

Santo was just starting to smile when she added, "She thinks it is hopeless, though."

"What?" he asked with alarm. "Why?"

"Because you are immortal, and she is mortal," Julius answered for his wife with a shrug. "She thinks she is just a diversion to you."

"And she believes you will be leaving soon. That you will just walk away and forget her," Marguerite added, and then glanced at him solemnly. "You are going to have to explain life mates to her soon and tell her she is yours."

Too right he'd tell her soon, Santo thought. He'd tell her as soon as he got off his shift. He'd get there, rouse the apartment manager, take control of him, and make the man let him into the building and Pet's apartment. Then he'd creep into her room, take off his clothes, climb into bed with her, and kiss and lick his way down her body until she woke up and then . . . well, honestly they'd probably finish what he'd started, and the talking part—where he told her about life mates and that she was his—would have to wait until they woke up from their post-coital faints.

"Post-coital faints?" Bricker asked, wincing. "Who talks like that?"

"He was not talking," Marguerite pointed out.

"Yeah, but he could have thought something like

after they woke from their post belly-bumping faint or something."

"Belly bumping?"

"Bonestorming?" he suggested.

"Bricker."

"Bumping uglies?"

"If you are through with your recitation of the most disgusting ways to describe making love," Marguerite said dryly.

"Oh, those aren't the most disgusting ones," he assured her.

"You have worse ones?" Zani asked with a grin.

"Oh, yeah," Bricker bragged.

"Let's hear them," Zani said with amusement.

"Dear God," Marguerite muttered, scowling at her cards.

"Let's see." Bricker thought briefly and then started to spout some out just as the phone began to ring. "Launching the meat missile, the tube-snake boogie, thumping thighs, a little bit of lust-and-thrust, splitting the beard, a hot beef injection, paddling up Coochie Creek, dipping the—"

"Santo?"

Bricker stopped abruptly and they all turned toward the doorway with surprise. The phone had rung several times since they'd started staying here, but they'd always ignored it, leaving the answering machine to get it. It had mostly been sales calls, with a handful of calls from family. Hearing that small voice calling out Santo's name from the kitchen answering machine shocked all of them. The sob that followed, though, had Santo on his feet and hurrying out of the den.

"Please be there! Aunt Pet said to call. She said

you'd be there!" Parker's voice was full of panic, desperation, and accusation as he cried those words. They made Santo's heart squeeze with dread as he crossed the hall and hurried into the kitchen with everyone following.

"Please! We need you! I don't know what to do. I—"

"Parker?" Santo barked as he grabbed up the phone.

Broken sobs of fear, worry, and relief were his answer, both in the phone and from the answering machine as it continued to tape the message. The sound seemed to surround Santo and he squeezed the wireless receiver until he heard a crack, and then forced his hand to relax and tried to sound soothing as he said, "It's okay, Parker. I'm here. What's wrong, son?"

"There's someone here. I can hear things breaking in the kitchen. But—"

"Where's Pet?" Santo interrupted grimly. "Where's your aunt?"

"She's here, but she won't wake up, and I don't know what to do. There's so much blood. She's covered in it. She said to call you and then . . . I can't wake her up and I'm scared!"

Santo froze at those words, horror sucking at his brain, but then Marguerite touched his arm and he cleared his throat. All he could manage was, "I'm on my way."

He held the phone out to her, barely waiting for Marguerite to take the wireless receiver before letting go and running for the door.

"Zani, go pick up the phone in the living room," he heard Marguerite order as he hit the hall. Her voice seemed to follow him, but he didn't understand why until she said to Parker, "Sweetheart, everything is going to be fine. Julius, Santo, and I are on our way. Zani is going to stay on the phone with you until we get there, okay? Now where are you?"

"In my bedroom. Aunt Pet had me put a chair under the doorknob, but what if he gets in?" Santo heard the boy ask as he reached the front entry. Jaw tightening, he dragged the door open and rushed out onto the porch but glanced over his shoulder as he did to see his aunt and uncle hard on his heels.

"Then you hide under your bed or in the closet until we get there," Marguerite said.

"But what about Aunt Pet?" Parker asked worriedly as Santo broke into a run at immortal speed.

"She will be fine," Marguerite assured him. "And we will be there soon. Now there is Zani on the other phone, and I am going to lose your call on this phone. But you just talk to Zani. He will tell you what to do. Okay?"

Santo didn't hear the answer this time. He was rounding the hedge to get to the SUV and was too far away from the house to hear the answering machine anymore.

"I am driving," Julius growled, coming up beside him as he reached the driver's door. When Santo opened his mouth to protest, he added, "You are in no shape to drive. Besides, I have the keys. You gave them to me when you got back. I will drive quickly, but get us there in one piece."

After the briefest hesitation, Santo nodded abruptly. Seeing that Marguerite was already opening the front passenger door, the now dead house phone still in her hand, he got in the back seat.

The ride to Pet's apartment building was silent and tense. Julius did drive fast, far above the speed limit. Marguerite even had to control and send away three different policemen in three different cars in the short distance. Still, it was not fast enough for Santo. He wanted to be there *now*. His mind was roaring with fear and dread that Pet was dead. That he'd lost her before he could claim her.

With anxiety shredding his heart, Santo was out of the car before Julius had finished parking. He heard a second door close and Marguerite call out, but didn't slow or look around to verify that she too had got out before Julius was quite parked.

A couple was approaching the door as he ran up to the building. Santo controlled them and made them open the door for him to enter. He'd just crossed the lobby and reached the hall that ran both left and right to the main floor apartments when Marguerite caught his arm and pointed out, "We need the manager to give us a key to get in."

"There is no time," Santo growled, and then movement drew his gaze up the hall to the left and he saw the apartment manager staring at them suspiciously from his door. Santo slid into the man's mind at once, verified that he had his key ring with all the apartment keys on him, and took control, making him wait where he was as Santo moved around his aunt. He spotted Julius hurrying through the door the mortal couple still held open, but ignored him and burst into immortal speed to reach the old man.

Once he had the key, Santo continued up the hall to the stairwell door, sure he could reach Pet's floor faster that way than by elevator. Julius and Marguerite followed, all of them silent until they burst through the door into the hall.

"Do you know which key it is?" Marguerite asked, eyeing the large ring of keys anxiously as they hurried to Pet's door.

"I got it from the manager's mind," Santo growled, and wasn't surprised by her amazed expression. Even he was shocked that he'd thought of it in the state he was in.

The apartment was silent and dark when he opened the door. Santo hit the switch on the wall as he entered, and the entry's overhead light blazed to life, chasing the shadows back almost to the end of the kitchen. The sight that met them, though, brought Santo to a halt. There was a wooden knife block on the floor with its knives scattered everywhere, two chairs knocked over by the dining room table, and the blinds beyond the table were swinging in the night breeze coming in through the open balcony doors. But it was the blood splattered across the cupboards and refrigerator door that held his attention. The words *arterial spray* slid through his head. It was a sign that a major artery had been severed. Without help, it took only twenty seconds to a couple of minutes for a mortal to die from a wound like that. It had taken them ten minutes to get here.

Pet had probably been dead before they'd even got Parker's call.

Santo was vaguely aware of Marguerite slipping past him to start up the hall, and then Julius moved up beside him to put a hand on his shoulder.

"I am sorry, Santo," he offered quietly.

Santo closed his eyes at this verification that he was

right. His Pet was dead, he acknowledged, and then opened his eyes again, and simply stood staring at the kitchen and imagining Pet's last moments and the violence that must have preceded her death.

"Parker? It is Marguerite, honey. Can you move the chair?" The words drifted to them from the hall.

"Marguerite?" There was no missing the relief in the boy's voice.

"Yes, honey. Can you move the chair so I can come in?"

"Yes. But Aunt Pet is in front of the door and won't wake up, and she's too heavy, I can't move her."

"That's okay. Just move the chair, sweetheart and I will slip in and move her," Marguerite said firmly.

They heard a door open and then close, and then silence filled the apartment before Julius asked solemnly, "Do you want to see her?"

Santo closed his eyes, his shoulders sagging briefly, but then he forced them back up, only to have them droop back down again in defeat.

"I—I need a minute," he said huskily.

Julius patted his back and then slid past him to follow the path Marguerite had taken.

Santo waited until he was gone, and then moved silently forward to the end of the island, memories of his time here tearing at his heart. Helping Pet unpack her groceries, teasing her about her cooking, eating their meal from the restaurant . . . He turned to the right then, peering into the living room at the chair by the window. In his mind, he could see Pet standing there in her red dress, staring out over the city at night.

"Santo!"

He turned at that urgent call from his uncle. The hall light was on now and Julius was waving him over.

"She is alive," Julius hissed.

Eyes widening incredulously, Santo broke into a run, rushing past him into the room. Parker stood at the foot of the bed, Mrs. Wiggles in his arms, and fear and worry on his face. Marguerite stood on the far side of the bed, bent forward over Pet who lay in it. And Pet . . . Santo's heart stuttered as he looked at her. There was so much blood. It covered her face and chest. It was hard to believe she yet lived, and he stopped halfway across the room to ask uncertainly, "She is not dead?"

Marguerite straightened with a frown. "No. But—"

"No?" Santo barked, shock and hope warring within him as he thought there was still a chance if he was quick enough. He was at the bed in a heartbeat, his fangs already out and wrist rising to his mouth.

"She's alive," Marguerite assured him on a sigh. "But she appears—Santo, no!" she cried with shock when she glanced up and saw what he was doing. But it was too late. He'd already ripped a six-inch swath of skin from his wrist and crawled across the bed to press the gushing wound to Pet's mouth.

"Santo, she is not—I do not think—the blood does not seem to be hers," Marguerite got out at last.

Santo glanced up with shock. "What?"

"I could not find any wounds on her," she told him quickly. "She has a couple of bumps on her head, but I do not think you need to turn her."

Eyes widening, Santo pulled his wrist away and stared down at Pet with a confusion of emotion.

They were all silent for a moment, and then Julius

approached the bed and peered down at Pet's still face. Letting out a slow breath, he said hopefully, "Maybe she did not get enough."

Pet disabused them all of that notion by suddenly sitting up in bed on a shriek of agony. Her eyes were wide open, revealing the silver specks pouring into their dark depths.

Santo stared, Julius cursed, and Marguerite punched Pet in the face, knocking her out.

"Take Pet down to the SUV, Santo."

When he turned a shocked and angry face to Marguerite, she clucked impatiently and pointed out, "This is an apartment building, Santo. We will have the police at the door if she wakes and starts screaming again, and the next time I do not think she will be subdued as easily. So *move!*"

She didn't wait to see if he followed her order, but hurried to the end of the bed to scoop up Parker and his cat. "Come along, darling. Everything will be fine. We are taking you and your Aunt Pet back to the Caprellis' house where you will be safe and we can take care of her."

"You punched Aunt Pet," Parker pointed out with dismay, his eyes wide.

"Yes, I did, dear, but it was for her own good," Marguerite assured the boy as she carried him out of the room.

Santo watched them go, gave his head a shake, and then bent to pick up Pet.

"Well," Julius said, following him to the door. "On the bright side, you do not have to convince her to turn now."

"No, I just have to beg her forgiveness for doing it

without her permission," he said grimly. "I will be lucky to keep my head."

"I am sure that is not a concern. You thought you were saving her life. The North American Council will understand," Julius assured him.

"It is not the Council I am worried about," Santo said dryly.

"You do not mean Pet?" his uncle asked on a laugh as they started up the hall.

Santo didn't laugh with him. Instead he said, "You did notice the blood everywhere and the bloody butcher knife on the floor of the bedroom, did you not?"

"Well, yes but . . ."

"A mortal could not survive that kind of blood loss," he pointed out. "Yet there was no body."

"You think Pet fought off an *immortal*?" Julius asked with surprise as they stepped out of the hall.

Santo paused at the end of the kitchen and cast one more glance over the mess.

"There is not even a blood trail," he pointed out. "Just arterial spray on the counters and refrigerator, and a small amount of blood on the floor."

"And more on Pet," Julius murmured, looking down at her.

"Yet Marguerite says all she has is a bump or two on the head," Santo growled.

"Damn," Julius breathed with realization. "You are right. That little girl fought off an immortal."

Santo grunted, and peered down at the petite woman in his arms.

"And she took a round out of the bastard too," Julius said now, sounding like a proud papa.

Grunting again, Santo turned and headed for the entry door.

They were silent as they left the apartment and started up the hall toward the elevators where Marguerite and Parker were waiting, and then Julius said, "A word of advice, nephew."

"Sì?" Santo asked.

"Do not anger your little life mate there, if you can help it."

"A bit late for that, uncle," Santo said on a sigh as he stopped a few steps from Marguerite and studied Pet's sleeping face. He suspected she would not be at all happy when she woke up and learned she had been turned without her permission. Santo saw a lot of groveling and making up to do in his future. Despite that, he found a smile slowly taking over his face. He hadn't lost her. Pet was alive.

Seventeen

Pet woke up in a rose garden. At least that's what she thought when she first opened her eyes. She was surrounded by the delicate blooms in every color imaginable. It took her a moment to realize that the flowers were actually in vases that covered every surface of the guest room she and Parker had used the night they'd stayed at her sister's neighbors, the Caprellis'. Alarm immediately claimed her, and Pet scrambled to sit up against the headboard, her eyes skating over the overlarge T-shirt she was wearing as the sheet and duvet that had been covering her slid to her waist.

"You are awake."

Her head turned at that soft rumble, but all Pet saw was a large bouquet of multicolored roses mixed with baby's breath and greens and then Santo's face appeared around the flowers. She blinked at him with confusion until he stood, and then she realized he'd been sitting in a chair next to the bed.

She started to relax, but then frowned and asked, "Am I dying?"

"No, of course not," he said, looking shocked. "Why would you think that?"

Pet gestured at the flowers around the room. "The last time I saw this many flowers was in Grandma Stone's hospital room when she was dying of cancer," she said wryly. "What's happened?"

Santo looked wary. "You do not remember last night?"

"Last night?" she asked with bewilderment.

"What is the last thing you remember?"

Pet searched her mind briefly, and then her eyes widened. "The immortal! We fought in the kitchen, and I cut off his head."

"You did?" Santo asked with surprise.

"Well . . . no," she admitted slowly as her memories became clearer. "I stuck the knife in his neck and pulled it out the front. I guess I half cut through his neck. Not that it seemed to affect him much," she added dryly. "He didn't even go down. Just stood there holding his neck. I suppose I should have finished the job, but I was dizzy and nauseous and I was afraid I was going to pass out, so I stumbled down the hall to Park—where's Parker?" she interrupted herself to ask anxiously. Her gaze shot to Santo's face. "Is he all right? I think I told him to call you, but—"

"Parker is fine. He's at school," Santo assured her before she could get too wound up.

"Oh, good," she breathed. "So I guess he did call you guys?"

"*Sì.* He called, and Marguerite, Julius, and I headed straight over. I took control of your apartment manager to get the keys to get in, and then we brought both of you back here."

"Oh." Pet sighed the word.

"Did you recognize your attacker?" Santo asked after a moment.

Pet pictured the figure in her mind, but that was all she'd really seen—a figure silhouetted in her door, and then a dark shape she'd battled with.

"No," she said finally. "It was a man . . . tall, slim, short hair, I think . . . That's it."

"That fits the description Parker gave of Purdy's cousin," Santo murmured thoughtfully.

"You think it was Dressler?"

He hesitated and then shook his head. "We did not see him leave the house, but the rogue next door is the only one we know of in the area. If he is Dressler, then . . ."

"Huh," Pet muttered, and then scowled. "Well, what's his beef with me then?"

"Who can say with rogues? They are usually at least half insane," Santo said on a sigh.

"Yeah, well, this Dressler sounds like he was wholly insane as a mortal, so I doubt becoming immortal helped that much."

"No." Santo smiled.

They were both silent, and then she glanced around at the flowers. "Are these all for me?"

"*Sì.*" Santo glanced at the blooms.

Pet nodded but then frowned. "You're sure I'm not dying?"

"No," he said firmly. "You are definitely not dying, Pet."

"Okay," she said with a grin. "I mean, my head

doesn't hurt or anything, so I guess I didn't hit it as hard as I thought. I just . . ." Pet glanced around the room again and shrugged. "I just didn't know immortals went so crazy with flowers when a person got a little banged up. I mean . . . who are they all from?"

"Me," he said quietly, bringing her gaze back around his way with surprise.

"All of them?"

"*Sì.*"

She stared at him wide-eyed for a minute and then shifted to her knees and crawled the few feet to the edge of the bed in front of him so that she could slide her arms around his neck. With her mouth just inches from his, she said, "Thank you. They are beautiful," before pressing her lips to his.

Santo was still and unresponsive at first as she brushed her lips over his, but when she slid her tongue out to taste his lips, he groaned and opened his mouth. His hands moved around her body to grasp her behind and he lifted her slightly against him as he took over the kiss. He briefly allowed it to get more heated, but then just as quickly caught her elbows and urged her back as he broke the kiss.

"We have to talk." His voice was a husky growl that had her eyes narrowing at once.

"Well, that's never a good preface to any conversation," she said dryly, and then pulled away to drop back to sit on the bed. "If you're about to give me the whole, *this has been fun but it's done* speech, write it in a letter and stick it."

"What?" he asked with shock.

"I'm sorry, that was unfair," Pet said on a sigh and ran a hand through her hair. "Look, it's okay. I knew you weren't going to be around long, so if you raided Purdy's place while I was sleeping, are done, and ready to go, there's no need for long, drawn-out, kiss-off speeches."

"We have not raided Purdy's place. I am not done, and if I went, I would want to take you with me," he said firmly. "I will never give you a kiss-off speech, Pet. I want to spend my life with you."

"Really?" Pet asked with surprise.

"Really."

"But I'm mortal, and you're—wait," she said suddenly as her common sense kicked in. "We can't—I mean, I like you and all. A lot. I might maybe even be a little bit in lo—" She couldn't get the word out and grimaced. "But it's a bit soon to be talking forever, don't you think?"

Santo hesitated, and then crawled onto the bed next to her, sat with his back against the headboard, and opened his arms.

Pet barely hesitated before climbing into his lap and cuddling up against his chest.

His arms closed around her, and then Santo kissed the top of her head and merely held her for a minute before saying, "Parker's call scared the hell out of me. He was terrified, of course, and he said there was someone banging around in the kitchen, but he also said there was a lot of blood and that you were covered with it." His voice was a husky growl as he told her that, but got even huskier as he added, "When we got there, there was sooo much blood. You were covered with it and there was arterial spray across your kitchen cupboards. I thought you were dying."

"Oh," Pet breathed, and then said, "I'm sorry," although she wasn't sure why.

"You have nothing to apologize for," he assured her. "In fact, it is I who owe you an apology."

She felt her eyebrows rise on her forehead and tilted her head back to look at him. "Why?"

"Because, in my desperation to save you, I did something . . ." His voice trailed off, and then he frowned and pushed her face back down under his chin. He held her like that for a minute, and then said, "For immortals, there is a thing called life mates."

Pet waited, but when he stopped there, she said, "I've heard you use the term before. I think you said my mom was Meng Tian's life mate or something. I'm not sure."

"I might have, I do not recall either, but in any case, she must have been."

"Why?" she asked, leaning back to look up at him again. "What is a life mate? I assumed at the time that it was just another word for wife, but I'm guessing I was wrong?"

Rather than answer, Santo pressed her face back to his chest and rubbed her back briefly. "You see, it is difficult for immortals to be around others."

"Okay," she said quietly, wondering if the fact that this conversation wasn't making sense to her was because of her head wound or because he was doing a piss-poor job of making sense. He seemed to be bouncing all over the place.

"We tend to avoid immortals who are older because they can read us if we do not constantly shield our thoughts."

"Are there any immortals older than you?" she asked dryly.

"Sì," Santo said with exasperation.

"How many?" she asked at once.

"Enough," he said and she could hear the scowl in his voice.

"So you can read each other too, not just mortals?" she asked with interest.

"Sì. Although, an immortal can learn to shield their thoughts. But that gets a bit wearying after a while, and of course, we can read the thoughts of immortals younger than us, which might sound okay, but really . . ."

"Isn't?" she suggested when he paused again.

"Exactly," he agreed.

Pet pulled back again and asked, "Why?"

Santo grimaced. "Because you hear it all. Not just what they want you to hear, or what they think is polite. But everything. And it is sometimes hard to hear what other people think of you. Their worries for you. Their irritation with you. That they think you should stop shaving your head and looking like a wannabe biker. Or that the rings you wear make you look like a pansy."

"Who thought that?" she barked, outraged on his behalf.

Santo waved her question away and pushed her back to his chest. "The point is it can be difficult having access to everyone's thoughts all the time. Again, you have to shield yourself from their minds to avoid hearing them."

"Why aren't they shielding their thoughts?" she asked at once. "Younger immortals, I mean."

"They do. But there are times when the shield drops and thoughts slip out."

"Oh," she said, and then added slowly, "So, immortals avoid other immortals to get some peace of mind."

"*Sì*. But we also avoid mortals because we can hear their thoughts most of the time too."

"So, Marguerite isn't actually reading my mind on purpose?" she asked uncertainly.

"It is hard to say . . . the older you get, the less effort it takes to read minds. I find I have to actually shield myself or I hear it. The easiest way to explain it is like with a radio. When you first learn to read minds, it takes a while to tune in to the right station. But after a while, you automatically tune to the right spot. For me, I am always tuned in unless I deliberately tune out. For Marguerite, she might still have to tune in, or she might not realize she is always tuned in."

"So you avoid mortals to avoid having to tune out," she reasoned quietly.

"*Sì* . . . and because they have a short life span," he added.

Pet rolled her eyes. "Well, there isn't much we can do about that."

"No," he agreed.

Leaning back, she suggested, "So, basically you're saying that immortals are a bunch of lonely losers?"

"Well, I would not put it that way," he protested, looking disgruntled.

When she arched her eyebrows at that, Santo pressed her head back to his chest and sighed. "*Sì*, fine, perhaps we are," he muttered. "But all of that is what makes life mates important. A life mate is someone an immortal can neither read nor control. They can relax with them without the constant need to shield their own thoughts or put up barriers against the other's thoughts. And they cannot control them, so can have a healthy relationship."

Pet took a moment to process that and then suddenly stiffened and jerked away from him again. "But you can't read or control me!"

"*Sì*," he agreed solemnly.

She stared at him for a minute and then asked, "You aren't saying that I'm your . . ."

"Life mate, *sì*," he assured her.

Pet stared at him wide-eyed, not sure what to think of that claim, and then asked slowly, needing the extra verification, "You think I am your life mate?"

"I know you are, *tesoro mio*."

"But—are you sure? I mean, what if you're wrong?"

"I am not wrong. All the symptoms are there."

"What symptoms?" she asked at once.

"I cannot read you. I cannot control you. I am eating food again, real food, not just the steak and raw eggs I occasionally consumed like a supplement. And I have found my passion again. I cannot keep my hands off you. The depth of my desire for you is most telling. And then there is the shared pleasure and the post-coital fainting too. That only happens with life mates."

"Post-coital . . . You mean you faint too when we have sex?" she asked with surprise.

Santo nodded.

"Well, damn skippy, you could have told me that," she said, smacking him in the chest. "I was starting to think there was something wrong with me and I should make an appointment with my doctor."

"There is nothing wrong. It is the shared pleasure.

The mind is not made to accept so much excitement. It is like a sudden surge of power blowing a fuse. The brain has to reset."

"So every time we do it, we're going to faint?" Pet asked with dismay, and thought that could be a bit inconvenient, not to mention limiting. No chance for quickies if you were going to take an enforced nap every time. And no outdoor sex, sneaking into a closet at a party, no . . . damn. It was going to be straight in-your-house-every-time sex from now on.

"We will only faint every time for the next year or two," Santo said soothingly. "After that our brains will adjust to the double pleasure and the fainting will stop."

"Double pleasure," she murmured thoughtfully, and then asked, "Is that what that thing was when I was doing stuff to you, but I was feeling it like it was being done to me?"

"*Sì*. You were experiencing my pleasure along with your own. But it keeps ramping up, my pleasure becomes your pleasure, and yours mine, and then it bounces back and forth between us, growing every time like a snowball rolling downhill, and then . . ." He shrugged.

"And then it hits a wall and explodes and blows your mind. Literally," she added dryly, thinking of his comparing it to a blown fuse. Frowning, she asked, "Is it something to do with the nanos?"

"I would imagine so. From all accounts, it only started after they were introduced for those originally from Atlantis."

Pet shook her head. "Why would the nanos do that? I mean, think about it, if you and I had just had sex when the intruder entered, we'd have been passed out like flakes and he could have killed us both. It's not really a smart survival thing."

"It is for the overall survival of immortals," he said solemnly. "We need life mates to withstand our long lives with any hope of not losing our minds. The double pleasure makes for very good sex between life mates and ensures they have a serious reason, even a need, to work things out that otherwise might break them up. They will not find that pleasure elsewhere. So unless they wish to live a lonely, sexless life, they treat each other with respect and work on their relationship."

"Still, it seems dangerous," Pet murmured. "I don't like the idea of being unconscious and vulnerable every time we do it."

"It is fine," Santo assured her, pressing her face to his chest again. "We just must be careful for the next year or two to only make love when somewhere safe or at home."

"I thought I was safe in my home last night when that guy came in and attacked me," she pointed out grimly. "And what if there is a fire?"

"Pet, no one is ever one hundred percent safe. Look at your mom and dad. They were attacked and killed at home. But," he added, holding her head in place when she would have raised her head to look at him again, "I do have a fortified bunker under my home in Italy, with a secret entrance in the bedroom. We can sleep there for the next year or two if it makes you feel better."

"A fortified bunker?" she asked, leaning back with disbelief.

Santo shrugged. "Everyone was building them during the Cold War. Most are gone now, but I kept mine, updated it over time, and it is well stocked and fireproof, with its own water supply."

"Why would you keep it?" Pet asked with surprise.

"Why destroy it when another Cold War or something similar might come around?" he countered, and pointed out, "I have lived many years. Eventually, all hell will break loose, and when it does, I am prepared."

"Wow." She stared at him. "Do you wear aluminum foil hats too?"

"What?" he asked with confusion.

"Nothing," Pet muttered and cuddled up against him again, but after a moment she asked, "So you really meant it when you said you want to spend your life with me?"

"*Sì.*"

She nodded against his chest, but then asked worriedly, "Does this mean you'll want to turn me?"

Santo stiffened briefly, and then asked, "Would you be all right with that?"

Pet grimaced. "Well, that depends. Is it painful?"

"You will not suffer any pain," he assured her firmly.

"Oh." Pet sighed with relief. She was thinking it would be some terribly agonizing deal. "Well, I guess maybe I could . . . I mean, you know, if things work out and stuff."

"Pet," he said solemnly.

"Yes?"

"I thought you were dying when we got to your apartment last night."

"Yes, you said that."

"Sì," he breathed out, and then took a big breath in and admitted, "But what I did not tell you was that in my desperation to save you, I turned you."

Pet pulled back slowly to stare at him. "What?"

"I turned you, *cara*. There was so much blood when we got there. I thought I only had moments to save you, and I . . . turned you there in Parker's room before Marguerite could tell me that the blood was not yours."

Pet blinked. Thought. Blinked again, and then lunged out of his lap.

Santo immediately began to follow, babbling rapidly in Italian. Every other word seemed to be her name, though. She was quite sure he was apologizing or explaining or begging, she wasn't positive which, but she didn't stop until she'd reached the dresser and the mirror above it. Leaning forward then, Pet stared at the silver flecks floating in her irises.

"Damn," she breathed.

"Pet?"

Stepping back, she whipped the huge T-shirt up and off and then examined herself expectantly in the mirror, only to sag with disappointment.

"What is it, *tesoro mio*?"

Pet sighed and gave a shrug. "I was hoping I'd have grown boobs, and maybe get some more curve on my hips or something."

"Your breasts are perfect," Santo growled, moving up behind her. "And I like your hips."

"Do you?" she asked, meeting his gaze in the mirror, and watching as his hungry gaze slid over her body. The silver in his eyes was growing, she noted, and then shifted her gaze to her own eyes and saw that

they were silvering too. Pet stared at them with fascination for a minute before grinning and saying, "It's
kind of like having an erection on your face, isn't it?
I mean, everyone knows what you're thinking about
when your eyes go silver."

She saw Santo's eyes shift to meet hers in the mirror
and his expression became uncertain.

"You are not angry with me for turning you without
gaining your permission first?"

"No. You thought you were saving me," she said
gently, and then grimaced and added, "Mostly what
I'm feeling is horny. Is that bad?"

Judging by how quickly he was suddenly pressed up
against her from behind, his arms sliding around her
so that his hands could cover and fondle her breasts,
Pet guessed he didn't think so.

"Oh, God, *tesoro mio*, I was so worried you would be
upset with me," he muttered, pressing kisses on the top
of her head as his hands caressed her. "I do not deserve
such a wonderful . . ." he nuzzled her hair aside and
nipped at her ear gently ". . . beautiful . . ." his teeth
scraped down her neck, and then paused so his lips
could gently suck the tender skin ". . . forgiving . . ." he
caught her chin and raised her face to kiss her passion-
ately, and then picked her up in his arms and carried her
back to the bed, whispering, ". . . woman."

Eighteen

Pet woke up splayed on Santo's chest, her head tucked under his chin, her hand curled up in front of her mouth, and his hand resting next to it, flat on his chest. She studied that hand that had given her so much pleasure, and then at the rings on his fingers, and eyed them with curiosity. She'd never really looked at them before. They were all silver or white gold, she wasn't sure, but they looked like old silver. The one on his pinky was smaller than the others. It had a ruby in the middle and writing above and below it that she thought said *Bruni* and *Notte*. The other three rings were much larger. Two had the same image on it, two people on a horse, and *Bruni* and *Notte* on them too, but the third ring had what seemed to be a family crest and some kind of Latin inscription.

Pet stared at them silently for a minute, but then stiffened as she recalled that she was immortal now, they'd just had unprotected sex, and he was very fertile.

"What is it?" Santo asked, apparently awake and feeling her sudden tension.

"We didn't use protection," she said, pushing herself up to peer at him with alarm. "And I'm immortal now, and you're fertile, and it only took one try for Dardi."

"It is fine," he assured her, rubbing his hands up and down her back soothingly. "You are not likely to get pregnant now. The nanos are using up the blood we gave you to finish your turn. They will not allow you to get pregnant, or at least not to stay pregnant. They would see the fetus as a parasite using up blood they need for you, and would not let it grow."

Oh," she murmured, but thought that sounded a little . . .

"When an immortal wishes to have a child, she must take in extra blood to support the child or she will not keep it," he continued. "That is the only form of protection we need, and the only way we have managed to stick to the one-child-every-hundred-years rule."

"What?" Pet gasped. "One child every hundred years?"

"*Sì*. It is to ensure we do not outgrow our food source," he explained.

"You mean people," she said dryly.

Santo shrugged, jostling her a bit on his chest. "It is a fact of life that we need extra blood to survive, *tesoro mio*. But it would be risky to allow our numbers to flourish too high. Aside from outstripping our blood source, there is the increased risk of exposure."

"Right," Pet sighed and laid her head down again, then ran one finger lightly over his rings. "Why do you have two exactly the same?"

"I have three exactly the same. One is on my other

hand." He held up his other hand in front of her face so she could see the third ring. "They are my sons' rings. The only things left of them after their death."

"The ones on your pinkies match too," she pointed out. "They look like women's rings."

"My daughters' rings. I had to have them enlarged to fit."

"And the one on your ring finger?" she asked.

"My family ring, given to me when I became a man," he explained. "The one on my right hand is my father's ring. And the last ring on my right hand belonged to the mother of my children."

"She wasn't a life mate, though," Pet murmured. "And they all died in the same house fire?"

"It was not a house fire," he admitted, his voice rough.

Pet knew he planned to explain, or he wouldn't have admitted the truth. So, she simply waited.

"Back at that time, there was a thing called *vindicta*. It later became vendetta in Italy," he said, his voice a soft rumble.

"If a member of a family was insulted, harmed, or killed, the victim's family would seek revenge on the other family, which would then seek revenge for this new hurt and so on," she said, shifting off of him to sit cross-legged on the bed facing him. When his eyebrows rose slightly at her words, Pet said, "History professor, remember?"

"Oh, *sì*." Santo smiled and then shook his head. "Well, Honorata, the mother of my children, was from the Bruni family, who had a blood feud with the Vilani family. It started quite small, with some sort of perceived insult. I cannot even remember what it was, if I was ever told. But it was not important, a small thing when Honorata and I first decided to have a child together."

"How did you decide to have a child together?" Pet asked with curiosity.

"Her brother, Anselmus, and I were friends, and I was visiting with him in 1035 A.D., shortly before my two thousandth birthday. We got to talking and . . ." Pausing, Santo rubbed a hand over his head. "I was about to turn two thousand years old. I was also without a life mate and in a bad place." He shrugged. "It is not unusual for immortals to go rogue after so long without a life mate. There have even been immortals who broke and went rogue after just three or four centuries, so . . ."

"So making it to two thousand without going rogue was doing well," Pet suggested solemnly.

"*Sì.*" He smiled wryly and nodded. "Anyway, I was no doubt very morose and perhaps even moaning about such things. Honorata overheard and commented that having a child might reinvigorate me and make life more bearable." Santo smiled faintly at the memory, and then admitted, "Of course, Anselmus and I laughed at the suggestion. He said something about children being a woman's answer to everything, and we left to go hunting. But—" He ran his hand over his skull again, the rings on his fingers catching the light, and finally admitted, "But the idea stuck with me. At first it just niggled at me, and then it intrigued me, and then it plagued me, and finally I could not get it out of my head. A child, a son or daughter of my own to love and care for. To raise and protect." He said the words with wonder even now, but then sighed. "It is not the right reason to have a child, but I needed something to live for."

Pet nodded in understanding.

"Finally, I decided to do it," he continued. "But I did not know how to go about it."

"You didn't?" she asked teasingly, her gaze dropping down over his body. "You seem to know what you're doing with me."

"Not the sex, Pet," Santo said with exasperated amusement. "I was not even interested in that part, really, other than that I would have to perform to impregnate a woman. I was more concerned with how to find an immortal woman who would be interested in such a thing. Having a child with a man not her life mate."

"Ah," she murmured.

"After thinking about it for a while, I went back to see Honorata. It had been her suggestion, after all. So I thought perhaps she would have some idea of how I would find a mother for my children."

"And she volunteered?" Pet guessed.

Santo nodded. "Honorata was eight hundred years old herself, and tiring of life. She wanted to have a child. It seems that was why she had suggested it to me in the first place. We were friends, she trusted me, and had hoped I would be interested. Fortunately, while she had been looking, she had not settled on another man while I dallied."

"How long did you dally?" she asked with curiosity.

Santo frowned, apparently doing the math, and then said, "Seventy-two, maybe seventy-three years."

"What?" Pet gasped with amazement. "And she couldn't find a man to get her pregnant in that time?

Not likely! Good Lord. She just wanted you to be her baby-daddy. Maybe she just wanted you, period. I mean, you are a big sexy beau hunk of a guy. She probably had a huge old immortal crush on you and wanted to get you into her bed and this was a way to do it."

Santo waited patiently until she ended her rant, and then arched one eyebrow. "Bohunk? Is that not an insult?"

"No," she assured him solemnly. "*B-o-h-u-n-k* is an insult. I'm calling you beau hunk, spelled *b-e-a-u h-u-n-k*. 'Cause you're my beau, and you're hunky. It's a completely different thing."

"Hmm." He didn't look convinced.

"Anyway," she said, prodding him past that subject. "So she jumped your bones and nine months later a baby was born?"

Santo winced at her words. "She did not jump my bones. We . . . performed sexual congress."

"Oh, wow," Pet breathed. "There's a term that takes the sexy out of sex."

"You are hopeless," Santo said on a chuckle, but caught her hand, tugged her against his chest, and hugged her close as he did. After a moment, though, he said, "And the baby was not born until ten months later. The first time did not take, so a month later we tried again, and nine months after that our twins were born."

"Ah," Pet murmured. "Cataldo and Romaso."

"You remember their names," he said with surprise.

"They're your sons. It's important," she said quietly, and he squeezed her again. Pet hugged him back, and then as they relaxed once more, asked, "So, did having them help? And how did this work? Did you move in together?"

"*Sì*, having them helped a great deal. They were wonderful boys. But, no, we did not move in together. I visited often over the first three years, and then the twins would come and stay with me for a while, and then return to her for a while and so on."

"Shared custody," Pet murmured, running her finger absently over his chest. "Like a divorced couple."

"*Sì*. Only without the acrimonious relationship. We were still good friends. Just without sex."

"Until you decided to have another son with her about a century later," she pointed out. "Dardi?"

"*Sì*. Honorata wanted to try for a little girl," he said solemnly.

"Ah, which explains the twin baby girls after that, Claricia and—" Pausing, she frowned, trying to remember the name.

"Fenicia," Santo said for her. "*Sì*. They were beautiful little babies. So sweet."

"Wait." She tilted her head up to look at him. "Didn't you tell me there was a one-child-every-hundred-years rule or something?"

"*Sì*, but they do not punish you for having twins."

"So, you had two beautiful little girls."

"*Sì*." Santo smiled softly. "While Honorata was the one most interested in having girls, they ended up being my little *tesoros*. I loved them dearly."

"What is a *tesoro*? You call me that sometimes."

"Treasure," he explained, his voice a gentle rumble.

"Oh." She smiled. "Well, I think you're a *tesoro* too."

Pet felt him kiss the top of her head, but he was silent for several minutes before continuing.

"My baby girls were my treasures, but they had very short lives."

"The vendetta," she said quietly. "Tell me."

Santo sighed, his chest moving under her. "Well, as I said the vendetta was just a piddling thing when we first decided to have children together. Nothing even worth noting. It was perhaps a little more troublesome when we tried for girls and had Dardi, but still nothing too bad. No one had really got hurt, it was still mostly insults cast back and forth and—" Frowning, he asked, "Rustling? Reive? I am not sure of the English word."

"Stealing their animals?" Pet asked, just to be sure she was understanding correctly, and when he nodded, said, "Either, I guess."

"Then they would reive back and forth a bit."

"Okay. Not great neighbors then."

"No," he said with a sigh. "But still not so bad either."

"If you say so," she said dubiously.

"It was a different world," he pointed out solemnly.

Pet merely nodded. "So what changed things?"

"Vanittus Vilani," Santo said, loathing in his voice. "He was born the same year as Dardi."

"Vilani was the family the Brunis were feuding with?" she asked, just trying to keep the names straight.

"*Sì*. The original feud was with his father, Vincente Vilani. Vincente met his life mate five years or so before they had Vanittus. He was their first son. Their only son as it turned out."

"Why?"

"Reivers from the Bruni family went on a raid, stole several sheep, and set what they thought was an old abandoned hut on fire as they left."

"But it wasn't abandoned," Pet guessed.

Santo shook his head. "Lady Vilani was inside. She had been to visit friends at court, but was delayed on her return. The sun rose as they reached the edge of Vilani land, and she took shelter in the hut. She kept her maid with her, but there was not room for everyone, and she did not expect any trouble, so sent the other servants and the soldiers on ahead. Old Vilani was sleeping when they arrived. But when darkness fell and Vincente rose, the servants explained their lady's absence. Vicente rode out to meet her as soon as he got word, but arrived only to see the hut ablaze. He ran in to try to save his life mate, and both died."

"We're very flammable," she murmured, remembering him saying that.

"*Sì.* Vicente was running to his death when he went into the burning hut and knew it. That is how important life mates are to us."

Pet merely asked, "So the son . . . ?"

"He blamed Anselmus," Santo said solemnly.

"Did he do it?"

"No. But his men did, and Vanittus held him responsible. I think Anselmus felt responsible too, otherwise he surely would not have been so easily captured."

"Vanittus killed Anselmus?" she asked, and when he nodded, said, "I'm sorry."

Santo grunted sadly, and then sighed and continued, "Honorata wanted revenge. But the vendetta was getting out of hand. Two had died on one side, and one on the other. I tried to reason with her and convince her to let it lie." His mouth tightened. "I thought I had talked her out of it. But I should have known better. The moment I left, she started plotting her revenge."

"I'm guessing something went wrong," Pet murmured solemnly.

"*Sì.* You could say that," he said dryly. "Her men attacked Vanittus and brought him to her so she could kill him personally as Honorata wished. But once they had him at Bruni keep, it turned out she could not read or control him. He was a possible life mate to her."

"No way," Pet gasped with dismay.

"*Sì,*" Santo said grimly.

"What did she do?"

"She could not bring herself to kill him, so let him go," Santo said wearily. "It was the biggest mistake of her life, and ended up causing the deaths of herself and our children."

Pet remained silent. She really didn't know what to say. Fortunately, Santo didn't seem to expect her to say anything and continued.

"I knew none of this until long after it happened. Otherwise, I might have been able to prevent what occurred." His hand lifted to his head, and she knew without tipping her face up that Santo was running it over his scalp. His hand dropped, and he went on, "In the meantime, she came to me about trying again for a girl. Knowing not what had happened and understanding her desire for a female, I agreed and we tried. Nothing came of that attempt, and we tried twice more before she got with child. But the pregnancy was an easy one, and the girls were born beautiful and perfect. Everything seemed fine for the next five years."

"But it wasn't," she said on a sigh.

"No. Nothing was fine. Vanittus was young and—"

"What?" Pet interrupted with a snort. "He was over

one hundred years old if he was born the same year as Dardi."

"Young for an immortal," Santo amended. "So . . . headstrong and arrogant. He was also grieving his parents, lusting after Honorata, and enraged that he was. He was equally enraged that she would have nothing to do with him."

"So, basically Vanittus was screwed up in the head," she suggested, and then added, "Although, I'm a little surprised that she could resist. I find you completely irresistible. And I did try," Pet admitted, although she knew she hadn't tried very hard. Santo was like a drug she couldn't do without. If Vanittus had been like that for Honorata . . .

"If you found out that I was a member of the Brass Circle who killed your parents . . ." He let the question drift off when she scowled.

"That is different," Pet said grimly. "The fire was an accident. They didn't realize anyone was inside. My parents were beheaded and burned to death on purpose."

"And perhaps that is why Vanittus was more willing to have Honorata as life mate. His parents' deaths were not deliberate murders. But Vanittus had Anselmus tortured before having him set on fire," he said solemnly.

"Oh." Pet sighed.

"But I do think Honorata was tempted anyway," Santo said sadly. "I think that is why she was so desperate for another baby. She said it was because she wanted girls. But afterward, I wondered if it was to distract her from her desire for Vanittus."

"What made you think that?" she asked with curiosity.

"Because Vanittus later told me she did lie with him one night. Which just made matters worse for him. He was young enough that he was still sexually active. Or had been. After sex with a life mate, however, no mortal or immortal woman would be able to satisfy him."

"It must have been hard for Honorata too," Pet pointed out.

"*Sì*, but Honorata was eight hundred years old. Wiser, more disciplined, and after six or seven hundred years with no appetite for sex, was used to going without."

They were both silent for a minute, and then Santo said, "The girls were five when it happened."

Pet didn't ask what; she suspected she knew.

"Dardi no longer lived with his mother, but he was visiting her and his sisters. He was not within the walls, though, when Vanittus and his army attacked. There was a small lake a half hour's walk from the castle, and Dardi had taken a young maid there for a moonlight tryst and to feed."

Pet glanced up at him with surprise.

"There were no blood banks then," Santo reminded her gently.

"Oh, right," she murmured, and lowered her head again.

"Dardi saw what was happening on his return. The gates were closed, and Vanittus was being held at bay for the moment. Dardi came looking for me. He had no horse and had to make his way on foot. He ran through the night and well after dawn, arriving at mid-morning." Santo paused, and his voice was grim when he said, "Unfortunately, Romaso and Cataldo were visiting me."

She didn't have to ask why he thought that was unfortunate. If they had not been there, no doubt they would still be alive.

"We gathered the men together and rode out."

"Were your men immortal too?"

"No. Mortal. All the servants and soldiers were mortal."

"And no one ever saw you . . . feeding. Or thought it odd that you slept all day and were up all night?" Pet asked with surprise.

"We were always careful not to be caught feeding," Santo assured her. "Often we rode out to find our hosts in nearby villages rather than feed on those at home. As for the hours we kept, the nobles and wealthy were always considered eccentric layabouts who partied all night and slept all day. Although, that was more true in the Regency period, but even that early in history some nobles were like that."

Pet shook her head, but then asked, "Dardi didn't stay behind? He'd run all night and part of the morning. He must have been exhausted."

"No. Extra blood took care of the exhaustion. It was one of the few times he was allowed to feed in the keep. And he was as determined as the rest of us to save the girls and Honorata."

"Oh," Pet said. She understood what he meant about the extra blood taking care of exhaustion. The body repaired itself while mortals were sleeping, but the nanos repaired immortals all the time. Give immortals enough blood and they probably hardly had to sleep at all.

"Vanittus and his men had breached the walls by the time we arrived at Bruni. Our men attacked from behind, while the boys and I plowed down the center, battling our way inside the wall. What I did not know was that one of his men had caught the maid that had been with Dardi, and learned he was fetching me back. Vanittus had sent for the rest of his men, and those of a nearby ally. He'd ordered them to wait in the woods on the other side of the keep and attack our flank once we arrived and set to.

"I should have expected that," Santo said wearily after a moment. "Had I stopped to think, rather than gathering my men and charging out in a panic, I might have considered the possibility of his doing something like that and planned ahead to—"

"Santo," Pet protested with a frown. "You can't anticipate every move that will be made. What if you had known, and had sent for your own allies, to attack their second army's flank when they attacked you? Perhaps Vanittus would have anticipated that and had a second backup to attack your backup. You can't foresee everything, and this was not your fault."

He looked like he wanted to argue that, but merely rubbed his hand over his head and said in a flat voice, "Unbeknownst to me, by the time we hacked our way up the middle and into the courtyard, most of my men were dead behind us. The few remaining would soon follow. There was a pyre burning in the center of the courtyard. Several men were holding Honorata, and several more held Claricia and Fenicia. Vanittus was demanding Honorata agree to be his life mate."

"They needed several men to hold on to two little five-year-olds?" Pet asked with surprise.

"Immortal children are strong. One male each would not have done," he said quietly.

"Oh," she said with surprise, and wondered how strong she was now.

"I had just stopped to take in the situation in the courtyard when I heard one of my son's cry out. The three of them had been guarding my back, but when I turned . . ."

Pet held her breath and ran her hand soothingly over his chest. She didn't look up. She didn't need to. She'd heard the pain in his voice before it had cracked.

Santo cleared his throat after a minute. "My boys had been beheaded and a wall of men twenty deep stood behind their bodies. As I stood gaping in shock, several men picked up their remains, carried them past me, and threw them on the pyre.

"Honorata let loose a terrible scream," he said sadly. "The men closed in on me then. I fought hard and killed perhaps two dozen, but there were just too many and eventually I was subdued. I thought they would behead me too, and I would join my sons, but instead they dragged me forward, and forced me to kneel by Honorata. She had collapsed to the dirt in front of the pyre.

"Vanittus made his ultimatum to her then. Agree to be his life mate or her daughters and lover would follow her sons onto the pyre. I thought she would do it to save our daughters," Santo said with bewilderment. "They were our daughters . . . And she could always have killed him later to gain her freedom." He shook his head. "But she stood up, spat at Vanittus, and leapt onto the pyre."

Pet swallowed a sudden thickness in her throat and whispered, "Maybe she thought he would leave the rest of you alone if she was dead."

"She was wrong," he said harshly. "Vanittus roared with fury as we watched her burn. She did not make a sound. Our daughters did, though, when Vanittus then turned and ordered them to be thrown on the pyre alive. I struggled to get to them, to stop what was happening, but there were too many men holding me back. I had to watch as they were tossed on the fire and shrieked and strove to get out. One of them did manage to crawl out of the flames, but the soldiers used long poles to push her back in."

Pet sucked in a deep gasp of air and closed her eyes, unable to even imagine what he must have gone through witnessing that.

"I still hear their screams in my sleep and fight to get to them," he whispered.

Pet could feel tears running down her face, but didn't move to wipe them away. She didn't want to do anything to distract Santo. She wanted him to finish this horrible tale as quickly as possible and never have to tell, and relive, it again.

"I fully expected to be thrown on the pyre next, but by then I had stopped fighting. I did not care. I had lost the will to live." A long sigh eased from him, making his chest move under her and then he said, "Instead, I was chained, thrown over a horse, and dragged back to Vilani keep. I was shackled to the wall of his dungeon, and there I remained for the next one hundred and sixty-two years."

"What?" Pet gasped, sitting up abruptly. "But, why—?"

She had meant to ask why no one had rescued him. Why he had been left to rot there for so long, but Santo apparently thought she was asking why Vanittus had bothered to chain him up, and said, "So that he could take out his frustration and fury at losing his life mate on me, and he did so every day at first. He would torture me for hours using one device or another, and then leave me to suffer more agony as the nanos began harvesting blood from organs to keep me alive. The next day he would force-feed me several of his servants so that I would heal, and then he would start again with a different torture."

"This happened every day?" Pet asked, horrified at how he must have suffered.

"For about fifty years or so. Then he grew bored, and the torture was reduced to every other day, and then after another twenty years, only twice a week, and so on."

"No one came to break you out, or help you?" she asked, wondering where his family was while this was happening.

"My family all thought I had died in the fire along with Honorata and our children. There was no one left alive at Bruni to say otherwise. Not servant nor soldier. And they found my ring in the ashes along with Honorata and the children's."

"How did it get there?"

"I am not sure. I presume Vanittus took it off me— either before we left Bruni, or during our first torture session—and had it thrown in the fire to ensure I was thought to be dead."

Pet stared at him silently for a minute, and then finally wiped her eyes and asked, "How did you get away? Did he release you?"

"No. A young maid who worked in the castle and had been force-fed to me a time or two ran away from Vilani. Without his parents there to control him, Vanittus fed on his servants and soldiers. They were all terrified of him. The maid who ran away had a sister at Vilani still. She went to my mother and told her I was there in exchange for the promise that she would save her sister when she went to save me.

"Mother raised an army four times the size of Vilani's forces and led them in the attack. She was inside the castle and cutting his head off before Vanittus knew what hit him and could order me killed. Then she found and set me free."

"Your mother sounds fierce," Pet said solemnly.

"She is a force to be reckoned with when her ire is up," Santo said with a fond smile. "And her ire was up. I am her son."

"Her favorite son?" she suggested with a smile.

"Her oldest son," he said after a hesitation.

Pet shook her head with amusement. She'd known he wouldn't admit it even if he was his mother's favorite, but she let it go and asked, "And the maid's sister? Did your mother keep her safe?"

"She did one better. Mother not only saved the maid's sister, she also settled a great deal of wealth on them both. If there are any descendants of theirs alive today, they are no doubt still wealthy."

They were both silent for a minute, and then Pet muttered, "Well . . . and here I thought I had a tough past."

Santo blinked at her words, and then shook his head with disbelief. "That is all you have to say?"

Pet arched one eyebrow. "Were you hoping for pity?"

"No," he assured her solemnly. "I take that no better than you."

Pet smiled. "That's what I thought."

"But I was hoping for some naked comfort," Santo added softly, the silver in his eyes growing as his gaze slid over her.

"Yeah?" she asked, remembering how his kisses and caresses had seemed to restore her soul in the restaurant parking lot. Shifting, Pet turned slightly and lay down with her head above his groin and her feet toward the top of the bed. Closing her hand gently around his hardening penis, she kissed the tip and then murmured, "I think I can manage that."

Pet had barely taken him into her mouth and paused as it sent a shaft of pleasure through her, when his hand slid up her thigh and between her legs sending another jolt along to join and double the first. They both groaned and then the door opened and Pet glanced around in shock as a stranger burst in, yelling something in Italian.

Squealing, Pet released Santo and dove under the covers.

Nineteen

"Thank God I stopped you when I did."

Santo rolled his eyes at those words as he stomped down the hall behind Christian Notte. He couldn't believe his cousin had just barged in like that, shouting, "Stop! Stop! You cannot do it!" in Italian, and he had no idea why he would, but intended to find out. To that end, he'd quickly dragged on his jeans and ushered his cousin out of the room. He was hoping to get to the bottom of things quickly so that he could return to Pet and finish what they'd started.

"I never would have forgiven myself if she had died because we kept quiet," Christian added.

"What?" Santo caught his cousin's arm and jerked him to a halt. "Kept what quiet?"

Rather than answer, Christian said, "You have to convince Pet to turn before you can sleep with her, cousin. Otherwise you could be dangerous to her."

Santo stiffened at the suggestion. "I would never hurt Pet."

"Not on purpose," Christian allowed. "But you could by accident."

"No." Santo shook his head with certainty. "I would sooner die than harm Pet."

"Of course, but you are not in control while you are asleep," Christian said insistently, and when Santo continued to shake his head firmly, asked, "Would you ever think you could hurt myself or our cousins Raffaele and Marcus?"

"No, of course not," he growled. The idea was ridiculous.

"But you have," Christian told him solemnly. "You have hurt all three of us."

"What?" he asked with alarm.

Christian nodded regretfully. "You do not just scream in your sleep when the nightmares are on you, cousin. You thrash and fight and have even choked each one of us on those rare occasions when we were forced to double up for a night, or we were foolish enough to try to wake you from a night terror."

Santo stared at him with disbelief. "You are joking. I would know if—"

"It's not a joke," Christian hissed. "You shattered my jaw once when I tried to wake you, crushed Raffaele's windpipe another time, and broke Marcus's back."

Santo stared at him with horror. "I did not. I could not—"

"You did," he insisted.

"How could I not know this?" Santo asked with dismay.

"Because we hid it from you," Christian admitted

solemnly. "We piled on the blood and healed quickly. At least Raff and I did. Marcus took longer to heal the time you hurt him, but he just stayed in his room and avoided you until it was done."

Santo gaped at him. "And you never told me?"

"You did not harm us intentionally, and we knew you would suffer guilt if you knew, so we avoided thinking about it so you couldn't read what had happened from our minds," Christian said wearily.

"Dear God." Santo ran one hand over his head, his mind racing.

"I'm sorry," Christian murmured. "But I am glad I got to you in time. I could not believe it when we arrived and mother said you were up here with your life mate. I rushed right up to make sure you did not sleep with her. I realized then that we should have told you before. I mean, Raff, Marcus, and I are immortal and healed quickly, Pet is not. If you crushed her windpipe or broke her back, she could die." He shook his head. "You cannot risk having life mate sex with her, passing out, and then possibly killing her in your sleep, or damaging her so badly she dies before you wake, Santo."

"She is turned."

Both men swung around to see Julius Notte approaching from the stairs. Pausing in front of them, he scowled at Christian. "You should not have kept that from him, son. Pet could have died."

"I know," Christian admitted. "But she has been turned? She is safe?"

"Sì," Julius murmured

"Good, good," Christian said, nodding. "It is all right then."

Santo almost winced at the claim. It didn't seem all right to him.

"I guess we should head downstairs," Christian said now. "Lucian wants to plan our approach for raiding the Purdy house."

"Lucian is here?" Santo asked, startled to learn the head of the North American council had arrived.

"Sì," Christian said. "He wants Dressler as much as the rest of us. Several Enforcers came with us too. Decker, Nicholas and Jo, Mirabeau and Tiny and Eshe all came as well. They want a piece of the bastard too."

Santo nodded. Most of the enforcers mentioned were family or friends of Marguerite on the Argeneau side. He wasn't surprised they had come, but merely turned back toward the bedroom, murmuring, "I must let Pet know I have to go below."

Pet glanced up when the door opened, relaxing when she saw that it was Santo. Raising her eyebrows in question, she asked, "Who was that?"

"My cousin Christian," he said quietly, remaining near the door. "The men are here. We are going to have a meeting to plot our strategy and then raid the Purdy house."

"Oh," Pet said with disappointment. "So, no naked comfort for now?"

She saw something flicker in Santo's eyes and then his expression hardened. "No." He turned back to the door, and then paused and looked back at her sadly as he added, "I am sorry."

Pet stared at the door after he left. There had been

something off about Santo. Something . . . wrong. She didn't know what, but she had a bad feeling. His last words . . . It had sounded as if he didn't expect to see her again.

"Well?"

Santo turned from searching the entry closet at that barked question from Lucian Argeneau, and followed the tall blond man's gaze to Nicholas Argeneau as the Enforcer led his wife, Jo, and his cousin Decker out of the basement near the end of the hall.

Nicholas shook his head. "Dressler was not there."

"But there are a dozen or more bodies downstairs. All drained dry," Decker announced grimly. "And we found Purdy locked in the cold cellar. He's in a bad way. Tiny's bringing him up."

"He'll need medical care," Jo added, even as a man nearly as large as Santo brought a shriveled old man dressed in filthy clothes out of the basement.

"Were you able to learn anything about who the rogue was here?" Lucian asked, eyeing the old man in Tiny's arms with a frown.

"It was Dressler," Nicholas assured him. "But he left four or five days ago after some kind of disturbance. Before Purdy lost consciousness, he managed to tell us that someone came by, causing a fuss, he thought it was Pete somebody. He heard a scuffle, and then later, he wasn't sure how much later, he heard his own car start in the garage and drive away. He hasn't heard anything since, but he's been in and out of consciousness. Dressler took a lot of blood from him and then left him locked up for days down there. Unfortunately, the only thing Purdy keeps in his cold cellar is bottled water, juices, and soda."

"Which is actually good or he'd be dead," Jo pointed out dryly. "Although some food too would have been better."

"We weren't able to get much more than that from him," Decker added as Eshe and Mirabeau came downstairs with Zani from searching that floor. "He's in a bad way, his thoughts disorganized and hard to read after what he's been through. But he was able to tell us that Dressler asked after two other relatives when he first got here. Where they live now, what their circumstances are, that sort of thing. He gave us the names, so at least we have a direction to go in now."

Lucian released a long sigh and nodded. "Mirabeau, you and Tiny take Mr. Purdy to the hospital and stay with him. Hopefully after a little care, his thinking will be clearer and we can learn more from him."

Santo watched the tall woman with fuchsia highlights in her hair lead Tiny to the door. She opened and held it for him to carry the man out, and then followed silently.

"Anything upstairs, Eshe? Zani?" Lucian asked, turning on the pair.

"A cell phone." Zani held up a black phone. "But I'll have to work on it. It's locked. Other than that, I didn't find anything else."

"Me either," Eshe said, shaking her head and making the flame-colored tips of her dark hair move so that it looked on fire.

Lucian's mouth compressed, but he merely said, "Decker, go back to the Caprelli house and call Mortimer. Give him the names and whatever information you got from Purdy on those relatives. We'll need addresses."

When Decker nodded and headed for the door, Lucian glanced around and continued grimly, "We had best start cleaning up. We need to remove the bodies and get them to a hospital morgue so their families aren't left wondering what happened to their loved ones. And we need to . . ." His mouth tightened as he surveyed the room. Santo followed his gaze around the garbage strewn entry and then into the living room, which was in even worse shape.

Santo knew the rest of the main floor was in the same condition. He, Lucian, and Bricker had searched the main floor while the others had dispersed to search the other floors.

"Let's just clean this place up. The poor old bastard does not need to come home to this." As everyone started to move, Lucian turned narrowed eyes Santo's way and barked, "Porch. Now."

Eyebrows rising, Santo ambled calmly to the door, but then paused and gestured for Lucian to lead the way. He'd learned long ago never to turn his back on a threat, and he suspected Lucian was about to threaten him. He wasn't surprised when, once they were on the porch, the man turned his ice-blue eyes with their fringe of silver his way, and went on the attack.

"I do not know how it is done in Italy, but here in North America, when you turn them, you train them. You are not abandoning your life mate and flying home."

"I will not risk hurting her by remaining," Santo responded, expression tightening. "And my position here was voluntary. You are not my boss and cannot order me around."

"But I *am* the head of the North American Council," Lucian responded in a smooth, cold tone. "And as such, anything that happens in North America is under my purview."

"There is no law that says I have to train her," Santo growled. "Only that I have to see that she is trained. I will arrange for her training."

Lucian opened his mouth to speak again, but Santo forestalled him, saying, "Do not bother threatening to kick my ass. You are only about five hundred and seventy years older than me, Lucian. Which means there is very little difference in strength between us."

Lucian's eyes narrowed dangerously and he warned, "I could still have a 3-on-1 done on you, Santo. The agreement made between you, Julius, and myself was that you would allow Greg to counsel you. If you try to fly home, you are breaking that agreement."

Santo shifted grimly, his gaze sliding over the quiet neighborhood, and then he turned back. "I will speak to Greg before I leave. That is all I will promise, though. And I will not go near Pet in the meantime. I will not risk hurting her."

"One more."

Pet grimaced at Marguerite's order as she tore the empty bag of blood away from her mouth and exchanged it for the full one the woman was holding out. Raising the new bag, she thrust it up quickly, relaxing a little when it slid smoothly onto her new fangs and didn't burst and send blood flying everywhere like two of the last six bags had done.

After Santo left, Pet had pulled on the overlarge T-shirt she'd woken up in and headed out of her room. Only to encounter Marguerite in the hall. The woman had turned her around and urged her into the bathroom for a shower, promising to bring her some clothes to wear. Pet's shower had turned into a nice relaxing soak since the bathroom she'd found herself in didn't have a shower. She hadn't minded too much. She'd always loved bubble baths and Mrs. Caprelli had the loveliest smelling vanilla bubble bath. Conscious that it wasn't hers, she'd used it sparingly, but still got a lot of bubbles from it.

Marguerite had popped her head in while she was soaking and set a tank top, shorts, and a belt on the sink counter, and then smiled at her before disappearing again. By the time Pet had managed to drag herself out of the cooling water, she'd been starved. She'd dressed in the clothes provided, relieved to find that while the shorts were large on her, the belt helped with that, and the tank top had at least fit. She wasn't exactly a fashion plate, but didn't look too bad.

Her stomach had been aching with hunger when she'd come below. It was only when she'd found Marguerite and J in the kitchen with several bags of blood in hand that she'd realized what her hunger was really for. Well, Marguerite had been holding the blood. Her big dog, J, had been lying by the table looking lazy.

As Marguerite taught her to feed on the bagged blood, she'd explained that the men were all next door plotting their raid on Purdy's house. Then four bags in, Julius appeared in the kitchen with the announcement that the raid was starting now, and he was to stay with them in case Dressler gave the men the slip and headed this way.

Now Pet was waiting anxiously to hear what happened with the raid.

"You will need to take in a lot of blood for the next little while," Marguerite announced as she deposited the empty bag in the garbage. "Your body is still changing. In fact, you came out of the worst of the turn rather quickly." Marguerite said that as if Pet had done something clever, when she didn't think she'd had anything to do with it at all.

"Perhaps it is because she is so petite," Julius commented as he walked by the kitchen door, no doubt headed for the dining room and the window there. He'd been pacing back and forth, checking the front and then the back since returning to tell them that the raid was on.

"Perhaps," Marguerite allowed. "But I do not recall Livy's turn being especially quick."

When Pet turned raised eyebrows to her, Marguerite explained, "Livy is Olivia. My niece, Jeanne Louise's, stepdaughter. She was turned at four years old."

"Five," Julius corrected as he walked past again, headed for the front.

"Five," Marguerite amended with a faint smile, and then added, "Much smaller than you."

"Mirabeau and Tiny just came out of Purdy's carrying someone," Julius announced from the front of the house. "It looks like an old man. I think it might be Purdy."

"Is he alive, dear?" Marguerite asked what Pet was wondering. Parker would be heartbroken if the old man died. He seemed very attached to the neighbor.

"I believe so," Julius answered. "Tiny is being very gentle with him. They're putting him in one of the rental cars they drove from the airport. Probably taking him to a hospital."

"Probably," Marguerite agreed as she tugged the now empty bag from Pet's mouth. Smiling, she said, "That should be good for now. But you'll need more before bed."

Pet murmured a "thank you," and then glanced toward the doorway as Julius called out, "Decker is coming out now. He is headed this way."

"Then we shall soon find out what is happening," Marguerite said with satisfaction. "That's good."

Pet couldn't agree more.

"Haven't you figured out the damned code for that phone yet, Zani?"

Pet glanced up at Lucian's impatient question, and then glanced to Santo's cousin as he growled, "Do you know how many permutations there are for six number codes? One million," he answered his own question. "And these phones lock up if the wrong number is entered too many times. We have to be careful."

Pet noted Lucian's annoyed expression, and then turned back to the game of checkers she was playing with Marguerite. She'd suggested cards at first, but Marguerite had reminded her she could read her mind and would know what cards she held, so they'd settled

for checkers instead. Pet just had to be sure she didn't
plan her moves ahead to keep it fair.

"Santo seems to be taking a long time picking up
Parker," Pet commented as she watched Marguerite
take two of her game pieces. Santo had returned to the
house after helping to clean up Mr. Purdy's place, taken
one look at her, and turned around to head back out the
door, muttering, "I'll go pick up Parker."

On the surface, it had seemed a really sweet thing
for him to do, and Pet had been grateful for it, especially since she'd forgotten all about the need to pick
up her nephew from school. But Pet had a niggling
worry that his performing the chore had been a handy
excuse for him to avoid her. She told herself that she
was being silly. Santo had told her only hours ago that
she was his life mate and he wanted to spend his life
with her. He'd also said that when he left, he wanted
to take her with him. But for some reason, Pet had a
feeling that everything had suddenly changed on that
subject, and she didn't know why.

"They shall return shortly, I am sure," Marguerite
said, her voice soothing, and then raising her head, she
gave her a sympathetic smile and added, "Everything
will work out fine, Pet. You must not worry."

The woman's expression and words only managed
to worry Pet more. They seemed to acknowledge that
there *was* something wrong, even if the woman thought
it would work. She hesitated briefly, her gaze sliding
over the pieces on the board, but rather than make a
move, she glanced up to Marguerite again, and asked,
"Has something happened that I should know about?"

Marguerite paused, seeming to consider what she
should say, and then sighed and opened her mouth to

answer, only to be forestalled when Bricker suddenly stepped through the front door and said, "Hey, Pet? A taxi just pulled up next door, and a woman who looks just like you got out with a suitcase. I think your sister's home."

Panic hitting her like a freight train, Pet leapt up from the table, catching the checkerboard with her hand and sending it tumbling. She didn't even notice what she'd done or hear the clatter of the pieces crashing all over the floor as she turned in an agitated circle, her mind suddenly spinning out in several directions. The house! Was it clean, or was there evidence that more than just she and Parker had been there the last several days? None of the Enforcers were over there right now, were they? She should go over there. Would Quinn be able to tell there was something different about her? Dear God, she couldn't go over there! Quinn would expect her to be picking up Parker. Oh, damn, she couldn't even go over once Parker and Santo came back. Her car was at her apartment, at least she assumed it was. How was she supposed to explain how she'd picked up Parker without a car? Dammit! What was Quinn doing home? It was only Friday. She wasn't supposed to be back until tomorrow. The conference—

"Calm. Calm."

Pet turned to Marguerite as she finally heard that soothing word repeated.

"There are no Enforcers at your sister's house," Bricker assured her, moving up to the table and eyeing her with concern.

"And we cleaned up before we left and locked up. It's all good," Zani assured her.

"Here." The tall dark beauty named Eshe approached her suddenly and took off the reflective sunglasses that had hidden her eyes since Pet had first watched her enter the house with the other Enforcers after they'd cleaned up Mr. Purdy's place. Turning them, the woman slid the glasses onto Pet's face and stood back to nod her approval. "Now she will not be able to tell there is anything different about you."

Pet gazed into the woman's gorgeous gold and black eyes and whispered, "Thank you."

"Now, just sit down and relax," Marguerite suggested quietly. "You cannot go over there until Santo returns with Parker and then takes you both to collect your car anyway."

"Right," Pet breathed, and settled back in her seat. Noticing then that the others had bent to pick up the board and pieces she'd knocked over, she started to get back up to help, only to be waved back to her seat by Marguerite.

"We have it. Sit."

"You and your sister are twins?"

Pet glanced around at that quiet question, and smiled crookedly at the woman who had spoken. Marguerite had introduced her as Jo Argeneau. The brunette was attractive, only a couple inches taller than her, and wore her brown hair pulled back into a ponytail. Pet knew she was married to the dark-haired Enforcer named Nicholas and thought they made a lovely couple. They'd both broken off the conversation they'd been having about what they'd found at the house in favor of offering her kind smiles as they'd entered, and been introduced.

"Yes," Pet sighed finally, as she realized she was just staring at the woman.

"I have two older sisters, but used to wish I had a twin," Jo told her with a grin. "Is it as awesome as they make it seem in TV shows and movies? Did the two of you switch places and stuff?"

"Never," Pet admitted wryly, knowing the woman was just trying to distract her, but appreciating it. "Quinn and I might look a lot alike, but personality-wise we're polar opposites. Besides, she's always worn her hair shorter while I prefer longer."

The sound of a car made them all turn toward the front window and Bricker moved over to look out before announcing, "Santo's back with Parker. He's driving your Toyota instead of the SUV he left in, though," he added with surprise, before continuing, "He parked it beside the RV, and your car is lower than the hedge. I don't think your sister will see it if she happens to look out."

"Right," Marguerite said, sliding her arm around Pet and urging her toward the door. "So, you just take the keys from Santo, drive Parker next door, and act like everything is normal. Then come back here after."

"But don't tell Parker his mother is home," Eshe suggested, following them. "That way at least one of you will look surprised to see her."

Pet was nodding at that advice when the screen door opened and Santo ushered Parker in. Her gaze moved hungrily over the man before dropping to Parker as he suddenly rushed forward, shrieking, "Aunt Pet! You're okay. Santo said you were, but I was so worried. You were screaming all night and I thought for sure you were dying."

Pet smiled down as her nephew slammed against her, his arms reaching around her upper legs to hug her. She slid her own arms around the boy and hugged him back. "I'm fine, sweetie."

"But, Parker, you understand that when your parents come home, you should not mention anything that happened while they were away, do you not?" Marguerite said now, eyeing the boy with concern.

"Yeah. Santo already warned me that this was secret spy stuff and I can't talk about it. I won't tell," he assured her earnestly as he let his arms drop and stepped back from Pet. He then added, "But he said I could tell her about the night the police came, and our staying here. Right?"

"Yes, that's fine," Marguerite assured him.

Nodding, Parker turned back to Pet and said, "We stopped and got your car on the way back. Santo said you'd want it, and he could pick up the SUV later."

"I see," Pet said, and suspected she did. Having her car meant he didn't have to drive her home. She'd caught the part about Santo's *picking up the SUV later*. He hadn't said he'd ride back with them to get it and wouldn't even have to buzz her, or come up to the apartment to pick up the SUV. Forcing a smile, she said, "Well, let's get going then, shall we?"

"Okay," Parker said easily, and turned to move to the door where Santo still stood. "Thank you for picking me up, Santo. I'll see you later, okay?"

Santo grunted and smiled at the boy, then opened the door for him to head out.

Pet followed Parker, her eyes watching Santo, but

he simply held the door and stared after Parker, not even looking at her, let alone giving her a kiss or soft word.

Swallowing her anger at the obvious rejection, she moved past him and followed her nephew to her car.

"I'm really glad you're feeling better, Aunt Pet. I was worried about you," Parker said solemnly as he did up his seat belt.

Pet smiled, some of the tension leaving her body. "Well, thank you for worrying, but I'm fine," she assured him as she started the engine.

"I like Santo," Parker announced suddenly as she backed onto the road.

"Do you?" Pet asked grimly, and thought she used to like the big jerk too.

"Can we—hey! Why are we going here?" Parker asked with a frown when Pet turned into his own driveway.

"I just wanted to check and be sure everything is okay," Pet lied as she slowed to a stop. "Grab your bag there, kiddo. We'll take it with us in case you think of something you want to bring back to my place."

"Okay." He gathered his school knapsack off the floor where he'd set it, and dragged it up onto his lap before commenting, "I can't wait to get my license someday."

"I can't wait to see your mom teach you how to drive," Pet shot back, striving for normalcy as she turned off the engine and undid her seat belt.

"Dad will probably teach me. He says women make terrible drivers," Parker announced as he opened his door.

"Does he?" Pet asked dryly, as she slid out of the

car. "Well, that's a sexist comment that you should never repeat."

"What's sexist?" Parker asked as they walked toward the front porch.

"Google it," Pet suggested.

"Okay. I—Mom!" Parker cried suddenly, rushing forward, and Pet glanced up to see that her sister had opened the front door and was smiling in greeting.

"Hi, baby!" Quinn hugged her son close and rocked him from side to side briefly, murmuring, "I missed you."

"I missed you too," he said at once. "But everything was normal around here, except that someone tried to break into the house the first night. But the neighbors scared him off, and the police came and we had to stay at the Caprellis' with Marguerite and Julius because Santo was so worried about us that he broke the door, and we couldn't stay in the house without a door. And Marguerite and Julius have a big black dog named J, but he and Mrs. Wiggles liked each other, so—oh, no!" He turned toward Pet with alarm. "I forgot Mrs. Wiggles! She's still at the Caprellis'."

Dropping his book bag, he fled down the porch steps and took off across the yard.

Twenty

"Someone tried to break in?"

Sighing, Pet turned toward her sister and shrugged. "Yeah. The police figured it was some perv. He was looming outside of Parker's bedroom window when I went to check on him. I grabbed Parker and took him into the bathroom with me while I called 911. But like he said, the people staying at the Caprellis' scared him off before the police got here."

"But they broke the door?" Quinn asked with concern, and turned to peer at her new door. "Dear God, I didn't even notice this isn't my door," she said with amazement, and then moved forward to run a hand over the wood. "It looks good, though."

"Yeah. Marguerite felt bad about Santo breaking the original and had it replaced."

"Santo?" Quinn glanced over her shoulder with interest. "Who is he? I thought it was just Marguerite and Julius staying next door."

"He's their nephew. He stopped by for a visit," Pet murmured, moving past her and into the house in the hopes of ending the conversation.

"Yeah?" Quinn asked, following her. "Is he as good-looking as Julius?"

"He's . . ."

Pet was struggling for what to say when her sister suddenly said, "Wait a minute. Mrs. Wiggles? Isn't that Mr. Purdy's cat? Why is Parker going to get Mr. Purdy's cat?"

"Mr. Purdy's in the hospital," Pet said calmly, glad she could say that honestly. "Parker's been looking after Mrs. Wiggles for him."

"Oh, Patrick isn't going to like that," Quinn said with a grimace.

"Patrick doesn't like anything," Pet said with amusement.

"No, he doesn't," her sister agreed with a sigh, and then frowned and asked, "Has he called home at all?"

"Not that I know of," Pet said with a shrug. "But I suppose I could have missed it if he called while I was picking up Parker or something."

It wasn't until Quinn moved to the phone that Pet began to worry about what she might hear. Pet knew Parker had called last night after she'd stumbled into his room. She also knew they'd been letting the answering machine take all calls while they were here. If Parker's call had been recorded . . .

"Delete," Quinn muttered, and pushed the button as a voice started talking about free vacations, all you had to do was buy . . .

Pet stood tensely as Quinn went through call after call, only relaxing when the last message ended.

There had been three calls from their mother, one from a friend suggesting she and Quinn get together for drinks, but the rest of the calls had been sales. If Parker's no doubt frantic call had been recorded, someone had had the good sense to erase it.

"Bastard," Quinn growled as she erased the last sales call. "I can't believe Patrick is being such a jerk. He hasn't answered my calls, called me, or even texted. I have no idea when he's coming back."

"Speaking of which," Pet said now, "I wasn't expecting you back until tomorrow. What happened?"

"Oh. I didn't feel like staying for tonight's dinner. It's usually just a drunk-fest the last night at these conventions anyway, so I switched tomorrow's flight for one this afternoon." Quinn moved to the refrigerator and opened the door. "I was going to text you, but then I thought I'd surprise you instead."

"Cool," Pet murmured, but couldn't help thinking it was a good thing Quinn hadn't "surprised" them that morning, or she'd have walked into a houseful of immortal Enforcers holding a strategy meeting.

"Man. What did you do? Buy out the whole grocery store? Look at all this food," Quinn murmured, bending to peer at the lower shelves. "And it's all healthy food too. Jeez, Pet, what's going on? You don't eat healthy."

What was going on was Pet hadn't bought the food. All she could think was that Marguerite had arranged for the groceries as a thank-you for the use of the house, but she had no idea when the groceries had been bought or by whom. She supposed they'd picked healthy stuff, though, because she'd mentioned that Quinn was a health nut when she'd explained the chocolate chip and bacon cookies to Santo. He must have passed on that tidbit to Marguerite. She couldn't say any of that, though, so lied . . . again.

"I just figured you'd be tired after your trip and not want to bother with shopping," she mumbled.

"Wow. Thank you." Quinn closed the door and rushed over to give her a hug. "Sometimes you're the best!"

"Yeah." Pet relaxed on a laugh and hugged her back. "Sometimes you are too."

Grinning at each other, they separated and Quinn moved to her purse and began to dig through it as she asked, "So. Want to stay for dinner?"

"No. I have some essays to grade," Pet lied, using the excuse she always used in a pinch. Sometimes it was handy being a professor, she thought.

"Are you sure?" Quinn asked, distractedly, frowning into the dark depths of her suitcase-sized shoulder bag. "You have all weekend for that, and we could open a bottle of wine or four."

"If we get started on the wine, I'll be hungover all weekend and won't be able to *read* the essays, let alone grade them. Besides, you could probably use an early night after all that rushing around at the conference," Pet commented, wondering what Quinn was looking for. She got her answer when Quinn pulled out a small set of keys.

"Damn." She eyed them malevolently. "These are Patrick's keys. I used his car Monday to go to work and we switched keys."

"Is that a problem?" Pet asked, eyebrows raising.

"Yes. I was going to check the mailbox. I forgot to do it before I left. It hasn't been picked up since Monday, and you know how small those community mailboxes are. It's probably crammed full of junk mail and nonsense," she said with a sigh.

"Doesn't Patrick have a key to the cluster mailbox on his key ring?" Pet asked with amusement.

Quinn snorted at the suggestion. "You don't think Patrick would do anything as plebian as collect the mail, do you? He's an *oncologist*." She opened her eyes wide and waved her hands around as if to pantomime fanfare as she named her husband's profession.

"And you're a *surgeon*," Pet said, imitating her pantomime.

"Yeah," Quinn mumbled on a sigh.

Pet frowned at her expression. "Are you and Patrick having problems?"

Quinn straightened abruptly and shook her head. "No, it's fine. I'm just tired from the conference."

"Right," Pet murmured, and debated pushing the issue, but then let it go and took advantage of the opening. "Then I should head out and let you get some rest."

Quinn didn't protest, but followed when Pet turned to head out of the kitchen. "Thanks for stepping into the breach and looking after Parker, Pet."

"No problem," she said lightly as she reached the front door and opened it. "You know I love the little twerp."

"Yep." Quinn grinned and hugged her when Pet turned back, then suddenly gasped and stepped back. "You forgot your overnight bag."

"Oh." Pet frowned. Her bag was at the apartment where she'd taken it when she'd taken Parker there Wednesday after school. She couldn't say that, though, so lied. "It's in my trunk."

Quinn blinked at the claim. "Why is it in your trunk? You didn't know I was coming."

"No. But I didn't bring enough clothes, so took the dirty ones home and grabbed fresh clothes on my lunch hour today. By the time I picked up Parker after school and drove here, I guess I'd forgotten all about it."

"Oh." Quinn nodded, appearing to buy the lie. "Handy in the end, I guess. At least you didn't schlepp it in just to have to schlepp it back."

"True." Pet forced a smile and turned away before anything else could come up that she'd have to lie about.

"Thanks again," Quinn called, watching her jog down the porch stairs and head for the driveway.

"Anytime," Pet assured her, and then paused next to her car door when Parker came running around the hedge with Mrs. Wiggles in his arms.

"Are you leaving?" he asked with obvious disappointment when he saw her by the car.

"Your mom's home," she pointed out, bending to hug him and Mrs. Wiggles when he moved to her. Giving him a squeeze, she whispered, "No mention of staying at my place or anything else but the guy at your window. We mostly played video games and watched movies after school all week."

"I remember," he whispered back, but frowned and pointed out. "My stuff is at your place. My television and PlayStation and—"

"Right," Pet breathed, interrupting him, and then shook her head helplessly and said, "I'll get them back here tonight. Tomorrow at the latest," she promised, but wondered how the hell she was supposed to do that without her sister seeing and asking questions.

It looked like she was going to have to stop next door before going home, after all, she thought grimly. While Marguerite had told her to return when she left her sister's, after Santo's behavior, Pet had decided to just go straight home. But she was going to need someone to control Quinn to get Parker's things to him.

"Go on. I'll see you later," Pet said on a sigh, and straightened to watch him walk to his mother with Mrs. Wiggles in his arms. She then got in her car. As she turned the engine over, she wondered if it made her a horrible aunt to encourage the boy to lie like this. But she knew it was for the best. Anything he told Quinn would just lead to questions she couldn't answer. Not that Quinn would want the answers anyway. At least, not if the way she'd refused to acknowledge anything to do with immortals and such from their childhood was any indication.

Forcing a smile, she waved out the window at her sister and Parker, and then backed out of the driveway. Much to her relief, the pair turned and walked into the house as she shifted into Drive. Even so, Pet drove up the block a bit in case Quinn looked out the window after closing the door. She parked on the road several houses down and walked quickly back to the Caprellis', confident the RV would block Quinn's view of her return to the neighbor's house.

"I was afraid you were just going to drive home and not come back here," Marguerite said quietly, opening the screen door as Pet mounted the porch stairs.

Pet shook her head. "We have a small problem. All of Parker's things are at my place. Television, gaming gear, clothes . . ." Grimacing, she pointed out, "I'm going to need help getting his stuff back into the house without my sister noticing and asking questions. I think a little mind control is going to be needed."

"Oh, my, yes," Marguerite agreed, ushering her into the house.

"Where did everyone go?" Pet asked with surprise as she saw that the only people still in the living room were Eshe and Zani. The pair were hovering over the phone they'd found in Mr. Purdy's house.

"Santo and Julius are having a little chat in the kitchen. Lucian went out in the backyard to call his wife, Leigh. Nicholas and Jo went for a walk. Decker went upstairs to take a nap. He came straight from another job and didn't get a chance to rest first," she explained, and then finished, "And Christian and Bricker went out to pick up some dinner for everyone. I hope you like fried chicken, because that's what everyone voted for."

"Yes, but I'm not hungry," Pet murmured, and then hesitated, unsure where to go or what to do. She *wanted* to go talk to Santo, but if he was talking to his uncle . . .

"Sit down and relax, Pet," Marguerite suggested lightly. "Julius and Santo should not be long, and then we can all decide what to do about Parker's things."

Pet nodded and moved to take the chair next to the couch where Eshe and Zani were murmuring and punching numbers into the phone. They both glanced up and smiled at her distractedly, but then returned to what they were doing. Pet watched them silently, but her thoughts were spinning. She was feeling uncertain and confused by Santo's behavior since Christian had crashed in on them earlier. It seemed obvious to her that he'd changed his mind and decided she wasn't his life mate, after all. She just didn't know why, or what she'd done wrong to change his mind.

Unfortunately, Pet didn't handle emotions like uncertainty and anxiety well, and they were quickly turning into anger. Which is why she scowled at Santo when he followed his uncle into the living room a few minutes later. The way Julius shook his head sadly when Marguerite raised her eyebrows at him didn't help any. She got the distinct impression that the "talk" Julius had been having with Santo had been about her, and it hadn't gone the way the other couple had hoped. Which she suspected she would have hoped for too.

The door opened then and Jo and Nicholas entered, holding hands. Noting the loving look they exchanged, Pet felt jealousy rise up within her. Santo had looked at her like that just that morning, and now . . .

Mouth compressing, she stood up abruptly. "I should get going."

Marguerite hesitated, but then glanced to her husband and said, "All of Parker's things are at the apartment, and Pet's concerned about getting them back. If her sister sees, she will undoubtedly have questions."

"Oh, yes," Julius said with a frown, and turned to Santo. "I suppose you will have to accompany her home, Santo, and help her get the items back, and then control her sister and—"

"That's not necessary. I'll figure it out," Pet said grimly, moving toward the door. She'd noted the way Santo had stiffened at the suggestion that he accompany her, and she'd be damned if she—

"Pet." Marguerite touched her arm as she passed, bringing her to a halt. "You cannot do this on your own. And you do not need to. We are your family now, and keeping the events that took place here and the knowledge of immortals and that you yourself are now one falls on all our shoulders. Does it not, Santo?" she added firmly, turning to stare at her nephew.

Santo's jaw clenched, and for a minute, Pet thought he wouldn't agree, but then he sighed and nodded. "I will come with you. I can bring the SUV back that way. And I suppose I had better see to your door too. I should have taken care of it before this."

Pet had glanced to the door as he spoke, her attention drawn by its opening to allow Christian and Bricker to enter. Both men carried several bags of something that smelled heavenly in their arms, but Santo's comment about her door surprised her and managed to briefly dislodge her anger.

Turning to Santo as Lucian entered from the hall to the kitchen, she asked, "What's wrong with my door?"

"I thought to put a dead bolt on it that wouldn't be so easily picked. At least, I presume that's how they got in," he added, and then arched one eyebrow and asked, "Or did they come over the balcony? Your balcony door was open."

Pet stared at him, recalling the jingling sound followed by the scrape of a key in the lock before her door had opened last night. "No," she said finally, "the intruder used a key to get in."

"What?" Marguerite asked with surprise.

"A key," Pet repeated, and scowled as she thought of it. She'd forgotten all about that what with one thing and another. Or perhaps what it meant just hadn't registered. Life had seemed to be moving fast the last couple of days.

"Your attacker had a key?" Santo asked slowly. "Who has a key to your apartment?"

"My sister and Mr. Laurier. But it wasn't either of them," she said with certainty.

"I thought you said you didn't get a good look at the intruder?" Santo reminded her with a frown.

"I didn't get a good look at his face, but I saw his silhouette. Mr. Laurier's an old guy with stooped shoulder and a potbelly. This guy looked young and fit, not . . ." She paused as the image flashed in her mind and she recalled something she hadn't really noticed at the time. "He had a coat on."

"A coat?" Julius asked with surprise.

"It's been rather warm for a coat," Marguerite pointed out.

"Yes," Pet agreed, and then shrugged helplessly. "A long coat that didn't reach quite to the knees. Like . . ."

"A doctor's coat?" Marguerite said, obviously reading her mind when she paused.

"Patrick wears a lab coat to work," Pet said slowly, her thoughts turning in her head. "He puts it on at home before he leaves for work and takes it off and throws it in the wash when he gets back. Quinn says he's obsessive compulsive about it. I think he just likes the world to know he's a doctor. He thinks it gives him a prestige."

"He has your sister's keys?" Marguerite asked sharply, obviously having pulled that thought from her mind. "And you think he was the intruder that night."

That was exactly what she was thinking. In fact, several things that Pet hadn't really thought much of were starting to paint a scenario in her mind that she didn't like.

"But why would he try to break into his own house?" Santo asked, his eyes narrowed. "He has keys."

"There are dead bolts on the front and back doors. I made sure both were bolted before bed that first night. Even if he'd unlocked the door, the barrel bolts would have kept him from opening the door," Pet murmured, her thoughts tracking other things.

"But he could have knocked to get in," Zani said, joining the conversation now. "He didn't have to try to break in."

"Wait a minute." Bricker set the bags of food on the coffee table before turning to peer at her. "Are you thinking it was your brother-in-law who broke into your apartment and attacked you?"

Was she? Pet wondered. Or . . . Biting her lip, she pointed out, "It was Parker's window the intruder was at the first night, and Parker was at my place during the second attack."

When silence fell over the room, she sighed and added, "And Patrick hasn't been answering Quinn's calls." Pet hesitated, but then turned to Nicholas and said, "You guys were talking as you returned from cleaning Mr. Purdy's house and I thought I heard you say he mentioned that someone named Pete came to the house and there was a scuffle?"

She'd asked Nicholas, but both he and Jo nodded.

"Are you sure he wasn't trying to say Peters?" she asked. "That's my sister and her husband's last name. Peters."

No one spoke, and Pet stood silent and still, her stomach churning. If Patrick had gone over first thing in the morning as he'd promised Parker . . . But why didn't he take the cat? And why had he not just come home afterward? Had Dressler turned him? Was he hiding?

"Zani," Lucian barked suddenly. "Show Pet the phone you found in Purdy's house."

The younger immortal stood at once and carried the phone to Pet. He held it out, but she just looked at it silently.

"Could that be your brother-in-law's phone?" Lucian asked grimly.

Pet shrugged helplessly. "I don't know. I've never really noticed what kind of phone Patrick has. Open it up."

"It's locked," Zani reminded her. "We've been trying to figure out the combination."

"Oh, right," she sighed, and stared at the phone. There were six blank circles above the number pad on the screen.

"Try 052209," Pet said quietly, and then explained, "It's their wedding anniversary."

Zani punched in the numbers, but shook his head. "No."

She thought briefly and then suggested, "070611."

As he tapped in the numbers, she added, "Parker's birthday."

"Bingo," Zani said triumphantly as the number page slid away revealing several icons.

Feeling faint, Pet watched as Zani opened the photo icon and flipped quickly through the pics. "There are a lot of pictures here of you and Parker."

"Not me. Quinn," Pet breathed, dropping to sit on the end of the couch. "Oh, God. He's not out of town."

"No," Marguerite agreed quietly.

"Dressler turned him, didn't he?" Pet said unhappily.

There was silence and then Marguerite admitted, "That seems likely."

"But why didn't he just come home and tell us?" Pet asked with frustration. She didn't like her brother-in-law much, but he was Parker's father and her sister's husband. She'd have done what she could to help him.

"Does he know about your past with immortals?" Marguerite asked quietly.

"Probably not," Pet admitted on a sigh. "Quinn won't even talk about it with me, I doubt she'd tell him. I certainly never did. He's such a sarcastic prick, he'd have decided I was crazy and taunted me every time I saw him. *If* I saw him and he didn't just refuse to let me anywhere near Parker and Quinn. *And* if he didn't just have me locked up in an institution."

"I doubt Dressler explained things to him," Nicholas murmured suddenly. "The bastard probably turned him and then took off."

"Probably," Eshe agreed. "But what I want to know is why Dressler took off at all. What spooked him? And how did he leave without you guys seeing him?"

"If he was watching from the house the night we were looking for whoever it was that tried to break in, he might have seen our eyes," Zani pointed out.

Pet glanced at him. She didn't have to ask what he meant. Immortal eyes reflected light in the dark like a cat's.

"And Santo's tearing the door apart would have given away that we are immortals," Bricker pointed out solemnly.

"If so, he could have slipped away while we were all inside talking to the police," Julius said grimly. "In fact, that's the only time there wasn't someone watching the house after we got here."

Pet glanced around at the people in the room. They all looked dour and angry. She knew they were upset about Dressler, but her concern was her family and she asked, "What will Patrick do now?"

Silence reigned for a moment, and Pet noticed that all eyes turned to Lucian. The tall icy eyed man didn't look happy when he said, "We have to find him before we leave."

There were several curses in response to that, but Lucian ignored that and said, "I want a guard on the house twenty-four-seven in case he tries to come back again. We need to protect Pet's sister and nephew."

She frowned at this. "You don't really think he'd hurt Quinn and Parker, do you?" she asked with concern. "I know he attacked me, but maybe that was because he was trying to get to Parker."

"Pet," Marguerite said gently, "if Dressler didn't train him, or explain anything, he basically . . ."

"Your brother-in-law woke up with fangs, hungry for blood, and no one to tell him that he's immortal and not a vampire," Julius finished for her.

"He'll assume he's basically the son of Dracula now," Bricker said on a sigh.

"Elvi did," Marguerite murmured, and when Pet peered at her in question, waved away her interest. "A sister-in-law. She was accidentally turned, had no training, so simply went by what she knew about vampires. Coffins, no crosses or mirrors, etc. It's most likely your brother-in-law reacted the same way."

"Elvi had an incredible support system, though,"

Julius said quietly. "Patrick doesn't. At least, he isn't trying to approach those who would be his support system. He's gone after his son, twice."

Pet was on her feet at once. "Oh, God, I have to warn Quinn."

"I'll come with you," Marguerite said, following her to the door. "You might need help if she takes this poorly."

"She'll take it poorly," Pet predicted as she hurried outside and down the driveway. The minute she hurried around the hedge, she saw that the front door of her sister's house was open. *Home invasion*, she heard Oksana squawking in her head, and burst into a run.

"Wait," Marguerite said sharply, grabbing her arm to stop her as she reached the door and started to push it. But it was too late, the door swung open revealing Quinn on the tile floor at the base of the stairs. Pet spotted the blood on her face, and nothing could have stopped her from rushing in.

She heard Marguerite curse behind her, and glanced back to see her waving toward the Caprelli house. Signaling that there was trouble, Pet supposed, as she knelt by Quinn and checked for a pulse.

"She's alive," Marguerite said grimly as she reached her. "I can hear her heartbeat."

Pet merely nodded. She could hear it now as well, but she'd also found a pulse, strong but too fast. Frowning, she started checking Quinn for an injury, looking for the source of the blood, but . . . "I don't see a wound."

Marguerite immediately leaned over and lifted one of Quinn's eyelids.

Pet gasped when she saw the silver coalescing in her eyes. "He turned her."

A curse drew her gaze up as Lucian led the others into the house. He'd obviously heard her words and now barked, "Bricker, take Quinn back to the Caprelli house, chain her up, and pump her full of the drugs Mortimer sent for Pet. The rest of you start searching the—"

A high-pitched shriek of terror from upstairs brought his words to a halt.

"Parker!" Pet screamed, already on her feet and running for the stairs.

She heard Lucian and Santo both bark at her to stop, but ignored them, and there was a sudden thunder of feet pounding as several of them apparently followed her.

Pet ran flat out up the hall, one part of her brain amazed at how much faster she was now. But then she had reached Parker's room. Halting abruptly inside the door, Pet took in the scene at a glance. Mrs. Wiggles was on the bed, growling and hissing at the man holding Parker. Her nephew's headphones lay on his bed next to one of his schoolbooks. He'd obviously been playing a game and never heard his father attack his mother below and then creep up here after him.

Pet shifted her gaze to the man backing toward the windows with Parker held to his chest. She didn't dare look at her nephew. The confusion and terror on his face would have undone her, so she concentrated on her brother-in-law. Patrick Peters hardly looked like the arrogant asshat she knew and tried to love for her sister's sake. He was filthy, greasy, his clothing torn and bloodstained, and his eyes were wild and desperate.

"Stay back," he cried, sounding panicked.

Forcing herself to remain calm, Pet said, "Let him go, Patrick."

"Just don't come closer!" He'd reached the window and now slid his free hand behind him to feel around for the window latch.

"There's nowhere to go," she said firmly, moving forward.

"Pet," Santo growled behind her.

She ignored him. "Let him go, Patrick. You don't want to do this."

"Shut up, Petronella," Patrick growled. "He's my son."

"Yes, he is," she agreed. "But you need help, Patrick, and these people can help you."

Her brother-in-law snorted at that. "Dressler told me about the kind of help they give. I'll not let them kill me."

"You talked to Dressler?" Lucian barked behind her. "Where is he?"

"Gone," Patrick growled, and then nodding to Santo, he said, "He recognized the big guy there. Said the hunters were running him to ground." His mouth tightened. "He wanted me to go with him, but I couldn't. Not without Quinny and Parker." The words were almost a whine, and then Patrick scowled. "Where is Quinn?"

"Safe," Pet assured him.

"Bring her to me," he demanded.

"Let Parker go and we'll talk about it," Santo said grimly.

Pet heard the click of the window latch. Knowing what was coming, she lunged forward and just managed to grab onto Parker's arm as Patrick pushed it open and started to climb out, dragging the boy with him. Tugging her nephew against her chest, Pet turned toward the people crowded inside the door. When her hair was suddenly caught and yanked backward, Pet gave Parker a push toward the others, and then she was swung around to face Patrick's furious face.

"You always were a stupid bitch," he snarled, tugging her head sideways and exposing her throat. Patrick lunged for her neck, fangs extended, and Pet closed her eyes, sure she was toast, and then she felt someone grab her from behind and pull her free. She heard the hiss of a blade whistling past even as the hands at her waist turned her away and against a hard, wide chest. But Pet heard the sound behind her, remembered it from her childhood. The sound of a head being lopped off, followed by a splat as it hit the floor.

A moan slid from her lips then, and a shudder ran through her. Then she was scooped up and carried from the room. Pet didn't have to open her eyes to know it was Santo carrying her. She recognized his scent and curled against his chest, trying not to imagine the state her brother-in-law was in now.

"Pet?"

"Yes?" Pet's voice was flat, her gaze never leaving her nephew's sleeping face. She hadn't stopped looking at Parker since Santo had carried her here to the Caprellis' home from her sister's house and then walked out. Pet had stared at Parker's face while she'd listened to Marguerite ask Santo how he could do this, followed by her begging him to reconsider, and as she heard him respond that it was for Pet's own good. She'd stared at Parker while she'd listened to Julius yelling at Santo that he was being foolish and needlessly cruel, and as Santo had responded that he wouldn't risk breaking her back or crushing her larynx. And she'd stared at Parker while she'd listened as Christian had tried to convince Santo to at least talk to her and explain that he'd asked his mother to come train her as an immortal rather than risk hurting her while in the throes of his nightmares, and as Santo had responded with a grim, "You just did."

And he was right, of course. Christian and Julius and even Marguerite had all given her the pieces she'd needed to understand, and now she knew why Santo's plans for them had changed. Oddly enough, it didn't make it hurt any less.

"Calandra Notte is here," Marguerite said now, and then asked gently, "Do you want me to stay?"

"No," Pet said quietly, but didn't stand and turn to face Santo's mother even after she heard the bedroom door close.

A moment of silence passed, and then Calandra Notte asked, "Have you nothing to say to me?"

"Your son is an idiot," Pet said in a flat voice.

Another moment of silence passed, and then Calandra Notte barked, "Turn around."

Sighing, Pet stood up and turned, the dead expression she'd worn on her face for the past several hours evaporating as her jaw dropped in shock. Calandra Notte was no taller than herself. No bigger either. After hearing how the woman had saved her son, Pet had imagined her to be an Amazon. Tall and strong and powerful. Not this tiny woman with dark brown hair and a lovely face.

"My son may be acting like an idiot, but he is not one," Calandra Notte announced solemnly. "And while I am small, bullets are tiny, yet also powerful."

When Pet managed to close her mouth, Santo's mother moved to peer down at Parker. "He is still turning."

"Yes," Pet agreed. "So is his mother. She's in the next room."

Calandra nodded. "He will be coming with us. She will not."

Pet glanced at her quickly, but asked, "Is there a reason?"

"Smart girl," Calandra said with a smile of approval. "You think first." Turning back to Parker, she nodded. "From all I have been told, and from what I have read from your mind and hers, Quinn is not likely to take what has happened to her well."

"No. She won't," Pet agreed.

"Parker has to deal with much. Becoming something he did not know existed, his father's attack on him, seeing his father die——"

"He saw?" she asked with alarm.

"It is there in his mind. He saw it over Marguerite's shoulder as she carried him from the room." She raised her gaze to Pet. "The last thing he needs as he adjusts to his new life is a mother who is distraught and unbalanced. He needs love and support, and only those who can offer that should be near him. You can do that."

Pet nodded but asked, "After they've both adjusted, though . . ."

"If Quinn retains her sanity when she comes out of the turn, we shall reunite them after their training," Calandra announced and then turned to face her head on. "Are you ready to be trained so you can be free to teach Santo how stupid he is being?"

When Pet's eyebrows rose, Calandra added, "I have read you, Petronella Stone. You are smart, courageous, and a fighter. You are perfect for my son . . . and he needs you very much."

"I'm ready," Pet said quietly.

Nodding, Calandra turned to stride to the door. "Then bring your nephew and we will go. My plane is waiting at the airport."

Pet bent to pick up Parker, and then turned to watch Calandra walk out of the room. A small smile started tugging at her lips as she followed. By the time she'd reached the hall, it had spread across her face.

Glancing down at Parker's unconscious face, she whispered, "I like her."

Twenty-one

Santo wasn't sure what woke him. Perhaps it was the cold or perhaps the pain grinding through his body, but his eyes snapped open and he found himself staring at the hard-packed dirt he knelt on. He was in a dark, dingy room, lit only by a couple of burning torches. He was chained to a cold, damp stone wall, dressed only in filthy, tattered breeches that left his mangled chest bare and revealed the bloody patchwork of burns, cuts, and gouges that hadn't yet healed. Santo's body simply didn't have the blood needed to manage the feat. But the torture would start again eventually, he knew. It always did. He might be left hours, days, or even months or years to suffer in dread, but his captor always returned and the pain began anew.

He would fight it at first, suffering in silence rather than give them the satisfaction of screaming. But eventually Santo wouldn't be able to bear it so stoically, and he would begin to scream. Once that happened, he wouldn't be able to stop until his throat ruptured and he found himself choking on his own blood.

Sighing, Santo closed his eyes wearily. With each round of torture, a little more of his spirit was worn away and he felt as if he lost another chunk of his soul. He used to search for ways to escape, and then he'd prayed for rescue, now he just longed for death to end his misery.

The screech of the metal cell door opening made Santo stiffen. His waiting was over. Vanittus had returned. He wondered wearily what torture would be visited on him this time. They had used nearly every known torture device on him as far as he could tell. Aside from the more mundane whipping, burning him with a hot poker, and slicing him repeatedly with swords, they'd used the thumbscrew to break every one of his fingers and toes, torn out his tongue with the tongue tearer, broken his body on the wheel, blinded and tormented him with the lead sprinkler, and once even left him in an iron maiden for months.

But the worst had been the rat torture. Santo shuddered at the memory. He had never been bothered much by rats, not until the night they'd chained him to a table, set a small cage with no top or bottom to it on his stomach, placed several large rats inside and then laid a torch over the top opening. Desperate to escape the heat and flames, the rats had taken the only path left to them and had tried to escape by burrowing through his body. Santo had nightmares of the pain as they'd clawed and dug their way into his stomach, their little bodies writhing inside him.

"Santo?"

He shot up in shock at that soft voice, and he stared with amazement at the woman moving through the cell toward him.

"Pet?" he said with bewilderment. She was wearing a short red nightgown made of a sheer material that merely veiled the flesh it covered. His eyes locked on her breasts as she approached, and Santo's mouth immediately filled with saliva as he imagined closing his lips around her tender nipples and tonguing her through the wispy cloth.

When she paused before him, Santo's hungry gaze lifted to her face, and he frowned when he saw that her eyes were full of sorrow as she looked him over. He almost flinched when she raised her hand, but she merely cupped his cheek and whispered, "Oh, my love. What are you doing to yourself?"

Santo blinked in surprise. "I did not do this. It was Vanittus Vilani."

"Vanittus is dead," she said gently. "Your mother killed him. You know that. You saw it. He is not doing this."

Santo frowned with confusion. "But he—"

"Would you really stay here in your past rather than join me in your future?"

When he simply stared at her with confusion, Pet leaned down the little bit necessary to press a gentle kiss to his lips.

Santo sighed at the feel of her mouth on his. When her tongue traced the seam where his lips met, he let them part and groaned as she deepened the kiss. She tasted so damned good it brought tears to his eyes, and he slid his arms around her waist without thinking . . . the chains forgotten. When her arms immediately wrapped around him as well, it was like coming home and he pulled her closer as his mouth ravaged hers, his tongue thrusting and dueling with her smaller one.

"Make love to me, Santo," she moaned by his ear. "I need you to love me. It's been so long."

Growling, he clasped her close, lunged to his feet, and then carried her to the table where they had performed the rat torture. Sitting her there, he stepped between her knees and allowed his hands to roam her body as he claimed her mouth with all the passion he had denied himself these last six weeks, and then a surprised chuckle escaped his lips as she licked one of his feet.

Frowning, Santo pulled back to look at Pet with confusion. She could not be licking his foot, she was sitting before him.

"What is it?" Pet asked, skimming her hands over his chest. It should have hurt, but didn't, and he peered down to see that the wounds and scorching were gone. His skin was unblemished.

"Nothing," he murmured, and then bent his head to kiss her again, only to chuckle against her mouth as she licked his foot again.

"What the—?" Santo muttered, and glanced down the length of his body just in time to see a golden Lab lick his foot for a third time. The dungeon and Pet had been a dream. He was awake now and in bed in his home, he realized, staring blankly at the unknown dog as it sat down and let out a soft woof.

"Good boy, Bear."

Santo sat up abruptly at those soft words and watched the dog pad over to the couch by the fireplace at the opposite end of his large bedroom. His eyes grew round with amazement when a sleepy Pet sat up on the couch to pet the animal.

"Good boy," she repeated, grabbing the golden Lab by the cheeks and rubbing the fur affectionately. "Good Bear."

After giving the dog one last pet, Pet stood and moved toward the bed. The dog immediately followed. When she stopped at the foot of the bed, the dog sat beside her and then peered up at Pet. Seeing that she was looking at Santo, though, he then turned to look at him too.

"This is Bear," Pet announced calmly as Santo took in the red tank top, black leather pants and black knee-high boots she wore. The heels had to be four inches high.

"What are you doing here, Pet?" Santo growled, dragging his eyes back to her face and tugging his sheets and blankets up to his chin.

"Bear is a service dog," Pet said, ignoring his question. Glancing down, she smiled at the Lab and stroked his head. "I had a student once who was an army vet. Well, I've had many of them. But this one had a dog with him at all times. Her name was Jazz. She was beautiful and so well behaved. It turned out she was a service animal."

"Pet," he growled in warning. "You need to get out now."

"No. You need to listen now," she said unperturbed, and kept petting Bear as she continued, "My student suffered from PTSD. Anxiety, depression, and night terrors. Jazz comforted him when he was depressed, soothed him when he was anxious, and woke him up when he had nightmares. He didn't go anywhere without her."

Leaving her hand resting on Bear's head, she turned back to Santo. "Jazz was trained to wake him by jumping on his chest and lying down, becoming a warm, furry blanket of sorts. But that wouldn't do for you. You might kill the poor thing."

Santo winced at the words, and then realizing he was clutching the bedclothes to his chin like a Victorian miss, he scowled and let them lower a bit as she said, "So we trained Bear to lick your feet, and if that didn't work, bark."

"Who is we?" Santo asked, his voice a rough growl.

"Your mother and Parker and I."

His eyebrows flew up on his forehead. "Mother is training *both* of you?"

"Yes. She decided to train Parker because she didn't think he should be around Quinn until we were sure she was handling everything okay," she explained, and then added, "And she had to train me, because you asked her to and wouldn't do it yourself."

There was no accusation in her tone, it was stated as a simple fact, but Santo flinched anyway. Mouth tightening against the guilt assailing him, he asked, "How is Parker?"

"Good. He's adjusted really well, and learned fast. He likes your mother," she added, and then said, "So do I. If you care."

"Of course I care," he growled miserably. "You are my life mate, Pet. I love you. But I cannot sleep with you and risk hurting you."

"And yet I hurt," she said quietly, and then turned on her heel and headed for the door. "Enjoy Bear. He's a good dog."

"Pet, wait!" Throwing the blankets aside, he slid off the bed and hurried after her. "Pet!"

Catching up to her in the hall, he grabbed her arm to swing her around. Pet spun back all right, but Santo suddenly found his feet swept out from under him. He crashed to the floor with a grunt and then stared up at her with amazement.

"That's Wing Chun," Pet said calmly, her gaze sliding over his bare chest and the loose black pajama bottoms he was wearing. "It's what I used with Patrick when he attacked me in my apartment. I couldn't have defeated him with it alone, but it kept me alive long enough to grab a knife that did save me."

She took a step back when Santo started to stand up, and then added, "I like to tell people it was something I took up when I was going through my Everything-Chinese phase as a teenager, but it's not true."

Santo smiled crookedly at that. "Your Everything-Chinese phase?"

"When I insisted on studying everything that was Chinese," she said dryly. "I studied Chinese writing, feng shui, Chinese architecture, wouldn't eat anything but Chinese food, and studied the Chinese zodiac."

His eyebrows rose in surprise. "The Chinese zodiac?"

"Yes, you know, its origins, the twelve animals, and their traits. It was really interesting and very informative. For instance, from my studies I know that I'm the dog, and you're an ass."

Santo blinked. "There is no ass in the Chinese zodiac."

Pet shrugged. "You're still an ass."

For some reason that made him smile, but then

Santo sighed and asked, "What is the truth behind your taking Wing Chun?"

"I started training in it at six when I landed in America as a scared child who had watched her parents and sister murdered. I wanted to feel safe."

Santo nodded. It was what he'd expected. Running a hand wearily over his scalp, he said, "I am sorry, Pet. Truly, I am. But I want to keep you safe too. I cannot risk making love to you, fainting and then possibly harming you in my sleep. I am doing this for *you*."

"Well, that's a lie," she said dryly.

"What?" he asked with amazement.

"That's a lie," she repeated. "You're a liar, and a selfish one at that."

"How can you say that?" Santo demanded, and suddenly furious, he roared, "I have done nothing but try to keep you safe from the beginning."

"I don't need you to keep me safe," Pet roared right back. "And you are a liar because you are not doing this for me, you are doing it for you. So you don't have to feel guilty if you should accidentally hurt me."

While Santo stood blinking at her, Pet added, "And if you really cared about hurting me, you would care that you are putting me in pain by refusing to have me as your life mate, and you would do something to fix that. Because you did this to me. You wooed me and made me fall in love with you, and then you turned me and gave me hope, and then you *walked away*. And let me tell you, while a broken bone might hurt for a few minutes to an hour until the nanos fix it, my heart has hurt every single minute of every day of the last six weeks since you walked away from me."

Pet turned her back on him then and started to walk away.

Santo stood staring after Pet, her words echoing in his ears, and then blurted, "How? How can I fix this?"

Pet paused and turned slowly back. For one moment, she just stared at him, and then she walked back until she was a foot in front of him. "You stop pushing me away. You trust that I might be able to help you out of the dungeon by sharing our dreams, and that Bear will wake you up if you have a nightmare." Smiling wryly, she added, "And apparently if we're making love in our dreams."

Santo smiled crookedly too, but asked, "But what if those two things do not work and I hurt you?"

"Then we sleep in separate rooms and I chain you to the bed when we make love, so you can't hurt me, but we do not give up. We never give up."

Santo let his breath out on a long sigh as he gave up, not on her, but on fighting his need for her. He could not live without Pet. The last six weeks had been hell. He had to try. Santo had waited too long for her to give up now.

"Are you ready to stop being an idiot?" she asked solemnly.

Santo smiled faintly. "I have been an idiot, haven't I?"

"Yes. But you're my idiot," she said, her voice husky. "I love you, Santo."

"I love you too, *tesoro*," he breathed, closing the small space between them and wrapping her in his arms. "I'll try not to be an idiot in future."

Pet shrugged in his embrace. "You can't help it. You're an ass in the Chinese zodiac. It's in your stars."

"There's no ass in the Chinese zodiac," he said with

exasperation, scooping her up and turning to carry her back toward the bedroom.

"Who studied it? You or me?" she asked.

Santo rolled his eyes. "You. Fine. There is an ass, and I am one."

"Yes." Smiling, she cuddled against his chest. "But you are my ass."

Chuckling, he carried her into the bedroom, no longer afraid of making love to her. They had shared dreams, Bear, and if necessary, he had some chains in his garage somewhere. There were worse things than being chained to a bed while your woman made love to you, but Santo didn't think that would be necessary. He was ready to let go of the past . . . especially if he had a future with Pet.

Read on for a sneak peek at one of
Lynsay's classic historical romances!

A LADY IN DISGUISE
(formerly called *The Reluctant Reformer*)

Coming July 2019 with a beautiful new cover!

One

$\mathbf{M}$aggie shifted her feet slightly, trying to ease the ache her cramped position was causing in her legs. The small movement was enough to cause her to bang her knees against the door of the armoire she presently sat in, making it rattle. Wincing at the pain that shot up her leg, Maggie was busily rubbing the appendage when the cupboard door opened and soft candlelight spilled in over her.

"Stop yer banging about, or ye'll be givin' away that ye're in there."

Ceasing her leg-rubbing, Maggie managed an apologetic smile for the scantily clad young woman glaring in at her. "I am sorry," she began in conciliatory tones, then paused and heaved out a breath. She straightened and began to step from the small closet. "No, actually, I am not. Er, Daisy, is it?"

"Maisey," the girl corrected.

"Yes, well . . . Maisey, then," Maggie said. The girl's put-upon air was irritating, as were the wrinkles that Maggie was futilely trying to brush out of her gown. "This is all really rather silly, and quite beyond the information for which I was looking. All I really wanted was to—"

The sound of a rap at the door made Maggie pause, alarmed. The young woman before her stiffened, then steel seemed to enter her eyes and she shoved Maggie firmly back into the armoire. Maggie landed on her behind with a grunt.

"It's too late to be changing yer mind now, milady," she announced, bending to shove Maggie's feet inside the closet before she could regain her balance. "Madame says ye're to watch, and watch you will. Now keep quiet," she said in a hiss. The door pushed closed with a decided snap.

"Damn," Maggie said under her breath, then struggled to a sitting position. The door rattled slightly, nearly covering the sound of a bolt being slid home. Pressing one eye to the crack where the doors did not quite meet, she saw Maisey nod with a grunt of satisfaction and whirl away to answer the door. Frowning, Maggie lifted a hand to push experimentally forward, but the door stayed firmly shut. The girl had locked her in!

Well, this is just bloody beautiful, she thought irritably. *Brilliant! I do tend to get myself into fixes, don't I?*

Not that she could have gotten out now, anyway. Maggie considered herself a thoroughly modern young woman: highly intelligent, independent, and uncaring of what others thought of her—but only to a certain degree. Even she, thoroughly modern as she was, hesitated to deliberately draw the wrath and scorn of the ton down upon herself. Especially when she merely had to sit quietly for a short time to avoid scandal completely. Patience was not one of her natural virtues, but she had been attempting to cultivate it of late. Yes, she would simply have to look at this as a chance to develop herself. A learning experience, one might say.

She had barely finished that thought when it occurred to her that she was crouching down in a small armoire in one of the rooms of the infamous Madame Dubarry's—this was a brothel, for God's sake! What she would learn in this room . . . well, she just shouldn't know yet! What was more, she certainly couldn't write about it.

Good Lord, how had she ended up here? Madame Dubarry, of course. The woman had been slow to warm to the idea of allowing Maggie to interview her and some of her girls for a story for the *Daily Express*. Once the madam had agreed to the undertaking, however, she had become quite enthusiastic. The older woman had bustled Maggie from girl to girl, attending the interviews to be sure each girl told the juiciest stories; then she had rounded off this most peculiar day by offering Maggie refreshment in her own private drawing room. It was while the two had chatted over tea that Madame Dubarry devised this harebrained scheme. Clattering her teacup down in its saucer, she had sat up abruptly, her eyes on the clock in the corner.

"What time is it, nearly seven? Oh, really, this is perfect timing! You *must* witness this, Lady Maggie. Really, you must. You shall thank me for it, I promise."

So saying, the woman had stood quickly, grasped Maggie's hand and dragged her from her chair, then hurried from the room and along the hall. Before Maggie could even collect herself enough to ask what she must see and why, they had reached this chamber. Madame Dubarry shoved her inside, installed her in the cupboard with admonitions to remain quiet and see, then had instructed young Maisey that Maggie was to witness the night's proceedings. She had fled the room nearly as hurriedly as she'd ushered Maggie into it.

Maggie, stunned by the abruptness of the event, had remained still and silent for a moment before the cramping of her muscles had forced her to shift positions and draw the wrath of the shapely young Maisey.

Really, had she been a bit quicker, Maggie might have managed to flee the room before Maisey's customer arrived. Now it appeared she was quite stuck. She sighed irritably and tried to ignore the murmur of voices from the room outside. Maggie had no desire to learn anything more than she'd learned in her interviews. And I won't, she assured herself. I simply will not look through the crack to see who Maisey's client is or what they are doing.

She frowned as the voices drew closer. The man's slightly deeper-timbered voice struck a chord of recognition within her. It sounded amazingly like . . .

Her gaze slid to the crack despite her best intentions, and Maggie drew her breath in with a hiss. Good Lord, it *was* him: Pastor Frances. Her eyes narrowed on the man. She had just been discussing the fact that he was paying her court, and that she thought he might soon propose, when Madame Dubarry had rushed her up here. Maggie was distracted from further thought by an odd question from Maisey.

"Who am I to be tonight, milord? Yer mother?"

Maggie's eyes widened in shocked dismay at that, but they nearly fell out of her head at Frances's answer.

"Nay. Tonight you shall be my dear Margaret."

"Sweet Lady Wentworth, is it?" Maggie was almost too shocked by Frances's presence to notice the irony in the young prostitute's voice. Almost. "The woman who personifies the very word 'lady'? The woman who never sets a foot wrong? Who is discretion herself?"

Maggie couldn't help but wince slightly at the pointy edges of Maisey's words. She also experienced a touch of alarm as she realized that, in her excitement, Madame Dubarry had addressed her by her real name when she'd brought her up to this room.

She forgot all such concerns when Frances answered, "Aye: my sweet Maggie. I have decided to propose to her. I arranged to take her to the Cousins' ball tonight. I shall propose to her afterward. I believe she will accept."

"Oh, 'course she will, guv'nor, a great, strapping man like yerself . . ." There was no missing the irony in Maisey's voice then. At least, Maggie caught it; the gibe seemed to slip right past the rather thin and emaciated Frances.

"Fine. You be Maggie then, and I shall practice on you." There was a moment of critical silence before he murmured, "You had best put something else on."

"Something else?"

"Well, Maggie would never greet me so scantily clad."

"Not even if the house were afire," Maggie agreed

under her breath. Through the crack in the armoire
doors, she took in Maisey's costume—what there was
of it. Sheer silk and red, it covered absolutely nothing.
It was scandalous.

There came a moment of uncertain silence; then
Maisey heaved an impatient sigh. "Fine, then. Ye step
on out into the hall, and I shall change. Give me five
minutes; then knock."

"Why must I wait in the hall?" Frances whined.

"Well, ye want it to be as if ye were proposing to
Lady Wentworth, don't ye? Would she dress in front
of ye? Get on with ye. I'll only be a minute, and this
will seem more real."

Through the crack, Maggie saw Maisey usher Frances out of the room as firmly as she herself had been
shoved into the armoire. The prostitute closed the
door behind the pastor with a snap, then locked it. She
was a no-nonsense type of woman, it seemed.

"Thank God." Maggie burst out of the armoire as
Maisey unbolted it. "I thought I should suffocate in
there. Now get me out of here."

"You know where the door is," came Maisey's un-
concerned response. The young woman was digging
through her clothing, picking up and discarding gown
after gown.

Maggie frowned and glanced from the door to the
girl. "I can hardly exit *that* way. Pastor Frances is out
there."

"Then I guess ye'll just have to get back in the
closet, won't ye?" Maisey snapped, discarding yet another gown.

"Get back in?" Maggie was confused. "Did you not
let me out to slip me from the room?"

"No. I let you out so I could find a gown suitable enough to play the likes of ye. I could hardly dig about with you sitting in my armoire just waiting to be discovered by the pastor, could I? Damn! I ain't got a single dress as drab as the one ye're wearing." Throwing her last garment down in disgust, she glared at her as if the lack of wardrobe were somehow Maggie's fault. Then a catty look came over her face. "You wouldn't consider letting me borrow yer gown fer a bit, would ye?"

"Certainly not," Maggie snapped. She looked desperately around the room. "There simply has to be a way out of here."

"There isn't," the girl assured her. "Unless ye can fly out the window."

"The window!" Maggie hurried over to it, then pushed it open and leaned out. They were on the third floor. The ground was a long way down. She was about to give up on the idea when her gaze dropped to the wall, and she saw a ledge a couple of feet below the window. It was just wide enough that she could walk it—if she were careful.

She would be careful, she decided.

"Here!" Maisey grabbed her arm as Maggie sat on the sill and made to climb out. "What? Are ye daft? Ye'll break yer bones jumpin' from here."

"I am not going to jump," Maggie said with a hiss of exasperation, tugging her arm free. "I am going to walk that ledge to the next room, climb in through the window there, and get away."

Leaning out, Maisey peered down, her eyes widening slightly in surprise. "Oh . . . well." The girl hesitated slightly, her gaze calculating; then she announced, "Well, that would be nice, wouldn't it? Except that Lady X and Lord Hastings are in one of the rooms next door. Yer climbin' in on them would cause the scandal of the decade."

Maggie frowned at the news. Everyone, absolutely everyone, had heard of the infamous Lady X. She was the most famous of Agatha Dubarry's prostitutes, and as such, Maggie had not been allowed to speak to her—though she had caught a glimpse of the woman earlier while interviewing the others. From what she had spied, Lady X was a lovely blonde with a perfect figure, full lips, and deep, mysterious eyes. That was all she had seen.

Actually, it was all anyone ever saw. Her face was always covered by a blazing red mask that never came off. Men paid highly for the privilege of bedding her, each trying to discover her true identity, but no one had yet figured it out. It was rumored that the woman was actually a lady of nobility who worked thusly on the side to help shore her sagging family coffers. While many disputed the idea, claiming that surely no lady would risk being discovered in such an endeavor, there were enough men willing to dig deep into their pockets to try to find out, and Madame Dubarry was doing very well.

Maggie definitely did not need the scandal of walking in on the woman while she was entertaining—especially if she was with Lord Hastings, one of the most distinguished royal councilors.

"Which room are they in?" she asked.

Maisey smiled, the expression of a cat who has cornered a mouse. "Let me use your gown."

Maggie stiffened, then shook her head. "I shall find out for myself," she declared. Sliding her legs over onto the window ledge, she straightened slowly, clinging nervously to the sill as she fought to maintain her balance.

"Have it your way," Maisey said with amusement, watching. "But it does look a long way down. And I know I shouldn't like to make it all the way along that ledge to a window, simply to have to turn back and travel twice the distance to another." At Maggie's obvious uncertainty, Maisey pressed her advantage. "'Tis just a gown. I'll give ye one o' me own to wear in its place. Then I'll send yers back to ye first thing on the morrow—once it's been cleaned."

Maggie took in the hopeful gaze of the prostitute, peered at the ground such a long way down, then shifted cautiously on the ledge. Her mind was made up by her jumping stomach. Cursing under her breath, she maneuvered back into the room and eyed Maisey unhappily. "The other room is empty, isn't it?"

The prostitute nodded solemnly.

"Fine. But—" A tap at the door cut her off, and both women glanced over sharply as the doorknob jiggled.

"Are you ready yet, my dear?" Frances cooed in a sickening tone. Maggie had never heard it from the usually dignified man.

"Oh, keep yer pants on. I'm hurryin' as fast as I can," Maisey snapped, then grimly turned to Maggie. "Well?"

"Oh . . . stuff!" Maggie huffed. She set to work disrobing as quickly as she could. Looking pleased, Maisey began to undress as well. The two worked in virtual silence until Maggie got her gown off. She handed it over, then crossed her arms, rubbing them as goose bumps began to form on her flesh.

"Yer shift and bloomers too."

"What?"

When Maggie stared at her in dismay, the prostitute rolled her eyes. "I'm supposed to be dressed like you. 'Sides, ye'll be caught fer sure if ye run around with those bloomers showing through my gown."

Maggie frowned at the transparent garment the girl held out, then shook her head in misery. "I will be recognized anyway if my face is seen. Oh, why did I leave my veil in Madame Dubarry's drawing room?"

Whirling, Maisey hurried to her armoire, returning a moment later with a plain red silk mask for Maggie to wear. "Here; put this on. With the mask, my clothes, and yer cloak, ye should escape all right."

Maggie glanced at it curiously. "Is this Lady X's mask?"

"Nay. Mine. Lady X's mask is far fancier." When Maggie continued to stare at her questioningly, the prostitute heaved a sigh. "Men like to play all sorts o' games. I . . ." She paused, scowling as there was another tap at the door, louder and more insistent this time.

"Maisey?" Frances sounded somewhat put out.

"Only just another moment, milord," Maisey called back. She shoved the mask at Maggie and said in a hiss, "Take it."

"Are you absolutely sure of this, Johnstone?" James Huttledon, Lord Ramsey, was finally moved to set aside the book he'd been reading when the Bow Street runner was announced. Carefully marking his spot with one of the many cloth bookmarks his aunt had made him over the years, he set the tome on a side table for later and sat up to give his full attention to this troubling turn of events.

"Aye, m'lord. I tried to find you right away. I knew you'd be wanting to know right prompt, but when I went by your town house, they told me you were at your club. By the time I got there, they said you'd left just moments earlier. I had to begin searching—"

"Yes, yes." James waved the explanation away and turned to stare out the window at the tranquil scene of the garden lining the back of his town house library.

Johnstone was silent for a moment, allowing Ramsey his thoughts, then pointed out gently, "It would explain where she's been getting the money to keep up the house and servants."

James jerked his head around to stare ferociously at the man. "You are not thinking that she *works* there?"

Johnstone appeared as surprised at the question as could be. "Well . . . what other business could a lady have at Madame Dubarry's?"

"For God's sake, Johnstone; she is a lady!"

"Aye, well, the claim is that Lady X is a woman of nobility."

James's mouth dropped open, but he quickly snapped it shut. "Good God," he got out between gritted teeth. He turned toward the window again.

They were both silent; then Johnstone said uncertainly, "I left Henries there to keep an eye out while I came to see what ye wanted me to do."

James remained quiet for a moment, then stood abruptly and strode toward the door of his library. "Hethers!" he bellowed as he stepped into the hall, relief filling him when he spied his valet approaching. "My coat. I am going out."

The servant hurriedly fetched his overcoat, hat, and gloves. As the man assisted him in donning them, James added, "Have some things packed. I am leaving tonight."

"Tonight, my lord?"

"Yes. I shall be staying at Ramsey for a while."

"Yes, my lord."

Maggie peered in at the scene taking place in the room next to Maisey's, and she groaned aloud. Her fingers tightening on the cold wall, she leaned her head unhappily against it. After trading clothes, Maisey had helped her climb back out onto this ledge, hissing that Lady X and Lord Hastings were in the room on the left. She had then left and hurried to attend the impatiently pounding Frances.

Relieved to be out of her predicament Maggie had immediately inched along the ledge to the next window, expecting to find the room empty. Unfortunately, what she had not realized was that Maisey had been referring to her own left—which, of course, with Maggie clinging to the wall facing her, was Maggie's right. Which meant Maggie should have gone right. Which she hadn't. She had ended up coming all this way for nothing, for while curtains shrouded the window, making the images beyond blurred and foggy, the figures were discernible enough to see two people engaged in the most energetic round of ride-the-pony it had ever been Maggie's misfortune to witness.

Resignedly Maggie turned to glance back along the ledge, took a deep breath, then began the long return the way she had come, clinging like a limpet to the wall as she did. She was nearly back at Maisey's window before she realized that in her haste, the prostitute had neglected to close it. Grimacing, she paused to the side and peered around its edge.

The time since she had crept from the room seemed like a century to Maggie, and while she knew that it was just the stress of the moment making it seem so, she was surprised to see that she must have indeed been gone for quite a length of time. A good ten minutes must have passed, at least, for Maisey—playing Maggie—had already served Frances a drink by a small table and chairs near the bed. Their refreshments finished and whatever passed for small talk between them done, Frances now knelt at Maisey's feet, the prostitute's hands clasped gently in his, heartfelt longing on the pastor's reverent face.

"I have known you for quite a while now, Margaret," he was saying. "Long enough to know that you are the woman for me. I would be most honored if you would consent to be my bride."

"Yes," Maisey agreed in a bored tone.

The pastor frowned. "Surely she wouldn't just say yes like that?"

"What would she say then?"

"Well, I don't know. Just . . . try to sound a bit more enthusiastic, please."

"Yes," the prostitute cooed.

Frances continued to frown, but apparently decided he wouldn't get much more out of the girl. Shrugging slightly, he surged to his feet, drawing Maisey up and into his arms with the same move. "You shan't be sorry, my dear. I shall make an outstanding husband—I promise you, we shall have a marvelous marriage." This he managed to gasp out between slobbery kisses across Maisey's cheeks and down her neck. When he reached the top of the prim black gown she now wore, he paused and pulled back to leer at her. "I love the proper little things you wear. They hide your lovely body from the eyes of other men, but there is no need to hide from me any longer." With that, he grasped the collar of the gown and ripped downward, rending it nearly to the waist before lifting wide eyes to Maisey's dismayed face. "Oops," he said lightly. "Now you shall have to punish me."

"Ye're damn right I will," the girl snapped irritably. "And ye'll be replacin' that gown, too. It weren't even mine."

"Then I, of course, shall replace it," Frances promised, unperturbed by her obvious anger. Releasing Maisey, he stepped back and began doffing his clothes.

Maggie turned away, unwilling to watch what would follow. She tried judging the space between where she stood and the other side of the window, wondering if she could traverse the distance quickly enough that she might not be detected. She supposed it depended on how distracted the two in the room were. Glancing back inside reluctantly, she saw Frances slide out of his top and drape it across the chair he had just vacated. Glimpsing welts on his back, Maggie paused in dismay, her gaze moving to Maisey to see that the girl had retrieved a long, wide leather belt from the armoire and was now eyeing Frances with a decidedly jaundiced eye. He continued stripping.

Staring in surprise at the pastor as he shed his trousers, Maggie saw that welts covered not just his back, but his buttocks and the rear of his upper thighs as well. She frowned in bewilderment. Was this what Madame Dubarry had wanted her to see? Did Frances really pay Maisey to beat him with a belt? Some of the girls had told her such tales in their interviews: stories of men who enjoyed odd or even unhealthy diversions during their sexual encounters. Was Frances one of those? It would seem so.

She shook her head with a sort of pity combined with disgust. What would make a man turn to such games? Frances had seemed such a normal, well-mannered, polite sort.

The first crack of the belt across Frances's back dragged Maggie from her ponderings to the realization that she was perched on a ledge outside the third-floor window of a brothel, balanced delicately between breaking her neck and being discovered and ruined. This was no time to be reflecting on Frances's foibles. She should just be grateful she had learned of them ere he proposed. Imagine if she had accepted, never knowing that just hours before the man had been whipped, among other things, by one of Madame Dubarry's girls.

Would he have expected her to beat him once they were married? Maggie immediately pushed the question out of her head with a shudder. She had no time for such thoughts. She would *not* be accepting his proposal. On that determined note, she peeked into the room once more, relieved to see that Pastor Frances and Maisey were suitably distracted, then forced herself to move past the window and continue on toward the next window along the wall.

James stood uncomfortably inside the foyer at Madame Dubarry's, waiting impatiently for Johnstone to conclude his whispered conversation with the madam herself. Ramsey had already been approached by, and turned down the offers of, three of the madam's girls, one of whom had offered to do a thing or two that he had never considered trying before. He certainly did not wish to attempt it now, here in this place.

"It's done, yer lordship. Madame says Lady X is with Lord Hastings now, but you can have a go at her next."

"I do not intend to 'have a go at her,' as you so delicately put it," James said in a hiss.

A flicker of irritation crossed Johnstone's face before the runner controlled it. "I didn't think you would, my lord. But I could hardly tell her ye wished to kidnap the girl, now, could I?"

"I am not kidnapping her. I am rescuing her."

"Aye. Well, I'd guess that there is a matter of perspective, ain't it?" Pausing, the man shook his head. "Either way, it'll cost ye deep," he announced, then mentioned a shocking sum.

"You must be joking."

"I never joke about money, m'lord. But ye'll either be paying that amount or waiting till a week from Sunday to lay hands on her. She's booked full for the night—a different man every half hour. Dubarry was willing to bump everyone back, but she wants to be paid well for the trouble. What should I tell her?"

James considered walking out the door, getting in his carriage, and riding to Lady Wentworth's home to await her return there, but his conscience would not let him. He had made a promise to look after the girl—and looking after her did not mean glancing the other way while she bedded some two dozen or so men. Muttering under his breath, he pulled a bag of coins from his pocket and dropped it in the hand the Bow Street runner extended. "How long until Hastings's half hour is up?"

Johnstone's gaze slid to a clock in the hall. "About ten minutes. I'll just give Dubarry the money; then we'll go have a look around and see if there's another way out of here."

"Another way out?"

"Surely you didn't think to march out the front door with her, did ye? Dubarry ain't gonna like that. The girl is her golden goose."

"Ah, yes." James sighed; then he, too, stared at the clock on the wall. Ten minutes.

Maggie grabbed the edge of the window with relief and paused to rest her face on the cold glass. She was sweating. Amazingly enough, she was more terrified of falling than of discovery, which was surprising, because she could remember a time when the prospect of social ruin had been more frightful than anything. But that had been when she could afford such petty concerns as her reputation, before she'd had the burden of so many lives piled on her shoulders.

"Damn you, Gerald, for dying, anyway," she cursed in a whisper, then immediately—if silently—apologized to her poor brother for cussing him so. Gerald had loved life. He had lived every moment of his short time on earth as if it might be his last. He had not complained when he was ordered off to fight Napoléon. And she had no doubt he had given his life in battle with as much passion and as little regret as with which he had lived. It was just too damn bad he'd been forced to leave her in such a fix.

As a woman, Maggie had been unable to inherit her brother's title and estates. While he had bequeathed her his town house in London—a purchase he had made with money from investments before inheriting his title and station from their father—everything else had been entailed to some blasted second or third cousin . . . if they had found the bloody man. The only money Maggie had to live off of was a small investment she had made with her own inheritance from their mother.

It wasn't really that small an investment. In fact, she could have lived quite comfortably off of it for her entire life—had she not been saddled with Gerald's property and servants. It was a town house fit for a duke, with lots of rooms, and nearly as many employees in attendance.

The practical side of Maggie had ordered her to release the servants, close the house, sell it, and move to a small cottage in the country. There she might have lived very comfortably with one or two hired hands. However, sentiment had not allowed her to sell the property. Gerald had loved the place. He had rarely even bothered to ride out to the estate he had inherited with his title, but his town house—there his spirit seemed to linger still. Maggie simply could not part with his home; it was her last link to her now all-but-deceased family. And as for the servants . . . faced with closing up part of the house and releasing a large portion of the staff, Maggie simply hadn't been able to do it. Gerald's staff were hardworking, cheerful individuals. She hadn't been able to look a single one of them in the face and tell him he was no longer wanted.

Such being the case, she had been forced to find a way to support the large staff. The answer had come by chance. While sorting through her brother's papers, Maggie had come across the knowledge that her brother had led a double life. He'd been Lord Gerald Wentworth, Duke of Clarendon, and also G. W. Clark—the adventurist writer who wrote columns for the *Daily Express*. He'd provided articles about the seedier side of London life: rumors, truths, stories of gaming hells, fortunes won and lost, affairs, everything. From Gerald's papers Maggie had learned he had met with Mr. Hartwick—the editor of the *Express*—only once, and then he'd been in disguise to protect his identity. Members of the nobility did not do anything so crass as to work.

She had also learned that he wrote the articles and dispatched them via Banks, his butler. Which was when Maggie'd had her brilliant idea: she would become G. W. Clark. She could do it—and she had for the last three months. She had gone to great lengths to continue her brother's column, going so far as to dress up as a young buck and travel to the seedier sections

of London with Banks in tow to protect her—for all
the good the elderly butler was.

All that was how she had ended up standing here on
the ledge outside the third-floor window of Madame
Dubarry's. The woman had apparently been a great
friend of her brother's, at least according to his notes.
Certainly Madame Dubarry had been privy to the fact
that her brother was G. W. Clark, for when the column
had started up again three weeks after his death, she
had paid a visit to Maggie.

With a sense of adventure equal to Maggie's and
her brother's, Madame Dubarry had arrived on the
Wentworth doorstep dressed as a poor fruitseller. On
being shown in to see Maggie, the madame had announced her true identity, revealed that Gerald had
been G. W. Clark, and complained that some "das-
tardly devil" had stolen his name. Maggie had been
forced to confess herself the culprit. By the end of a
pot of tea, she and Dubarry had struck up an unlikely
friendship. They had been in cahoots ever since—
although the woman had only recently given in to the
interviews of her employees.

Amazing, Maggie thought. For the first time, she
considered that perhaps Agatha Dubarry had been
right when she had suggested Maggie come dressed as
a man to this night's activities. Maggie had shrugged
away the suggestion, thinking that the madam's girls
might be more forthcoming with information while
talking to another of their gender. It had worked, too.
She had been introduced as the sister of G. W. Clark,
sent to interview them, and the girls had responded
very easily. And no one had known her true identity,
not until Agatha had slipped up in Maisey's room.

Maggie found she wasn't too concerned about Maisey, though. She had no doubt that Madame Dubarry could keep the girl quiet. Her real problem would be if some member of the *ton* saw her; then she would be recognized and ruined for sure. There was no way Agatha Dubarry could keep all of London quiet.

Yes, now would indeed be a beneficial time to be disguised as a man. And, she thought as she glanced down nervously past her long skirts, such a disguise would also have made climbing about on ledges more seemly.

"Lord Ramsey, we'll have to sneak her down the back stairs and smuggle her through the kitchen."

James nodded at Johnstone's suggestion. After he'd made a brief but thorough examination of the brothel, it indeed seemed the best bet to get the girl out. "Go have my driver move the carriage to the alley," he instructed, his eyes on the clock in the hall. "Hastings's time is up. I'll go see if he has left yet."

Nodding, Johnstone hurried away toward the front door, and James started upstairs. He was at the top of the steps before he realized that the runner hadn't told him in which room Lady X was supposed to be. He was about to return downstairs to ask Madame Dubarry when he changed his mind. He would recognize Hastings. Everyone knew of Hastings, if not in person, then by reputation. He was second only to the crown in power. Whichever room Hastings exited, James would enter.

He had just come to that conclusion when the thud of

a door made him turn back around on the landing. A glance up the hall showed Hastings strolling jauntily toward him, whistling under his breath as he straightened his cravat. James almost cursed aloud. He had been too slow; he couldn't be sure from which room the man had come. There were several possibilities.

He would try them all, he decided resolutely. Giving Hastings a curt nod, he moved purposely past him to set about his work.

The thud of a closing door tore Maggie from her thoughts, and she glanced through the window into the empty room to which she had inched. If her thoughts had distracted her so long that this room was now occupied, too, she thought she might very well throw up. She did not think she had the stamina or nerve to traverse the length of the ledge again. It was with some relief that she saw that the room appeared empty. Letting her breath out, she reached down, opened the window, and silently slipped inside.

Now that they were on solid ground, her legs were more than just a bit rubbery. Ordering them to stand firm, Maggie strode quickly across the room, pausing at the door to take a breath and listen for sounds in the hallway. When she heard only silence, she eased the door open. About to step out of the room, Maggie recalled the mask Maisey had given her—she had shoved it into her pocket in her rush to finish dressing and escape. It would be better to wear the thing. So thinking, she turned back into the room and started to lift the flimsy red silk mask to her face. Her eyes fell on a bed and a woman gaping at her from the shadows within. The two females gaped at each other briefly; then the sound of footsteps in the hall reminded Maggie that she had to get out of here. She quickly finished raising the mask to her face, tied the strings of it in place, then slipped from the room without a murmur of apology.

She had just finished pulling the door closed when a hand slid around her from behind, covering her mouth and smothering her startled cry. She was lifted bodily, bundled in her cape, and carted swiftly down the hall.

*G*ive in to your Impulses!

These unforgettable stories only take a second to buy and give you hours of reading pleasure!

Go to *www.AvonImpulse.com* and see what we have to offer.

Available wherever e-books are sold.

AVONIMPULSE

IMP 0811